T0274286

SWEETEST DARKNESS

LESLIE LUTZ

HOLIDAY HOUSE   NEW YORK

Library of Congress Cataloging-in-Publication Data is available.

ISBN: 978-0-8234-5494-5 (hardcover)

For all the caretakers of the world,
who give up so much

This is the Dark Place.

I sing it.

This is the Dark Place.

I hum it in my little cave.

My voice keeps me company.

And I can feel it,

the starlight beating

on the outside,

like rain.

A hailstorm.

A hurricane of light.

CHAPTER
ONE

We had no business going to the Alvarado that night.

Then again, it wasn't like we had a choice.

June and I shivered in the parking lot, watching the broken-down hotel watch us. Above the tiled roof, the Milky Way stretched, bright and fathomless. Gram used to call it a highway to nowhere in particular.

Tonight, I felt it leading us here.

"What's taking Selena so freakin' long?" I buttoned up my jacket, the denim collar scraping the stubble on my chin.

June didn't answer. Instead she blew on her hands, blond hair gleaming under the pale light of the waxing crescent moon. She fished a black beanie out of the pocket of her hoodie and slipped it on.

Around the Alvarado's dark shadows and opulent rot, the desert rolled out on every side. A lonely mile away were the squat buildings of Gypsum's outskirts—too far to hear us scream, which June had already pointed out.

"Got a joke for you," I said.

June shivered and stamped her feet to keep warm.

"Two girls and a guy walk into a haunted hotel—"

"Quinn, I think we should go home."

"—and one of them says, 'Quinn, I think we should go home.'"

"Then why don't we?"

I had no follow-up joke. No punch line. None of us had planned this little excursion. None of us called, or texted, or spoke about it, even though we saw each other every day at school, spent every weekend together. I'd arrived first, on foot, after telling my brother I needed to take a walk, which turned into a two-mile hike. My feet just led me here. Then June showed, materializing out of a pickup with Texas Longhorn plates, waving goodbye to some stranger she'd just hitched a ride from. And of course Selena would come.

She had to.

We'd spent the last four months resisting it, the urge to give in to this place. Every night, I'd had the same bizarre dream—and so had they. In the lunchroom last week, June had casually mentioned her "nightmares," and we'd all fessed up. Compared stories. Realized an abandoned hotel on the edge of town was *calling* to us, sweet as a lullaby. Then the three of us sat in a pocket of silence in the cafeteria, speechless, in the aftermath of an earthquake only we felt.

Now, here we were, at 11 p.m. on the first night of winter break, waiting for Selena, letting the Alvarado tell us what to do.

A crunch of gravel from behind, and Selena appeared out of the dark, rolling in on her bicycle, a lithe shadow swallowed by her dad's old sheriff's jacket, black hair spilling out of her hood. She stepped off and let the bike fall, expression bewildered, like she'd sleepwalked here. Without a word, she stepped up next to us, and we stood shoulder to shoulder, staring at the Alvarado.

The hotel loomed over us, all that darkness inside pressing against the windowpanes.

"I'm pretty sure I've seen this movie before," I said.

June nodded. "The one where the blond chick gets whacked in the opening scene."

Selena frowned and pulled a flashlight out of her pocket, then flicked it on, her breath fogging in the cold. "Let's just peek in the windows, then go."

"Won't be enough," I said. The sudden glare of Selena's flashlight blinded me, and I held up a hand to shield my eyes. "We'll just end up back here tomorrow night."

She huffed. "Quinn O'Brien, when you talk like that, you really freak me out."

"Because you know it's true."

A peppering of stars reflected in the windows. I tilted my head. The hotel seemed to tilt too, following me. No, it wasn't following me. Was I following it? I blinked and my tiny reflection caught and stretched, then warped until my stomach flipped.

Behind us, on the edge of town, the Gun Barrel Trailer Park glimmered as a sea of blacks and grays. I used to go there when I still read tea leaves, selling a glimpse of the future for twenty dollars a pop. Maybe I shouldn't put Selena through this. The first trailer was only a half mile away by foot. Maybe I should take my two friends by the hand and leave.

The thought seemed to pull some kind of trigger. A tug inside my chest. The Alvarado . . . it was disappointed. I always disappointed people. Even my brother thought so. Ollie's voice played in my head: *Why you gotta make everything so hard?*

I sighed.

"Uh-oh," Selena said.

"Uh-oh, what?"

"I *know* that sigh."

"Come on," I said. "Let's get this over with."

———————————

I led the way across the parking lot. Clumps of prickly pear had broken right through the concrete, reaching their paddles toward the sky. I stepped up on the porch, my boots thudding hollow on the boards, and stopped short of the door. Selena ran into me from behind and yelped.

After four months of the same maddening sequence playing every night, it wasn't like I didn't know what to do.

Up the grand staircase.

Through the spa.

Down the corridor.

Past the row of six framed photos.

Find room 336.

And then...and then what? That was when the dream always ended and everything faded to black, like a movie changing scenes. And every morning, I'd wake up and ask myself, *What happens next?*

Something good?

Or would we end up like those ghost hunters a few years ago? Just *gone,* their beat-up car out front, keys still in the ignition?

But I had to know.

I grabbed the doorknob and pulled. It came off in my hand. A pane of glass in the door fell and shattered. Behind me, Selena grabbed the back of my jacket.

June walked right past, wedged the door open with her boot, and slipped through, the white graphic on the back of her hoodie—WEST TEXAS REGIONAL CHAMPS—melting into the dark, along with the coiled outline of a snake, poised to strike.

I dropped the doorknob and followed, my boots crunching over broken glass.

The inside of the hotel was colder than out. I drew in a breath that tasted musty, then shivered. June had disappeared. Typical. Now that she'd made up her mind, she put her fear in a box and brought out the false bravado.

I flicked on my flashlight. "June?" I called out, then raked my beam over the mahogany paneling, the checkout desk, the cavernous ceiling.

June wandered near the bar, then disappeared behind the staircase that wound majestically to the second story. Selena stayed by my side.

Gram's stories about the Alvarado came back to me: what it was like in the glittering thirties, all lit up and freshly painted, the front porch brimming with parties and cocktails and big-money deals, actresses holding court on the upper balconies, where the beautiful people would wait for sunset, to *ooh* and *ahh* over the night stars as they appeared, like frozen fireworks.

At the top of the stairs, the black thickened. From nowhere came the thought that the darkness on the other side wasn't just creepy or endless. That the darkness was *sweet*. But not a normal, good kind of sweet. I could almost taste it on my tongue.

I pointed my flashlight at the top landing, squinting. Torn wallpaper. Doorways. Nothing but—

From behind, a pair of hands closed in on my shoulders. "Boo!"

I jumped a foot. Selena screamed. June's laugh echoed in the lobby.

"And I thought you were a big tough guy, Quinn," June said.

"You thought wrong."

Selena looked at the doors we'd just come in, as if considering making a break for it, but turned back to June and whisper-hissed, "Stop creeping around with your flashlight off."

June didn't need one, because she was June, but I dug in my pocket for my small backup, then handed it to her. "Just humor us, okay?"

A grumble, followed by a pencil-thin glow. We swept the beams up the grand staircase.

I'd seen it all before—in the daytime. There wasn't a kid in Gypsum who hadn't come out here on a dare, slipped past the NO TRESPASSING sign to play "Chopsticks" on the haunted piano, which only sounded haunted because it was out of tune. In middle school, when Gram got sick, we came dozens of times. Explored the jumble of furniture on the west side, made up stories about how it was a barricade to keep out zombies. Then we'd sit on the checkout desk and flick the broken bits of wasp hives at each other, yell swear words and listen to them echo, the sunbeams turning the Alvarado into nothing but a playground.

But everyone in Gypsum knew the Alvarado changed at night.

I started up the stairs, past the line of broken beer bottles that marked the edge of the zone where locals were willing to go. June and Selena followed, the chandelier I'd seen in my dreams catching our beams, shattering them. I stared at the glimmer, not fighting—just accepting—the urge to count each teardrop. That was what the dreams nudged me to do. *Count them,* the dream said, without uttering a single word.

I'd almost reached the top when my phone rang.

"Feliz Navidad…"

I fumbled for the phone in my pocket as José Feliciano's voice echoed through the cavernous space, cursing my decision to let Selena mess around with my ringtones. Then I stumbled into the banister. The wood cracked.

"Quinn!"

Selena pulled me back from the edge just as the railing detached and plummeted to the floor below. The song echoed off the walls. I searched blindly for the side button.

"Shut that off!" Selena said in a whisper-hiss.

"I'm trying!" I pulled away from her. My brother's name appeared. *Missed call.*

I started to type a text, my face heating up. Ollie, always hovering. So that's what I typed.

stop hovering

Before I could press send, the phone rang again. Selena grabbed for it.

And it slid out of my hand, hit the stair, bounced off. A second of silence followed by a sharp crack as it slammed into the floor.

June peered over the edge. "Well, that's not optimal."

While June and Selena stayed up on the stairs, I collected the shattered remains of my phone. Cradled it in my hands and swore into the dark. Three months of side hustles at the Gun Barrel Trailer Park. Three months of reading tea leaves. Three months of seeing *those expressions* on the faces of the people who'd asked me—even begged me—to tell them the future. Gratitude. Wonder. Fear. Then Ollie's expression when he'd found out what I'd been doing and shut everything down, acting like a warden rather than an older brother.

I looked up at Selena, who watched me with her hands clasped in front, her signature *I'm sorry* pose.

My anger carried me back upstairs but evaporated as I followed June and Selena to the hallway beyond, which led to a set of double doors. This was the point in the dream where I took the lead, put my palm on the doors, pushed and watched them swing wide open. How satisfying it felt to open things. That was what four months of the dream whispered to me. *Open everything.*

I directed my flashlight inside, sliding the beam over the metal tubs. It was the spa, where the movie stars and gangsters and well-heeled city folk went to sink their bodies into Gypsum waters. Trying to stay young forever, Gram used to say.

June brushed by me. I swept my beam over fancy cabinets, glass bottles coated in dust, a tiled shower, spiderwebs trailing from the ivory handles.

Then June tilted her head back and whooped.

Selena pointed the flashlight in her face. "Stop it!"

"No," June said. "Listen." She whooped again.

June stood only a few feet away, but her voice seemed distant, like it was funneling down a long tunnel. I'd always heard that the Alvarado played tricks with sound at night, like the gypsum mines did, but in the darkness of the spa, the echo of June's voice coming from somewhere behind me made gooseflesh erupt on my arms.

"That's so cool," June said, her voice full of false courage that was too easy to recognize.

Selena's beam skittered over the edges of a ragged hole in the wall. "Oh yeah, *so* cool, just like a haunted carnival. Can we leave now?"

June ignored her and moved between the tubs, starting up a whisper-sing of "Old Town Road," which seemed like it was coming from my left rather than my front. I searched the corners, my light cutting into the soft darkness.

A passageway out of the spa, lined with doors. At the end, a T junction.

Next to me came Selena's quiet voice. "Honeycomb."

"What?"

She shook her head, like she was trying to shake something loose. "Remember? In the dream, this is where it all becomes a honeycomb."

Although our destination was always the same—room 336—our individual dreams had strange differences. For her, the deep passages of the hotel became a honeycomb; for me, stone tunnels, coming apart; for June, masses of tangled string.

We started down the hall, my heart picking up speed, like it knew any moment the walls would crumble and I'd be buried under tons of plaster and stone.

I firehosed my light around, pausing on the brass numbers. Room 251, where Judy Garland once slept. Room 247, Bonnie and Clyde's supposed hideaway. Room 241, where the chambermaid was murdered. A half dozen other names slipped through my mind—the dead, the famous, the forgotten.

We kept going. Searching. For what, we had no idea.

Another stairway led us into another hall of suites. The stagnant air clogged every breath. We reached a line of six framed photos full of strangers in sepia tones. Next to them was a door with a brass plaque.

Room 336, where that Hollywood director died, the one who shot *Dead for Dollars* and *Dark Noose* and all those other B Westerns that almost everyone had forgotten.

I looked at Selena, then June. We were finally here.

I pushed the door open with my boot.

Inside, outlined in moonglow, was a sitting room, and beyond that—past a door hanging from its hinge like a lolling tongue—were a bed, a nightstand, and a closet. A window yawned halfway open. The fresh smell of the desert replaced the musty scent of the halls.

June stepped into the room and turned in a circle. "This is it. Three thirty-six." She looked at me, triumphant. "We did it."

I swung my light around the room. It was bigger than the others we'd passed; less dilapidated, too, although the wallpaper still sagged and the fancy sconces dripped with cobwebs.

"Now what?" June asked.

"We should look for clues," I said.

"Clues?" Selena asked.

"I don't know." I put my head in the closet. "A bloody knife? A ghostly message?"

"It's just a room," Selena said. "Like all the others."

A cold wind blew through the window. On the bare mattress next to it, a flutter. My beam caught a stack of white paper, marked up with ink. I stepped closer. Picked up a page.

It was covered in numbers.

I dropped it and picked up another. And another. More numbers. Random, scrawled, endless. There had to be a hundred pages of them.

Then a voice came into my head.

Whispering and urgent, but too garbled to understand. I pressed the heel of my hand against my forehead and willed it to stop.

"Can you hear that?" I asked.

Selena turned to me. "What?"

A rustle. Not inside my head this time, but out there, in the hall. Selena's light swung to the doorway. Lit up the torn wallpaper.

The rustle again. The hairs on the back of my neck rose, and the urge to run hit me. I glanced at the window. Three stories down from there. Then I looked back at the doorway. Maybe it was nothing? Just something soft running along the floors. A rat, perhaps. Only...

I met Selena's eyes. She didn't want to check. I didn't want to check.

But I closed my eyes for a second, opened them, and then forced myself to step past June and lean into the corridor.

To the left, darkness. But to the right...

The last door of the hall was open. And there was a light on.

The sound came again. Something moving, thumping. Like the flutter of moth wings against a spiderweb. Large moth wings.

I motioned to June and Selena, and they slipped past me. Then the three of us retreated on silent feet around the corner, away into the pitch black.

We paused there, backs pressed against the wall, just breathing. I checked around us: pointed my beam down a hall that stretched long, its line of doors closed, until I caught a glimmer on a mirror at the far end. Empty. We needed to leave. Now.

"What *was* that?" came Selena's quiet whisper.

A tug on my flashlight. Before I could react, it was gone. June had taken it right out of my hand. The glow flicked off.

"What are you doing?" I whispered.

Selena's beam jittered wildly. "No, June, I need it!"

"I need to *see*. Just trust me, okay? Can't you just trust me?"

I reached out for my flashlight, a spike of panic in my chest. Fumbling in the gloom, I hit something, and a clatter followed.

Complete darkness. The world turned into velvet, crushed against my face. I couldn't breathe. "June?"

Selena's voice came from the floor, whimpering. I heard the soft scrape of her bare hands on the hardwood. "The batteries came out. June, where are you?"

"Trust me!" Her footsteps receded, softening down the hall, deeper into the hotel.

I dropped down beside Selena, feeling blindly over the floor for the batteries. Along the walls, in the drifts of leaves. Gone. I stood. "Selena, let's just get out of here."

"No freaking way," she said, her voice thin, panicked. "I'm not walking around in the pitch black."

"It's not like we don't know the way..."

"No! June'll be back soon. She never leaves us for long!"

Selena had a point. And I didn't much want to feel my way blind through the Alvarado.

I thought about our games of Marco Polo on moonless nights, when the darkness was a blindfold for Selena and me, but not June—who, for God knows what reason, saw best in the dark, like a cat. There were a lot of things like that in Gypsum, things you couldn't explain.

Marco Polo. That's all this was. A game, and the hotel was our swimming pool. We'd call out, and soon enough, she'd come back...

I leaned against the wallpaper, my shoulder touching Selena's. The cold insides of the hotel seeped through my skin, the faint smell of mold passing over me like a breath.

Selena shifted. Then her fingers brushed once through the hair at the base of my neck, where it curled by the collar. I was so surprised I didn't react at first, flashing back to the kiss last year, the one we never talked about. The warmth of her hand left, then returned, this time a nudge against my palm. It felt like a question.

She was afraid. So was I.

I threaded my fingers through hers. Blinked into the inky air, breathed in the sweetness. And suddenly it dawned on me why that word kept welling up in my head.

Sweet...like the inside of a pitcher plant.

"Quinn?" Selena asked, her voice soft, like it was far away, like June's voice had sounded in the spa. The Alvarado, playing tricks on me again.

I squeezed her fingers. "Yeah, I'm here."

"Where are you?" Her voice was farther away now. "I can't find you."

It took a moment for me to put it together: Selena here, Selena there. Impossible.

And then the hand holding mine wasn't warm anymore.

CHAPTER
TWO

A t first, I didn't let go. My mind tried to make sense of it: Selena's hand losing all its warmth, her voice so far away. It's what you do when you're faced with something that shouldn't exist.

Fingernails pressed gently into my palm. Short. Ragged. And that's what broke the spell. Selena's fingernails were always long.

I yanked my hand away. Scrambled right, stumbled left, right into someone. We went down in a tangle of limbs. Then somehow I was up, dragging a confused Selena down the hall, sprinting toward the exit, running my hands over walls, counting doors, drawing a map of the hotel in my mind. I picked up speed, becoming a riot of breath and adrenaline. Something heavy clipped my shoulder—a doorway. I dragged Selena through—and we kept going until we reached the spa, my memory drawing a straight line through the tubs.

We turned a corner, and the black gave way to faint moonglow. We were back on the second-floor landing at the top of the stairs, the wide-open lobby below us.

I hurtled down the steps, ignoring Selena's panicked questions, a sick feeling building inside me, cold and slow.

Like I wasn't supposed to leave.

And then it was as if someone had just slipped an icy hook around my spine. The hook tightened, pulled.

I careened sideways, taking Selena with me. She threw out a hand for the banister that was no longer there, the one I'd sent crashing to the floor not twenty minutes ago. And then she fell.

I lunged for her, catching her wrist. She yelled for me to pull her up, but my sweaty hand greased right over her skin, and it was all I could do to hold on. No way could I drop her—not down the mouth of the pitcher plant. Something in the hotel *wanted* me to drop her. I could feel it. I held tight, the muscles in my forearm taut as piano wire, my knees locked.

Her hand slipped an inch more. I let go of the broken banister edge to get a hold on her jacket collar.

Then a chill breath touched my neck again. Two palms on my back. A final push.

The stairs were there, and then they weren't. And I was weightless and falling, holding Selena's hand tight.

The floor slammed into me. Wooden boards groaned and splintered, and before I could grab hold of anything, we both crashed through—right into the dark heart of the basement.

One, two seconds falling, and then another hammer, this time to my head and back. My lungs stopped working. For a desperate moment, I was afraid they'd never work again. Finally, I drew a breath, peering up at the weak glimmer pouring through a hole in the ceiling.

From beside me came a groan. Selena rolled on her side, holding a palm over one eye.

"You okay?" I managed.

"Can we…please…go home now?"

I stood, my legs shaking, and scanned the dark around me. A small room. The shadows against the walls were furniture. And in the center sat what looked like a safe, waist-high, its silver dial glinting in the moonlight.

The hotel was quiet, like it was holding its breath.

"What happened?" Selena whispered.

"Something pushed us right off the stairs."

"Something?"

"I don't know what it was."

"You mean it's up there right now?" she asked, her voice small.

I searched for a door, turning in circles. There was nothing but smooth plaster.

"What kind of psycho builds a room with *no door?*" Selena breathed.

We both looked at the hole in the ceiling again. The only way out.

I checked the distance from the top of the safe to the ceiling. I could give Selena a boost. Then, if I could reach the light fixture, maybe I could swing my feet to catch the edge and . . .

I put one hand on the safe to climb up. And all those thoughts evaporated.

It was warm under my palm. Like skin. Like it had been sitting in the sun. I jerked away.

Selena said something, but her voice faded. Numbers spilled through the dam in my head. This room, this safe, I'd dreamt about both dozens of times—a part of the dream that I'd forget as soon as I woke, that I only now remembered.

My palm crawled with imaginary ants. *This was it.* This was what we'd come to find. And in the oily light, I could swear the safe moved. I stumbled back, my heart stuttering.

Footsteps pounded over our heads, and a silhouette appeared. "What are you two doing down there?"

I wiped a shaking hand over my face. "Planning your murder. Now get us out of here."

I pulled a table from the wall and made Selena climb that instead of the safe, ignoring her *Why*s and *What is wrong with you*s. With June's help, we climbed up and out, the safe watching us.

No strange hands came out of the dark to push us back in. The hotel was quiet now. Sleeping.

We stumbled outside, down the steps, and out into the desert. Selena sprinted away from the Alvarado toward the Gun Barrel Trailer Park. June and I followed, running through the cacti that formed a strange forest around us, a forest etched in dark lines by the crescent moon.

Halfway there, Selena stopped to catch her breath, leaning on her knees. The sky stretched above us like a dark lake, its black surface pebbled with stars. She yanked her shoe off and shook out a rock. "That was great, June. Just great. Leave us there in the dark. Abandon us, people you've known all your life…"

As Selena and June argued, I tilted my face up, savoring the freedom of it, the luminous moonlight pouring down. The starlight felt like rain.

"But we're all okay!" June said. "It's okay now. We're out!"

"Okay?" I said, running a hand across my forehead, my fingers coming away sticky with blood. "You call this okay? Where the hell did you go?"

"I…thought I saw the way we were supposed to go, and…I needed to make sure!" she said, but the tremor in her voice told me she was holding something back.

Our voices tangled together. Arguing. I didn't mention the safe.

We fell silent. Something jabbed through my jeans into my calf. Lechuguilla. I'd need pliers to get it out before the barb worked its way in, like a fishhook. Some things were like that, Gram used to say—did more damage coming out than going in. Sometimes, she said, you just left it well enough alone and lived with it.

Maybe she was right. She usually was.

Probably should have left the dreams alone.

The three of us walked through the last stretch of desert, toward the Gun Barrel. The moon followed us. I lied to myself and said the dreams would stop now. That the safe I'd seen in the dark, in the strange room without doors, wouldn't be a part of my future.

I glanced over my shoulder once, back at the Alvarado. Somewhere in the upper rooms a light winked out.

CHAPTER
THREE

My phone buzzed in my pack, vibrating at the base of my spine. I clung to the cliff face, reaching up for the next handhold. Stretch, shift, press the ball of my foot into a shallow crack. Push myself up. Pull another quickdraw off my harness and clip it into the anchor. And, like a spider, I made my way up toward the summit.

The phone buzzed again. I ignored it.

Sorry, June, your nonapology will have to wait.

I made it halfway to the summit and paused for a few breaths just shy of a wicked overhang. I found two good handholds and let my feet leave the cliff face. An act of faith, my brother, Ollie, once told me. Faith in yourself. Faith that your equipment and your muscles and your will can work together to defy gravity, push you higher.

I dragged the toe of my shoe up the rock, into a crevice I knew from memory, feeling its familiar shape through the thin leather.

Out of the corner of my eye, I glimpsed the number one reason I'd come out to climb today. The reason I came any day. The desert: a hundred shades of earth and stone, stretching out for miles. Blue sky. No clouds. Down below lay the round O of the spring-fed pond ringed with six empty campsites and one bright orange tent.

My arms shook and sweat dripped between my shoulder blades as I pulled myself over the lip. Reason number two I came out here today:

nothing cleared my head like sweating it out on the toughest route of the Horse Crippler.

I reached the last handhold, another overhang, and pulled myself up and over, the jagged sandstone scraping across my jeans. Then I made my way over to the three old movie theater seats my brother had hauled up to the top of the cliff last spring, when he thought being quirky would help our campground compete with El Cosmico in Marfa. I fished a Snickers from my pack and sat in a seat to take in the show. I'd seen this movie before, but I never tired of it.

The Chihuahuan Desert stretched out in front of me, rolling, jagged, and still, the kind of place the rest of the world thought was full of bandits hiding from the long arm of the law. Gypsum rose up in the distance, a small scattering of low buildings that grew into a cluster of tidy streets with shops and small restaurants. At the end of Main Street, the county courthouse towered, a stone fortress, full of courtrooms no one used.

Nothing much of note happened in Gypsum anymore, unless you counted the Rattlesnake Roundup in July or the Gypsum Chili Cookoff in August (neither of which seemed to draw tourists). Other than that, there were only enterprising locals who ran ghost tours and spook-light tours and silver screen tours, parking a healthy distance from the sagging front porch of the Alvarado and telling tall tales about the old days.

Or, in my case, yesterday.

For a second, I felt those cold hands on my back again. A tiny push. That was all it would take, and I'd plummet ten stories off the Horse Crippler to the unforgiving ground…

My phone buzzed in my pack. I reached in and glanced at the screen. I could barely make the words out through the spiderweb of cracks.

Ur avoiding me cmon was it really that bad

I slipped my phone back into my pack. Was it that bad? Really?

I glanced west, past Bud Pilsner's sprawling land—which we never crossed for fear of death or dismemberment—toward the Alvarado Hotel, a mere two miles away. *Yeah, June, it really was that bad.*

Down below, a flash of movement caught my eye, and for a happy second I thought Selena had changed her mind about coming today. Whenever school was out, she was here, climbing these cliffs over and over, like she was made of air.

But it wasn't Selena. It was a man, coming out of his bright orange stargazing tent, followed by a little boy and a woman. I guessed when Selena said she wanted to keep her feet on the ground for a while, she meant it.

The three campers had shown up yesterday morning, city campers in their North Face quilted jackets and fancy boots, and completely blew off my offer to show the kid how to rock climb. Told me they wanted to start out on something easier than the Horse Crippler, which I told them sounded a lot worse than it was. That it was named for a cactus, not for its level of difficulty, at least not the route I would lead them on. We'd belay them the whole way, me and Ollie. My brother would stay at the bottom holding the safety line, and I'd lead them up to the glorious top of the world. At least the top of Gypsum, which for me meant the top of the world.

They'd said, *No, too much for us. We'll stick with stargazing and s'mores, thank you very much.*

My phone buzzed again. Another text from June.

I'm off work at noon. Wanna grab burgers at the diner?

June was probably at the Gun Barrel Trailer Park, caring for Ms. Durbin, who was so old she used to hang with my great-grandparents, back when the Alvarado was still a working hotel and attracted big-time directors and all their glittering crew. Taking care of Mrs. Durbin and listening to her endless stories about her starlet days was something June had started doing when she'd lost her job at the Stoplight Café for being late something like five hundred times. Most of the inmates at Gypsum High had jobs like that, running the register at the Gas 'n' Sip or changing diapers or driving up to Alpine to wash dishes at the Applebee's. Or in my case, sweet-talking tourists into rock-climbing lessons.

I slipped my phone back in my pack before I could change my mind. June could stay at work and drink Ensure for lunch, for all I cared.

Below, the woman placed a log on the fire, which was dying, while the man and the boy took cooking gear from a gray Sterlite tub. Only tent in the Starlight Campgrounds. And the new cabin Ollie had built, the one he claimed would push the balance sheet from red to black, had a sum total of nobody in it. Business was always quieter in December. The fifteen-dollar camping fee barely covered the water the family had already used.

I repacked my bag and slung it over my shoulder, ready to rappel down, let gravity do her work. In the distance, a fancy hybrid kicked up a dust trail on the road to Gypsum and pulled into the parking lot of the diner—probably tourists stopping on their way to Marfa. Macie would try to send them our way, tell them our campsite was cheaper than Marfa's overpriced El Cosmico, that our stars were just as bright and the water better. But like Gram always said, some people liked the packaging more than the gift.

The lean months. And since they didn't want the best guided rock-climbing tour in West Texas, I guessed I had to sell them something else. A half mile away, our house rose up, three stories of dilapidated white. The gravel road out front was still empty. Maybe I had just enough time to do it before my brother got home to stop me.

Down below, the man and the woman picked their way along the rocky edge of the spring to fill their canteens. I called down to them, and they waved at me. The wife had agreed to the reading last night, over a tin mug filled two fingers high with some of Gram's whiskey, because campfire circles make good atmosphere for psychics to hawk their wares to half-drunk housewives. One reading, twenty bucks. Just a hundred more of those, Ollie and I might actually clear the mortgage.

I watched the little boy taking a drink from the spring with cupped hands, hoping he didn't show up in my cup.

Still, twenty bucks was twenty bucks.

June's tiny message appeared at the top of the screen.

Marco.

Yeah, June, I'm sorry too. Sorry about the dreams that come from I don't know where. Sorry I don't have rock climbers paying to climb the Horse Crippler in December. Sorry Ollie and I are about to lose our grandmother's house. Sorry you don't know why the world is strange, or why we're in it, or what we're supposed to do next.

———————————•———————————

The woman with the bright orange tent tried to get me to call her Susan, rather than Ms. Johanis, but Gram taught me better than that. Ms. Johanis pulled out a camp chair and set it by the fire. I checked out the brand on her gear—all from REI—and wished I'd doubled my price. She looked the type to pay too much and not mind.

Ms. Johanis set an aluminum coffeepot on the coals.

"I've never done this before," she said, talking more to the pot than to me. She glanced up to the rise, where the sun lay a handsbreadth above the horizon and her husband and son were nothing but dots, walking along the mile-long desert trail.

I looked over my shoulder toward the house, but Ollie wasn't back yet. I checked the time: 9:36 a.m., which meant he was still in the middle of the job interview at the Gas 'n' Sip, and Jim Betleman was a talker. If I was lucky, Ollie would slip and mention politics, and Jim would keep him there for hours.

From the bottom of my day pack, I pulled a bundle of cloth and unwrapped it. Inside lay a single china cup, its outer skin dotted with small yellow flowers and green leaves, the inside white and empty.

"So that's how you're going to do it?" she said, watching me pull a small cellophane package from a side pocket like I was about to sell her crack.

"That's the idea. Is it boiling yet?" I dumped the contents into the cup, and the scent of black tea and prickly pear rose up to mix with woodsmoke.

"We made coffee in it this morning, so I hope I cleaned it out good enough," she said. She was a nervous talker, like Selena. She lifted the lid and peered inside. "I guess the tea might taste funny. Will that ruin things? I hope it doesn't ruin things. Should I dump it out and start over?"

"A few coffee grounds won't hurt."

"What's in the tea?"

"Just regular Irish breakfast."

"You're kidding."

"The magic's not in the tea."

She gave me a knowing smile, like she understood, which she didn't. Neither did I.

"What else's in there?" she asked, eyeing the green and red bits, the little flakes of pink there among the dark brown tea.

"Nothing special."

She tended the pot and went on about how the coals weren't hot enough, talking nonstop about nothing. Which was good, since I hadn't really told her the truth about what was in the tea. It was hard to explain anyway. Why I gathered prickly pear flowers, then laid them out on the roof of Gram's house to shrivel in the sun. Why I used the flesh of tree cholla, and stems of the creosote bush. Little bits of the desert, selected and dried and mixed with the tea. Gram always said I didn't need it, but she also said it would help, having the land you lived on in the cup. If I ran out and used only regular tea from the market, I just made sure to use Gypsum water. Better than a telescope into the soul, she always said. I nodded to the camp chair across from me. "Sit. You'll need to hold it, or it won't work."

"Oh, okay, sorry." She placed the pot of water next to my boots and sat across from me, knees tightly pressed together and back straight, like she was applying for a job.

"Relax." I passed her the cup. "This doesn't hurt."

She laughed and took it. It was a good laugh, and she had a kind face, and I hoped the leaves gave her good news.

I directed her through the motions. *Hold the cup as I pour. Drink. Near the bottom, drink and turn at the same time, letting the bits of tea cling to the sides.* From that, I would read the patterns that would tell me what was inside her.

She was a slow drinker, and we sat in uncomfortable silence while she finished, sip by sip. I watched her face, wondering if her future would bring the good, or the bad, or something in between.

I glanced up the trail, toward the house, remembering my fight with Ollie six months ago, before the dreams had come, when I made the mistake of telling him what it was like to read someone's future. Sometimes, when I read the cup, I was afraid I was doing something wrong, stepping over a threshold I wasn't supposed to touch. It almost felt like swimming, or like I'd touched the edge of a membrane with my fingertips. It was cottony, like a spiderweb, tea leaves caught in the silk. Then when I pushed through, I'd find water on the other side.

Deep. Vast. I didn't know why I knew this, but I drank that water through the skin of my fingers. I wasn't supposed to be there. That I knew. But I kept coming back and pushing through.

I told him all this, pent up too long, and I was going to tell him more, but then I saw his expression. My cocky brother gone, replaced by someone I didn't know. Unsure, shaken. So I didn't tell him about the fear. That one day when I went into the Dark Place, I wouldn't be alone in there anymore. Something would be on the other side, a breath away. I'd reach out blind, past the spiderweb, into the abyss, and this time, it would grab me. Sink its claws in my arms and pull me right through.

And the thing that scared me the most, the thing I couldn't say, was that part of me wanted it to. Just let go and give in, let gravity take me until I knew everything there was to know, until I was bursting with it.

Ms. Johanis finished her last sip and set the cup on the saucer.

"All right," I said, "turn the cup upside down on the saucer and put your hands over it."

"Why?"

"I have no idea. It's how my gram taught me."

We sat awhile, waiting. I watched her, worrying the silver stud in my left ear, the one I'd worn since the day we put Gram in the ground. What Gram always said came back to me, that the insides of a teacup made you feel big and small at the same time, like looking at the night sky.

I took the cup from Ms. Johanis, balanced the saucer on my knee, and flipped the cup over. The tea leaves clung to the white porcelain. The urge to count the leaves rose in me. I focused instead on the symbols.

A cross. A dog. A razor. A star.

She leaned forward in her camp chair. "What do you see?"

The cry of a desert bird reached me, a pyrrhuloxia winging its way overhead, the clipped notes tumbling down from the top of the Horse Crippler. Miles away, a truck without a muffler roared down Gypsum's Main Street. A breeze pushed a bank of clouds over the sun. But inside me, the world had gone still.

"I see…" The rustle and pulse of the world were fading, along with the light. "I see…"

And then, as if someone had turned a switch in the sky, I stood in the Dark Place. The veil of spiderweb stretched in front of me.

"What do you see?" Her voice came from far away, along with the birdsong, and the brush of wind over the Horse Crippler. But my eyes were made of sackcloth.

I stepped toward the web, reaching out in the dark, until I felt it. Cottony. I pulled back and it clung to my fingertips, stretching like taffy.

Something moved on the other side, but distant. A breeze maybe. Or a current.

I ran my fingers over the patterns of the tea in the web. Cross. Dog. Hanged man. Star. Her future flowed into me, electric and beautiful. My fingers sifted through the moments.

On the other side, the breeze, or current, or whatever it was, changed. Something big and small at the same time, sprinting for the membrane, toward me. But it was too far away, and it would be too late. Because

I had to know. My hands, my skin, my whole self, wanted it. Not just for her, but for me.

Images flowed. Her future, moments and decades. Smiling faces, weeping faces, accomplishments and dreams and sorrows, all flowing through my hands and up my arms and into my mind. I sank deeper, to the knuckle, stretching the web. Soft, cottony...

Something solid, there in the dark, stopping my hands. Not a web.

I drew back, confused. The Dark Place didn't contain anything solid. Ever. The world here was soft, sticky.

The current on the other side quickened. It was coming, whatever it was. But I had a few seconds left. I had time.

The web felt broken in one spot. I pushed my hands through and ran my palms over a smooth, hard surface. Like an actual *thing*, not a memory or a wisp of the future. This had an edge. I followed it, even though the prickly sensation running up my arms, into my throat, told me to stop, to pull back.

It was a big boxy thing. An image from an old movie flashed through my head, of an obelisk. It could be something like that. Which meant what? Was it real, or a symbol I was supposed to read? Was it for her, or for me? Yes, it was for me, I was sure of it.

I started to draw back, and my skin dragged across a raised circle on the front of the box. It felt like a...

"Quinn!"

The screen in front of my eyes filled with sunlight. Rock and sky and the bright orange city campers' tent. The woman's hopeful face. My hands felt empty.

Ms. Johanis looked past me, her brows coming together.

"It's just my brother." I turned away from the cup and the woman with all the hope on her face. At the edge of the campground, Ollie stood, outlined by the morning sun behind him, our house in the distance.

I ignored the urge to examine my new discovery, peck it apart, and figure it out. Instead, I turned back to give Ms. Johanis everything I could before Ollie got down the hill. "You're going to have another baby." She wasn't showing yet, but I could smell it in the leaves.

The woman put a palm over her mouth. "I only found out yesterday."

"You're going to Paris in two years. Don't eat the food on the plane. And that weird ceramics business you're starting up, that friend with the red hair? Don't partner with her."

"You mean Amber?"

"Whatever. The one with the overbite. She's going to screw it up and make you crazy."

"Wow, you really can see," she said softly, and there it was, a little bit of fear, right there in her eyes.

Ollie's footsteps grew louder and quicker, and I talked faster. Ms. Johanis had a fight coming with her husband's family at Thanksgiving, so I told her to go for a walk when they brought up politics, and don't come back until dessert. And then I gave her other things, the ones that came to me in soft focus, that her daughter, the one she was still carrying in her belly, would be two weeks early, but healthy. That she'd hate softball and love soccer. And her husband and his coworker—the one she'd always been jealous of—he'd like the coworker a little too much, but he wouldn't do anything about it. Her son would visit often after he got out of college, like a good son should.

I wrapped up the cup and shoved it in the bottom of my pack. "And if you'd give me the twenty without my brother seeing it, I'd really appreciate it."

CHAPTER
FOUR

Ms. Johanis slipped the money into my hand, and I tucked the bill in my pocket just as my brother entered the campsite. With the dark hair brushing his collar and his thick brows knitting together, no wonder Ms. Johanis shrank in her seat.

"Hey, Ollie. What's up?"

He stared at me a moment longer before turning to Ms. Johanis, his expression softening. "You enjoying your stay?"

"Yes...yes, I am, thank you."

"Good, good." He put on a stiff smile and grabbed me by the upper arm, then pulled me up from my seat. "Excuse us."

He waited until Ms. Johanis was out of earshot before he spoke. "Tell me you didn't." His grip was like a metal cuff on my arm.

"Didn't do what?"

"Don't give me that."

And the lecture began. It kept going until we'd passed the empty cabin and the six vacant campsites. About how I shouldn't read anyone ever again, how I shouldn't mess with forces that I didn't understand. I argued, said he never minded when Gram did it. And what about her father, our great-grandfather, who'd done the same—read the fortunes for half the town? No one ever told him to stop. They put Liam O'Brien's picture up in the courthouse, gave him a brass plaque. Called him the Oracle of Gypsum. Ollie told me that was different, but refused to explain why.

He was only looking out for me, he said. And just because school was out for Christmas break didn't mean he'd let me run wild for three weeks, doing whatever I pleased and breaking the house rules, which were *his* rules.

And then I noticed the smell.

I'd caught a whiff of the chalk that dusted his jacket. Not fresh and clean like climbing chalk or new drywall (which he sometimes put up when the work came his way). No, this smelled old, with a hint of mildew and spider husks. He was covered with it, like he'd been . . .

I stopped walking.

"What?" he said. "You gonna backtalk me now?"

"You didn't go to your job interview today."

He frowned. "How in the world would you know that?"

"Because you smell like the Alvarado."

His expression changed. The anger melted into shock, and then into something so fleeting I wasn't sure I'd seen it right. Fear. Right there in his eyes.

I shouldn't have said that, given him a hint that I'd been out there. He'd told me a thousand times not to go poking around. But I was boiling inside. No job interview! No money! And a bank just waiting to take everything. "We're running on fumes. And you didn't even go?"

"Gas 'n' Sip's a no-future job."

"But it's a job."

He went on like he hadn't heard me. "Minimum wage. Running a cash register all damn day, selling tampons and motor oil. I got a better idea. You'll see. I got it in the truck right now."

I rounded a bend in the trail, and Gram's white house lay dead ahead, the familiar shape of Ollie's pickup parked beside it. My heart stuttered, and I came to a dead standstill.

There, in the bed of his old Toyota 4Runner, was a familiar safe, its silver dial staring at me like an eye.

My vision narrowed, the edges of the world disappearing. Here. How was it here?

"Well, c'mon," Ollie said, hooking his arm around my neck and pulling me forward. "Come take a look."

It was as high as my chest, and black. The words THE SCHWAB SAFE COMPANY were stenciled in gold across the door, E. C. WEIST printed across the top. Part of the *E* and the *I* were missing.

Its body was so dark it seemed to absorb light. That was my first thought, as the safe grew larger with every step, the letters more distinct. My second thought was that the safe was just big enough for a six-year-old to fit himself inside.

I glanced over at the cluster of old refrigerators near Gram's house, dumped thirty years ago by some repairman who wanted to get them out of his garage. (My grandparents took everyone's junk, just in case it was worth something.) The refrigerators had been rusting there ever since, their unnaturally straight bodies lying against the knotty limbs of ocotillo, the pointed barbs of the lechuguilla, the bulbous ends of prickly pear. Gram made us take the hinges off after I locked myself inside one, brilliant kid that I was. She'd found me—lips blue, unconscious—by reading the sheriff's cup, the horrible future sitting there in the leaves like a cluster of black widows.

I don't know why, but staring at that safe...I couldn't stop thinking about how awful it was to pound on the inside of that door, trapped and alone and about to run out of air.

"Quinn," Ollie said, "are you hearing *anything* I'm saying?"

I turned to face him slowly, like I was coming out of a dream.

"Thank you for your attention. Geez. So anyway, Enrique called me about some people in the Alvarado last night, and how he could hear them trashing it, breaking things, and then he couldn't stop thinking about how much damage they coulda done, so he just had to go over there to take a look, make sure everything was okay. Asked if I'd come. You know how Gram loved that old place! And sure enough, they did a number on the lobby, probably some tourists with a ghost guide, running around without a care in the—"

"Why in the world did you bring that thing home?"

"Are you kidding me? This is a Schwab safe."

"I can read."

"It's like catnip for collectors."

My brain finally put it together. "You are not putting another piece of unsellable junk in our house."

"*My* house. Gram left it to me."

"Because she thought you were man enough not to be a total wanker about it."

Ollie stepped up on the truck wheel to climb into the bed, turning to face me and putting a hand on top of the safe like he'd brought home a prize hog. "This here Schwab safe is a *collector's item*."

"Uh-huh."

He did a slow little sweep with his arm, like a girl in a car showroom. "Even empty, some folks would drop five C-notes for this. We crack it without drilling into it, and we get what's inside, *plus* the money for the safe itself. Make a fortune."

"Normal people don't solve their money problems this way."

"What do you know about normal?" He eyed me, his lips pressed together. "Our family's been getting themselves out of trouble this way for over a hundred years. Find a long shot. Bet on it. Wait and watch. Seems normal to me."

"Normal people get *jobs*. Regular jobs with a regular paycheck."

He pushed up his hat and scratched his forehead. "It probably belongs to us anyway. The hotel *is* kinda our legacy."

"The bank owns that land."

"Yeah, but—"

"You want a sure thing? I'll bet you twenty bucks if that safe belonged to anyone in our family, they spent what was inside a long time ago."

He frowned at me. "All right, fine. Be like that. You're still helping me get it off the truck."

We stood a few feet apart on the gravel drive, staring each other down. Tater slinked out from under the porch and padded over, weaving in and out of my boots, purring and leaving her orange fur all over my jeans. She blinked up at me, expectant, then moved her eyes to Ollie, letting out a hungry mew.

The angry glint in his eye softened. He sighed and went to the cab, pulling out a brown lunch sack and fishing around in a half-eaten sandwich for a piece of bacon. Then he dropped it on the ground in front of Tater. "Here ya go, good girl."

"Bacon's bad for her. The vet said so."

"A little bacon never hurt anybody. Did it, Tater Tot?"

Except Gram, I almost said.

Ollie wiped his fingers on his jeans and threw the bag back in the cab.

I walked over to the safe. The urge to touch the dial was suddenly so strong that I reached halfway out, then let my hand fall by my side.

"Uncut diamonds," Ollie said. "Gold ingots. Secrets you can sell for a mint. Just imagine it."

And despite myself, I did. Imagined what it would do for our lives.

"Make more in one day than I would *all year* at the Gas 'n' Sip. One look at it and I knew I had to take it," he said, his gaze on the safe. He seemed fascinated by its lines, in love with its angles. "Absolutely had to."

A shiver crawled up my back, watching him watch it like...

I snapped my fingers in front of his eyes. "Ollie."

He blinked, then went on, "I mean, if Gypsum is gonna get all that money from the government to renovate the hotel, I might as well get a piece." He patted the top of the safe again. "It's a sure thing."

Sure thing. Last year, Ollie had mortgaged the house and the land for one of his sure things. Two hundred fifty thousand dollars. The business—bottling Gypsum mineral water and selling it all over Texas—failed spectacularly, until we had nothing but an old building full of bottling equipment that we couldn't pay anyone to run. And here we were, about to lose it all.

"Half our junkyard's full of your sure things," I said bitterly.

He had the good grace to look guilty. "This is different."

"Yeah? How?"

"Because things are worth more if they have a story attached to them." Ollie leaned forward, like he had a secret that was about to blow me out of the water. "What you don't know is where I found it."

"Just because you found it in the basement of the Alvarado doesn't mean anyone will buy it."

Ollie's smile, along with the glint in his eye, faded. "How'd you know I found it in the basement?"

I leaned down to pet Tater, searching in my box of lies for a good one. "Just a good guess."

Ollie put one foot on the side of the truck bed and leaned on his knee. He rested there a bit, not looking at me. "You've been reading me again."

"Reading you? No."

"Without my permission."

"No. No way."

"Taking my cup from the sink and looking at the leaves."

"I didn't."

The look in his eyes went sharp, distant, and he glanced at the house. "I swear I'm switching to coffee."

"Ollie—"

"You're really gonna lie to me and say you're not reading again?" With a curse, he reached into my front pocket, and, before I could stop him, pulled out the twenty from Ms. Johanis and slammed it down on the tailgate. He yanked off his hat, ran his fingers through his dark hair. "Why you gotta pry into people's lives like that?"

I felt his disappointment like a cactus barb.

"It's not like you've never tried it," I snapped.

"That was a long time ago."

"You're just bitter because you can't do it."

His mouth pressed into a thin line. "*Can't* and *won't* are two different things, Quinn."

"Ms. Johanis asked me to. So it's fine."

"But—"

"And I didn't read your cup. Gram taught me better than that. No family. No close friends. Never do it at school. I always follow the rules."

"Then how did you know where I got the safe?"

"It just... flew into my head."

"Flew into your head," he said, his look measuring.

"Last night, when I was..." I coughed to stall for time, searching through my mental filing cabinet of misdirection. "I was on the roof, helping Selena with her photography thing, you know, the school project she's working on. Because she didn't get the memo that we're on break, because... Selena, you know."

Ollie stared at me blankly.

"She's taking pictures of the Milky Way." I could feel myself babbling, but I couldn't seem to stop. Ollie's hard gaze just made me babble more. "And she was setting up her tripod, and I was looking up, and bam! I just saw it. Which is a thing, you know, telling the future with... stars and all that. Gram said her father did it all the time, so... there you go."

Ollie didn't respond at first, his eyes searching mine. Then he let out a defeated sigh. "You're a terrible liar, Quinn."

I was. But I wasn't about to tell him the truth about where Selena and June and I were last night. I hadn't told him about the dreams. He already thought I was strange enough.

"You gonna give me a hand or not?" Ollie asked, a challenge in his eyes.

I almost said yes. Thought about the foreclosure notice in my backpack; all his talk of riches. But then I took another look at the safe, and I swear it stared back at me.

"No."

He spit out a curse and threw his hat on the front porch, where it missed the rocking chair by a foot. Him doing that was probably the only thing keeping him from clocking me across the jaw.

Ollie made his way across the gravel drive and away from me, stirring up a little puff of dust with his boots, pulling his cell phone from his pocket, muttering the whole time about how he couldn't call Enrique because it was the middle of the breakfast rush at the Gypsum Lights, how he had nothing left but to call Bud Pilsner, and how now Ollie would owe Bud a favor. How he'd probably have to walk over to Bud's the next time the man was out of town to feed his damn snakes, and how he wouldn't do it, no sirree. How *I'd* be the one going over there with a bag of frozen pinkie mice.

Before Ollie disappeared up the drive and a clump of prickly pear blocked my view, I caught the last words, because he always had the last word: something about how he didn't sign up to be a father.

Yeah, Ollie, I didn't sign up for this either.

I stayed outside near the truck. Maybe I'd drive to the edge of town and dump the safe in the desert. That way no one would have to feed Bud's snakes, and I'd be able to sleep tonight.

A small mew drifted up from behind the back wheel. The twenty-dollar bill had fallen off the side of the truck and lay there in the gravel. Tater had finished her bacon and was now sniffing the twenty. I picked it up and slipped it in my pocket again. Money was money.

Tater blinked up at me, a question in her eyes. She wasn't used to me ignoring her. Then her eyes shifted to the truck bed, as if she was noticing it for the first time. Her back arched, and she danced sideways behind my legs.

"It's probably empty anyway," I said to her.

It's not, a small voice said.

Ollie came back down the drive, phone against his ear, pretending I wasn't there, talking to Bud, barking short yeses and nos every so often. He stopped at the truck, opened the door, and grabbed a small brown sack and tossed it at my face.

I fumbled it, and the bag fell to the ground. The house's front door slammed. The Christmas wreath tumbled off its nail and landed on the welcome mat.

I picked up the bag and dusted it off. GYPSUM LIGHTS DINER was printed on the side, and a receipt was stapled to the top for $8.23. Inside were a sandwich wrapped in butcher paper, a bag of chips, and a pickle. Probably my favorite, a Cuban. Ollie always got me my favorite. I closed the bag, a rock settling somewhere in my throat. Tater came out from under the truck to sit at my feet, staring at the bag, until she let out one plaintive mew.

CHAPTER
FIVE

The buzz of the motorcycle engine, the rough road vibrating through me until my teeth hurt, almost cleared the argument from my head. Almost.

I slowed on Main Street, passing boarded-up windows and faded paint, and slipped into the parking lot of the Gypsum Lights. As soon as the engine died, I sat back on the seat, looking west into the desert, which stretched out long to the Chinati Mountains. My ancestors had come over those, carrying their water and their dreams until they found this place and set down their packs, ready to call it home.

I watched the hills, letting the stillness settle around me. Quiet, like the bottom of a pond.

Without really meaning to, I reached back toward the key. I could keep going, right past the town's welcome sign. Forget about family and all that. Take Highway 67 and head toward the interstate. Drive north until I reached Dallas, and then, a few hours past that, I'd be in the Wichita Mountains. Trade readings for rock-climbing gear. Live in a tent. Explore the Dark Place whenever I wanted, without Ollie telling me it was wrong. That *I* was wrong.

I could do it. Just leave the dreams and the safe and the fights about what the friggin' cat ate.

I imagined it. Me, on my dirt bike, racing north across the asphalt. Sun on my face. Cut those roots and be free.

Then I imagined the phone call from Ollie. *The bank's taken the house, Quinn.*

A wave of sick rolled through me.

I took the key out of my bike, then headed into the Gypsum Lights. The building glinted in the sun, practically blinding me, all shiny chrome and sleek lines, like a classic car morphed into a restaurant. I reached for the handle. Macie behind the counter caught my eye and pointed at my boots. I wiped them on the welcome mat and pushed open the second door to the smell of bacon and coffee, and to the murmur of the midmorning crowd.

The Gypsum Lights, which my aunt Macie owned, was the only place worth hanging out in a dying town like Gypsum. It had the best burger for a hundred miles and a pool table in the back. It also served as the local post office, notary, and only live music venue. Everyone came to the Gypsum Lights.

"Hey, Quinn," Aunt Macie said, with a broad smile that crinkled her eyes. "What brings you in today?"

"Pie."

"Ah, I should have known. Growing boy like you needs pie."

I let the door shut behind me, the Christmas bells on the handle jingling. "What's the special?"

"Mixed berry."

"Can I have two pieces?"

She lifted the glass dome and pulled out the pie. "You want one to go? For Ollie?"

"No."

"June? Or...Selena?" On the last name she waggled her eyebrows. Aunt Macie had been trying to get us together since junior high. If Macie knew I was here to meet up with her, I'd never hear the end of it.

"Nope. It's all for me. Today's a double-slice day."

"If that's the case, you can have *one*."

"Aunt Macie, why are you so mean to me?"

"I'll fix you a salad first." She tucked a strand of gray that had escaped her bun behind her ear and opened the enormous old fridge behind the counter to pull out a bowl of greens. There was no use fighting; the salad was free, anyway.

I set my pack down by the bulletin board near the entrance, next to the 1950s counter that lined the front window, the one Macie had put in so tourists could sit at night and watch for the spook lights and whisper about aliens and ghosts and God knows what. Most people went to Marfa to see the lights, but we had them too, if you were patient enough to watch the darkness that long.

I looked at the parking lot, then craned my neck to peer north down Main Street. Selena was late. Well, fine. I opened my pack and fished out the flyer I'd made that morning after I'd seen the foreclosure notice.

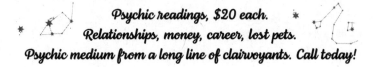

Psychic readings, $20 each.
Relationships, money, career, lost pets.
Psychic medium from a long line of clairvoyants. Call today!

Standing in front of the board with my homemade flyer in my fist, I could see the future without having to read it: me, the first day after winter break, walking into class and hearing all conversations die. *Psychic boy, at it again. What a showboating freak.* My mother had the same trouble when she went to Gypsum High. But she used her sight to bet on football games and pry into her friends' lives. I wasn't like her. I didn't take what wasn't freely offered.

The bulletin board was almost full, so I moved a few things to make space. A flyer about a Tejano band playing in Alpine on December 23. A birthday card June had stapled to the board covered in signatures for Mrs. Durbin, oldest resident and ex–film star, whose measly minimum wage kept June in Cheetos and Steam cards. Another flyer announcing the winner of the artist-in-residence grant, Gypsum's latest sad effort to compete with hoity-toity Marfa. Then an article from six months ago in the *Big Bend Sentinel* announcing A. J. Garcia as the youngest mayor in Gypsum history.

I signed the birthday card in my left-handed scrawl, then hung my flyer right next to A.J.'s smiling face, dark hair pulled up in a fancy do that made her look like a professor, trying to look older than twenty-six. Ollie's ex-girlfriend.

Three bites into the best pie Aunt Macie had ever put under glass, the door opened, and Selena breezed in, her dark hair lying loose over her shoulder, her button-down untucked but ironed to perfection. A couple of guys from school at the front viewing counter gave her a once-over as she passed.

"Hey, Quinn," she said, sliding onto the seat next to mine and setting her small backpack on the checkered black-and-white tiles.

"Missed you this morning," I said. "I had to belay myself."

"Poor baby."

"Clear day. I could see all the way to Mexico."

"Dude, it's winter break. Sleep in every once in a while." She peered around the restaurant. "Where's Macie?"

At that moment, Macie swept in from the back room, the door flapping closed behind her. When her eyes lit on Selena, her face broke into a broad smile. "Hey, girlie! Quinn wants to buy you a slice of pie." She threw a sly look at me. "He told me so."

"Gee, thanks, Quinn," Selena said, giving me a fake *I'm so into you* look. "Does it come with a corsage?"

Macie waved Selena's comment away. "My matchmaking skills will be appreciated one day. You know I got your brother and A.J. together. That's right. *Me.*" She pointed at herself with the spatula.

"Look how well that turned out," I said.

"Ah, c'mon. They're the second-most-famous couple in Gypsum High history...no matter what happened after."

I didn't have to ask who the first was. The picture of Aunt Macie and Enrique at age eighteen, wearing crowns at the 1972 Gypsum prom, hung above the stove. I'd seen a similar one on the wall of their cramped trailer at Gun Barrel, stuck in with the family pictures of Gram and Great-Grandpa Liam. Macie held an armful of red roses, blond hair trailing in loops over her shoulder. Enrique, in a tux, with his broad smiling face, stood with his arm around her.

Macie looked wistful, then turned to shout through the double doors that led to the prep room. "You remember that, baby?"

"Yep" drifted through the door.

"Those were the times, weren't they, baby?" she said to the double doors.

"Yep."

Selena pretended to gag and slipped off her stool to head to the jukebox, doing a double take as she passed the bulletin board and my flyer. She slipped a quarter in the slot, punched number 16, and kicked the side twice. A Van Halen song came on.

She climbed back on her stool and leaned close. "So . . . you wanted to talk? Spill."

I did. I told her how I'd read Ms. Johanis's cup. Sank myself wrist-deep beyond the veil. How for the first time I'd felt something solid, a smooth surface, like an insect's carapace, horrible and beautiful. And that dial, right in the center, begging me to spin it. Then Ollie coming home with *that safe* in the bed of his truck.

A guitar riff filled the restaurant. My phone buzzed. Ollie's name popped up on the screen. Selena watched me switch off the phone and turn it facedown on the counter. I dug into more pie while she rested her chin on her hand, tapping out a rhythm on her cheek with one finger, thoughts somewhere else. A bruise had bloomed there overnight, just below her eye, from our fall off the grand staircase. I owed her an apology, or an ice pack, but before I could give her either of those things, she turned to me.

"Maybe we've been thinking about this all wrong."

"Wrong how?"

"We've been thinking the dreams we've all been having were a *bad* thing, sent by something evil."

The cold hand in mine. The push over the edge of the staircase. "I mean, that something *did* try to off us two nights ago."

"But it didn't," she said. "It could have strangled us, or bashed our heads against a wall, or—"

"You sure are a lot braver with the lights on."

"What I'm saying is... I think it just wanted us to find the safe."

She had a point. A one-story drop wasn't the best way to off someone.

"Think about it. Maybe someone in the great beyond is sending us dreams to *help* us. I mean, an old safe, in a hidden room, in the Alvarado? It probably has gold in it!"

I scratched my cheek. "So the Alvarado has a magic fairy that wants to help me and Ollie make two hundred fifty thousand dollars to keep Gram's house. That makes sense."

"Or a bag of diamonds," she said, ignoring my sarcasm, "from all those Hollywood executives, when they brought their fancy dames down here."

"Dames?"

"You know, that's how they talked then. It was all fox furs and dames and gumshoes."

"You watch too much AMC with your abuela."

"Bonnie and Clyde," she said, her eyes brightening. "They could've put something in there."

"Yeah, the severed head of one of their enemies."

"More likely it's a stash of their ill-gotten booty."

"You keep talking dirty to me like that, and Macie's gonna put our picture next to hers above the grill."

"You know what I mean."

Before she turned away to pick up her fork again, she blushed. Then I pictured it too, Selena and me, dressed up and smiling for the camera, my arm around her waist, a corsage on her wrist. Heat trailed up my neck. I stared at my plate.

Everything had been so much easier when we had our feet firmly planted in the friend zone.

We ate in silence while another guitar riff filled the room, the lyrics blotting out any weird thoughts. I caught a couple of words about danger in the rearview mirror.

"I don't know, Selena. I took one look at it and got a really bad vibe."

Selena checked over her shoulder and lowered her voice. "I know it's a burden, what you see sometimes. But it's also... not always accurate," she finished softly, as if afraid to hurt my feelings.

She was right. Sometimes my predictions came to a big fat nothing. In eighth grade, I'd stupidly told the entire school that I knew—psychically *knew*—that the Rattlers' basketball team would beat the Fightin' Bucks of Alpine, our archrivals. We lost. A week later, I found a dead deer on our property with a rattlesnake bite in its leg. Not quite the same thing. And eight months ago, I told Gram she'd be going on a trip this Christmas without us, because in my vision I saw a letter arriving from her a few days before New Year's. She took a trip all right, in July. To the hospital, and then to the grave.

I put my face in my hands and groaned. Maybe the risk was worth it, and when we cracked the safe, we'd be rich. No, not *when*. *If.*

"And I hope you're not refusing to open it just to spite Ollie."

"What? No."

She held up a palm. "I'm just saying, if Ollie told you to get out of the rain, you'd stand there, soaking wet, and tell him the sun was shining."

"I do not do that."

"Yeah, you don't sound stubborn at all."

I took another bite of pie, which was starting to taste like cardboard. "Like you get along with your sister."

"That's different."

"How?"

"Because A.J. is so..." I could see the word *perfect* bouncing around her head. *Dad's golden child.* She pressed her lips together. "Just because."

"God, you're worse than June. Can't admit when you're wrong."

She put her fork down. "That's not true."

"Uh-huh."

I caught a flash of anger in her eyes before she looked away, toward the grill, where Macie threw on a pile of hash browns. The sizzle filled the silence. Selena wrapped her hands around the water glass and peered into it, swirling the ice like the answers were there.

That feeling rose up again, seeping out of my bones, that spinning that dial would let something awful loose.

I dropped my fork on my plate with a clatter. "How are we even gonna crack it open? Neither me nor my brother has the skills for that. So that means drilling, which means if it's empty, we can't even sell it because it'll be damaged."

Selena sighed. "Try having faith that it's *not* empty, maybe?"

"You have to admit, this is not the best way to make money. Especially money we need like...yesterday."

The Christmas bells on the front door jingled, and Selena's big sister slipped in, a laptop bag over her shoulder. Selena stopped chewing, watching A.J. make her way through the diner, doing her mayorly duty and saying her hellos to the regulars. Then Selena turned to me, a bright little spark in her eye.

———•————————•———

It was a good idea. Selena always had good ideas. And what I was about to ask A.J. for wasn't charity, I told myself. It wasn't charity if you worked for it.

I waited until A.J. finished chatting up the regulars, giving them a politician's smile and a lot of fluffy answers about the upcoming renovations to the Alvarado, grant-funded and meant to turn it back into a working hotel. She lingered by a table of tourists—two long-haired guys who looked like they kept Austin weird—then slid into her usual booth, the one next to the autographed headshots of movie stars like John Wayne and Myrna Loy and our own Eva Durbin.

I sat down across from her just as she was booting up her laptop.

She looked up from her screen, expression grim. "They're like a plague of locusts, I swear."

"Who?"

She nodded to the two long-haired guys at the next table. "Them. I mean, just look at what they're driving."

In the parking lot, I spotted a VW van parked next to the entrance, a hokey yellow moon and cartoon forests spray painted on the door. In the center of the moon, creepy dripping black letters spelled TPS, with a smaller TRIPP'S PARANORMAL SHOW underneath. People like them wandered around town with EMF readers and little flashing gadgets, frequently getting lost in the mines. They were the type who wrote articles about our "backwater" town and how spooky we were. A.J. hated them.

"At least they spend their money here and not in Alpine," I said.

"Not nearly enough. Macie says those two are asking about the apartment above Sal Lumpkin's shop. That's all we need, that ridiculous van parked on Main Street, scaring away the holiday shoppers." A.J. typed something. "Probably looking for the ghost of Judy Garland or something." She read the screen, her expression darkening. "Look at this. They have a YouTube channel."

"Everyone has a YouTube channel."

"I don't."

I watched her obsess for a bit, her eyes on the screen. "A.J., if you want, I can hide in the halls of the Alvarado Hotel and break out into 'Somewhere over the Rainbow' and scare the crap out of them."

"That sounds fun," she said, her eyes still on the screen. "Ugh, they have, like, a million views on each video. Who watches this nonsense?" Then she glanced at me, doing a double take and closing the laptop. "All right, what do you want?"

"How do you know I want something?"

"Worst poker face in Gypsum."

"Okay, you got me," I said, throwing my hands up in mock surrender.

"Wow, you give in a lot easier than you used to."

"I'm not eight anymore."

She smiled warmly and met my eyes, reaching across the table to muss my hair. "I know. I mean, look at you, Quinn. You're a full head taller than me now."

I batted her hand away. "You done treating me like a baby? 'Cause I need a favor. A big one."

Her smile faded. "Does... Ollie know you're here?" She stumbled over the name. "Asking me for favors?"

"He doesn't have to know."

A clink on the table startled me, but it was just Macie, setting down a plate of chilaquiles and a cup of coffee. I waited for her to leave. "The artist-in-residence thing that Gypsum's doing. That's government money, right?"

"Yeah, so?"

"Which means it's a lot of money."

She eyed me strangely, taking a sip instead of answering me.

"The painter who won the prize, where they gonna stay?" I asked.

The curious glint in her eyes dimmed. "It's a sculptor, not a painter. And they're at the Dawes Ranch. In the cabin by the creek."

I pressed my lips together and waited for her to put two and two together.

"No way," she said.

"C'mon. The Starlight Campgrounds are practically empty. We could really use the money. Send them to us instead."

"Ollie hates charity, you know that." She contemplated the inside of the cup. "Especially from me."

I looked over my shoulder at Selena, who glanced at my backpack meaningfully. This was the one part of the plan that really sucked.

I unzipped the top compartment and pulled out the foreclosure notice, hoping Gram wasn't looking down from heaven right now. She always said O'Briens should never beg for anything. I started to show it to A.J. but froze. Heat crept up my neck and I folded it in half instead.

"I'm not asking for charity. We'll earn it. I'll make the cabin look nice."

She gave me a wary look. "The cabin? It's drafty and full of scorpions."

"I cleaned out the scorpions last week. It's totally fine." When her expression didn't alter, I kept going. "Ollie's had me painting and doing all sorts of HGTV things in there. All I need to do is put up frilly curtains and the linens and stuff. And I'll deliver muffins in a basket to their door every day." I watched her face, and I could see she was on the edge of tipping over to my side. "Selena said she'd help."

A.J.'s expression hardened, and I realized I'd made a terrible mistake. She put her coffee cup down with a *plunk*. "Oh my God. My sister put you up to this?"

"She knows a good bet when she sees one."

I didn't need psychic abilities to read her next move. "I'm sorry, Quinn. The Daweses are already expecting them. There's nothing I can do."

We sat in uncomfortable silence for a moment. Then I unfolded the foreclosure notice and slid it facedown across the table.

She picked it up, her eyes scanning the words. Halfway down, shock registered in her eyes. "Oh my God."

"They're gonna love it in the cabin," I said. "Best place in town."

She set it down on the table between us. The red numbers—$10,158 DUE NOW—screaming in the space between us. "How long has this been going on?"

"Doesn't matter. We just need to get caught up on the mortgage."

She rubbed a hand over her face and looked to the parking lot, as if she couldn't bear to meet my eyes. "Same old Ollie. Throwing money into wishing wells rather than . . ." She looked at me then, her expression filled with disappointment. "If everything's not perfect, Gypsum will never get one of these grants again."

"Weekly laundry service."

"Quinn, I—"

"Free rock-climbing lessons."

"No. Just no."

We sat in silence. Then I stuffed the foreclosure notice back in my bag so hard it tore down the middle. I was sure the bank would be happy to send us another one.

A.J. looked sorry. She really did. "I'm trying to change things here, you know," she said. "Make it more than the ghost town everyone keeps saying it is. Make this a place the artists come to, like Marfa. Make this place thrive, just like Dad..."

I could feel the sentence finish in her head. One deathbed comment from Sheriff Garcia about the empty spot on the mayor's ballot and how he loved Gypsum almost as much as he loved his girls, and abracadabra, here she was, trying to do CPR on a town that had been dead for twenty years.

"Look, I know there's only one reason you came back to Gypsum. And I loved your dad too. So did Ollie."

She sat back in the booth. "It's more than that now. I've got a responsibility to make this town *something* again. And I can. If I play it right."

"But what good is it to be mayor of a one-stoplight town if you can't help the people who live here?"

A.J. took a dainty sip of her coffee. "Gypsum has three stoplights, thank you very much."

"Yeah, but only one of them works."

A.J. smiled in spite of herself. I watched my words register. *Helping the people who live here,* that was what her father meant when he said he loved the town. Gypsum wasn't anything without its people.

Her expression shifted, an idea brightening in her eyes. "Look, I can't send you the artist. But maybe I can send you someone else. I mean, money is money, right?"

Something about her tone set off a warning bell. "Who'd you have in mind?"

A.J.'s phone rang, and Ollie's name showed up on the screen. Her eyes widened. She picked it up like she was afraid a snake would come out of the speaker. "Hello?"

A rapid buzz of Ollie's voice bled through the speaker, and A.J.'s expression changed from wary to concerned. She gave me the phone. "It's for you."

I put it up to my ear. "What, you can't give me one hour of peace?"

"Why'd you turn your phone off? I tried everyone. Aunt Macie wasn't answering and—"

"Yes, I turned my stupid phone off."

"Quinn, you have to come home."

I was about to tell him off—tell him I wasn't going to drag that safe into the house—but I stopped short. His voice. The last time I'd heard that tone, Gram had died.

"What's wrong?"

A long silence filled the line. "There's been an accident."

CHAPTER
SIX

I pulled up into the mouth of our long snaking gravel drive just as EMS did. In the distance sat Gram's big white house, at least a mile of empty desert on every side, the Chinati Mountains behind pressing their spines into the blue sky. A police car was parked next to Ollie's truck. The small figure with sloped shoulders and tan uniform standing next to my brother had to be Selena's uncle, Deputy Cruz. It was too far away to see who was sitting on the steps of the front porch, head in hands, but after what Ollie had told me, I knew exactly who it was.

June.

And I wasn't sure how I was going to face her. Because while I was shredding the speed limit, heading for home, it dawned on me that this wouldn't have happened if I'd just unloaded the safe like Ollie wanted.

I turned the last corner and pulled up behind the police car, which blocked my view of the "accident." Ollie glanced my way. June looked up from her hands, her eyes swollen and red.

She hadn't been within ten feet of her father's front door since the spring, when she finally moved out and got a place with her mom in the Gun Barrel Trailer Park. I hadn't seen much of him since then either, but I knew him well enough. Her dad, Bud.

I cut my engine and stepped off my bike, not knowing where to look.

"Quinn." Ollie called my name softly.

I rounded the cop car as the EMS pulled up behind me.

The safe lay facedown, on the gravel drive, an orange nylon strap around it, the dolly still attached to the side. Next to it was one of Gram's old blankets, and under the blanket was a shape. I could make out the shape of shoulders, hips. A body. And I recognized the snakeskin boots.

Ollie came to me, blocking my view of the blanket, putting an arm around my shoulders and turning me away.

"What happened?" I managed.

Ollie rubbed a palm over his ashen face, glanced at Deputy Cruz. "Bud was helping me get the safe down from the truck and..."

He kept talking. Something about how it was all going fine, until suddenly it wasn't. How they'd been flapping gums while moving it, talking about what might be inside, how he'd split the goodies with Bud if he helped him crack it, and Bud saying they should just sell it, unopened, in an auction in San Antonio. Distracted with talk, Ollie said. Not paying good enough attention. Then the safe shifted suddenly, tipped before Ollie could catch it. How it seemed to slip through their fingers, like it was greased.

Deputy Cruz's voice came from my left, but it was like his words had been strained through cheesecloth. Something about accidents like this happening more than you think they do. That Bud had died instantly, taking the full force of the blow to his face like that.

A dark stain had spread out beyond the edges of the blanket, trickling downhill toward the police car. The wind shifted, and the smell came with it, copper and earth and...

Without a word, I turned and walked away from the house. Ollie called after me, but I didn't stop. As soon as I'd passed the refrigerators, it was like my stomach knew I was finally alone.

Voices gathered just beyond the clump of junkyard where I was hiding. Like a coward, I stayed put. My stomach wasn't done emptying itself, so I braced myself on my thighs and stared at the ground. The creak of van doors reached me, followed by the grind and rattle of a gurney bumping across the rutted gravel, and for the first time in my life, I hated the land I lived on. We needed a regular paved drive. Why didn't we have one? And money. Why didn't we have enough money to hire movers when we needed something moved? And why hadn't I stayed, like I was supposed to?

Then another question elbowed past the others.

Why hadn't I seen this coming?

I kicked the refrigerator nearest me, and it groaned, its door swinging open wider, like a mouth, until I could see where Ollie and Gram had drilled out the handles so they would never lock again. A sickly odor wafted out, a sweet sort of mildew. I kicked the door hard again and watched it fall off its hinges. Then I sat with my back to it, a chill breeze picking up until my face went numb, along with the rest of me. Why did the Dark Place tell me what kind of pie Macie was gonna serve at the Gypsum Lights tomorrow, but not tell me Bud Pilsner was gonna die in our driveway?

Ollie called my name. I walked back to the house, to face June and my brother and the police and the whole horrible lot of it.

The next three hours were a blur, a swirl of color and voices around me as I sat next to June on the porch steps, my arm around her shoulders, while people moved about our driveway. Her mom was on her way but still an hour out, coming back from a day trip to El Paso to see their cousin. Deputy Cruz took notes, while Ollie stood beside the safe, nodding every so often and giving brusque answers to Cruz's questions. From under the porch shadows, Tater blinked at me, her shoulders tensed, her tail hidden underneath her; then she slinked out and sat beside June.

June reached out and stroked Tater's head absently, as if she couldn't sit any longer without something for her hands to do. There was no love lost between her and her father, but still, your father was your father.

A.J. rolled up in her Jeep Cherokee just as two EMTs were putting Bud Pilsner in a black bag. She stepped out and made her way to Ollie, who for once didn't look like he was about to throw her off his land. Then an EMT came over to the porch, put a hand on June's shoulder, and asked if she wanted to go with Bud in the van. June shook her head.

Six months ago, when June had left home, she told us only part of the truth. What it was like to live with someone like her dad, who was arguably the strangest person in Gypsum (which was saying something). Withdrawn. Paranoid. He talked more to the snakes than he did to his wife or his daughter, spending most of his time collecting venom to sell for some weird side hustle. And then he began setting up booby traps on their land. He had an overwhelming fear of the big bad government coming in to take his stuff, so he turned their home and land into a fortress. "To prepare for the future," Bud would say. June told us it was the last straw for her mother, and for her. It wasn't until just before Thanksgiving that I found out the reason they left. *Me.*

I'd gotten so used to what I could do that I forgot sometimes how freaky it was, like watching a person sprout a third arm. And June's dad, well, apparently, he'd cracked open a beer one day and told June and her mother that she wasn't allowed to hang out with me anymore. That gifts like mine weren't really gifts at all, but a sign of something more sinister. Her mom, who was already on the edge of leaving, only needed a little push, and June told her she was moving, whether her mother planned to come along or not.

I went inside to fetch a Coke from the fridge and came back out to set it beside her. June was a lot of things. Unreliable, inconsiderate, less funny than she thought she was. But she was loyal with a capital *L*.

June looked at the Coke, and then finally met my eyes. I thought she would break down. But she bit her lip, which was quivering. Maybe she would blame me, or ask me if I could take her back to the Gun Barrel, or tell me she never wanted to see me again.

"I shouldn't have left you in the dark."

"What are you talking about?"

"Like, I *actually* left you sitting in the dark, back in the Alvarado, without any lights to get you out. You're my best friend, and I can't believe I did that to you. I'm sorry."

"It's okay. We don't need to worry about that right now."

"Yeah, we do." I watched her pick at her cuticles until they bled. Then she grabbed the Coke, popped the top, and finished half of it in one long drink. She put the can next to her on the step. "There's this voice, in my head sometimes."

My breath snagged on something in my chest.

She went on. "When I hear it, I always think it's me—at first."

A voice. In her head. She said it so casually, like she'd gotten used to that voice long ago.

"It's only later I realize it *isn't* my voice."

If I hadn't experienced the same thing, I'd have thought she was losing her mind. I tried to keep my tone even. "And what did the voice say?"

She crossed her arms over her chest and rocked forward. "That you would be safer in the dark. That the ghosts, or whatever, would pass right by you then. And that I needed to see what was in that next room. Really *see* it."

"So you were trying to protect us."

"I guess."

"So . . . what did you see?"

"Nothing. That room was empty." Her voice cracked on the last word. We sat for a while, watching the sun inch down in the afternoon sky. "Quinn?"

"Yeah?"

"Did you know this was going to happen?"

"I had no idea."

"You didn't see it coming down the road? Maybe in a dream?"

"I swear, I would have told you if I'd known."

We sat without speaking for a while. She leaned her head on my shoulder, and I could feel her body trembling.

"I should've made you read my cup," she said, and then she finally let go.

I watched the clouds on the horizon, sweeping over the mountains, as I let her cry it out. I wondered if her cup would have been honest with us.

By the time the EMTs left with Bud, the sun was dipping low, along with the temperature. A.J. and Ollie talked alone out of earshot, their heads closer together than I'd seen them in years.

Deputy Cruz walked up to the porch and stopped, the sun behind him, throwing his craggy face in shadow. He zipped up his jacket against the cold, his breath fogging. "Your mom just called, June. She'll be at the Gun Barrel by sunset. I can take you."

"I'll take her," I said.

She turned to me. I expected grief, but she just looked lost. "No, I'll go with him."

Cruz gently pulled June away and helped her into the cruiser. A.J. gave Ollie a rare hug. I stared at my boots until A.J.'s engine roared to life and her tires crunched down the road. Then the world became quiet again, everyone gone, like the end of a really bad party.

Ollie settled next to me. The safe was still there. The EMTs had hauled it off Bud, but they'd left it on its side. I watched it, wondering which of us would speak first.

"I know you hate me right now," I said.

Ollie turned me to him so I would meet his eyes. "Why the hell would I hate you?"

Because everything was my fault. If I had just let sleeping dogs lie, like Gram taught me, the floor of the Alvarado would be whole, the safe wouldn't be here, Ollie would be looking for a different for-sure thing, and everyone would be okay. But I couldn't say any of that.

"I should have been here. Helping you."

He shook his head slowly, like he couldn't believe he had to explain himself to me. "No, man. I'm relieved."

"Relieved?"

"That could have been *you* under that thing. Not that I'm happy poor Bud . . . Look, it wasn't anyone's fault. It was a freak accident."

But somehow, deep down, I *knew* it wasn't an accident.

Ollie reached toward me, pausing halfway like he wasn't quite sure how to finish the motion. Then he let his hand fall by his side. "Quinn, I might yell and cuss and give you a hard time, but you're a serious dumbass if you think I would ever *hate* you, okay?"

My throat felt thick, maybe because I believed him, maybe because I didn't.

I stared at the safe, thinking again about the way it felt when I touched the smooth surface in the Dark Place. Like skin and metal at the same time. I squeezed my eyes shut. Selena's voice came back to me, something about me being the Grim Reaper.

Ollie sighed, pulling up his hat to scratch his forehead before settling it back on his head. He usually loved this place—the hush of empty spaces, the brilliant night sky—but his eyes were fixed on the northern horizon, like he wanted to be on the road, be anywhere but here.

A cloud of dust rose in the distance, near the entrance to our driveway. Ollie squinted. "You got to be kidding me."

"What?"

A familiar van rounded the bend, TRIPP'S PARANORMAL SHOW airbrushed on its side. It took me a moment to put it together: A.J.'s refusal at lunch to send the fancy-pants artist here to stay in our cabin…her telling me she had someone else in mind…

"Oh no," I muttered.

"We can't have campers showing up today! Not after what…" Ollie gestured to the dark stain on the driveway without looking at it.

"I'm pretty sure these guys want the cabin." I wasn't about to tell him how I knew.

He met my eye. We sat so close I could see the brown flecks in the green of his irises. I could smell his stress sweat. We were both thinking of the foreclosure notice, burning a hole in the kitchen counter. That $10,158 DUE NOW, glaring at us in red letters.

"You remember Gram's motto?" Ollie asked, looking over his shoulder at the empty rocking chair on the porch, like he expected to see her there. "*Money—*"

"—*is money. Get it where you can.* Yeah, I didn't forget."

I stared at the safe, and a creeping sensation swept up my back. I didn't know why, but it looked like it had shifted on its own, moved an inch closer to me. And for a second, I caught a sound on the wind, below the engine rumble from the van and the soft mewing of Tater on the porch. A hum, coming from inside.

Ollie nudged me. His eyes were on the van. He waved, putting on his best fake *Welcome to the Starlight Campgrounds* smile.

"Quinn," he said softly, his eye on the new customers, the wooden smile never leaving his face, "get your ass inside and grab sheets and towels and whatever else Gram would do to make that place look like something other than a glorified toolshed. I'll stall. You have thirty minutes."

●————————————●

When it comes to hanging curtains, nails work just as well as spring rods. A potted cactus on the cabin's small kitchen table works just as well as flowers. They'd be looking at the view anyway. And fancy coffee and a French press? Forget it. A bag of my special-blend tea and a decent spritzing of Glade to cover the smell of the recent paint job would do the place just fine. The weirdos would love it. Well, I didn't know what weirdos liked, but it would have to do.

Out the cabin's front window, two people came into view. The first seemed about Ollie's age, a tall guy with shoulder-length blond hair. He reminded me of surfers I'd seen on YouTube, with their casual tans and loping gait. The only thing out of place was the T-shirt he wore, which was two sizes too small and read DO YOU KNOW WHAT'S LIVING IN YOUR BASEMENT? It seemed to be designed to show off his abs.

In front of him a short guy with a ponytail walked backward, a camera trained on T-shirt guy's face, which was beaming with a smile I could only describe as real-estate fabulous. I caught a few words, like *charming* and *dilapidated,* and wasn't sure if he was talking about the town or the cabin.

Hurriedly, I did another quick sweep. The wood-framed pictures next to the TV were things I'd found in Gram's shed: black-and-white photos of Liam O'Brien and a few other guys in old-fashioned climbing gear, standing at the base of the Horse Crippler. The clock, which was set in the belly of an armadillo, had apparently run out of battery, its hands stuck on 1:23 p.m. The free calendar hanging on the small bathroom door was turned to the wrong month.

And standing there, the footsteps outside growing louder, I breathed in the saccharine smell of Glade, catching a whiff of mustiness underneath, and saw the place clearly for the first time. A wood-paneled nightmare with a rickety towel rack and a deer head on the wall.

I turned back to the window, a sick feeling rising in my stomach. They'd be moving out by sundown. And taking their money with them.

But then I saw the look on the surfer dude's face.

The short one was staring at his phone, but the other guy couldn't stop looking at the desert, the sky, the mountains—and the expression there, I'd seen it before.

That guy, he wouldn't care.

I slipped out the back just as their boots hit the porch, taking the deer head with me. I spent most of the walk back thinking about Bud, and then thinking about what was in the safe, and then feeling guilty about not thinking about Bud more. Back at the house, I fed Tater, who heard the rattle in the food dish and shot out from under the porch like she was on fire. Then I threw some grain and scraps into the coop, gathered eggs from the nesting boxes, and cleaned the soiled pine shavings. I fixed a hole in the henhouse with some spare chicken wire I found in the shed, hidden next to Gram's boxes of picture albums and old family journals. Swept the back porch and washed it down with a bucket of water. I'd never felt so restless.

The porch door creaked open behind me. I didn't turn.

"Quinn, come help me get the safe out of here."

I got up and made my way around the house to the driveway, where the safe still lay on its side. Ollie had a long silver ramp set up at the tailgate, so that no one would have to be under the thing ever again. After he got the guests settled, he'd probably gone down to the hardware store and blown seventy bucks on that ramp. But the money was worth it, if just for the relief, knowing that the thing would be gone within the hour.

Ollie turned his cap backward and pulled some chewing gum from his pocket, started popping. "Let's get this over with."

"Where are we taking it?"

He shrugged. "Let's drive it out to the edge of the junkyard and put it under some plastic."

I stared at the safe, my insides tugging. Yes, away from the house. And then maybe Ollie would forget all about it. Out of sight, out of mind.

Turning the safe upright wasn't hard. I just grabbed the hand truck and pulled while Ollie lifted from the other side. Then we carefully maneuvered it to the end of the ramp.

"I'll bring up the rear," Ollie said, pointing for me to step up.

I didn't want it backslide on him like it had Bud. "No, I'll do it."

This set off a fifteen-minute argument that I was sure everyone in the campground could hear. The sun set an inch more. The rooster weather vane threw long shadows in the yard. Finally, I gave up and stepped on the ramp, grabbing the handle of the hand truck to tip the safe.

It didn't budge.

"All right, Ollie, you got me up here. Would you damn well push?"

Ollie stepped behind it, grimacing, and placed two palms on the top. "On three."

We counted. On three, I pulled, he pushed. Nothing. Suddenly, the safe weighed a thousand pounds, as if someone had bolted it to the ground.

My arms broke out in gooseflesh that had nothing to do with the cold.

Ollie adjusted his hat and tipped his head. "What the hell."

We tried again. And again. It wouldn't move even a millimeter.

By the time the sun had set, we sat sweating on the tailgate, on either side of the ramp, staring at it. The safe stared back.

Thrumming bass drifted to us from the direction of the road, and a minute later, a beat-up car rounded the bend stuffed full of college kids, most of them already drunk.

A.J., being helpful. I could almost hear her voice. *You want campers? Here ya go, Quinn. Enjoy.*

Ollie shot me a look that said *When it rains, it pours,* then waved them over to park beside the van, while I hid on the porch, in no mood for chitchat. Ollie took their fifteen dollars and handed them a paper map of the campground. I came back down just in time to see them disappear down the trail, their backpacks bobbing as they walked, carrying a case of beer between them.

"It's fillin' up," Ollie said.

"Yes, three whole campsites are full."

Ollie turned to look at me. "Dude, shout it out on social media! Tell 'em we've still got vacancies!" Then he started babbling about the social media plan and how it was working just like he said it would. A sure thing. I didn't have the heart to tell him the campers were here because of A.J. spreading the word, and our forty-three followers were just townies.

We tried to move the safe one last time, until even Ollie, the most stubborn person in the universe, had to admit defeat. "Maybe we're just tired," he said.

"Yeah, that makes sense. Being tired definitely changes the laws of physics."

"It's been a long day."

"We rolled that thing to the end of the ramp, but now it weighs as much as a battleship."

He placed his palms on top again, and a strange expression crossed his face. "You know, it's still warm. From the sun."

Another chill went down my arms. The metal tailgate I was sitting on was so cold that it hurt.

"Maybe we should call someone to come help," I said. "Enrique would do it." Bud's face popped into my head, like a habit. A sharp edge of fear followed, pressing right into my spine, the feeling that no one—no one—could get this safe on the truck bed.

Ollie rubbed his fingers across the top of it. "No," he said softly. "It's okay. We'll try again in the morning." He looked up, peering past me, rather than at me. "Get some rest."

"We haven't had dinner."

He turned and walked up the steps. "I'm beat. There's a pizza in the freezer."

"But—"

"Good night, Quinn." He shut the door. A few seconds later the Christmas lights on the porch flicked on.

I sat out on the tailgate until the fear gave way to cold numbing my fingers, seeping through the soles of my boots. I shoved my thoughts away—let the cold wind take them. It wasn't like the safe could grow legs and come inside.

The darkness grew thick in the yard. The sun put itself out in the mountains, like an ember in a lake. Ollie would give me hell if I didn't snap a few pics, post them on Instagram. *Quinn, you need to earn your keep,* he'd say. *Make something other than a mess around here.*

I opened our account to see my last post—a "sculpture" of an old Thunderbird rusting in our junkyard, cactus sprouting up around its tires, a sparrow perched on its steering wheel. I'd titled it *Sculpture #12: Plenty.* There were no Sculptures #1 through #11, but hey, if Marfa could leave metal to rust in the desert and call it art, so could I.

I thumbed through the feed, pausing on the pictures of places I wanted to visit one day, stops on the way up to British Columbia, a motorcycle trip my brother and I talked about sometimes, when we weren't fighting. Cathedral Grove, where it was so green and the trees so tall it made my head spin. I swiped, and the mountains surrounding Whistler appeared. Another swipe, street scene in Vancouver. Swipe. Café in Victoria. I imagined the ride, the adventure of it. The hostels my brother and I would stay in. How cool it would be to come back to Gypsum with a battered backpack and a year's worth of stories.

After a ridiculously beautiful vista of the Pacific coast, up came a post from June. *Best Friends,* it read. It was a picture posted a few days ago, but she'd taken it much earlier. The three of us at the Gypsum High Art Show, where Selena had taken top prize *again* for photography. June's and Selena's faces were pressed on either side of mine, me pretending I hated it, them smiling wildly; Selena's eyes done up with glitter, June with a small cactus covered in Christmas lights painted on her pale cheek, a purple streak entwined in her blond braid. And me, I looked just like June always said I did, with a wild head of O'Brien curls and my don't-talk-to-me black denim. Like someone who was trying to disappear into the crowd. In this shot, with the dour expression and the camera flash picking up the glint of silver on my left ear, I looked like a guy about to write a poem about death, get on a bus to Seattle, and leave Gypsum forever.

I studied the safe in the driveway, a clump of ocotillo behind it. Selena would take a look and call it found art. A new sculpture. Lucky #13. I framed my camera on it, mostly as a joke, lining up the shot. I wouldn't actually post it, not after what happened today.

But the flash went off, and a tumble of images rolled through my head like a waking dream. The Alvarado's chandelier; pictures lined up on the wall; room numbers shifting and tumbling over each other, the flapping wings of birds breaking into flight.

I pulled the phone down, my hands shaking. Flipped into my photos, afraid I'd see it all captured there. But I just saw the safe, looking like nothing at all. A black box, contents unknown.

Eyes closed, I told myself to get a grip. Focus on what's real, not the horror show in my head.

I framed a few shots of the sunset over the Horse Crippler, posting the best one on the campground account. *End of another amazing day at the Starlight Lounge. It's fillin' up fast, so book your spot now!*

Ollie was wrong about me. I was an excellent liar.

CHAPTER
SEVEN

The Alvarado welled up in my mind, like a bead of blood from a wound that just wouldn't heal. Black birds, picture frames, a jumble of images cutting into me and telling me to count. And the silver dial of the safe, always watching, its numbers like ants marching in circles.

The blue sky at noon. I was a kid in the junkyard, playing hide-and-seek. I'd win this time, for sure. The old refrigerator, listing there by a clump of rocks and an old bedspring. Its door hanging open like a flap of skin. I didn't want to, but I was so sick of losing to June, sick of her crowing and celebrating and calling me a loser.

The dark insides of the refrigerator whispered to me, saying it was the best place for children to hide.

Suddenly, I was pulling air through a straw. Pressure—on my chest, my face. I struggled, fighting my way up out of the dream. Six years old again, banging on the door to be let out.

I jerked upright, my heart trying to beat its way out of my rib cage. The darkness thickened around me like water in my lungs. I thrashed through the sheets and Gram's quilt, stumbling out of the bed and making my way to the window, ripping the curtains aside to let the moonlight in.

The room felt wrong. Tense, like a bowstring, like a held breath. Down the hall, Ollie cried out in his sleep too, then fell quiet.

I wandered into the bathroom and fumbled in the dark for the pull chain on the bulb above the mirror. The room flooded with light, lit up my face and my wide staring eyes. The bedhead, the silver earring, the pale skin—I looked like I'd just woken up after a week dead in the desert.

I blinked. Leaned in close to the mirror. Across my mouth, my right cheek . . . the skin looked strange. Reddened, like I'd broken out with some kind of rash. Maybe a new detergent? Ollie was always searching for a good deal at the dollar store. God, one day he would poison us both.

Turning my jaw, I examined the rash. No, not a rash, just swelling. Five stripes of pale red, one shorter than the others. I touched it and found the flesh tender, like a bruise would form tomorrow.

I froze. Five marks, like fingers would leave.

A handprint.

I turned on the tap and splashed cold water on my face. A sweat broke out on my back. No, it *wasn't* a handprint. No way. That was just a dream.

Leaning my forearms on the sink edge, I watched the water swirl, the earthy scent rising up and filling me. Healing waters. When she was younger, Gram swam in the spring every day, she said, floated on her back fully clothed, looking up at the wide blue sky. Told me Gypsum waters could fix anything that ailed me.

I threaded my fingers through my hair and gripped until the roots burned. Maybe they could fix paranoia. Maybe I could inject water into my brain with a hypodermic needle.

A prickle on my back made me stiffen. When I stood to look at myself in the mirror again, I wasn't alone.

A flash of gray behind me.

I spun around. Flowered wallpaper. A wet towel hanging on a hook. And the kind of quiet you'd find if you were trapped inside a jar. But . . . nothing else. No shadow or smoke, or—God forbid I should even think it to myself—ghost.

The bathroom was empty. Whatever had been there had disappeared.

———•———

Sleep wasn't happening, so I put on my black denim jacket and beanie and climbed out the bedroom window, up the trellis, and onto the roof.

I always felt better when I could see the sky, and tonight there were no clouds.

Like a container that had been stuffed too full, I couldn't take one more thing. If Gram were here, she'd sit me down on the front porch, hand me a glass of sweet tea, and tell me the mind has a limit. She once told me it's why people laugh and joke after funerals. Or why a kid who'd almost suffocated in a junkyard refrigerator could be found later that very night, eating ice cream and watching reruns of *M*A*S*H* with his grandmother. Or why a guy who just might have a malevolent spirit following him could lie back on the roof and lose himself in the view.

There's only so much fear a body can absorb.

The scattering of stars glowed bright and clear in the icy air. Near the horizon I spotted Venus, next to the waxing moon, curved like a scythe. Then the Milky Way. Tonight it felt less like the highway Gram talked about, and more like a bird's wing, stretching over our house and the campgrounds.

I looked toward downtown, the lights dim to keep the dark sky intact, and wondered what Mom was doing, out there in the world somewhere. If she was the type to worry, about me and the strange things happening in my life. If she'd do something to help. But it had been a long time since I'd wondered about Mom at all, or where she went to after she left us. I had no face to remember, just stories and vague comments—the same kind Gram offered whenever I asked who my father had been.

They weren't the kind of parents that stay, she'd say.

Ollie's descriptions of Mom weren't any better, but she left when he was six, so I guess he couldn't remember much. He said we didn't need people who didn't need us. That he and Gram were all the family I'd ever need.

Sometimes, though, I'd wondered about what makes someone the kind of person who stays. If you inherit that, or if you choose it.

I exhaled, and the stars trembled in the fog of my breath. The cold seeped up through the roof tiles, bit through my jeans, but I felt better than I had all day. I uncapped my water bottle and drank, watching the sediment at the bottom swirl and glimmer in the starlight, remembering dinners at June's place, back when I was still learning how to throw a baseball, and Bud was a second father.

Finish your water, son. It's good for you.

I swirled it again, watching the sediment turn into a little twister. The tourists who came to the diner complained, sometimes sent their glasses back and asked for a Pellegrino or an Evian or some snob water like that. All the locals knew the truth, though. That you should always finish your water—the stuff at the bottom was the best part. And Bud, back then, he was always looking out for me.

The crackle of tires on gravel drifted up to me, but no engine. Bike tires. I'd recognize them anywhere.

When Ollie said that he and Gram were the only family I'd need, he should have added June and Selena to the list.

They crawled up the trellis without a word—they knew better than to wake Ollie and get sent home—settling themselves on either side of me, June smelling of mint gum and a faint whiff of stale cigarettes from Mrs. Durbin's trailer, and Selena of spice and sandalwood perfume. Selena plunked a small backpack next to me, and I caught it before it slid right off the roof.

"What's this?" I asked. "Please tell me you brought candy."

"You do know me, right?" She unzipped the bag and took out a glass container full of berries.

June and I exchanged a glance.

Selena and her big sister were more alike than she wanted to admit. Healthy snacks and academic planners and prepping for the SAT a year early, which, of course, was easy when you had a photographic memory like Selena did. Usually I found her prissy tendencies annoying, but tonight it was comforting. Tonight it was good to know some things never changed.

I nudged June. "You okay?"

June shrugged. I didn't push.

We ate berries and some sort of horrible seaweed "treat" while Selena fished a camera and tripod out of her bag. We knew June well enough to know she wasn't ready to talk yet, so Selena set up the tripod to catch the night sky and went on a rant about how her house was bursting with cousins and aunts, and how her sister was "ruining" Christmas by bossing everyone around and rearranging the ornaments on the tree, which wouldn't have bothered me one bit. At least they had a tree. Then we listened to June complain about Mrs. Durbin, who'd "fired" June *again,* this time because June had found the old woman's hidden fifth of whiskey tucked between two couch cushions and poured it down the sink. Of course, no one else wanted the job, so June would be back tomorrow with her usual peace offering—a pack of Marlboro Lights and new support hose.

As they talked, my gaze kept drifting back to the dark stain on the driveway. June rattled on and on, but Selena fell quiet.

"—like it's even gonna matter anymore," June said. "She's leaving town anyway."

I stopped and blinked and then replayed that statement. "Mrs. Durbin is leaving? As in, forever?"

"She doesn't know yet. Her people are coming to get her, take her home to San Antonio." Her voice held a bitter edge, like she couldn't quite believe it either. "They asked me to keep her busy while they pack tomorrow. Keep her looking the other way."

"They'll have to drag her out of that trailer."

Her expression softened. "At this point, she might not even notice."

June always complained about Mrs. Durbin, how she couldn't seem to let go of all that fame, gnawing on memories like she was looking for a tooth that was no longer there. But this wasn't the best timing for the universe to take away another fixture of June's life.

I nudged June's side with the toe of my shoe. She looked up, a warning bright in her eyes. I ignored it. "Really, though. How're you doing?"

She shrugged. "I'll get another job."

"That's not what I mean."

"I'm fine."

"How in the world are you fine?"

"I'm better than Bud, that's for sure." June looked from Selena's face to mine. "Too soon?" She shrugged, and a lump rose in my throat.

My gaze slipped again to the spot by Ollie's truck, where the police had been earlier, where Bud Pilsner's body had been. The shadow of the safe stood there, a cutout in the night. It wasn't like a piece of furniture could have a will of its own. Make itself fall over.

Then another thought came, louder than the others. *Yes, yes it could.*

June wrapped her arms around her knees and peered out into the dark. "I'll survive. My mom is a mess, but that's nothing new. If she would be honest with herself for once, we lost him years ago."

Something in her tone said she was done talking about it.

June's eyes flicked to my mouth. "Hey, what happened to your face?"

I mumbled something about laundry detergent and rubbed my palm across the stubble on my chin. The skin still felt sore. I looked down into the driveway again, then back at my room. Through the roof tiles, the feel of the house holding its breath reached up to me.

I let my hand drop, unease growing. "Have the dreams been...I don't know...getting worse for you two?"

"Not really," June said.

"Actually, they're kinda...softer now," Selena said. "I don't know how else to describe it."

I rubbed my face again. "Not for me. Tonight it was..." I let my hand fall. "I don't know. More real or something."

Selena and June exchanged a coded look.

"What?"

Selena turned on her side and propped her chin on her elbow. She looked back at June, like she was asking permission, before she turned back to me. "The dreams have always been worse for you. You ever wonder why that is?"

I had wondered, but I was honestly too scared of the answer to look that hard. Whenever we compared details, Selena and June reported it all like it was a movie playing in their heads. But I didn't just *see* myself walking up those stairs, which crumbled like stone. I could actually *smell* it. The damp and rot. *Feel* the cold wrapping itself up my spine. *Hear* the scrape of my boots on the floorboards.

"Nope, never really thought about it."

"We were talking," Selena said, "and we thought…all those readings you do, maybe you're…causing this somehow? The dreams, I mean."

"What?"

Selena held up her hands in surrender. "We're not saying you're doing it on purpose."

"We're not saying that at all," June said. "When Selena brought it up, actually, it seemed kind of farfetched—"

Selena's expression pinched. "So now it's my idea?"

"You're the one who was all *Where's this coming from* and *He's got some seriously weird energy* and—"

"Oh, please," Selena scoffed.

"I'm not causing this," I cut in. "I mean, why would you even go there?"

Selena turned back to me. "Just hear us out. And it is *us*." Selena shot a quick poison look over her shoulder. "You've got a sixth sense, and you keep opening that door, over and over again. Reading leaves, telling fortunes. Maybe, just maybe, you're…channeling something. Maybe you're sending *your* dreams to *us* without really meaning to."

Not once in the last year had I considered this. The dreams were just a mysterious force weaving themselves through the town. Hell, sometimes I even thought Ollie had them, calling out in the middle of the night, thrashing in his sleep.

"I'm not doing this to you."

Selena pressed her lips together.

"Maybe June has them because we're second cousins," I offered.

"What about me?" Selena asked.

"You, well, maybe you're just psychic and you don't know it. Hell, these could be in *everyone's* heads, for all we know."

Selena threw up her hands. "Okay, you're right. Totally right."

"You're starting to sound like Ollie. *Stop messin' with forces you don't understand.* Are you kidding me? You're saying I'm hurting you? It's coming from the hotel, not me! And besides, what am I, anyway? I don't have telekinetic powers or firestarter powers or anything like that. I just *see* things, and not even lottery numbers, just useless stupid things. Did my fancy abilities stop *that* from happening?" I gestured toward the driveway. "No, they didn't. I couldn't send you dreams even if I tried."

This set off a flurry of *Oh, of course* and *It was just a theory,* each of them stumbling over the other until I was sure they didn't mean a word they said.

Like Ollie, they thought there was something wrong with me.

The grind of a window opening beneath slid up the side of the house. A familiar voice thundered up from below the roofline. "Quinn!"

I put my finger to my lips. They nodded and kept quiet. They knew the drill. I crab-walked to the edge until Ollie's head and shoulders were visible, leaning out of my window, his dour expression bathed in yellow light.

"Don't you think it's late?"

"No."

Ollie sighed. "Get your butt down off the roof. You're gonna kill yourself." Then he looked past me, although he couldn't see a thing but the starry sky. "And girls?"

Both June and Selena froze for a moment, then answered in unison. "Yeah?"

"Go home."

———————————●———————————

A few minutes later, Selena and June were two dark figures on bicycles, while Ollie and I argued about whether or not it was dangerous to sleep on a roof. I wouldn't budge.

"What are you, my jailer?"

"No, I'm your brother. Now get off the damn roof."

"Gram and I sat up here a hundred times, and neither of us rolled off."

A pause, a heavy sigh. Then the window slammed shut.

I stayed there until the cold numbed me through, thinking about what Selena and June had said. In all the years Gram taught me how to read, how to *see*, she never said anything about opening a door we couldn't shut.

I lay back and put my hands behind my head.

My phone pinged. It was a text from Bill Winter at the Gun Barrel Trailer Park.

I hear ur back in business. Come by tomorrow at one?

Bill Winter used to be one of Gram's best customers. Never made a big decision without getting a reading first. If I was lucky, Bill would spread the word, and soon I'd have all of the Gun Barrel Trailer Park feeding me twenties. By the time Ollie found out, maybe I'd have enough to keep the bank off our heels for a while. And June and Selena, they wouldn't even know.

I tapped out a quick sure and slipped the phone in my pocket.

You've got the gift, boy, Gram told me. *More than any of the O'Briens. So much of it a teacup can't hold it all. Nothing can.*

She went on about that a lot. How I was different. There were plenty of people in our family who could see, and we all had a little of the gift—even Cousin June had a warped version of *seeing,* seeing in the dark—but mine, Gram said, was the strongest she'd ever seen. Stronger than my mother's, and she threw hers away on petty gambling and blackmail. Stronger than Ollie's, and he could see just enough to know he didn't want to; and stronger than Gram's, and Gram read half the town and was loved for it, or her father's, Liam O'Brien's, and he always sat at the right hand of the mayor, whispering secrets. No, *I* was the most powerful.

And there was a story about the night I was born, something she told me every year on my birthday to remind me who I was. Gram said the night I came into the world, the sky was clear, the moon was new, and my mother demanded that a doula meet her out by the spring, where she sank herself into the waters for hours, going on and on about how the water would bless her child. And when it was time, she gave birth to me under full starlight. I opened my eyes looking at the Milky Way, not my mother. It claimed me, Gram always said. It was my first baby blanket, deep black and studded with pinpricks of fire.

I thought again about what I'd said to June and Selena—my excuses—and my face burned hot. I wasn't *that* kind of powerful. Was I?

I slid my legs over the edge to begin my climb down the side. Then I caught sight of the safe sitting there in the driveway. Darker than the washed-out sand and gravel under it, darker than the night around it. The silver dial gleamed in the starlight, its black numbers swirling.

I paused, one leg over the edge, hand on the trellis, and looked at it. Really looked at it. When we left it in the driveway, I could have sworn it was right at the end of the silver ramp, positioned to roll up. But now it stood cockeyed, only halfway in front of the ramp, and a foot closer to the porch steps.

A shiver ran up my arms. It had to be a false memory. We never really lined it up at all. We weren't professional movers, that was for sure. I climbed down into my bedroom, took one last look at it, sitting there in the starlight, and shut the curtains.

CHAPTER
EIGHT

I am not a monster. And look what they've done to me.

This is the Dark Place. The Dark Place. I sing it, for ninety years, I sing it. Each year presses in on me, like the push of a cactus barb, into my fingers, my toes. My whole being. They put me here to keep me still, to keep me down. I don't deserve it. I don't deserve anything they've done to me.

This is the Dark Place.

I sing it.

This is the Dark Place.

I hum it in my little cave. And my voice keeps me company.

Something's happening, where the starlight hums outside my little cave, missing me. The whole universe, missing what I once gave it, each night, my bare feet in the sand and rocks, my hands upstretched to the Milky Way. Oh, I gave the night sky so much of myself, and it gave pieces of itself back to me, to make me larger. Bigger. Better.

I danced under the new moon, when the starlight gave me the most, when the lights from the Alvarado finally went dark. Windows winked out, one by one, like candle flames. The champagne glasses lay empty on the long bar, and the ladies in silk tucked themselves into their beds upstairs, next to the balconies where the diamonds on their necks sparkled in lantern light. All of the Alvarado fell asleep, and the desert floor became a dance floor. I would sway and hum and fill myself with so much starlight I thought I would burst, and still I would make it back to the Alvarado before anyone knew I was gone.

I am not a monster. When they saw me, they did not turn away. And what I did, I didn't do it for money, or fame, like the ones who sleep in the Alvarado. I did it for love.

CHAPTER
NINE

I couldn't sleep until sunrise, and as soon as I dropped off, the dreams came.

Glimmer of a flashlight. Up the stairs. Through the spa. Then into the halls, crumbling like stone. Room 336 opened like a mouth. But this time, the safe stood inside. I slid my hands over its beetle-black metal, touched the silver dial. It hummed against my fingertips.

I jolted awake.

Tater slept on the pillow beside me, an orange pile of fur on white sheets. As I stirred, she opened one lazy eye, then closed it. The clock on the bedside table said 11:23 a.m.

I rolled over and pressed my fingers against my temples, trying to hold on to the details. The dream had changed. The Alvarado was fading, and the safe was taking over. And that feeling...a well of *want* pushing up something from the Dark Place.

Had there been a nursery rhyme, too? Singing?

I rolled out of bed, grabbed my phone to text June and Selena.
did you dream?

Dots appeared underneath, and from Selena I got a single yes. From June, I got a voice recording. I played it, and her voice raised the hair on my arms.

"*This is the Dark Place, I sing it. This is the Dark Place. I hum it in my little cave.* Yeah, Quinn, I'm sick of this. I say we go check out that room in the Alvarado, the one where we found the safe. I want to end this before what happened to Bud happens to us."

I texted her.

you're overreacting
am not
we're not gonna die
that's not what I meant

My phone chose that time to shut down—it had been all wonky since it took a nose dive off the balcony in the Alvarado—so I plugged it in and threw it on the rumpled sheets.

I pulled on jeans and a black T-shirt, rubbed the sleep out of my eyes, and checked the mirror above the dresser. Turned my face every which way and prodded the spots where the finger marks had been. Gone now, but just thinking about them felt like a foot on my chest.

I looked myself in the eyes. Maybe I shouldn't tell June everything would be okay. Maybe that was a lie.

In the left side of the mirror frame, I'd wedged a half dozen pictures. Me and Ollie fishing on the Rio Grande, Gram hugging me and Ollie at Ollie's graduation, Selena and her dad, in his sheriff's uniform. I took the top pic down, one of me and June and Selena, in first grade, at a book fair. Selena and I wore cheesy GYPSUM RATTLERS READ! T-shirts, but June had forgotten because Bud and her mom hadn't gotten the email, because they never got the emails.

That was the day Mrs. Palmer read *Pete the Cat* to us and June ended up in trouble. I still remember Mrs. Palmer's voice, how it rose and fell and sort of hypnotized us. I couldn't really remember the book, but we all thought it was the coolest story ever, and then the popcorn arrived, so we were all losing our minds and irritating Mrs. Palmer past her breaking point.

The teacher read us the refrain one more time—"Don't be shy, don't be blue, there is something everyone can do"—then asked us how each of us was special.

I said I could pick up things with my toes. Selena said she could bake lemon bars. Jake next to me said he could fart in time with "Twinkle Twinkle," which got him sent to the office in five seconds flat, although we all thought it was totally worth it. Bobby and José and Charlotte, they raised their hands and told the teacher why they were different. They sang, they danced, they could shoot a rattlesnake from across the yard and get him right in the eye.

Then June's arm shot up. "I can see in the dark. Better than in the daytime. It's like I have built-in night vision goggles or something."

June went on and on, not noticing the unnatural stillness of the room. She talked about how sharp and clear things were at night, and how she'd seen a possum that had broken into the chicken coop out back eat one of the chicks, and how the other night creatures that came out thought she couldn't see them, but she could! She could! How everyone in her family could do this special thing, but they'd always told her not to tell anyone, but she thought that was just silly.

That afternoon, Selena and I got in trouble on purpose, just to spend time with June in recess detention, so she wouldn't be alone.

Across the bedroom, my phone powered up, then pinged. I glanced at the screen. Instagram alerts, but nothing from June. I thumbed out a text.

everything's gonna be okay

Three dots appeared, shimmering.

promise?

I'll make sure of it

I slipped on my boots, put Ollie's old Texas Rangers ball cap over my bedhead, and grabbed my black denim jacket off the chair before heading for the door. But when I passed the window, I stopped and froze. A strange thought rose, and I pulled aside Gram's gauzy white curtains. The safe *wanted* me to look.

In the distance, the ridge of the mountains rose, pale and covered in scrub. Down below in the gravel drive, Ollie's truck gathered dust. Behind the open tailgate was a patch of bare gravel.

The safe was gone.

I blinked, then rubbed my eyes. What in the world...? Maybe someone came into our driveway and filched it?

I let go of the curtain, relief flooding through me, thick and sweet. Gone! It was gone. I decided Ollie had hired someone to come get it and they'd taken it in the early hours. Thank God. We'd get the money another way. Me and Ollie, we'd figure it out. And maybe, just maybe, I wasn't lying to June when I said everything was gonna be okay.

Drifting from the other side of the house came the crack of an axe on wood. Ollie, hacking up a pile of campfire fuel big enough for our four guests and fifty of their closest friends. Ever hopeful, that was Ollie.

I shouldered open my bedroom door, which stuck on the hall's shag carpet, and made my way down to the other side of the house and into Ollie's room, which had a view of the backyard and the campgrounds. I stopped next to the unmade bed and the cluttered nightstand, which was covered with half-empty water glasses and his money jar. I picked it up, the sunlight catching the glass, sliding over the stickers that read *Shannon Falls* and *Yellowknife* and *Prince Edward Island,* and all the places Ollie used to talk about going, a dream trip riding a Harley from Texas to the top of Canada. There was at least a hundred dollars in the jar, which he should already have sent to the bank.

I set it down in the same place and turned it so he wouldn't know. Ollie hated me touching his stuff.

"You know what you're really gonna hate?" I said to the empty room. "The bank, touching all your stuff, and putting it on the curb."

I made it down the stairs, fed Tater. The chickens weren't out yet, which was weird, since they were usually pecking the yard by dawn. I peeked inside the dark henhouse and saw all six of them huddled, perched up on their roosts.

"Good morning, ladies."

Pumpkin turned her head to the side and blinked, eyeing me.

"You sleeping in?"

She shifted, then huddled back into her feathers, jostling the chicken next to her, who drooped her head farther and let out a plaintive warble, low in her throat.

There was definitely something off about the flock.

I left a message on the feedstore's voicemail, hoping Hugo could come out and take a look. I searched for Ollie but all I found was the axe, its blade wedged in the stump. Heading to the campsite to make nice with the rich people, probably.

Back in the house, Tater started yowling at the front door to be let out, and when I cracked it to let her slip through, she took her sweet time, weaving through my feet a few times. Then she took two steps out onto the porch and froze. A second later, she scrambled back into the living room, a hurricane of claws on wood, and disappeared under the couch.

"What's wrong, buddy? Coyote?"

I edged the door wider and peeked around the corner, trying not to startle whatever wild thing had set up shop on our porch.

I expected a racoon. A rattlesnake. Even a javelina.

But there, at the top of the porch stairs, was the safe. Beetle black, its silver eye looking at me.

I backpedaled, stumbling. To my left, the grandfather clock clicked and then chimed, and I tripped over the threshold. And then I was frozen, staring at the safe. My bones throbbing with a feeling... that it was *moving*. Not fast enough for me to see, but *moving* toward me, toward the front door, toward our lives. Slowly, the way a vine grows.

I waited for it to speak, to open, to explode, to rush at me.

The clock filled the house with its twelfth hollow note. The safe still sat there, doing absolutely nothing.

Of course it was doing absolutely nothing. It was a piece of furniture.

I pulled my ball cap off and threw it against the wall. The chickens were sick, I was imagining things, and somehow Ollie must've gotten the safe onto the porch *by himself.* Which meant he'd changed his mind about putting it under a tarp somewhere out in the junkyard.

I eyed it, and it eyed me back, just an inch from the edge.

It would be staring at me for weeks, I was sure now. Ollie would drag it inside, into the living room, where he would mess with the dial while I tried to watch TV. It would be with us for years until he gave up. Of course, by then, we would already have lost the house, so...

I kicked it once. Then twice.

A pressure cooker of fury built in my chest. Ollie never listened to me. Treated me like a child. Like I was some stray he'd adopted from the pound and was sorry he had to feed. And he was heartless—still fixated on this stupid thing when the whole town had to bury Bud Pilsner on Tuesday.

"The hell with it!"

I put both hands on the door of that safe and pushed, trying to tip it down the porch stairs. See what Ollie thought of his precious safe in pieces on the driveway! I put my back into it, dug my boot heels against an uneven board for leverage, and shoved.

The board under my foot cracked in half. The safe didn't budge.

In the bed of Ollie's truck, I fished around the clutter for the chain he kept there, my hands shaking, a volcano inside me. Then I wrapped it around the safe's middle and attached the other end to the back of my motorcycle. I'd drag it off the porch. Down the road. Let it bust open like a piñata.

With a satisfying kick, I started the engine and peeled out. The chain caught. I fishtailed on the gravel, stirring up a monster-sized cloud of dust.

I stopped the engine and looked over my shoulder. The safe hadn't moved an inch. If it was that heavy, it should have busted through our sagging porch. Busted right through and hit the ground. Plowed its way down until it hit the earth's core and melted there.

My anger faded, turned brittle. There was no way Ollie got the safe up there on his own. Which meant...

No, it was just a *thing*. A thing that could be moved if you applied enough force. I just needed more power. I glanced at Ollie's truck, which sat in the shade of house. I might not have my license yet, but I knew how to drive.

My bike had buzzed like an angry hornet, but Ollie's truck roared to life like a dragon. I backed it up, angling it around the porch, and got out to hook the chain to the trailer hitch. Then I got back in the cab, the adrenaline singing in my veins.

I floored it. The chain caught with a jerk and the wheels spun, and a cloud of dust drifted over my windshield. And then the tension was gone, and with a grinding groan and tear that resonated through my seat and the steering wheel, I shot forward.

Two seconds of victory, that's what I had.

I hit the brakes, and the dust cleared. The chain, there in the rearview mirror, trailed down the porch steps. The bumper of Ollie's truck lay like a severed arm in the gravel.

"Oh God..." I closed my eyes and waited a few seconds before opening them, hoping the bumper would magically reattach itself.

I slowly reached up to shut off the engine, anger melting. Ollie was going to kill me; he was going to roast me. Ground me and take away my phone for a year...

I leaned my forehead on the steering wheel. Maybe I could put the bumper back on before Ollie saw it. Yeah. That was the ticket. I'd get the drill and a little superglue and—

Next to me came the stutter of a throat clearing, then Ollie's voice. "That's it."

I forced myself to face him.

Ollie, when he gets mad, spits fire. But when my brother's furious, he goes very still, and very quiet.

"All right," I said, "what are you gonna do?"

Ollie leaned on the open passenger window. Then his gaze drifted to my motorcycle, propped up against the house. When he met my eye again, he was smirking.

"No," I said. "Anything but that."

CHAPTER
TEN

Farm Road 323 was empty most of the way to the Gun Barrel Trailer Park. I walked on the shoulder, peeling off my jacket and kicking rocks and cursing the universe. Ollie was using my motorcycle, punishment for destroying his truck. Served me right.

A couple of cars passed, full of half the basketball team from school, yelling and whooping out of their windows, voices spilling out into the endless rolling desert. Then the silence came down again, like a blanket, leaving me alone with all my jumbled thoughts.

The safe should have tipped right over and tumbled down the steps. Three hundred pounds of metal versus Ollie's truck? It was no contest. But it hadn't budged.

And the dreams I'd had all year, full of endless numbers? I was lying to myself if I didn't admit that someone out there in the universe was trying to tell me the combination.

The shadow of a hawk swept across the road. I watched it fly east, toward the Chinati Mountains. If I tried hard enough, maybe I could read the signs in its flight. That was what Liam O'Brien could do, look up into the sky and see the future in the bend of a bird's wings. Gram did it once, back when Aunt Macie was just a kid and had come to Gram for advice, like everyone in town did. Gram had watched a hawk fly over the diner, back when my great-uncle Eamon O'Brien owned it, and told Macie she'd marry Enrique Salazar one day and they'd run Eamon's place together. And that's exactly what happened.

The hawk swerved, rose, and flew out of sight, leaving me with nothing but a half-mile walk.

Over the rise, the Gun Barrel Trailer Park came into view, a sprawling two-acre collection of RVs and trailers, peppered with saw grass and beat-up satellite dishes. I zigzagged my way through the lots until Bill Winter's tidy double-wide appeared. A dozen cars and trucks had parked on the gravel lot. A banner with HAPPY BIRTHDAY, KRISTA! hung underneath it.

Before I could process what I'd gotten myself into, the screen door on the trailer squealed and Bill Winter came out, hiking up his jeans over his sagging middle. I made my way across the scrubby yard and up his steps.

Bill gave me a meaty pat on the shoulder. "You're late."

"You didn't tell me I was reading at a kid's party."

"Krista likes magic."

"I'm not a magician."

Bill's eyes brightened like I'd just told a joke. "You'll do just fine."

I looked past Bill to peer through his front window. A crowd of at least twenty people milled about, with Krista in the center, wearing a wide grin and "I'm Twelve!" plastic tiara. I recognized almost everyone, which meant Ollie would know by dinnertime that I was doing readings again.

"I wouldn't have come if I'd known half the town was gonna be here," I muttered, not even trying to hide how pissed I was.

"Which is why I didn't tell you," Bill said, like it was all really funny.

I hesitated at the door, thought about turning back, going home. Then I remembered that Ollie had already taken away my bike, so I had nothing left to lose. And why was I so worried about what Ollie thought anyway? He wasn't my father.

I stepped inside Bill's trailer. The screen door squealed again and everyone turned. Then I got an avalanche of hugs and *Where you been*s and *We miss your gram*s. Sal Lumpkin and Jim Betleman and Enrique Salazar and half of last year's basketball team all heating up the double-wide, welcoming me back with open arms. Selena breezed in from the back stoop with her camera around her neck, clearly the hired photographer, waving hello to me and hugging Bill, who lifted her off the floor until she laughed and begged to be let down.

No matter where you went in Gypsum, someone was bound to make you feel like you'd just come home.

I spotted June through the crowd, standing next to Mrs. Durbin, who was haunting the corner of the room by the punch and cake. June must have decided to pick her battles this morning, because Mrs. Durbin's usual velour tracksuit was missing. In its place was what I could only describe as a *gown,* a silvery-gray floor-length thing. The rhinestones along the V-neck showed a constellation of age spots, the whole thing hanging loosely off the curved C of her back. Wispy gray hair trailed down over both shoulders, and an unlit cigarette dangled between her index and middle fingers.

I squinted. I'd seen enough pictures of Eva Durbin to recognize the dress. When I was really little, Gram would take me to Eva's place sometimes, and they'd take out her scrapbooks and talk about Hollywood days until my eyes glazed over. Eva having lunch with James Cagney. Eva linked arm in arm with Marlene Dietrich. My gram saying, "My goodness, look at that dress! What a dish."

As soon as June saw me, a smile touched the corner of her mouth, although her eyes looked a little red, like she'd just been crying in the bathroom. Last night on the roof, she'd been lying. She was nowhere near fine.

Selena and I exchanged a glance, a silent message. Bill dragged Selena away, telling her she had to take a group photo of the family on the porch, and I made my way to June, stopping every foot to say hello or shake a hand. June wasn't a hugger, but when I reached out to give her my usual slow punch on the shoulder, she walked right into my arms.

She pulled away first. "What are you doing here?"

I took off my backpack and unzipped it, then dug out my bundle with Gram's cup in it.

She did a slow nod, like it was all cool, but a hint of disapproval flashed in her eyes. "Opening that window again, huh?"

Mrs. Durbin twisted her neck and set her gaze on me, with those bright, childlike eyes, then slipped the unlit cigarette between her lips.

"Hey, Mrs. D."

"Well, if you're gonna stare at me that long," Mrs. Durbin said, the cigarette bobbing, "you might as well take a picture." She squinted up at me. "You're Liam's boy, aren't you?"

Somehow Mrs. Durbin had mistaken me for my grandfather. June made a rolling motion with her hand. *Go with it.*

"Sure."

"It's a good thing you've got June then, isn't it?" she said, glancing at June and nodding like it all made perfect sense. Then her eyes went distant and unfocused again.

Through the window behind Mrs. Durbin, I caught a flash of orange and white. The whir of an engine followed, and a U-Haul truck parked next door in front of Mrs. Durbin's place. June saw the direction of my gaze and nudged me, then held a finger to her lips.

I'd forgotten. Her people were coming to get her. I guessed they were waiting for the right moment to spring the bad news.

June handed me a plate of fajitas and I ate standing next to Mrs. Durbin, who fiddled with her cigarette and stared at her shoes. If Gram were here, she'd be going on and on about Mrs. Durbin, fussing over her. Talking about how much we all loved Gypsum's "star of the silver screen." Through the window I watched the U-Haul back up to Mrs. Durbin's trailer. I still had no idea why someone who once made out with Humphrey Bogart would give up all that glitter and fame to live here. And now I would never know.

Mrs. Durbin craned her neck again to look at me, like she could read my thoughts.

"It's...it's really good to see you, Mrs. D."

She gave me an odd look, like I was someone she hadn't seen in decades, then reached for my face. As soon as she touched me, an image welled up out of nowhere, soft and featherlight. Eva, young and beautiful, standing in the empty desert, looking up into the peppering of stars above. I could feel her feet, rooted to the ground, the tilt of her head as she watched the sky, her breath fogging the night air.

Then a patch of bright sky above her went dark.

I pulled away. The image faded, leaving behind a hollow space in my chest. I didn't know what it meant, but it didn't take a psychic to know that Eva Durbin's star was fading.

———•———

I set Gram's cup and the pot of tea on a card table Bill set up in the corner of the living room. Krista's mother and a few relatives lined up on the couch, eating birthday cake with plastic forks, watching me like I'd come out of a carnival show, right next to the two-headed lizard-turtle.

Gram once told me that I shouldn't worry about the looks we got. She told me folks like us had been doing this kind of thing for thousands of years, oracles and prophets and shamans, all of us the same, giving people what they desperately wanted.

"What do they want?" I'd asked her.

"They want to know there's some wonder left in the universe," she'd said. "And you, my sweet boy, *are* a wonder."

I handed a full steaming cup of tea to Krista, who sipped it suspiciously. The screen door squealed and slapped closed, and people went back and forth to the kitchen for Solo cups of sweet tea and bowls of guacamole. Krista finally finished the last drop, the china clinking against her braces, and when I took the cup from her, the sides were still warm.

Damp leaves clung in a ring around the rim, the near future. The bits trailing in patches down the sides marked the events of the next few years. And then came the symbols formed in the well of the cup, things to come decades from now.

The axe. A palm tree. The letter *L*. All close to the rim, happening now, or soon. The girl would have something she really wanted, this year. The letter *S*. Or maybe it was a serpent, I couldn't tell which. Ten years from now, she would love someone and lose him. Not great, but true.

Then lines. One led deep into the cup and ended at the bottom. Her journey would be long, and she would find sweetness in it.

But those were all parlor tricks. I was waiting. Waiting for the pull of the current, for the world to go dark. Waiting for the place where the real secrets lay, where they nested, and bred. The symbols shifted, the world dimmed, and then...

I stood in the Dark Place. The blackness in front of me vast, a corner of space where the stars hadn't been born yet.

I shifted my feet on the ground that wasn't ground. I breathed in air that wasn't air. All quiet. One step forward, reaching out, feeling blind, and I found the edge of the web. Pushed through the sticky fibers.

Years ago, when Gram first taught me to do readings, I was terrified of the web, so I came back from the Dark Place with nothing to show for it. Then, eventually, I made myself touch it. I'd imagined myself as Indiana Jones in a cave, reaching into a cobwebbed recess to find the lever. I'd open the ancient door. Find treasure, maybe save the girl. If I was lucky, both.

I sank wrist-deep into the web. There on the other side, whispers swelled, electric and sweet.

Bits of the girl's future jumbled through my mind. Her at a table, one hand wrapped around a ceramic mug, the other reaching across to grab hold of someone's hand. Another image of her and her mother packing boxes. Another, the girl sliding an urn on her bookshelf, the Twenty-Third Psalm etched into stone. The events came to me out of order. Then, now, tomorrow, the distant future, twisted like a mass of roots.

Then her whole future was swept away by the current.

I blinked into the darkness, my palms empty. Flexed my fingers, reached, pushed my arms in to the elbow. Nothing.

This didn't happen. When I had hold of an image, it never disappeared.

A crawling sensation began in my brain, shifted and sharpened like ants biting.

And images swept back into focus again. Three birds, on a windowsill inside the Alvarado. Six framed pictures from the hallway. Black-and-white photographs, unsmiling faces of long ago. The glimmering teardrop crystals of the chandelier appeared. Thirty-six of them.

That number, and others, tumbling in front of my eyes.

A step forward. A swell of new knowledge, the web clinging to my biceps. Because I had to know, once and for all, what the dreams wanted me to do. The crowd around me, the party, the reading, those could wait.

The numbers were a tangled mess, out of order. Then a shining sphere appeared, pushed into my mind as if by the finger of God. A silver dial. Impatience swelled in my chest . . . but part of me was sure that emotion wasn't my own.

It didn't matter. I knew what the safe needed me to do. Of course I knew. I always knew.

Not a thought, but an impulse, as strong as the need to eat or drink, made me grab hold of the numbers and search for order. I needed to do this. To find out the combination once and for all. I didn't have to use it, I told myself. I just had to know.

My lips moved, my tongue pressed against my teeth, forming a word I hadn't thought yet. I couldn't make out the shape of it, but it felt like a part of me, something that had come up out of my heart, spiky and real, and desperate to get out.

Which was why I didn't notice at first. The Dark Place wasn't quiet anymore.

The hiss of something being dragged, there in the dark, on the other side of the web. Something slouching, moving toward me. I froze and strained to hear. A dense prickle on my arm, the ants, biting my skin and running wild across my brain.

It's coming.

I knew I should let go—leave. That thought drifted through my head, muffled by the urge to add, subtract, combine. I still had time, a soft voice sang in my brain. Everything would be okay.

The smell of ozone followed, razor-sharp.

Something brushed against my nose and chin, and shock rolled through me as I realized what I'd done. I'd stepped forward, sunk my arms into the web all the way to my shoulders. My right leg was entirely on the other side.

I tried to step back and couldn't. I pulled wildly, like a fly in a web, three of my limbs dangling in the current on the other side. Then the current changed, pulled my right arm. A tug. Something there in the water on the other side, nipping at my fingers like fish.

I leaned back from the web with all my weight, sliding out inch by inch, but I was too slow. The low hiss of dragging on the other side of the web grew louder. The slouching thing, moving toward the web on the other side. It stopped. A draft of warm, damp air drifted over my hand. Like an exhale.

I pulled harder, a well of fear rushing up and out of me. And then, a tickle on my forearm. A clamp. Then a white-hot pain.

I yelled out. Something wrapped around my wrist, damp and sticky, tightening. I struggled, used my other hand to pry the vise grip off, and then pressure, and pain, and something ripping. Harder this time. I cried out again, struggling. Just before the Dark Place disappeared, before I snapped back into the real world, I felt knuckles. A thumb. A hand.

Blinding light, a roar of voices, coming at me like a wall.

I was back in the real world, inside Bill Winter's trailer, holding Gram's cup in both hands, panting like a sprinter.

I looked down into the cup, and on the edge of my vision, a red flower bloomed, right there on my arm. Like an omen, opening there on my sleeve. I blinked the cobwebs out of my eyes and realized what it really was.

Blood. A lot of blood.

I pushed up my sleeve and turned my arm. A crescent-shaped wound stretched from elbow to wrist.

Tooth marks.

Krista was looking past me, at the TV, half bored with her party and especially her magic show. I grabbed my jacket and covered my arm. There was a football game on. Half the crowd with their backs to me, yelling and whooping.

Then a voice came, rising up above the others.

A song.

This is the Dark Place. I hum it in my little cave. I sing it.

You did good, the voice said. *Now you have everything you need.*

CHAPTER
ELEVEN

'd never noticed before, but in twilight, blood looks like motor oil.

Bill Winter drove me home and didn't once ask me about the bloodstain on the sleeve of my jacket. He handed me my precious twenty dollars and pulled out of my drive, disappearing in a cloud of dust.

I walked up the steps, then paused by the safe. It had shifted, this time in the direction of the driveway, like Ollie couldn't make up his mind which way to drag it.

Like *it* couldn't decide which way to go.

I reached out to touch it, but when I got an inch away, my breath stalled. I circled the safe a few times. Looked under it, finally got up the courage and tapped the top like it was a hot pot. A hum reached me, faint, from inside.

I touched my bandaged arm, feeling the tender spots where the teeth had sliced so easily.

In the kitchen, I found Ollie pulling a pizza out of the oven.

"Again?"

"You love pepperoni."

"By the time I graduate from high school, I'll be about fifty percent pizza."

"Like you're going to graduate."

Another one of Ollie's knife-edged jokes. And that one stung, especially considering it would probably help if I turned things in.

Ollie took a look at my face and his expression softened. "I'm just kidding. Of course you're going to graduate. With honors. And if you don't, I'll beat you with a tire iron. Is that better?"

"Yeah, it helps a lot. You should be a motivational speaker."

"Come on, now, and help me get dinner on."

I set the table, which meant a roll of paper towels in the center, along with a basket of parmesan cheese packets.

"Got a call today."

I tensed, expecting the worst.

"From Hugo," he said. "He's coming by in the morning to check out the birds."

"For free?"

"I did a trade."

"What'd you promise?"

He pulled a two-liter bottle of Dr Pepper out of the fridge and handed it to me. "Your comic book collection."

"Seriously?!"

He gave me a knowing smirk. "Of course I didn't. That'd be worse than killing all your chickens."

A soft trill came from the coop outside, mournful and low. Last year, Gram had hatched every one of those birds from eggs, babied them under a heat lamp and fed them chick starter and called them her little ones. There was no way Ollie was putting them down.

"They're *our* chickens."

"That was you and Gram, not me." He reached into the cabinet for glasses, pulling down the first things he could reach, which were a coffee mug and a beer glass.

He went on about Gram's chickens, and how he hoped I appreciated how much work it would be for him, under the hood of Hugo's wife's 1995 Toyota Camry, to keep them alive and clucking. I didn't respond. Ollie said something about his aching feet, then poured his beer glass full of DP. When he finally glanced up long enough to take in the look on my face, his smug expression deflated.

"Anyway, we'll fix it, like we always do." He capped the bottle and took a long drink from his glass, then set it down with a heavy *thunk* before he met my eyes again. "Or we won't. Either way, we'll be okay."

Somehow, I didn't think he was talking about the chickens anymore. It wasn't until we were halfway through a Tombstone pepperoni that he finally spoke again. "You got your suit ready?"

"Why would I wear a suit?"

He stopped chewing. "Bud's funeral."

"Oh." I swallowed the bite I'd taken, which now seemed oily and tasteless. "There should a be a cosmic law that you can't go to two funerals in one year."

"Yeah," he said, taking a sip of his drink. "Yeah."

I waited for him to say something else. To ask how I was doing with that, with missing Gram, which was basically like missing my mother, since I didn't have a mother. He stared out the kitchen window, rubbed his palm once across his stubbled cheek.

"So . . . the suit?"

I guessed our moment was over. "It was already tight when I wore it last. And I think I've grown."

He took another monstrous bite and eyed me, like he was just noticing me for the first time. "Yeah, I guess you are taller." Tater wandered in and jumped up on the table. Ollie pulled a piece of pepperoni off his slice and fed it to her, sighing. "Just put on the suit and don't complain."

"I'm not going to Bud Pilsner's funeral in highwaters. And stop feeding her that."

He put another piece of pepperoni in front of her. "Just . . . hunch down while you walk," he said, a smile in his eyes.

"It doesn't work that way, Ollie."

His smile softened, like he was remembering something. "Doesn't matter what you wear, just matters that you show up."

The enjoyment of a rare moment when Ollie was being the actual Ollie, rather than a distant father, faded. June would never say she didn't want me there. She'd hug me and thank Ollie and me for coming, but all the while, she'd be thinking about how if Ollie hadn't called Bud and asked for help, they wouldn't be having a funeral. "Are you sure we should…"

"Sure we should what?"

"Go to the funeral?"

"I don't know, but we're going. To pay our respects."

"Maybe it's more respectful to stay away."

"Both Bud and June came to Gram's funeral, even though Bud didn't like you much. It was the right thing to do. Which means we're going to Bud's service."

"June and Bud didn't drop a safe on Gram."

"We're *going*." He gave me an up-and-down look. "Wear black socks and the highwaters won't show as much."

———•———

The lamp on the nightstand threw long shadows over the unmade bed and the green shag carpet. The closet door was cracked, the strip of darkness a thin mouth. The suit was somewhere inside, deep in the back, hanging behind the clothes I hadn't worn since summer. Those probably didn't fit me either. It would be awesome in the spring, when I needed new shirts and Ollie took me shopping in Alpine. I bet everyone in the senior class would see me get in the truck with a bag marked GOODWILL.

I sank down on the bed, my hands lying open on my lap, my bandaged arm throbbing, and stared at the closet door. I could root around for the suit, use Gram's trick of hanging it in the shower to let it steam. Even then it would take at least a day for the creases to come out. But the thought of even looking at my good shoes, two sizes too small, made me sick, and I shut the closet door with my foot. I'd do it tomorrow.

Tater jumped up on the bed, a warm pile of cat settling next to me, purring. I stroked her fur, wishing I could be like that, uncaring, sleeping without wondering about the future and what it would do to me.

A knock at the door startled me. I opened it to find Ollie. "Almost forgot." He handed me a manila envelope and walked away, calling back over his shoulder, "Selena left that for you on the front porch."

I sat at the end of my bed and tore open the envelope. A note and a photograph fell out. The photo was eight by ten, glossy black-and-white, a shot of me in Bill Winter's living room sitting across from Krista and holding Gram's teacup. She'd caught my unsmiling face, the small scar on my chin from the motorcycle wreck I'd had a year ago. In the image, I slouched in the folding chair, my black denim jacket rolled up at the sleeves, dark hair flopping in my eyes, curling on my collar. My gaze was locked on the cup. I didn't even know Selena had taken my picture.

I opened the note and read it.

We need to talk about this. Come find me tonight.

Talk about what? And why in the world had she printed this and left it at my door instead of just texting it to me?

I put the picture on my nightstand and picked up my phone, ready to ask Selena if the sun had gotten to her head. But the lamplight illuminated a darker spot on the print. Something so slight, I wouldn't have noticed it looking at a picture on my phone.

I brought the picture closer to the glow of the lamp.

A shadow hovered right behind me. Hands on either side of my head.

I dropped the picture, pinpricks of light forming at the edge of my vision. The note fluttered down to lie on top of the photo.

Selena's talk about opening a door too many times came back to me. No one had ever taken my picture before when I was reading. Invisible to me. Invisible to her. But not to the camera. Did Ollie bring this thing home with him, in the safe? Or...maybe that shadow had always been there, all these years?

There was one way to find out. A test.

I flicked off the light and leaned back against my headboard. Watched the shadows. The house felt normal, like a regular shell of wood and paint. Minutes ticked by, my body wound like a spring.

An hour passed, me watching the darkness, the darkness watching me. And nothing happened. Just a pile of laundry and junk I should clean up. My eyes felt heavy. I let them shut for one…two…three seconds. Opened them to watch the walls again. A dark wing of a curtain, drawn by moonlight. Ink in the corners of my room. Then the weights on my eyelashes drew them down for the last time.

I drifted into a dream.

A voice hummed and a sweet song rose up. *This is the Dark Place, I sing it. This is the Dark Place.*

I stood in the shadow of the Horse Crippler, next to the spring-fed pool at its base, writing *36* in the desert air. A voice hummed its approval, some kindergarten tune that made me feel calm and still. The numbers flamed, hovering in front of my eyes. I circled *36* a few times.

That one's first, my dream self said.

Other numbers came, and I added and subtracted as they became fireworks under my hands. The second key of the combination was right there in the darkness with me, but just out of reach. And I wanted it.

Six framed pictures formed in front of my eyes, on the wall of the Alvarado. Twenty people in the first. That meant the next number would be *26*. I waved that away, like smoke, and wrote *14*. Then rubbed my fist over it until it darkened, then wrote *6*.

I wrote different combinations, red glowing numbers against the black of night, my mouth dry, the numbers like water on my tongue. I couldn't get enough. When I tried to rest, fingers wrapped around my wrist and lifted my hand again. *Write,* the voice said.

"I don't want to anymore," I murmured, turning back and heading up the trail, toward the house, which loomed enormous on the hill.

My feet plodded on rock and sand. Hands on my leg and then a yank. The world tipped, and I fell hard, fingers digging into the ground, cactus barbs catching my clothes as the force dragged me backward.

"Quinn!"

I jerked awake, my head pounding. Dark room. A shadow in the doorway, moving slowly out of frame. Moonlight on my brother's face, the terror bright in his eyes, sliding out of view like a train inching out of a station.

No, he wasn't moving. I was. But not of my own accord.

The soft rasp of carpet against my cheek, my T-shirt. I was sliding across the floor, backward, as if the house had tipped.

Ollie rushed toward me, and my stomach dipped, bottomed out like I was on a roller coaster. The world turned over. The floor shrank and blurred.

Because I wasn't on the floor anymore.

Ollie stood under me, his wide eyes staring, the fear so stark in them I thought he would crack. Then he was gone, a blur of gray and black, smashing into the mirror. The bright shattering of glass followed.

My stomach swooped again, and the floor blurred—then ran into me, hard. I rolled over, trying to make my lungs work, then stumbled to my feet, fumbling across the wall for a light switch. The room flooded with light.

Ollie lay in a heap by our broken floor-length mirror, stirring weakly.

I think I called Ollie's name. Or Gram's. Or maybe I didn't say anything. A few slaps across his face, and his eyes fluttered open. Then I hauled him up and led him out.

CHAPTER
TWELVE

I pulled two frame backpacks from the hall closet and shoved one in Ollie's hand. "C'mon, pack up."

Ollie looked at the backpack, then behind him at the safe in the living room. I'd never seen him so lost. "Where are we going?"

I grabbed some clothes from the laundry basket and shoved them inside, then slipped my bare feet into my hiking boots and grabbed my jacket from its peg. "Anywhere but here."

We headed down the trail to the campgrounds, our breath fogging in the frigid night air. Ollie kept his eyes dead ahead, his gait unsteady. "Quinn, what the hell was that?"

"How would I know?"

"You *levitated*. Freaking. *Levitated*. And something threw me across the room." He slowed and turned, walking backward to look back at the house. I followed his gaze.

It loomed there against the starlit sky, quiet, still. Then, in the upper floors, a light winked on.

"Oh, you gotta be kidding me," Ollie said, turning back to face the trail, picking up speed.

Our thudding footsteps became our only conversation. The campgrounds, the hills, the landscape, the moon ahead hovering a handsbreadth over the horizon—all of it seemed so normal.

A half mile down the trail, we chose campsite 35, a spot on the far side of the Horse Crippler. I hadn't shared a tent with Ollie since we were kids, but we'd left too quickly to get more than one. A few campsites over, on the other side of the spring, the college kids were asleep in their hammocks.

I lit a Coleman lantern, the glow lighting up the green canvas ceiling as Ollie spread out a sleeping bag. I went through the motions of doing the same, numbly, wondering if I would ever be able to go home again. Ollie looked around the tent for something else to set up, but we were done. Then he looked me in the eye, and I could see what he did—that we both had a quart of adrenaline in our veins.

"Quinn," Ollie finally said. His voice had lost its hard edges. The old Ollie, like my brother, not a pretend father.

"Yeah?"

"You gotta tell me what's going on. And I mean everything. 'Cause there's something in our house, and I don't know what to do."

He was right. I'd been keeping secrets from him too long. And look where it had gotten us. I started small, with the trip to the Alvarado with June and Selena. The more I talked, the easier it was to confess.

That I'd been having dreams about numbers. What happened when I read the girl's cup.

He gave me an alarmed look—but oddly, he didn't seem surprised.

"Ollie...I get the feeling you know what I'm talking about."

He looked toward the tent flap, like he was searching for words—or an exit. "I've been having weird dreams for months. Nightmares, I thought. About the hotel. And like you, I keep seeing numbers." He stared into the middle distance, like he was trying to figure out a path through a place he didn't want to be.

You keep opening that door, over and over...

"What if we just get in the car and leave?" I asked.

"What?"

"We could pack our suitcases, get in the car, and just go. I think that thing will follow us, but it's slow. I can feel that much. We could stay ahead of it."

Ollie's expression softened, and for a second, he looked at me the way Gram did, like he knew me through and through and he didn't want me to suffer. A lump rose in my throat. It was good to know that Ollie finally got it, how much of a burden it was to see the things I did, to be who I was.

"We're not going anywhere," he said, almost an apology.

"Why not?"

"You have school."

"I can miss a few weeks. I'll bring my books."

"Quinn—"

"A long road trip. The one Gram used to talk about when I was little, back when—"

"—back when we had enough money to buy groceries? Or gas?"

I fell quiet, the sharp edges of his answer cutting.

"You're going nowhere, Quinn, and you know it. So let's deal with the reality in front of us."

Ollie lay back on his sleeping bag and shut off the lantern. I turned on my side in the dark, thought about Selena and June and what we would do when we graduated.

You're going nowhere.

"It'll just follow us out here, you know," I finally said.

"You said it yourself. It's slow. We pitch a tent. Check in the morning to see how far the safe traveled. Then move out of the way."

"Every night?"

"Until we can figure out what it wants, yeah."

I stared at the ceiling of the tent. We both knew what the safe wanted. I guessed both of us were afraid if we said it out loud, we'd actually do it. And my fingers *itched* to touch that dial. Spin it. Even the wisp of a thought sent a swell of satisfaction through me, and again, somehow I knew that feeling didn't belong to me.

CHAPTER
THIRTEEN

Morning light broke over the mountains. I came out of the tent to find the fire already made, hot biscuits in the Dutch oven, an aluminum coffeepot sitting on a rock, and no sign of Ollie. He'd probably gone to town to get supplies. Or to look for an exorcist. I ate one of the best breakfasts I'd had in a long time, drinking coffee from a camp mug. The air smelled of baked bread and green cactus and woodsmoke, and with the cold morning air waking me up the rest of the way, last night felt like a dream, something that would burn off like a mist. The warmth in my hands, and the yellow light spilling over the horizon...all of it felt like a gift.

Ollie had left a cardboard egg box by the tent, and somehow, after six biscuits, I was still hungry. He must have gathered the eggs from the coop at daybreak, while I was still asleep. Considering how off the chickens had been lately, I was surprised they were still laying. I set the cast-iron pan on the coals and waited for it to heat, thinking today would be a good day. Ollie and me, we'd figure it out. We'd be okay.

Then I cracked an egg. The shell opened and the insides spilled out.

I dropped the shell in the pan. Sat there, fingers dripping, stomach turning. Because it was like an egg, but not. There was no yellow yoke. No clear whites, bubbling there in the pan.

Something red, like a blood clot, sat at the center where the yolk should have been. It was threaded with pale veins, snaking out through the white, which was actually gray.

My stomach heaved and I swallowed hard, then pulled the Dutch oven off the coals. The egg, or whatever it was, had started to cook at the edges. I grabbed the camp fork Ollie had left lying on a rock and lifted the corner. Clots of something red there too.

I could imagine what Hugo from the feedstore would say. *A virus, boy, you got yourself a virus.* Although I'd never seen an egg look so disgusting in my life. What kind of virus did *that*?

I stood, my quiet, perfect morning gone, and paced in front of the tent, my skin crawling. This was no coincidence, the haunting in our house, and then this. And what would be next? All the food in our fridge? I stopped midstride. Or maybe *we'd* change too.

A thousand bad scenarios rained down on me. Five minutes later, I stood at the narrow crevasse at the edge of the campgrounds, Dutch oven in hand. I dumped the contents inside. The spatula was covered with blood, and I threw it in after. Next went the pot itself, spinning and bumping its way down the jagged rock, all the way to the bottom.

I stood there, looking into the earth, and racked my brains for the next step. There had to be a way to get rid of a ghost, like in the movies.

And suddenly...all I could think about was Ghost Hunter Tripp and his partner in our cabin. All the places Tripp and Nicco had been. The people they'd talked to. Other ghost hunters. Historians. People who'd been haunted.

And maybe people who weren't anymore.

———•———

I found them in the cabin, Nicco in front of a two-monitor setup in the kitchen, editing an episode of their show, and Tripp shirtless, performing sun salutations on a yoga mat in front of the fireplace.

I did the whole *How's your stay* kind of nonsense Ollie was in charge of, although I must have seemed anxious. Tripp invited me for "a cuppa joe." While he talked about his graduate thesis at Columbia (telekinesis?!), his longest meditation session (three hours and fifteen minutes), and his favorite way to put his hair in a man bun (something to do with cocoa butter), I watched Nicco edit footage of the two of them on a fishing boat in the middle of the ocean. Looking for water ghosts, I guessed. Could these guys really have the answers? God, I hoped so.

"You gotta subscribe to our channel," Tripp said, tipping his head toward the kitchen, where Nicco worked. "Got the best episode ever coming up. A whole Bermuda Triangle thing."

"Okay, yeah, of course," I said politely, trying to find a natural way to slide into my question. "Speaking of weird things, can I ask you something?"

"Shoot," he said, his gaze still on Nicco and the monitors. "Watch this. The earth's magnetic field goes all wonky."

"You've seen a lot of haunted places, right?"

"Loads. See that?" He pointed excitedly. Nicco's screen showed a close-up of Tripp's hand holding a compass. The needle spun wildly.

"Do those places ever get...unhaunted?"

Tripp kept his eye on the monitor, where Nicco had filmed him slipping on scuba gear. The soundtrack was low, but I could hear him going on about a boatload of missing divers, and how some "mysterious force" was behind it all.

"You mean cleansed?" Tripp asked, still distracted. "Nicco, don't cut that part. It's my best side."

"Yeah, cleansed, exorcised, whatever."

"Sometimes."

"Have you ever done it? Cleansed a place?"

"Nah. But I know of people who have."

"So, how do you—"

Tripp finally looked away from the screen, where he was rolling back off the side of the boat in full gear. He met my eye, as if he'd finally caught on. "Well, you've got your sage, your salt on the thresholds, holy oil—the usual trifecta. But really, you gotta know more about why the haunting is happening in the first place. If you don't know what a ghost wants, then how are you gonna make it leave?"

"And how do you find that out?"

He shrugged like the answer was obvious. "Ask it."

Across the room, Nicco rewound the footage, and Tripp's body came flying back out of the water to perch on the side of the boat.

"What if you know what it wants," I asked, "and you're not sure if it's such a good thing, you know, to give it to them."

"Hmmm, if you had access to a psychic or medium..." He turned to me. "That's usually what we do, when we need to know what's what. You know anyone like that?"

I didn't respond, but I also didn't look away.

"We can cut the crap," he said. "I saw your flyer at the diner."

The silence lengthened.

Tripp shook his head. "You townies, you're all so secretive, but you know all it does is make people like me more curious. Now, I don't know if this is about the Alvarado or something else, but if you're clairvoyant, spirits will naturally be attracted to you." He watched me with a curious expression. "Hey, are you for hire?"

"No thanks."

He gave me a crooked smile. "I pay much better than twenty bucks. Take a few road trips with us."

Much better than twenty bucks. "How much better?"

"How about a hundred bucks an hour? From everything I've heard around town, you're the real deal. I'll pay you to read haunted buildings for us."

I stopped with my coffee mug halfway to my mouth. "What did... you've been asking around about me?"

He tilted his head and gave me the side-eye. "In a small town, you can always tell if the psychic's real if people are just a little bit afraid of him."

I tried to take another sip of coffee, but a stone had lodged in my throat. I held out the mug, making to leave. "I'll think about it."

Tripp took the mug from my hand. "Seers, oracles, diviners, whatever you want to call yourself, you've always got a foot on the other side. Don't undervalue yourself."

How could I? He'd just told me that the only person who could help me with the safe was me.

CHAPTER
FOURTEEN

I stood at the doorway of my bedroom, Selena and June both peering warily over my shoulder. A sparrow flew outside the window, sending a brief shadow across the carpet. When we'd first entered the house, I'd barely been able to get past the safe, which had moved to the kitchen, as if making its way through the house to join us at the campgrounds. I'd slipped past and up the stairs, skin crawling.

June stepped inside, her hands shoved into her black hoodie, and turned in a slow circle, the white rattler printed on her back glaring at me. "God, look what the ghost did to your room." She took another step, and something crunched, probably a Dorito.

"Actually, my room always looks like this."

"I'm not sure I'd admit that if I were you," Selena said.

"Thanks, Miss Hospital Corners."

Selena moved closer to the bed, stepping over a tattered English notebook and a pair of Chuck Taylors. She crossed her arms tightly over her chest, as if suddenly feeling a chill. "You said it *dragged* you, right?"

"Yeah, I was having this dream and—"

"About what?" Selena asked.

I started to answer, and then Tripp's comment played in my head. *In a small town, you can always tell if the psychic's real if people are just a little bit afraid of him.* But Selena was one person I didn't want to lie to. "I was writing numbers. In ... flame."

Selena's brows drew together, a flash of unease passing over her expression.

"I wasn't standing in hell, Selena. I was in the desert—"

"Okay, okay."

"—and this voice wanted me to keep writing, adding, subtracting."

June stopped chewing her gum, and I got the feeling she was holding her breath. "A voice. *The* voice? The one we dream about?"

"Yeah, I think so. I wanted to stop, and it wouldn't let me."

Selena met my eye and looked quickly away. I hadn't called her last night about the photo, and with everything after, I'd completely forgotten to. And now she seemed distant. Or was it fear?

"What direction was it dragging you?" she asked.

I stepped across a pile of laundry and stood next to her, trying to remember the broken images of the night before. Our shoulders brushed, and for a moment I couldn't concentrate. "It...was dark, so I don't know, but...I think this way." I pointed to the south wall.

Selena went to the wall, most of which was covered by Harley-Davidson posters. She reached out to touch the map of North America, studded with red thumbtacks I'd used to mark Highway 101 along the Oregon coast.

I joined her there and looked at the map, the trip Ollie and I had planned out two years ago, back when we still felt like brothers. "Maybe it was trying to tell me to go?"

"Wanted you to leave the house?" Selena asked. "Maybe."

"Ghosts do that, right?" I asked. "Try to take the whole place for themselves?" The thought of leaving felt pretty awesome at the moment—but then the thought of never coming back ripped through me like a sharp wind. Free and homeless weren't the same thing.

Selena moved from the wall to the closet, which she opened with a creak. "What if it was trying to drag you into the closet?"

"Why would it do that?"

"Alternate dimension? I don't know."

June came to stand next to us and stare into the black maw, which was a narrow walk-in, packed with Ollie's old things and mine. "But there's nothing in here except more of your stuff." She pointed. "And I think a possum made a nest in the corner."

"That's a papier-mâché armadillo from sixth grade."

June gave me a strange look.

I shrugged. "I don't like to throw anything away."

"Obviously."

June's phone pinged. She took it out and groaned. "Great, I'm late for work."

"Shocker... wait a minute. You don't have a job anymore."

"I guess you didn't hear," Selena said with a smirk.

"Hear what?"

"Mrs. Durbin's back," June said. "My glamorous career as caretaker of the old and cranky continues."

"I thought her people came for her."

"She left them at a rest stop just outside of Alpine," Selena said. "Hitchhiked back to town."

"You're kidding."

"No lie. They gave up."

That frail, 109-year-old woman standing on the highway with her thumb out? In December of all months, the cold wind blowing through her, hitching her way back to Gypsum.

"You'd think for once in her life, she'd want to go somewhere other than here."

Selena looked at my bedside clock. "I gotta go too. A.J.'s got some Christmas tree lighting ceremony thing tomorrow, and she asked me to help with the setup." She looked at me. "You wanna come?"

"No, I'm not in the Christmas mood."

"Don't worry, my sister's got enough for all of us." The humor in her eyes shifted, became more serious. "I don't think you should stay here alone. Even though it's daytime."

"I won't. I'll just get a few things and go."

"And if you get sick of sleeping in a tent... you and Ollie can come stay with us."

"Like that'll ever happen." At Selena's hurt look, I added, "Ollie doesn't like charity, or your sister."

Selena tipped her head and gave me an *Are you kidding me* look. "Your brother is *in love* with my sister."

June slipped her backpack over her shoulder. "You know that's an O'Brien trait, not knowing what you want."

———•———

I promised them again I'd be right behind them, that I wouldn't stay in the haunted house all by myself. I wasn't that worried, though. It felt safe inside the room, quiet, like the aftermath of a storm.

Was it the darkness that had brought the ghost to me? Darkness or... sleep?

I stood at my closet and stared inside. My suit hung in the left corner, packed tightly with a letterman jacket from my short-lived stint on the basketball team. Then there were some winter coats I'd grown out of and a half dozen collared shirts Gram bought me that I never wore and then outgrew.

I pulled the suit off the rack, grabbed the church shoes, and started to leave, but halfway to the door, I stopped and dropped everything on the bed and turned back.

I grabbed jackets and shirts off the closet rod and threw them behind me. Old sweatshirts and button-downs from seventh grade and Gypsum High novelty hoodies—I ripped it all from the hangers until the back wall was completely exposed.

I hadn't seen that wall in a long time, not since Gram painted my room with a fresh coat of cream-colored paint two years ago. I remembered when she was done and I stepped into the closet and saw all the scuff marks covered up and cleaned, Gram with her paintbrush smiling at me.

The walls weren't blank and clean anymore. They were completely covered with hundreds of numbers.

The number *36*, written dozens of times and circled over and over, like someone had been obsessed. The number *23* was also circled multiple times. Straight, careful lines went from one number to the next, like constellations.

And on the floor, lined up against the baseboard, were five or six pencils, a square pink eraser, and a pencil sharpener. I remembered buying them, just before school started, when Ollie took me to Alpine to shop for supplies. Curled bits of wood shavings lay like the husks of insects on the carpet.

I reached out, my hand shaking, to touch the numbers. The bare bulb above my head sent shadows across the wall and my bandaged arm, like bruises. I imagined Ollie coming into my room at night, slipping inside the closet to write this. I wanted to believe that, as ridiculous as it was. Maybe it was him, dreaming of numbers, sleepwalking in here and trying figure out the combination to the safe. On my closet wall. Maybe it wasn't me.

My vision shrank. And as I scanned the lines and diagrams and additions and subtractions, a second whisper rose, the fairy-tale song from my dream.

The stack of papers, in the Alvarado, full of numbers. Could that be…

My legs stopped working, and I stumbled out of the closet and sank onto the bed. All the dreams I'd had, writing numbers in the desert air with my fingers. Now in the bright lights of my bedroom, I saw everything clearly. The desert air of my dream shimmered, and the landscape warped like a mirage, until it re-formed, became a wall. And there I was, standing in the closet in the middle of the night, my hanging clothes around me, sharpening my pencil.

Then, when that wasn't enough, wandering across *miles* of desert to the Alvarado, to sit in room 336 and do the *same thing*.

At my feet was a stack of clothes. On top was my basketball team shirt from eighth grade. Number 36. It wasn't just me. My coach assigned that to me. *Two years ago.* Or did I pick it? Those numbers had been following me everywhere I went. Number 23 on the jukebox. I'd picked it so many times, even though I didn't like the song!

I laced my fingers behind my head, cradling it, closing my eyes and trying to remember.

"What are you doing in here alone?"

Ollie stood at the doorway. I tried to answer but my mouth didn't work.

"After last night, I don't want either of us poking around in here without…"

I shook my head, and his expression pinched, like he was steeling himself for the next blow. "What's wrong?"

I pointed inside the closet, and as he turned to look, I felt that turn in my chest, like a screw tightening. Because *I* had done this. And he was about to find out that his brother *had* opened a door one too many times.

I leaned on my knees, trying to breathe. I couldn't get enough air. Then a weight settled next to me on the bed.

"It was me," I said, "in the middle of the night."

"Sleepwalking?" The tone of his voice was careful, like he was talking to a small child.

"Dreamwalking." I rubbed the bridge of my nose while Ollie digested that. *You've got a sixth sense, and you keep opening that door, over and over.* "Or…God, those weren't dreams at all."

Ollie asked questions, softly, like he was afraid I would shatter, but I didn't hear him. I finally opened my eyes to look at it, to face it. The wall. God, it was something you'd do if you'd come unhinged, scribbling all over it like that. And *I* had done that.

The two numbers I'd circled—*23* and *36*—they were the first two numbers of the combination, I knew it. And deep down, I knew what order they went in. First *36*. Then *23*. There was only one number left.

CHAPTER
FIFTEEN

My back still sore from sleeping in the tent, I went to Bud Pilsner's funeral in a daze. Ollie sat close beside me, sending me an occasional comforting look, the kind you give someone dying of cancer. And it wasn't like I could escape him. We were all packed in St. Christopher's Church so tight that if everyone exhaled at once, we'd blow out the stained-glass windows.

I tugged my collar and tried to listen to the sermon. They'd brought in a stranger, which made everything worse. Some churchy guy from Alpine with a powder-blue blazer and a president's haircut. He wasn't one of us. Everyone else in the room was someone I'd grown up with or seen every day of my life on Gypsum's main street or waved to as I passed the Gun Barrel Trailer Park.

Ms. Tabor from the T-shirt shop sat in the pew right ahead of me, with her helmet of gray hair, next to Javier Rivera from the library. Elvira Shulman, who ran the Stoplight Café on Main, her knitting bag beside her as always, sat a few rows over. Jim Betleman from the Gas 'n' Sip, hands washed clean of engine grease, sat in the pew just in front of hers, shoulder to shoulder with Gunter Moon, who looked like he'd showered and had skipped his usual 10 a.m. Heineken. When I'd come in, I'd passed the entire Gypsum High football team plus all their parents in the back rows, shifting and coughing and sniffling like one giant human raft of sound. Then there was every teacher June had ever had, shop owners, and the head of the trailer park HOA—they were all there, packed in the pews, using up all the oxygen in the room.

The claustrophobia became intense, and my fingers itched. I silently counted panes in the windows. A nudge on my shoulder made me turn.

"What's wrong with you?" Ollie whispered so low I could barely hear it. I mouthed *I don't know* at him.

"Stop squirming. God, what are you, five?"

A flare of anger blotted out the other sensations, and I faced front like a good O'Brien should.

Like most sermons in Gypsum, this one hovered somewhere between heaven and damnation. I wanted to pay attention, so I could forget how tight my suit had become and that the tie was cutting off the circulation to my brain, but most of it skipped over my thoughts like a stone on water.

Was there was something wrong with me, or just wrong in general? And were other people feeling this?

I turned, looking for June and Selena. Selena was easy to find, sitting next to A.J., her shoulders straight like she was at her desk in class, ready to raise her hand to be the first to answer any question. June sat three rows ahead, wearing a black dress with a grown-up set of pearls around her neck, her blond hair pulled into a bun. And she wore makeup, which June never did. Her jaw moved slightly and rhythmically, like she was chewing gum. This dressed-up stranger turned and looked at me, and stopped chewing, her solemn expression evaporating. She gave me a little eyebrow raise as if to say *Are you okay?*

I turned back to face the preacher again. I guessed it really was just me.

The preacher droned on. I wondered how long he was going to talk, and how long he had already been talking. I avoided looking at the coffin and counted the people in the front pew. Someone coughed behind me. Two rows ahead, two little girls whispered to each other, and their mother, one of the English teachers at Gypsum High, shushed them.

Ollie took a hymnal from the pew and opened it, the smell of paper rising up, dry and musty. He flipped a few pages in, then glanced at me disapprovingly. I realized the room was full of music.

I stood with the others and sang "Amazing Grace" without looking at the words—Gram had played it for us on the piano in the living room only a billion times—and thought about the risks of opening the safe. Would anything bad *really* happen? A voice in my head said no. It'd be just fine. No more haunting. All my paranoia about it was just that, paranoia. What was I waiting for?

Those thoughts didn't belong to me. I *knew* they didn't. But the warning was distant, as if it were coming down a long tunnel.

The music died, and a few heads turned my way, their eyes filled with confusion. I was still singing softly, like a whisper. Ollie nudged me and I stopped. It wasn't until the sermon resumed and it blurred into nonsense that I realized I'd been singing a different song.

This is the Dark Place. I hum it in my little cave. This is the Dark Place. I sing it.

I stared at the altar, my face on fire, trying to breathe through the fact that most of Gypsum was witness to me finally losing my mind.

The row in front of me shifted, and June came into view again, leaning against her mother. Enrique and Aunt Macie and Deputy Cruz shored up the other side. A sign hung on a small velvet rope that said RESERVED FOR FAMILY. But she had a lot less family now. Because of me, and whatever was haunting me.

Another voice competed with that one. Said that was ridiculous. It was just an accident, and if I opened the safe, I would feel better.

"Will you all please turn to page sixteen in your prayer book?" the preacher from Alpine asked.

Sixteen. The number floated through my head and settled, like a leaf falling from a tree. The claustrophobia that had been rising in me like a slowly heating pot of water suddenly boiled over.

Sixteen. It was the last number. I didn't know how I knew, but I knew.

My vision narrowed. The world was suffocating me, like the

refrigerator out in Gram's junkyard had. Dark and musty and full of mushroom smell. Any second, I would run out of air.

I tried to stand, and Ollie's hand was suddenly on my shoulder.

The service ended. People stood for the receiving line, all black suit coats and stiff raven-wing dresses. I slipped out the side door, into the open air, and gulped down lungfuls. I couldn't get enough. The sky was too heavy, pressing down on me, and the world spun.

I'd finally figured out the combination, without really trying. And now it was tearing me apart, from the inside out. If I didn't do something soon, it would burst out of my rib cage.

Somehow, I got home. I thought I walked inside the house, or crawled, and the room spun like I was on a carnival ride. The doorknob felt hot on my hand. Then Gram's hardwood floors rose up to meet me. My fingers itched.

Open me.

It wasn't my voice, in my head. But I didn't care anymore. My fingers were crawling with imaginary spiders. My head was about to pop.

If I never opened it, if I could leave Gypsum, would it follow me forever? What if I spent my life on the move? Would it find a way to kill me like it did Bud, or would it just watch me while I slept?

My lungs on fire, I crawled to the front of the safe to turn the dial.

36

The claustrophobia immediately vanished. I gulped in a lungful of air and reversed directions.

23

Inside me something swelled. An emotion. It felt huge, like a wave or a sirocco, and my heart felt laid bare under the sun, baking in its glorious heat.

I would finally know. What was inside.

As I touched the dial, I realized that all these years, I'd been afraid of myself. Afraid of what I could do. And why? Why fear it? I should just let gravity do its work, let it pull me down to the very bottom of this thing, whatever it was. Just stop resisting.

That was all I ever wanted. To know.

I spun the dial clockwise. Settled on the number *16*. A tick. Like the second hand of a clock. Soft, yet it reverberated through the room.

The yard.

Gypsum.

The universe.

I reached for the handle, my fingers shaking.

The grandfather clock ticked, its pendulum stirring the air. Late-afternoon sun cast an oily shadow through the front window. The Chinati Mountains lay broken on the horizon.

I twisted the handle, heard the deep grind of an old lock sliding, metal on metal.

A voice came from behind me. "Quinn, what are you doing?"

The front door stood open. I hadn't noticed the creak of the hinge and the sudden cold draft. Ollie stood on the front porch in his funeral suit, still gripping the knob, alarm growing in his eyes.

"It's okay," I said. "Everything's okay now."

The small door of the safe swung open.

My eyes were still on my brother when something brushed the top of my left hand. Rough, like a cat's tongue.

Sand.

A stream of it came from the mouth of the safe, pouring onto the hardwood.

"I can't believe you opened it." Ollie crossed the room in two strides to take a closer look. He pulled back, confused. "Sand?" He knelt in front of it, took a handful, and let it stream through his fingers. No money after all. No diamonds.

I expected the flow of sand to slow and trickle to a stop. But as it kept coming, at the same speed, a warning bell went off. I saw the same alarm growing in my brother's eyes.

Ollie tried to close the door, talking fast, but his words were a jumble. The sand kept pouring. More than could fit in that small compartment. It pooled around our feet. And it wasn't slowing down.

The sight of Ollie struggling with the door snapped me out of my trance. The world sharpened, and his voice pierced the fog. "Help me close it!"

I gripped the small metal door and pushed.

"C'mon!" he yelled. *"Shut it!"*

I shoved. Put my back into it, but the lock wouldn't catch. The sand built up until it burst the door open again.

A flash of something beyond the rushing grains, deep inside the safe. Something moving.

I scrambled back.

A foot slipped from the yawning opening, wearing a dark shoe. It was followed by a calf, and a knee. Tan slacks. Ollie pulled me back until we hit the wall.

After the knee came a thigh, then a second leg, until it slipped from a space no bigger than a six-year-old could fill. Arms, torso, noodling out of the entrance to the safe like a grotesque carnival show. Sinuous and unnatural. And expanding. Finally, a head emerged, and the thing unfolded itself, its limbs swelling, taking shape, bones locking into place, until it stood upright.

In our living room, in the slowly widening pile of sand, stood a man.

His eyes glinted with a series of emotions. Intense gratitude. Or maybe fury.

And then he looked around the room, and his expression shifted, like he'd just heard a really good joke. As the sand continued to pour, spilling out to reach the edges of the room, filling the space under the couch, he finally spoke.

"Well, it took you long enough."

CHAPTER
SIXTEEN

Ollie and I stared at him. At his dark eyes. At his even darker shock of hair, which brushed the top of his eyebrows. About Ollie's age, I guessed. Blue-and-white suspenders held up tan slacks, and his white linen shirt was as bright as July sun on top of the Horse Crippler.

He tilted his head, and a weird glimmer of recognition came over me. But I couldn't think of *where* I'd seen him.

He nodded to the safe door. "You better shut that thing, or we'll be buried."

Ollie stumbled over and shut the safe and locked the handle, while I stared at him. I'd opened it. I'd really done it.

The man started to laugh. "You should see both your faces! You look like cartoons who just got hit with a mallet!"

Neither of us responded.

"You know, a cartoon? Like someone's just dropped an anvil on your head and you're seeing the little birdies?"

He glanced around the living room, stepping out of the sand. "I remember this house. Liam O'Brien. Looks a little...worse for wear... but then, it *has* been ninety years since I was here." He walked over to the grandfather clock and touched it, almost lovingly. "This hasn't changed."

Somehow, I found my voice. "Who are you?"

A smile, like he'd just met me at a party, and then he held out his hand to shake mine. "I'm Kit."

"That's not what he meant," Ollie said.

"I know what he meant."

"So who are you?" I wanted to say *What are you,* given the way he'd unfolded from the space. Boneless. Unnatural. Snakelike.

"Don't worry," Kit said, retracting his hand, "I'm not going to hurt anybody. I know what you're thinking, but I am not a monster." He held his arms out and turned his hands side to side. "See? I look just like you, right?" He slipped his hands in his pockets and rocked back on his heels, like a man waiting for a bus. "So, you got anything to eat? I'm absolutely famished. Haven't eaten since 1933."

We fed him. *It.* Whatever it was. Partly because we didn't know what else to do, partly because I had a fear that he would eat one of *us.* Unhinge his jaw like one of Bud's snakes and slip his face over my head like a hood, covering my eyes, my shoulders, working down until all of me was gone. His dark eyes shone in the dome light that hung above the kitchen table. His hands tore the bagel in half and slathered cream cheese, and he never stopped talking, unless he was swallowing.

Then he started licking the cream cheese off the knife.

Ollie's expression tightened. "You want me to get you a bucket? You can just fill it up with snacks from the pantry."

"I like this. Creamy."

I exchanged a glance with Ollie. "Are you the one who's been sending me messages?"

"Yep, that was me."

"And what happened in my room two nights ago, that was you?"

"Yeah, sorry about that." He winced, embarrassed. "I have a bit of a temper."

"Can you give us a minute?" I asked, standing.

"By all means," he said, swallowing the remains of his bagel.

We stepped into the hall. Ollie looked like he was about to pop, and before I could speak, he lit into me. "Why'd you do it, Quinn?"

"Me? You're the one who brought the safe home in the first place!"

He went on like he hadn't heard me. "And why is that guy"—he pointed to the kitchen—"sitting at our breakfast table, eating all our bagels?"

A rustling came from the kitchen. We slowly rounded the corner. Kit was at our bookshelf, running his fingers along the spines. He stopped on one and pulled it out.

"I hope you don't mind." His gaze went to the box of Cheez-Its by the coffeemaker. "Are those crackers?"

As Kit consumed that entire box, Ollie and I sat across from him and gave him one-word answers and watched his Adam's apple move up and down as he swallowed. And I knew that I had made the biggest mistake of my life.

"You didn't," Kit said.

"What?"

"Make the biggest mistake of your life. That one's coming, though."

Ollie's expression paled. "You can..."

"Read your thoughts? Sort of. If they've got a ton of emotion with them. It amplifies the words. I can hear them like they're floating down a long empty tunnel." He pulled out another handful of Cheez-Its, his gaze on me, eyes sparkling with curiosity. "Is that what you're feeling right now, Quinn, that you're in a long empty tunnel?"

I didn't know what he meant, and I didn't want to know what he meant. I wanted him to go. His eyes bored into mine. Then they shifted to my brother.

"I'm sorry too."

"About what?" Ollie said.

"That there wasn't a pile of diamonds in the safe. Or gold ingots. Or... what was it you were thinking? German bearer bonds, and I don't even know what those are, but they sound valuable." He leaned forward and lowered his voice. "There was something in the safe a long time ago, but I ate it."

"So I guess you'll be on your way then," Ollie said, rising from his seat.

I put my hand on Ollie's arm, keeping my eyes on Kit. "What are you going to do now?"

"Nothing much. Just live. Mind if I take the spare bedroom?" He grinned. "Your face just now. I'm kidding! The desert's fine for me. I like sleeping under the stars, and I don't get cold." He stood and brushed the crumbs off his shirt. "Thank you for the bagel. It was adequate, but not delicious."

He gave me a two-fingered salute, tucked the book under his arm, and walked out of the back door. The screen door closed with a bang.

CHAPTER
SEVENTEEN
Kit

This is not the Dark Place.

This is the world.

Trails behind the house stretch out, long and snaking through the wide land. The cook fires send smoke up into the blue veil. Night's coming. Then she'll strip away the sky, like a mask she wears, and I'll see them again. A legion of stars. A hurricane of light.

Waiting for me to sing to them.

Across the miles of desert, I can feel her heart beating.

The way time moves, it's so cruel to all of you.

CHAPTER
EIGHTEEN

Money. Answers. A window into the great beyond. That was what I'd half hoped to get when I spun that dial. But as I stood at the window, watching Kit disappear around a bend in the trail, all I had now was fear.

Maybe I was still asleep. Any moment, I would wake up, and the world would be as it was. Weird, but not *this* weird. I'd wake up and Ollie and I would—

Glass shattered in the living room.

I found my brother standing by the front door. Next to him, the grandfather clock lay facedown, the leaded face in pieces.

"You wanna tell me what you're doing?" I asked.

Ollie went to the stack of mail on the old piano and pulled off the bottom envelope, then threw it at my feet. Then he sat on the couch and leaned on his knees, his hands on the back of his head, like he was afraid he'd pass out.

I opened it and the world tilted.

It was from the bank. The word "auction" glared up at me in bold print. Date: January 20. Location: Presidio County Courthouse.

"All that time," Ollie said, his voice quiet, "I really thought this could save us. And what's inside?"

I sat next to Ollie on the couch, holding the auction notice. We'd get a place at the Gun Barrel, maybe the one next to June's. Wake up every morning to Bill Winter's snoring through the walls of his double-wide. There was nothing wrong with living in a trailer, but this house was everything Gram worked for—the business, the chickens, four generations of memories. All of that would belong to someone else.

The safe sat a few feet away. On impulse, I reached out and turned the handle.

Ollie looked up sharply, his body tensing as the door swung open. But nothing spilled out. Nothing moved at all.

I leaned down to get a good look. Inside was an empty metal compartment, big enough to fit a bag of money, big enough to fit several trays of uncut diamonds, but it didn't have any of that. Pockmarked and beat up and completely ordinary.

Ollie stared at the remains of the clock on the rug. Then he put his face in his hands. "What are we gonna do now?"

———————●———————

I lay on my stomach on the ridge, binoculars up to my face, and searched for Kit. On my left, Selena did the same, a stash of seaweed snacks and apple slices laid out between us. On my right, June sat cross-legged, her attention on the horizon, her face pale and dark circles under her eyes. Her claim that she was "fine" wasn't fooling anyone.

My conversation with Ollie still burned, but I couldn't even think about the bank now. I needed to know what I'd let out. And I couldn't do that alone.

For hours we searched the trails and rocky outcroppings that were as familiar to me as the lines on my own palm. But something felt... off. I couldn't put my finger on it, but the desert seemed to have *thinned* somehow.

An uneasy feeling growing, I swept my binoculars over the empty campsites, then the college kids' tent. They had a fire going and a Dutch oven hanging over it. The acrid smell of burning drifted on the air. It wouldn't be the first time a camper had screwed up a campfire meal, going hiking instead of staying to watch.

After searching from every inch of Bud Pilsner's land in the east to the tall heights of the cliffs in the west, I spotted Kit.

"There!" I said, pointing. "Near the spring!"

In the distance, Kit carried a tattered olive-green armchair that looked suspiciously like something from our storage shed. In the seat he'd placed a small TV and a VCR, also ours. The whole lot must have weighed at least eighty pounds, but he carried it like it was made of feathers.

"What's he doing?" Selena asked.

The cliff reflected in the water at its base, a dark profile in a shimmer of sunlight. There, underneath the cool shadows of the overhang, a few feet from the dripping rocks, Kit set everything down and arranged it.

"Looks like he's…moving in?"

"That's what he's doing," June said, pulling her binoculars down to look at me, "but what are *we* doing?"

"Well, I don't know, June. I have no idea what to do when a magical man comes out of a piece of furniture. We're trying to figure out who he is."

In the distance, Kit sat in the armchair, slipped a VHS tape into the player, and touched the side of the TV with one finger. Even though the power cord lay coiled on the rock, plugged into nothing, the screen flickered to life.

"Or *what* he is," June added.

I focused on the screen of the TV, and a shaky image started up, white letters appearing and disappearing on a gray background full of cliffs and desert.

"You're kidding me," I said.

"He's just watching a movie?" June asked.

Selena brought her binoculars down. "Maybe he's harmless."

"No." I was sure of that.

June brought the binoculars back up to her eyes. "He killed my dad," she said, her tone so dry it could start a brush fire.

"Maybe a curse on the safe caused that," Selena said. "Maybe it wasn't Kit at all."

"Well, we need to do something other than watch and wait," June said.

"The three of us should head to the room in the Alvarado where we found the safe," Selena suggested. "It was full of objects."

I nodded, relieved. It was a good idea. We obviously needed something to do.

"There has to be something in there to tell us what kind of *thing* he is," I said. "What kind of danger we're in."

Selena turned to me. "Just because something's supernatural, doesn't mean it's bad."

"Name something supernatural that isn't bad," I said.

"Didn't Moses part the Red Sea?"

"C'mon, the Bible?"

"Okay then, you and June and your whole weird family line."

June and I exchanged a glance. "You think of us that way?" I asked.

"Well, yeah. June can see in the dark like a bat. And you, Quinn? You can see the future."

I brought my binoculars up again and focused them on Kit's face. "Me and him, we're not the same thing."

Kit's gaze slipped away from the TV screen and lit on me, as if he were staring right down both barrels of my binoculars. Before I yanked my head down and pulled Selena and June out of sight, I caught Kit's crooked half smile.

⸻

The walk back along the desert trail gave me time to think. June and Selena were already out of sight, their bikes flashing silver in the late-afternoon sun. Tomorrow, they'd said, we'd go to the Alvarado tomorrow. Try to find some answers.

I made my way up the trail, our house looming on the hill, three stories of faded white cupolas and sagging porches, and tried to recall exactly what was in the room we'd fallen into at the hotel. An old clock. A stuffed owl, its wings spread wide. A champagne glass, on its side.

Stacks of leather-bound books—I was pretty sure I saw books. All of it walled up with the safe like some sort of tomb.

I found Ollie in our mudroom, sitting next to the safe, drinking a Bud Light and dabbing at the hinges with a rag. "What are you doing?" I asked.

"Getting it ready for eBay."

"You're *selling* it?"

He shrugged, taking a sip from the bottle. "Trying to. Antique safes go for hundreds. I looked it up."

"We might need it!"

He took a sip of his beer, his gaze settling on me in a calculating way. "To do what? Put him back in? You know how to do that?"

"No."

"Okay then. I'm selling it." He took another swig and set it down with a clink and a sigh and a defeated shake of his head. "When you sign mortgage papers, there's a stack sky-high, but when they take everything from you, they just send a single page. Reminds me how much harder it is to build something than it is to burn it down."

"So, three weeks? That's really all we have?"

"Yep, and before you ask, I already called Jim Betleman, and he said I could come by the Gas 'n' Sip tomorrow. No guarantees, since I missed the first interview, but maybe he'll give me a job cleaning the floor."

I watched him rub at a dull spot until it shone. It occurred to me that the set of his shoulders belonged to an old man, not my brother.

"That's good, Ollie. That's something." Deep down, I knew how that would go. Minimum wage, and no advance. It wouldn't be enough.

Ollie rubbed gun oil on a scratched spot near the dial. "Some rich guy with money burning a hole in his pocket is going to snatch this up. You just wait and see. I'm selling it for five hundred dollars. It's a—"

"—sure thing. Yeah. Why would anybody spend that much on an antique safe?"

Ollie stopped rubbing for a second and gave me a sly look. "I may have mentioned something about it being haunted."

"Wouldn't that make someone *not* buy it?"

"People love that crap. Haunted dolls. Cursed watches. Trinkets with a connection to the great beyond."

"Why?"

"Everyone wants their lives to be something more than ordinary. If they can't be special, at least they can *buy* special."

I sat down across from him and watched him clean the dial. A fleck of red came off on the rag, and my stomach turned. Bud. That was Bud Pilsner's blood he was cleaning off.

"I wish Bud had let me read his cup at least once," I said. "Maybe things would have been different."

The swipe of the rag slowed, then stopped. Ollie gave me a darting glance before he picked up speed again.

"What?"

"Nothing."

I tilted my head and watched him, thinking again about Bud, about June, about the Pilsner fear of what I could do.

"Last year, what was it that Bud said to you to make you come down on me like a hammer?" I asked.

He kept on cleaning, his eyes intent on his task. "What are you talking about?"

"What did he say? Something that made you make *me* stop reading cups, I know that."

He gave me a look that said I'd hit a nerve.

"Okay, fine. Made me *hide* it from you."

"Bud just thought you don't need to be messing with forces you don't understand."

"You never minded when Gram did it."

He turned back to the safe and rubbed the hinge with his cloth.

"Ollie?"

"I don't know, but there's just something different about it when you do it. Bud knew that. And I knew too, even before you told me all that stuff about that weird mental place you go when you're reading. I just knew it wasn't healthy for you."

"You just knew."

"Yeah."

"A gut feeling."

"That's right."

We both fell silent, and the only sound in the room was the swish of the cloth.

"Must be an O'Brien trait," I said.

"What?"

"Bad liars."

Ollie turned and met my eye, resigned. "He said he'd had a dream about you."

I drew back. "What?"

"He went on and on, said if you kept dipping into that well, one day, you'd bring out something that didn't belong here."

A dream. A prophetic dream. From Bud Pilsner, of all people. "Bud Pilsner was a paranoid prepper who booby-trapped his land with home-made land mines. Why would you listen to him?"

"It wasn't him I listened to in the end."

"Then who? Was it June? Because I don't know why—"

"It was Gram."

I sat back. His words left a fist-sized hole in my chest. "No way."

"I'm sorry, Quinn."

"She taught me how to do it."

"True, but...you took it too far."

"And you didn't think to *tell me* this?"

"She was hooked up to about six machines, okay? And you were wandering around the hospital with that sad face of yours. So no, I didn't tell you. I thought if I just..."

"Ordered me to do something without explaining it—"

"Yes, I thought you might listen to me because you trusted me. Okay? Do you trust me? Hell no, you don't trust me." He threw the rag down.

I sat frozen, watching the anger burn. It had always been this way, when Ollie lost it. Him lecturing, me feeling nine years old again, watching a storm brewing on the horizon that was far too big for me.

"Quinn, what Gram used to do, she saw things that didn't matter much, like predicting a door falling off its hinge, or when a drought would break," he said in a strained voice. "And her predictions were often wrong. A lot. It was harmless, you know, like pulling out a Ouija board—but what you can do is just not natural. I wish it were different."

"You're afraid of me."

"I'm not afraid of you."

I gave him a level look to tell him I wasn't buying it.

"I just...I'm afraid of what's coming down the pipe, about what that power could do if you let it off the leash."

"If I read a few more cups, maybe I can find out."

"No, no, I don't want you doing that."

"Maybe if I read Kit's cup—"

"*No!*"

I blinked, surprised by the sudden flash of anger. "Why not? Everything points to him. He has the answers about what's happening in this town. If I can just—"

"Promise me. Promise me you won't do that."

"I won't go too far."

Ollie stood, using his extra foot of O'Brien height to look down at me and pin me with his gaze. "Promise me."

"Ollie."

"Kit's out, and there's nothing we can do about it!" His face flushed. "I want a promise."

I'd lied to Ollie a hundred times. Maybe a thousand. But this time, it hurt to do it, like sliding a splinter into a place that was already stretched too thin. "All right, I promise."

He nodded, but I saw the doubt in his eyes. He wiped his hands on his jeans, searching my face until something shifted in his eyes, shuttered. "I need another beer."

He left the room. I sat and leaned my head back against the wall. Looked into the open safe, like it was the entrance to the Dark Place itself. Like it had answers inside, the mouth of some oracle, ready to speak truth. It looked like an ordinary container. That was what it was now. Nothing more extraordinary than a chest of drawers.

Leaning forward, I peered into the small space, then stuck my entire head inside. The inside was peppered with marks. Damaged like this, Ollie was gonna get about twenty bucks for it. I turned my head to look at the ceiling of the compartment, pockmarked and scratched up. With the door closed, it would be so dark. How terrifying to be swallowed by this, living inside it for all those decades.

Claustrophobia sank its teeth into me. I edged out, filling my lungs with clean fresh open air. Something about those marks nagged at me, and I grabbed a flashlight from the table and pointed it inside.

They weren't random, like I'd originally thought. It looked like Kit had been trying to *write* on the inside. Maybe he was just trying to pass the time.

And that was when a weird sense of déjà vu hit me. Where had I seen these? Maybe I wasn't remembering something I'd seen. Maybe I was remembering what I *would* see. Future tense.

Unease rolling through me, I shut the door.

•————————•

That night, after A.J. had dragged Selena away to some family thing and June had gone off to be with one of our distant cousins who was still in town for the funeral, I lay in bed waiting for something awful to happen. It didn't. No dreams. No visitations. I stared at the map of North America, counting the pushpins over and over, thinking about what that would be like, spending an entire summer exploring. How good it would feel to come home and put pictures of all the places I'd been over these walls. Me and Ollie, standing cross-armed in front of our hogs, Mount Robson rising up in the background.

Morning finally broke, spilling its honey over the Chinati Mountains and into my bedroom. I'd slept a total of zero minutes, wondering what I'd let loose in Gypsum, and what was going to happen next.

Ten minutes later, I went into the mudroom for my boots, a bowl of cereal in my hands, and found the safe in pieces.

"Ollie!" I yelled up through the ceiling. "Get down here!"

The legs had been torn off and twisted, the sides had been broken in half, the way someone would break a loaf of bread. The door lay ripped off its hinges, facedown on the tile.

Ollie wandered into the room in his boxers, his bleary eyes widening as soon as he saw the destruction. "Well, ain't that great," he said, his tone bitter.

"Did you hear anything last night?"

"I was half in the bag, so I wouldn't've heard a rocket ship landing on the house."

I looked at the back door. "You didn't lock the door last night."

"I never lock that door," he said defensively, though he couldn't hide the regret in his voice.

I squatted and picked up one of the pieces of metal. "How strong would you have to be to do this?"

Ollie went to the mudroom window. He stared out until his phone pinged, then he read it and hung his head. "I gotta get showered and go. Jim's expecting me." He finally met my eye, and I could see the hangover in the pallor of his skin, in the puffy circles under his eyes. "Just stick the parts in the shed for now."

"That's what you're worried about? The mess? Aren't you worried he's gonna come back and do this to us?"

"I'm worried about a lot of things, Quinn," he said on his way out of the room. "Go ahead and add death and dismemberment to the list."

———————•———————

I texted Selena and June with the news, then got back nothing but an exclamation point from June, and an entire paragraph from Selena. They both agreed to meet me at the hotel today, just as soon as they could get away.

The desert stretched out ahead of me, the winter sun bouncing off the pale hills, throwing shadows. If I kept up the pace, I'd be at the Alvarado in an hour.

Somewhere behind me rose the growl of a car, and I stepped off the road. A familiar van with a yellow moon painted on the side passed me and pulled onto the rocky shoulder, tires grinding on gravel.

Tripp had the driver's-side window down, his beefy arm resting on the lip. When I reached his side, he slipped his aviator shades off, the way they do in those cop shows Gram used to watch. I wondered if this guy was always onstage. "Need a ride into town?"

"Thanks, but I'm not going to town."

He nodded, keeping his chin high, evaluating me. "Your brother tried to sell us a rock-climbing package. Said you're a pretty good guide. For someone so young, you've got some interesting side hustles going."

I gave him a tight smile. Ollie, taking his revenge.

"We're climbers too!" he said. "But we don't need a guide."

"Okay."

"You know, we're professionals. With our own gear and everything."

"Uh-huh."

"We even have shoes. Rock-climbing shoes."

"That's great."

He flashed me another toothy smile. "Where you headed?"

I looked over my shoulder, then back at Tripp. It wasn't like they didn't know about the hotel. "The Alvarado."

Tripp lifted his eyebrows. "Well, whaddaya know. So are we! Hop in."

The van reeked of incense, which barely covered the even sweeter smell of pot wafting up from the upholstery. Tripp had the unsettling habit of breaking into a sunny smile every time he looked my way. The mug in the cup rest said STANFORD, which seemed unlikely, but what did I know about colleges? I'd never been farther north than Alpine.

Behind me, Nicco moved about in the back of the cluttered van, stumbling as Tripp went over potholes. I sat with my backpack between my boots, hand on the strap, as he peppered me with questions.

"So why are you going to the Alvarado?"

The truth—that I was searching for clues in a room where I'd found a haunted safe, which I'd opened after years of prophetic dreams, which contained a weird guy who was now wandering around the desert—was juicy enough to keep him and his friend in our campground for months. Hard pass. "Just photographing the hotel."

"Why?"

"School project."

"It's winter break."

"I'm a good student."

"You ever been in the hotel before?"

"Yes."

"You ever seen anything weird in there?"

"No."

"Is it okay if we record you a bit?"

"No!"

Tripp frowned and looked over his shoulder. "Turn it off, Nicco."

I turned to find Nicco scowling and lowering a camera. "You better erase that," I said.

"Sure, we will," Nicco said with a sly little smile.

"So, why'd you take the long way?" Tripp asked, flipping stations. "I woulda just cut right through that stretch of desert and saved myself three miles."

"I wouldn't do that if I were you."

"Why not?"

"That's Bud Pilsner's land."

"So?"

"It's completely booby-trapped."

"No way."

"Mines and stuff." At his odd look, I shrugged. "He hated the government, or something. No one knows for sure. We just don't go there."

He fiddled with the radio some more and finally settled on an old Van Morrison song. "I guess they don't call it Weird Gypsum for nothing."

The long walk was starting to look better and better.

The landscape sped by in a blur of tans under a blue sky while they talked shop. Ghosts. Aliens. Houses in Savannah where the dead walked free, apparently. Then one of them mentioned locking themselves in the Alvarado last night, and how the whole thing was a bust.

"Wait, what?" I asked.

"Ah, he speaks. Yeah, we set up our gear at sunset on the third floor, you know, the room where the director was murdered? Drank coffee until sunrise."

"And what happened?"

From the back, Nicco spoke up. "Not much."

"You're kidding."

I must've given away too much in my tone, because Tripp turned and gave me a curious glance. "I thought you said you've never seen anything weird there."

"I haven't. But we've all heard the stories."

Tripp turned back to the road. "We caught some cold spots. The EMF reader went off a few times."

Nicco piped up. "Footsteps, up on the second floor. Too nice for my tastes."

"Run-of-the-mill stuff, really," Tripp said. "I mean, if I knew what a lightweight the Alvarado was, I'd've gone to El Paso instead."

Nicco nodded sagely. "The El Dorado. Now *there's* a place that knows how to deliver."

Tripp leaned over and raised his eyebrows, a conspiratorial glint in his eye. "Nicco once got bit by the Thing in the Basement."

His partner lifted up his tie-dye and showed me a scar.

For the rest of the drive, the two of them went on about the Thing in the Basement and the El Dorado, then how overrated the Alvarado was, while I tried to wrap my head around the idea that they'd seen nothing horrifying during twelve hours of darkness. No hands, reaching for them in the dark. No lights flicking on in the suites.

A cold realization grew in me as the Alvarado rose up in front of us in all its dilapidated grandeur. Could it be that the most dangerous thing in the Alvarado wasn't there anymore because it'd been set free? By me?

"Oh God," I murmured. Tripp and Nicco should be setting up their gear at our house, not the Alvarado.

"What?"

"Nothing."

By the time we'd pulled into the parking lot, I was convinced I'd set off the apocalypse. Kit could go anywhere. Do anything. But what did that look like? I needed answers.

Nicco and Tripp started unloading expensive-looking black cases from the back of the van.

"Thanks for the ride," I said.

By the time Nicco and Tripp had wandered inside, June had arrived on her ten-speed. She gave me a chin nod and set her bike against the pale stucco of the hotel, which in the sunlight had the texture of a thousand shotgun blasts. She looked better than yesterday, but her eyes were still bloodshot, her flannel shirt picked from the bottom of a laundry pile. She walked up to me without a word.

"You sure you want to do this today?" I asked.

"You're right, Quinn. I should go home and stare at the walls."

"Sorry."

We stood in silence awhile, waiting for Selena. The road was as empty as the sky. I handed June a piece of Juicy Fruit and she popped it in her mouth, her gaze set off in the desert, like she was looking for something. In the distance, her father's homestead was a blip of brown in a rolling sea of cactus.

"Mom told me this morning Bud left everything to me."

"Oh." I rifled through my head for the right response. What Gram would have said. "That's good, I mean, that he...really cared about you."

"It's okay, O'Brien. We can just stand here."

A cloud of dust announced Selena's arrival. She set her bike against the hotel. Then the three of us stood in front of the sagging entrance, staring the hotel in the mouth.

Selena seemed to be steeling herself for the next step. Then she took a deep breath and let it out in a rush. "Are we doing this again or what?"

I put on my head lamp, and the girls carried flashlights—we'd need them for the little room. Inside the lobby, the monstrous chandelier caught the sunlight and rained it down on us, sent it into the hushed corners. I had no urge to count the teardrop crystals. The building felt empty, like a cicada shell.

As we filled the echoey space with our footsteps, my mind snagged on those words: *empty shell.*

I stopped.

"What's wrong now?" June asked.

"Can you feel that? How different it is now?"

June and Selena looked at each other. "Feels like the same old creep show to me," June said.

I told myself to keep my psychic thoughts to myself, then rounded the mouth of the grand staircase. There was the gaping hole in the floor Selena and I had made a week ago. Someone—probably Ollie or Enrique—had set a piece of plywood over it, probably to keep kids from falling in and keep it hidden from local looters. I lifted it a foot above the lip and peered into the thick darkness. I was inside that refrigerator again, my fists beating against the door.

Selena took in my expression. "We could come back tomorrow. It'll still be here."

I wiped the dust off my hands, let my lungs take in a breath. "Will it?" But really I meant *Will I?* Because if I waited until tomorrow, what would Kit do to me tonight?

"Fine, go in," June said finally, "but if you pass out, I'm not giving you mouth-to-mouth."

"Okay. Here I go." I moved toward the opening, then stopped. Rested my forearms on my knees. Footsteps and voices came from the second floor, then faded while I tried to pull up some courage. God, we didn't have time for me to have an episode.

"Think of wide-open spaces," Selena said, watching me with an unreadable expression. "Blue skies."

"I am. Tahiti. Bahamas. Poconos."

"Don't go overboard."

I sorted through the fog in my head. Latched onto the image of Kit, roaming free in our campgrounds, in Gypsum. "I just need to focus on why we're here: discovering who Kit is."

"Right. Now drop down and tell me if there are any monsters."

I shimmied down, let go, and landed on the soft carpet below. A moment later, June and Selena dropped beside me.

The space was small, like a bedroom, and cold, but it wasn't as bad as I remembered. I took another deep breath, and this time my lungs felt like I owned them again. Shook the dust and cobwebs out of my hair.

June made a slow circle. "Whoa, look at all this creepy stuff."

Dust danced in the glow from my head lamp. Along one wall was a long table with thick, curved legs, the kind that took five guys to move. My light skipped over the tablecloth, a few dining chairs, the face of a brass clock, the stuffed owl. I traced the outlines of the room. The Persian rug under my feet covered almost the entire floor, its reds and blues dulled by a layer of grime.

Behind me came a rustle of papers. "Bingo!" Selena stood beside a stack of leather books, her face lit up like Christmas morning.

June wandered over. "Please tell me there's a SparkNotes version of these."

"No kidding," I said.

Selena shoved a book into June's hands and one into mine, then picked up another from the stack. At least twenty more sat on the table. The leather covers were cracked, the paper inside yellowed, the handwriting neat and cramped. They were *journals,* not books. A scan of the one Selena gave me didn't show much, so I picked up another and flipped through. The third wasn't much better.

I flipped through a fourth. A faded black-and-white picture fell out onto the carpet.

Three men wearing old-fashioned clothes leaned on pickaxes outside the ragged opening of the gypsum mines. I picked it up and flipped it over. On the back were the names *Hector Garcia, Robert Fitzwater, and Liam O'Brien. 1933.*

"Whoa." I pointed the light at the page while they both looked over my shoulders, then put my finger on the guy on the right. "That's Liam O'Brien, my great-grandfather. And look who he's standing next to." I pointed to Robert Fitzwater. "You look just like him."

June shot me an irritated look. "Just what a girl likes to hear."

"You know what I mean. There's a resemblance."

June took a closer look. "Yeah, that's my great-grandfather, all right. Mom keeps his picture on the wall next to the bathroom." She tilted her head. "He looks a lot like Bud. Before the accident, I mean."

I winced.

Selena took the photo from my hand and squinted at it. "And that's *my* great-grandfather, right there." She looked at me, and then at June. "Do you guys believe in fate? I mean, what are the chances the three of us would be friends?"

June sat on the table, sending up a cloud of particles. "We're a flyspeck town. Who else we gonna be friends with?"

Flipping back a few pages, I found the title page of the journal, which held the name of the owner. *Hector Garcia.* "Selena, look at this."

She took the book from my hand, and when she read the name, her eyes widened.

I reached for other journals, opened them to the front plates. "These two belong to Liam O'Brien. The rest are all Hector Garcia's."

"Your great-grandfather's stuff being here, that makes sense. He owned the place," Selena said. "But mine was a miner. Why would this room have his journals in it? And why wall it up?"

We lost ourselves reading: June and Selena lying on their bellies on the carpet, turning pages in the dark, me standing at the long, dusty table, trying to make out the slanted hand in the glow of my head lamp. Most of Hector's journal didn't tell me much beyond what Gram had taught me. That he, like most of the men who came here back in the 1920s, worked his butt off for fourteen hours a day, chipping gypsum out of the earth. Since the 1880s, that was who you were if you lived in Gypsum—a miner, someone who married a miner, or someone who served whiskey to miners.

Then the locals discovered the mineral waters, and they figured out that it cured everything. Which then brought businessmen to build a hotel and spa they called the Alvarado, which in turn brought the Hollywood types.

All that success, like a line of dominos falling.

Hector wrote about quitting the mines and helping my great-grandfather Liam, who'd sunk everything he had into the Alvarado. First Hector was a bartender, then an extra in *Dead for Dollars*. (According to him, Eva Durbin spent most of her time in a silk bathrobe, pouting and smoking in the film trailer. She hadn't changed much.) There was a whole entry on what it was like to serve the famous Fritz Von Sturnberg, the director (described as a showboating jerk), and the other rich men who sat in the Alvarado Hotel, profiting from the sweat of others. Hector sounded idealistic, like someone who'd change things if he could, and I wasn't surprised that his wife became Gypsum's mayor. I thought of Selena, lying back on my roof with her eyes on the heavens, making her plans. Of her sister, A.J., stepping up and taking the reins of the town when she was needed. I guessed it ran in the family.

Hector went on to mention that he and his wife went swimming at the spring at the base of the Horse Crippler, and that it blessed them, because she got pregnant soon after. The journal was full of bits like that—a mix of history and superstition.

I found an entry about the *Dead for Dollars* film crew and their wild parties at the Alvarado. I'd listened to Gram talk about that film endlessly:

how the production imploded when some of the crew went missing, how the movie had to be cobbled together by editors who spliced in extra footage, how it was said to be cursed. The Hollywood execs had probably been the ones to keep those rumors going. There was even supposed to be a ghostly figure in one corner of one scene, which you could only see if you were *really* working for it, a figure raising its arms to the night sky. I guessed they thought more people would come to the theaters to watch it if they thought the set was haunted.

Of course, the hotel was part of the set, so they were right. The film *was* haunted.

And then I found a tucked sheet of paper. Unfolded it.

A map.

The landscape was familiar. Chinati Mountains in the west, hills to the east, a whole lotta desert in between. A small X marked the corner of the page, and next to it was written *O'Brien Homestead*. Several more dotted the page, each with familiar names: Fitzwater. Betleman. Garcia. Rivera. Lumpkin. Pilsner. Not far away, another X marked the Alvarado. And over everything faint lines were drawn, twisting and turning and crossing each other.

"Selena, look at this."

She leaned over my shoulder. "The geography's right, but the roads make no sense. See?" She traced the lines with her finger. "Some of them run right through your campgrounds. And this one runs sideways through downtown, like they're passing *over* buildings. And these three roads go all the way to the Alvarado Hotel, shoot—right through the walls."

"Either this map is wrong, or…" I flipped it over and looked at the back, then flipped it over again. Suddenly, I was back in the halls of the Alvarado, the walls turning to stone, crumbling around me. "Oh my God."

"What else could it be?" June asked.

"It's a map of the *mines*. Under us."

"No way."

"I'm telling you, that's what it is."

"I've seen maps of the gypsum mines before," Selena insisted, "and the tunnels don't even come *close* to the hotel, or the town."

"Obviously, those maps are wrong."

"Why isn't this one wrong?"

"I just know." I looked up from the journal. "This map is important to understanding why Kit was here—I know that, too. Hell, I bet there's an entrance to the mines somewhere in this basement."

"You mean one ghost hunters and historians haven't found?" June scoffed. "This place is pretty well picked over."

"People miss stuff," I said. "And think about it. Gangsters stayed here in the thirties. They could've used it like a back door, for business."

"True…and after some of that film crew went missing, no one found any bodies," Selena added in an ominous tone.

"They're probably just buried out in the desert," June said.

Selena studied the map. "Or their corpses are rotting down in the tunnels under the Alvarado."

June gave Selena a look. "Sometimes I worry about you."

Selena folded the map carefully, then closed the journal. "Someone probably walled it up, like this room."

"Yeah," I said, "just bricked up the opening like…"

In the silence, we all looked down at the same time, at the dusty carpet covering the stone floor.

I grabbed the edge of the rug and pulled it back.

There, set dead center in the middle of the room, was a wooden hatch.

CHAPTER
NINETEEN

I lifted up the iron ring that served as a handle. With one strong pull, I opened the hatch a few inches. June and I both grabbed the lip and heaved. The hatch door fell over backward on the stone.

From beneath, a cold draft of air rushed at us, an exhale of stale breath. Selena and I knelt by the hole and directed our beams down. There was a jagged hole bored down through four feet of stone. My light barely made it to the pale stone floor thirty feet below that.

"That...is a great way to break both legs," June said.

At the far end of my head lamp's reach, the remains of a rope ladder lay in a pile. Not much else was visible. The thick stone lip of the hole blocked most of the view.

"What do you think's down there?" Selena asked.

"Mice. Things that eat mice. Dead people." A scent wafted up, something foul with an edge of sweet rot. The chill of the hatch's iron loop was numbing my fingers.

I could close this door. Pack up the journals and go home. Let Kit melt into Weird Gypsum. But as I stared into the darkness, I really did feel it staring back, and I was tired of being the one to blink first.

I stood and wiped my hands on my jeans. "I don't know what's down there, but we're about to find out. You think there's some rope up in the lobby?"

The girls stared at me.

"C'mon, you really think it's a coincidence that the entrance of the mines was hidden along with the safe?"

They couldn't argue. Thirty minutes later, I was lowering myself down into the hole, hand over hand. The nylon straps June and Selena had found behind the bar almost reached the stone floor below, once we'd knotted them together. My light shone jagged over stone, gravity's fingers digging into my shoulders, my face, my rib cage. A moment of vertigo hit me, traveled down my spine into the pit of my stomach.

From above, June's voice came, muffled by rock. "You know what movie this reminds me of?"

I could barely hear Selena's far-off reply. *The Sound of Music.*

"No, *The Descent.*"

"The one where the two girls get stuck in a shark cage in Mexico?"

"That's *47 Meters Down.* Why in the world would you think of that one?"

"Which one is *The Descent?*"

"The one with the caves and the girls and all the blood."

"Thanks, June, that's lovely."

"Welcome."

An image popped into my head: a clawed hand coming out of nowhere and wrapping around my skull.

"Not helping!" I called up. I told myself it wasn't a premonition. Just plain old fear. It wasn't the future. Just Hollywood.

None of that was real.

I touched bottom, and the hiss of the rope died. Then I arched my neck and swept the light across the walls. Stalactites, hundreds of them, dripped from the ceiling, glimmering in the beam. Not with moisture, though—the stone itself glimmered, like it was inlaid with mica.

Gram's words came back to me: *They want to know there's some wonder left in the universe.*

I was in a cavern. It looked big enough to fit the entire Alvarado Hotel inside.

"Wow," I whispered. My voice didn't echo, swallowed up by the darkness and all that space.

"What's down there?" June called out.

"Slavering beasts!"

"Ha ha."

"It's a cavern. Seriously, both of you gotta come down here."

I waited. The darkness just outside my beam felt dry and empty, like the shell of some great insect. Again, I had the feeling I was inside the skin of something that no longer lived there. It was quiet down here, too, the kind of quiet I heard when I woke far out in the desert. The quiet that drifted over a campsite like a soft hush.

As the heavy ceiling loomed over me, so many tons of it hovering above my fragile head, I remembered something Selena had told me once, last summer, when we'd left the tent flap open all night and a snake had crawled into her bag to sleep, coiled against the warm skin of her bare feet. She'd told me that the quiet I loved so much had a flip side. That it could be like the underside of a rock. Suffocating. Dangerous.

And that was what this place felt like.

June descended the line and stood beside me. Both of us looked up to the hole in the ceiling thirty feet above, and Selena's face appeared. She wore the same look as she did that day last summer, her eyes too wide, her mouth pressed in a thin, bloodless line. Fear. It had been the longest ten minutes of our lives, Ollie and me dragging Selena out of the sleeping bag in slow motion, inch by inch. Then she lay panting and trembling, the morning sun raining down on us as we watched the rattlesnake slither out and head into the desert.

"You coming?" I called up.

Selena's face disappeared as she looked over her shoulder, tested the line. Then she tested it again. She'd been climbing since she was old enough to walk, usually with us on the Horse Crippler, or on the White Bone Cliffs on the other side of town. Ollie'd taught her everything she knew, and he was the best climber in West Texas. She knew her knot was good. She didn't need to check it.

Finally, she made her way down the rope, hand over hand, and dropped next to me. I reached out to wipe some rock dust from her cheek, then thought better of it and let my hand drop by my side.

I swept my small circle of light around the cavern. My boots crunched softly on small bits of rock as I made my way west into the coiled darkness. The rhythmic drip of water hitting stone echoed. No matter where I directed the light, I couldn't find the source. It came from everywhere and nowhere at once.

A glimmer on the walls caught my eye, and I stopped. They were practically shining. Curious, I touched one. The sheen came off on my fingertips.

Selena reached out and touched the wall. "The walls are sweating as much as I am."

Drip, drip, drip.

"The springs must butt up against this."

The aquifer, just on the other side of the wall.

I stopped after about ten steps and shined my light back toward the dangling rope. "Are we heading west?" I asked.

"Do I look like a compass?" June turned in a circle, clearly with no idea.

My mouth was dry, so I unwrapped a piece of chewing gum and handed it to June. My light caught on the shiny foil as I crumpled it. Gram's bedtime stories came back to me, from when I was five and Ollie was in middle school. He pretended he was too old for bedtime stories, but even so, he would stand at the doorway, a little smile on his face as she read "Hansel and Gretel." Gram's worn fingers, her knuckles knotty, the pads of her fingers rough as she turned the page with a rasp.

I dropped the crumpled wrapper on the stone floor.

"Why are you littering?" Selena asked.

"I'm leaving a trail of bread crumbs."

"I can lead us out with the map."

"Just in case."

"Why are we whispering?" June asked.

"I don't know," Selena replied in a whisper.

I kept moving, unwrapping pieces of gum as I went. Darkness. My circle of light on the pale stone floor. By the time I'd almost finished the pack, my beam hit a wall. I'd reached the end of the line.

I stopped and firehosed my light around me, above me, over the stalactites that hung from the ceiling like stone icicles. The beam caught on two dots, close together, then another pair, and another, reflecting like the tinfoil wrappers I'd left behind.

"What is that? Mica?" I asked, counting up the pairs. A dozen, then two dozen. I took a clumsy step back toward the wall.

Eyes.

I covered the light with my hand, an instinct. *Don't be seen.* I tried to quiet my breathing, but my heart leapt in my chest. Eyes, all over the ceiling. It could be anything.

I forced myself to look again, redirect my light above. Small. Brown. Hanging upside down. Pointed ears. June's voice came from beside me, in a low ominous tone: "Bats. Why did it have to be bats."

"Shut *up,* June," Selena said. "Don't wake them."

I swept my light in both directions, following the wall until my light faded. "If there are bats, there has to be a way into the proper mining tunnels—and from there, to the outside."

I dropped the final silver gum wrapper at the place where the wall met the floor, and I headed left, scouring the stone with my light, looking for an entrance into the mines. But I was also looking for something else, although I couldn't put my finger on what it was. It was the same feeling I had when I read the leaves, when I stepped into the Dark Place and had an urge to throw my whole body past the veil, into the other side. The answers were down here. I could feel that, pressing down like pins on the marrow of my bones. I would find out why all this was happening to us.

After thirty steps or so, my light sliding over the rock like a finger, the wall abruptly cut off. An opening. "Hey, check this out."

Selena passed me to get a better look inside, but the light only penetrated so far.

"June, what do you see?"

No response.

I stopped and turned, swept my light in both directions. "June?"

Selena swept her flashlight's beam across the rock walls, sent it wildly into the darkness, where the ink ate it up. "*June!* I'm gonna *kill you* when you get back!"

June's voice came to me, faint and far away. "Just going back to check out the dark corners, see if we missed anything. You want something sneaking up on you? I don't think so." Her last words came out as a singsong.

"She can see her way back to the rope if she falls behind," Selena huffed.

Selena and I edged around the corner and shined our lights inside. A small cave off the cavern, not much bigger than my bedroom, with a stalagmite growing right out of the floor dead center. Next to it was a pool of water as big as a hot tub, the surface still and black.

As I examined the surface, I wondered if it would feel sticky, like the web.

Like the veil in the Dark Place.

A ridiculous thought. Of course it wouldn't feel sticky. It was just water.

I stepped inside the antechamber. At first, the texture of the stone's surface threw me. So many shades of dark and light, thin striations set into the rock. My head swam, trying to make sense of what I was seeing. I needed June, but she was out there in the cave, doing God knows what.

And then next to me, Selena made a little gasp. "Writing. The walls are covered with writing!"

We raked our lights over the stone. Symbols, some in white, some in black. Hash marks. Dots. Words in a language I didn't understand. Pictographs. All of it crowded so tightly that at first it looked like a mere pattern in the rock. I reached out to touch the image of a snake, a small unintelligible word above it. And then small dashes, followed by small circles of white, over and over, in different patterns.

I rubbed my fingers together. "This chalky stuff is alabaster."

Inside my stomach, the sudden swoop of vertigo hit me. My vision swam. The marks, spinning like fireflies. I closed my eyes.

"Oh my God," I murmured under my breath.

"What?" Selena stepped near, her eyes searching my face.

"These marks. I've seen them before. They were inside the safe."

We stood there for too long, sweeping our lights over the walls. I tried to wrap my mind around what this meant. Selena's eyes filled with that spark of wonder I always saw in her when she took out her camera to capture a small thing, like a beetle on a cliff wall, or a big thing, like a cloud bank. And now she had that look, inching her light over the walls, holding her breath.

"So, I'm guessing this used to be Kit's home?" Selena asked. "And he put these marks on the walls?"

I thought of the pieces of metal lying in our mudroom. Of the rage that tore those pieces apart and left them behind for us to find. "I have no idea."

"Seems like he had a lot of time on his hands," Selena said, her light raking the walls.

I followed the bright streaks of symbols and dots around the wall, dragging my beam across stone. Then I flashed the far corner of the cave and saw an opening. An old door lay on the stone floor, detached from the hinges, like it had been knocked down.

"Hey, Selena. Check this out. I think I just found an entrance to the mines."

Selena knelt and examined it, inching her light across the surface. "Look. This is covered with symbols, carved right into the wood."

A thrum of tumbling rock came from behind, far away. Somewhere out in the cavern, beyond the opening to this room, something had dislodged a rock.

Selena was still hyperfocused, crouched and still, her fingertips feeling the carvings on the fallen door.

I crossed the cave, back toward where we'd come from. "June?" I chanced one look behind me to make sure Selena was still there, then took two steps into the ink, trying to make sense out of the head lamp–lit shapes in front of me. Stalactites twenty feet long. Small bright eyes buried among them. Another step, my ears straining, my heart a little hammer in my chest, my light pointed too high.

On my fourth step, I caught nothing but air.

CHAPTER
TWENTY

I plummeted, yelling, flailing my arms and legs. The beam of light came with me, spinning uselessly in the dark.

I threw out my arm and grasped for a handhold. One, two long seconds, my life as heavy as a stone in a well, and then my hand found an edge. A blinding pain on my elbow, a hammer to my hip.

The fall ended. I'd caught hold of the wall.

I hung there by one hand, trembling with adrenaline. With the other, I searched the rock face, turning my head to direct the head lamp's beam. Looking for shadows, the cracks that would let me hold on. And a thought rose up, as I hung there, searching for the right hold. That I would never see Ollie again. That he would be so pissed at me for dying, and he would never forgive me for leaving him alone.

My light caught a shadow, and I got a second hold. My ligaments stretched, muscles shook. The rough rock scraped against my cheek as I turned to look down and find a foothold. I skittered my feet over the cliff face. Saw another shadow on the wall and slipped one toe into it. Another edge by my left calf took the other foot. I shifted my weight so my arms stopped shaking, then pressed my forehead against the cool surface.

As the rasp of my panicked breathing faded, I focused on the distant drip of water rather than the fear clawing its way up my throat. I was stable. I wouldn't fall. I wouldn't. I could do this. Crawl up the cliff face, the head lamp guiding me, find holds, and reach the summit. I'd done night climbing before. Climbed right up the toughest side of the Horse Crippler, then stood at the top and shouted at the moon.

I tilted my head back and the beam of the head lamp caught on a cluster of stalactites. The pinprick eyes of the bats nested between, watching me.

And then I made a huge mistake. I looked down. Not at my feet, but farther out, into the darkness.

Vast. Endless. A sheer drop that ate up my light.

I turned away. The head lamp caught on a protrusion of stone near my eyes, and the band slipped up an inch, to the top of my forehead. I froze and reached up to slip it back down. The light flashed haphazardly on something below.

Something pale gray. The size of me.

And it was climbing.

I fumbled the strap, the electric pulse of fear making my fingers numb and stupid. The band slipped. And my head lamp fell. I watched it tumble down, spinning.

Sweat dripping in my eyes, I clung to the rock and told myself June would come to look for me. And that there was *nothing* in the dark with me. That was a mirage, the thing moving. Climbing.

But a voice whispered, reminding me: *Gypsum's a strange place.* The Alvarado, pressing down above me, full of ghosts. The dozens of people lost in the mines before the town boarded up the entrance. The vanished film crew.

I opened my mouth to yell for June and Selena. Then I stopped. It would hear me, the thing that wasn't there. Maybe it couldn't find me if I stayed quiet...but staying quiet meant staying here.

"Selena!"

Seconds passed. I counted them. I counted because the numbers were comforting. Then the scrape of a shoe on rock.

"Quinn!" Selena's voice fell down to me like rain and I soaked it in. High-pitched, as if she'd scraped her vocal cords raw on her way to me. "I'm going to get the rope we used to climb down!"

"No! Then we'll be stuck down here. Find June!"

I listened to her footsteps fade, wondering if I'd ever hear them again. I let go of the rock with my right hand to wipe the sweat off on my shirt, then did the same with my left. I shifted my weight from leg to leg.

Rock crumbled somewhere beneath me. A little pattering of tumbling, scraping. Thirty feet below maybe.

But sound, in a cave, it was full of tricks. I thought of the picture on Gram's desk of Liam O'Brien, the lines on his forehead etched with gypsum dust. He'd tell her how sound traveled in strange ways in the mines. That it spiraled. That sometimes his own voice came at him from behind. And as I hung there, thinking of reaching up blind and feeling for a new handhold, I couldn't stop thinking about Gram's dad—of his picture at the hotel, his eyes following me up the stairs.

One, two, three, and I let go with my right hand, feeling up over the sandpaper rock. To the right, over a sharp point. To the left. But even if I found something to hold on to, I needed to know the route up. Which way to handholds? And which way to a sheer face?

A thumping came from above, far away, but building. Feet hitting ground. A rhythm. Someone running.

The tattoo of boots on rock grew until it echoed, then stopped above me.

"Good God, Quinn," a voice high above me said. It was June, her words full of so much panic I barely understood.

"I didn't get my morning climb in, so I thought I'd try something different."

"Where's Selena?"

"I'm sorry, I can't hear you that well, what with all the screaming in my head," I said. She'd left us, again. In the dark. If she'd just been here—

"Oh God. Is Selena . . . I can't see that far, the bottom's too far. Is she—"

"What do you mean *the bottom's too far?*"

"Did she fall?" June asked, her voice shaking.

"How far can you see?"

"Oh sweet Jesus, she's down there, isn't she?"

"She didn't fall. She went looking for *you*."

"Oh, thank God!"

"Help me! Guide me up!"

I heard her shifting above me as she tried to get a better look at my situation. "Right. Let me check out the holds, see if I can tell you how to climb. There are a few good jugs just to your left, two feet up, then—" A sharp intake of breath, then silence. My insides went cold.

"What?" I shouted up. "What'd you see?"

"I'll be back soon." And she was gone.

I counted again. There was nothing beneath me, I told myself, and I kept counting until the sweat had soaked through my T-shirt and gathered in the small of my back, the tendons of my fingers stretched like piano wires. Then the crumbling beneath me returned. My weight, probably, on the cliff, destabilizing it. Or . . .

I couldn't wait for June and Selena. Time to climb.

My boots felt rubbery and loose, an old pair of Ollie's that had too much air at the toe. *To grow on,* he'd said. I cursed them now. I couldn't feel the rock through the thick soles.

I reached down and pulled my right boot over my heel, let it fall. Did the same with my left. Then I slid one hand up over the rock, to the left, the surface a cat's tongue on my palm. I found a higher handhold. A good one. A nice jug to hold on to. My foot was next. I dragged it up, searching with my toes for another hold. When I found one, I pushed. The pull of gravity told me which way to go, and I moved against it—toward the top, toward salvation, feeling for an overhang or an underhang, every hold I'd ever learned spinning through my head. My fingers jittered across the wall. Right. Then left. Then up.

And then it was smooth. *All* smooth. And I was going to fall. I was going to find out what was at the bottom of the blackness. Join the head lamp at the bottom. Spin and fall and scream. Until I didn't.

I tamped down my panic and reached an inch higher. Suddenly, there was something warm, there in the dark. Pressing against the back of my hand.

I froze. Warm, clammy flesh. *Fingers.* They slid across the skin of my wrist, circling over and sliding underneath.

Sounds reached me. A strangled cry. Words maybe. A scream. They came from me, and I pressed my face against the rock and waited for my life to end. For a slice, a bite, for *it* to pull me off the cliff and throw me into the dark.

A pull on my wrist. Gentle. Pulling my hand farther up and to the right. Then it let go. Underneath my fingers was a handhold.

Footsteps returned, echoing through the cavern. "Quinn!" Selena's voice. "Thank God."

"I've found help!" June said. "They're coming."

"There's something in the dark with me."

She didn't answer. Two, three seconds.

"June?"

"I know. Just wait for the rope."

The rhythm of footsteps thumped in the distance. Then a man's voice tumbled down to me.

"The rope's coming. On three."

A flashlight swept down into the depth, blinding me, followed by a gasp from the guy who was holding it. Next to me, something scrambled away over the rock, disappearing into the depths. I clung to the handhold it had led me to.

"Nicco, did you see that? Did you?"

"Yeah, yeah, man, I saw it."

"Did you have the camera on?"

"Yes, I think... I got some of it."

My arms were shaking. I was going to come loose from the wall.

"Would you throw him the rope already?" June cried.

"Sorry, sorry!"

A slap, to my right. I fumbled in the dark and wrapped the line around my palm.

Selena's voice tumbled down to me. "We've got you, Quinn. We got you."

I let go of the rock and clung to the rope, and they dragged me to the top, inch by inch. Below, near the bottom, a small tumble of rock pierced the silence, then disappeared.

·———————·

I lay on my back, my hand flung over my face. Tripp and Nicco shined the flashlight in my eyes and asked me if I could see.

"Not with that light blinding me."

"Sorry, man, we're just checking your pupils—"

"—to make sure you don't have a concussion."

"—Yeah, exactly. A concussion."

As they poked and prodded and asked me if I knew what year it was, I managed to catch my breath and remind myself that yes, I was alive.

"Did you see that thing?" Nicco's shadow asked me.

"What thing?" I answered.

"That gray...shape...I don't know. What was it?"

I exchanged a look with June, then Selena, and turned back to Nicco, who I could now see had a GoPro firmly attached to his headband. And he was recording. "I have no idea what you're talking about."

"C'mon, it was right there."

June spoke up. "People see things down here all the time. Just tricks of the light. Means a whole lotta nothin'."

The three of us knew better to than to tell them anything. They weren't our people. It wasn't their business.

But no matter what we said, they wouldn't listen. They insisted a "monster" had been with me. This talk continued, as well as their bickering about how to use the camera, all the way back up into the lobby of the Alvarado. After I refused to be interviewed, Tripp and Nicco called me "ungrateful."

By the time we made our way to the Gun Barrel Trailer Park, sunset had arrived in all its glory, the hot-orange glow turning Eva Durbin's trailer into a dark rectangle. A breeze picked up, spinning the rooster weather vane in her yard, sending its rasping moan out into the desert scrub.

Ignoring June's questions as she tailed me, I marched up the steps to Ms. Durbin's door and held up my fist to knock.

June grabbed my wrist. "Hey, cowboy. Slow down."

Selena, who stood at the foot of the stairs with her hands in her pocket, shrugged as if to say *Talk to her, not me.*

"If anyone knows the history of this town," I said, "it's Eva Durbin. She's the only one left alive from when the journals were written."

"I know, but—"

"June, after what happened today, I don't think I'll sleep. Ever again. I need answers. Now, can I knock?"

"No."

"Why?"

"Because it's sundown."

"So?"

"So, Sherlock, Mrs. D. *sundowns.* This time of day, she's a little . . . off. Gets startled by loud noises, starts spiraling, thinks it's 1933, that sort of thing." She let go of my wrist and pulled a key out of her pocket. "So, no knocking."

We quietly entered the warm, sticky air of Mrs. Durbin's trailer, which smelled like chicken soup and hospital soap. Like every trailer in the park, Eva Durbin's living room was small, but instead of deer head décor and embroidered pillows, the whole place was a time warp. Black-and-white framed photos covered almost every inch of paneling.

Jimmy Cagney and Eva Durbin at a party.

Clark Gable and Eva Durbin linked arm in arm on the red carpet.

Alfred Hitchcock and Eva Durbin, caught deep in conversation.

And this Eva Durbin was stunning, smiling at the camera, glancing coyly over her shoulder, posing with a silver cigarette holder, rubbing elbows with people no one in Gypsum ever dreamed of meeting.

Only one spot on the wall had a splash of color—a picture of a much older Mrs. Durbin at one of June's volleyball games. Bud stood behind her wheelchair, his John Deere hat slightly off center, and June, in her gold-and-black uniform shorts and tank, leaning down to press her cheek to Mrs. Durbin's, a bright championship smile on her face.

At the kitchen table, Eva Durbin sat with hands folded in her lap, a messy gray braid lying over one shoulder. Her cat, who she called Mr. DeMille, formed a pile of white fur on a nearby barstool.

"Hi, Mrs. D," I said.

She didn't respond, shoulders hunched, chewing on her lip. Today she'd traded the gray silk ball gown she'd worn at Krista's party for sweat pants and a long-sleeved tee with DIVA written in swirly letters. By the velvet fainting couch across the room, *Sunset Boulevard* played on a flat-screen, the sound muted. But Mrs. Durbin wasn't watching, her gaze instead fixed through the window on the orange glow that now filled the whole western sky.

I sat next to her. At the scrape of the chair, Mr. DeMille jumped off the barstool. Mrs. Durbin turned, saw my face, and startled.

"What's wrong with you, boy?" she asked, clutching a hand to her chest.

I looked down at the bloodstains. My face probably looked worse. "Aw, this is nothing. Just fell."

"Fell? Good lord, young man, into what? A wood chipper?"

"No," I said. "I fell into a mine."

She peered at me, her wrinkles deepening, her eyes shining with suspicion. "Mine? Liam, is that you? I told you not to go down there." Her gaze flitted down to my shirt again, surprise filling her eyes, as if I'd just arrived. "Boy, what in the world happened to you?"

June sat beside her, shot me a *Told you so* look, and handed her a glass of water. Then she stood, grabbed me by the sleeve, and dragged me toward the bathroom. "It's okay, Mrs. D. I got this."

"Well, I certainly hope so."

The three of us squeezed into Mrs. Durbin's bathroom, and June smacked my arm with the back of her hand.

"Sorry," I said. "I just thought—"

"Let's clean you up," June said, "and try again. Not that you'll get anything useful from her. Unless you want to know what Clark Gable looks like naked, which I'm sure she'll tell you all about."

June reached into her backpack and brought out a first aid kit, and Selena took it without a word. They'd both patched me up before, during my daredevil-on-a-bike phase.

I slumped down on the tile, a thousand questions about what had happened in the mines still swirling in my head. Selena sat across from me, fishing around in the kit for supplies, arranging them in a neat line on her blue-jeaned thigh.

June pulled herself up on the vanity, her booted feet swinging. "I bet Mrs. D. can lend you a T-shirt."

"And there goes the last of my masculinity."

June grinned and slipped out, leaving me alone with a giggling Selena.

We fell silent as she worked on my face, the drip of the faucet filling the small bathroom.

Selena cleaned my forehead, leaning close enough for me to smell the scent of her sandalwood perfume. Her shirt gaped at little at the neck, exposing a sprinkling of freckles down her collarbone. She noticed my gaze and adjusted the collar. I looked away. My face flushed.

The door opened and hit me on the shoulder. I winced.

"Sorry," June said, slipping in and throwing me a clean tee. I caught it in one hand, eyes still on Selena. "Did I interrupt something?"

"Of course not," Selena snapped.

A little smile played on June's mouth, and she and Selena exchanged an unreadable glance. Selena found a butterfly Band-Aid, then attached it to my scalp.

"Ow."

Selena leaned close again, only inches away. "Just hold still," she said, her soft voice finding a place somewhere in my chest and pulling.

I concentrated on a small mole on her temple, trying to ignore how good she smelled, until she finished pressing the bandage in place.

When I stood to change my shirt, Selena covered her eyes—which made June crack up—and I slipped on the fresh tee, which was emblazoned with GYPSUM CHILI COOKOFF and an image of a rattlesnake taking a bath in a Crock-Pot. June gave me a once-over, then nodded. "You're no longer terrifying."

"Definitely not," Selena said, and before I could make out her tone, she grabbed June's bag to stuff the first aid kit inside, then paused, opening it wider, her brows coming together. She reached in and pulled out a white envelope.

On the front, written in pencil, was *For June, from Bud.*

"What's this?"

"You're nosy," June replied, her expression shuttered.

"I am. Now, what is it?"

June shrugged, picked at a cuticle. "Mom found it in Bud's office, tucked in with the will."

"What...what did it—"

"Dunno. Haven't opened it yet." June took the letter from Selena. "Probably something like *Hey June, would you like a hundred acres of worthless desert seeded with land mines? Love ya, baby girl.*" She stuffed it back in her bag.

"You gotta open it eventually."

"Or I could just move. Give the land to the military or whatever."

"Doesn't sound like something Uncle Sam would want."

"Uncle Sam loves fireworks. He'd be all over it." June's voice cracked a little on that last word. She turned away from us, suddenly very interested in the tiny bathroom window.

"Thank you," I said.

"For...?"

"For keeping me from falling ten stories and breaking both legs."

June turned to face me. "Like I would leave you in the dark full of monsters...Oh, wait a second..." She gave me the first real smile I'd seen from her all day.

We stepped out into the living room, ready to ask Eva Durbin,

Gypsum's oldest living resident, what in the world was going on in the mines, and what she knew about my grandfather back in the day, and all our ancestors for that matter. But the chair by the kitchen table was empty.

The three of us stood in front of the fainting couch, looking down at Eva, who lay with one arm draped dramatically over her forehead, sleeping peacefully.

On the flat-screen behind her, *Sunset Boulevard* played on. As Gloria Swanson, in all her black-and-white glory, stood at the top of a staircase, her face radiant in the flashbulb fire from a dozen cameras, June covered Mrs. Durbin with a blanket, tucking it under her chin gently.

I reached for the remote, and June stayed my hand. "Just let it play."

CHAPTER
TWENTY-ONE

Ollie didn't freak when he saw me. Just took one look at me and said, "What's the other guy look like?"

The rest of the night I tried to take it easy and let my wounds scab over, but sleep wouldn't come. Not with what had happened in the mines spinning through my head. I Googled *cave people* and went down a rabbit hole till 3 a.m. Then I scoured through two of the journals the three of us had taken home and split among us. I read for hours before I came upon the first hint of something out of the ordinary, an entry in Hector Garcia's journal:

> March 2, 1933
>
> This week a miner went missing. One of the Gonzales kids, barely 15. I remember the day he first went into the tunnels, he stood at the entrance and looked me in the face and asked me if it was safe.
>
> "Yes, mijo," I told him. "It's safe. Everyone comes out of the mines okay. And when you do, the stars will seem that much brighter."
>
> We've looked for him. Two days. His mother sits by the well off Agave Street, staring into the darkness there and crying. We told her to go

home, that he wasn't lost in the well, that we were looking for him in the mines west of town. But she won't leave. Says the water knows where he is.

Mrs. Gonzales been there two days now, sitting and rocking at the rock lip of the well, talking to the water.

I shut the journal and pushed it across the table from me. He was talking about Crying Woman's Well, east of the courthouse. I'd never heard that story, of how the well got its name. Now I wished I hadn't.

I slipped out my window and climbed up to the roof, watching the bowl of the sky rotate above me, full of stars. Familiar and real. Morning came, seeping into the black edges of the world until they became gray. Then a rose glow followed, brightening minute after minute. My body was stiff from the cold, but I didn't want this moment to end, when everything was simple. The sun rose. The sun set. People lived and died in Gypsum. I was one of those people.

These were facts. Comforting and stable. I knew these things, my place in the world, and the way things should be. But now, I felt the world changing, the way I could smell a rainstorm coming.

Something was coming. I was the one to let Kit out, and now I had to be the one to take care of it. Figure it out. Figure out the omen in the sky and how to stop what came next, if I could.

In my jacket pocket, my phone vibrated. I knew who it was before I looked at the screen.

Selena.

did you sleep?

no

I read journals all night.

Of course she did. My share of the journals still lay on my desk, open and full of tiny, cramped writing. Hector Garcia talking about cattle and grasslands. Liam O'Brien going on about his plans to make

Gypsum a world-class town and the Alvarado the best hotel west of the Mississippi. I hadn't found a thing that helped me.

they're hard to read, I thumbed out.

Her text popped up and made me smile.

it's your own fault for not learning cursive in third grade.

yes that's what's important right now – cursive

just saying

I stared at the phone, then the slowly brightening horizon, the dark backbone of the Chinati Mountains. Where was Kit? Watching the sunrise, like me? Sleeping? Did he sleep? What *was* he doing?

we need to see what he's up to

Selena didn't respond at first, although texting dots appeared, shimmering, then disappeared. Maybe Kit was the mind reader, but Selena knew me well enough to know where I was going with this.

no we should keep researching – Maybe we can figure it out, what they did, back when this all happened.

Reading was her happy place. It was safe. I tapped out a response.

i vote for FIELD research

She took her sweet time responding, the dots appearing and disappearing twice. I could almost hear the heavy sigh when the words popped up.

okay fine, but how?

———————●———————

An hour later both of us geared up at the base of the Horse Crippler, slipping into climbing harnesses, flaking the rope, checking knots. For a few brief minutes, life felt normal. Wonderful even. Almost like we weren't here to spy on a potentially dangerous supernatural being. We were just climbers.

But then I remembered we weren't. We were here to spy on Kit, see what he was made of. See if he had any ill intent toward me, Selena, or anyone in Gypsum.

The sun rose another inch, a molten coin hovering just above the horizon on the other side of the craggy cliff, throwing a cool rock shadow over us. Selena shivered and zipped up her black sport hoodie, which matched her climbing pants, which she probably picked because she wanted to be stealthy, which made no sense since the cliff was tan. I cupped my hands under the dripping stalactite until my hands were full and my fingers freezing, drinking most of the icy water down and rubbing the rest over my face.

Selena tied her long black hair into a bun at the base of her neck, watching me with a cool expression. "Is that the only shower you've taken today?"

"There's a reason I'm standing downwind of you."

She chuckled and slipped a pair of binoculars into the small pack on her waist. "You know, two people standing at the top of the cliff with binoculars is kind of conspicuous. He's gonna know we're trying to keep tabs on him."

"We'll be sneaky."

"I think you just wanted an excuse to climb." Selena went first, making her way across the underside of the west overhang like gravity meant nothing to her. I never got used to seeing someone—even myself—defy gravity like that, hair hanging straight down, hands and feet clinging to the stone like they'd grown tendrils and rooted into it.

She made it over the lip of the recess, making short work of the rest, yelling out "Clipping!" every so often and moving so fast I almost short-leashed her once. She was smart, working the cliff like she'd planned out every handhold. I had to keep my eye on her every moment—it was what a good belayer did—but I wasn't sure I could have taken my eyes off her if I'd wanted to.

When she summited, she reached into her pocket, then drew her hand out with nothing in her fingers. I knew what she'd done. Pressed stop on a small timer. Later, she'd copy down the numbers. I'd made fun of her for it before, so she'd started hiding it from me. I still didn't know what she was trying to prove.

Selena hung at the summit for a while, a small pair of binoculars pressed to her face, looking out over the campgrounds and the miles of rolling hills. A minute later she rappelled down, landing next to me like a member of the Mission: Impossible team.

"He's a mile away, due west, sitting on a boulder, just on this side of the Pilsner fence."

"That's it?"

"He was watching me."

"For real?"

"I had to come down."

I threaded my rope through the harness and tied a figure eight while Selena got ready to belay. Poised myself at the base, anticipation clawing up my throat.

Then I was climbing, my palms sliding over the rock, finding holds, zigzagging my way up the face. Yesterday's horrible experience fell away, like it was nothing. The wind was brisk, my fingers numb with cold. I knew the wall better than I knew Gypsum, or Ollie's face, or the honey of Gram's voice, or even the web of the Dark Place. Rough and mean and kind and beautiful. I was crawling up, like that thing I'd seen in the dark.

I forced that image away, laid it in the cellar of my memory, along with the thick, sweet darkness of the Alvarado. Here, there was light. I was weightless and made of air and *fast,* reaching up until the sun's golden honey spread over my face and I touched the top anchor.

I leaned back in my harness, feet planted on the cliff face, and scanned the landscape. The boulders Selena had mentioned were empty. My fingers tightened on the rope, and the back of my neck itched.

It was entirely irrational, but for a full skin-crawling five seconds, I thought I'd hear Kit's voice *next* to me, right there on the cliff face.

I fished the binoculars from my pocket and looked more closely, inching over the land. A flash of movement to the north drew my eye, and the hammer in my chest let up. Kit, hands in the pockets of his old-fashioned tan slacks, linen shirt open at the throat, walking toward the entrance to the mines. He slipped through the crumbling barrier, entered the mine shadow, and disappeared.

I started to put away the binoculars, then caught sight of campsite 25. The college kids' tent and gear were gone. I looked up toward the house, where their car sat, gathering desert dust. A current of unease moved through me, and I trained my sights back on the mine entrance, my heart in my throat.

By noon, Selena and I had set up a stakeout in the movie theater seats. Kit was a no-show, still off somewhere underneath Gypsum, rooting around in the dark for God knows what. I thought I'd feel better, having him out of my sight, but actually I felt worse.

Selena slipped out of her hoodie and her shoes and set her bare feet on the rock, flexing her toes. She'd painted her nails silver. Her dark hair had come loose from its tie, and she let it hang over one shoulder. A few pieces clung to her damp forehead, and I had the ridiculous urge to sweep them back.

She pulled a small pouch from her backpack and gave it to me. Raspberries. I took a couple and popped them in my mouth, the cool noon breeze sweeping up off the earth.

"When I'm up here," I said, "it's like yesterday didn't even happen."

"Yep," Selena said, throwing a raspberry up in the air and catching it in her mouth. "Denial is a beautiful thing." She turned to me, dark eyes curious. "What do you think Kit's doing in there?"

"Planning our murders."

"See why I call you the Grim Reaper?"

"I don't know what he's doing. I'll ask him later."

"Maybe…" She paused, her expression becoming distant. "Maybe it has to do with that thing we saw in the caves yesterday. Maybe he knows him."

"Could be a *her*."

"Her. Whatever."

"Just saying."

I fished a bandana out of my pack and wiped the sweat from my forehead and neck, then made a big clownish show of shaking the rock dust out of my hair.

Selena made a face. "Don't you ever comb that mop?"

"I swear, I'm buzz-cutting the whole thing off tomorrow."

"Don't you dare," she said with a smile, then lifted her hand toward me, as if to brush some of it out my eyes. Halfway up she stopped herself, a little blush coloring her cheeks. "I mean, your gram'll rise from her grave if you cut those curls off." She cleared her throat awkwardly, turning back to the view.

We finished half the container of berries, sitting there in the movie theater seats, watching the entrance to the mines, waiting for Kit to come out again. Down by the house, our junkyard looked thinner than usual. I guessed Ollie had finally sold some of his sure things on eBay. Strange that he hadn't said anything about it, or the money he'd gotten.

Before I could puzzle that out, Selena nudged me. "Tell me what you found in the journals."

"A bunch of ramblings. Stuff about my great-grandfather taking the Hollywood types out into the desert to find the perfect shot for a scene, that kind of thing. Mr. Fitz Von Sturnberg was fond of buttes, apparently. Nothing about a safe." I took another berry from the container. "And Hector Garcia's journal? There was this thing about the well, but I don't know what it means. And your great-grandfather worried a lot about cows. Kinda reminds me of someone I know."

"I don't worry about cows."

"You know what I mean. You worry."

"I'm just a planner."

"You're a worrier."

"Am not."

"Afraid of what'll happen if you're not the perfect daughter, the perfect student, the perfect climber."

"Since when did I want to be a perfect climber?"

I started to reach into the side pocket of her yoga pants, and she slapped my hand away. "You still keeping track of how fast you are?"

She flushed. "It's just to see if I can beat my last time."

"You know what I think? You go around all day thinking you're juggling glass."

"Excuse me?"

"It's this thing Gram used to tell me. That we're all juggling a bunch of balls, and some of them are plastic, and some of them are glass. You drop the plastic ones, and you can just pick them right back up. The glass ones, though..."

"Yeah, I get it." She looked at the middle distance between us.

"But really, most of what you're juggling is plastic, so go ahead and drop some. It's okay."

She crossed her arms and stared over the view. "I never thought about it that way before."

"I should add counseling to my services. For twenty dollars, I'll look in your head. For thirty dollars, I'll fix it."

"Ha. First you'd have to fix yourself."

"Ouch."

She gave me a smile to take the sting out of it. I faked being mad, and then she nudged me painfully with her elbow, which then ended with me dousing her with half of my water bottle. It was a pattern we'd fallen into a lot lately—and I was so busy laughing and trying to keep from being drenched, I didn't notice movement until it was directly below us, at the spring.

Kit stood at the base of the cliff, his hands hanging by his side, head tilted back, watching us. His black hair was peppered with gypsum dust, as were his clothes. But it was the look in his eyes that made my arms erupt in gooseflesh.

The laughing next to me cut off abruptly. Selena's fingers closed around my forearm.

Kit's eyes held a glint of knowing. Reading us, for how long, I had no idea. And I tried to shut it down, how happy I was to be sitting next to Selena at the top of the cliff, how confused I was about what was happening between us, and how embarrassed I was to have an audience. All that emotion, spilling out of me and down the Horse Crippler and right into Kit's head. Along with all my thoughts.

Kit gave me a close-lipped smile, one that said I had just become an open book.

I stood, and Selena followed my lead. Kit gave her a little head tilt, as if considering her, and I was struck with an image of a bird, watching something small, trying to decide if it was worth the hunt.

And with that one smile, I felt an invisible bubble pop. My arms felt weak, my hands numb. I couldn't think. I'd been walking around hopped up on some lotus flower, all this time, and the taste of it was suddenly gone.

We were all going to die. I knew it. I was reading the landscape like it was made of tea leaves.

"Quinn," Selena said, her voice trembling. "What just happened?"

Kit turned his back on us, put his thumbs in his pockets, and walked away, toward the boulders where he'd spent his afternoon. We didn't rappel down until he was small, a dot on the landscape. When I finally planted both feet again on the desert floor, my hands were still shaking.

CHAPTER
TWENTY-TWO

That night, the first constellation went missing.

For the rest of the day, I hadn't let Selena out of my sight. We read journals, found dead ends, drank all the mulled cider in the fridge. After nightfall, I'd pulled up into her driveway with her hands warm on my waist. She was slow to let go. She stood and pulled off her helmet, her hair spilling around her face. I was supposed to turn, walk her to her door. Instead I sat stock-still. Something hung there, in her expression, like she was holding her breath.

I fiddled with the strap on my own helmet, willing myself to take that step forward. Now. She was right there. I could just reach out and...

Her gaze slipped past me, then stuttered. "Quinn?"

"Yeah."

"Did you put vodka in the cider?"

"We were out, so I just used the rubbing alcohol from the first aid kit. I hope that's okay."

"I'm serious."

"No, it's just cider."

When she grabbed me by the shoulders, I thought that was it, that she would lean in. But instead she turned me and pointed up into the sky. "Then where is Cassiopeia?"

"It's right above Cepheus."

"No, it's not. It's gone."

I peered up into the Milky Way, but for once in my life, I couldn't get my bearings. Then I found the boxy shape of Cepheus, just as Selena stood close. "It's supposed to be right there."

I scanned the blanket of pinpricks, distracted by her warmth next to me. The desert's body was cold and black and rolled away from me for miles, and above it I tried to find the constellation. I knew this patch of sky like I knew my own house. The time of the year. The time of night. I knew what spot I stood on on Earth, what kind of view of the universe I'd have at 9:23 p.m., December 22.

And Cassiopeia was gone.

I left Selena at her front door, burned up the lonely trail home to my house, the engine's growl almost blotting out my fear.

Stars don't disappear. At least not in my lifetime. Maybe a million lifetimes of Quinns and Selenas and Junes. Maybe when people had fallen in love over and over, in a million versions of life, years and years of it, the stars would go out, but not now. Not *tonight*.

But when I stopped in front of my house, the chainsaw buzz of the engine died. I looked out into the desert. It looked back. I blinked first.

Eva Durbin. The strange vision that had swept over me when I'd hugged her—her looking up and seeing a patch of starlight, winking out—

An omen, that was what I'd thought at the time. A symbol in the Dark Place. I hadn't taken it literally. I didn't believe that it would *actually happen*. That the Dark Place was somehow spilling out into Gypsum Falls.

CHAPTER
TWENTY-THREE

From the Journal of Hector Garcia
March 4, 1933

Liam O'Brien practically busted down my door
this morning, hair wild and eyes full of fever.
Told me I had to come with him to the mines. That
he'd found some sort of nest.

We went down into the dark, into the tunnels
where I hadn't been in years, where I never wanted
to go again. Where that poor boy went missing.
Mrs. Gonzales still sits by the well.

There was damage to the tunnel, where someone chipped away at a big vein of gypsum and
half the wall had collapsed. They'd found a cave
on the other side, the walls covered with symbols.

"This isn't a nest," I said.

His eyes seemed haunted. Then he said something I'd never forget.

"Hector. Look at this. Look at every spot. I need
you to remember this. Just in case we need to write
it down again. In case something happens to it."

I put my hand on his shoulder, and he leaned
forward to brace himself on his knees. "Why?"

He shook his head. "I just know."

"I'm glad you came to me," Tripp said. "If this Kit guy is as real as you say, we all need to get our butts in gear."

I knelt at the edge of the hatch, looking down into the caves under the Alvarado's secret room. The darkness peered back at me. "No cameras in my face, right? You keep my name out of it. If you even catch my voice, you edit it out."

Tripp made a dismissive gesture, then opened his phone and used it like a mirror, arranging his hair loose around his shoulders. "Looking fly today," he said to himself, turning left, then right to check out his profile.

Nicco, who was still in the lobby directly above us, peering down at us through the hole in the floor, gave me a sly smile. "Buckle up. We're in for a wild ride."

I hated the idea. *Hated* it. But Ollie and I needed money and answers, and these guys had at least one of those. I had a brand-new hundred-dollar bill Tripp had given me burning a hole in my pocket, an "advance on future services." Selena and I weren't getting anywhere with the journals. Right now, Tripp was Gypsum's only expert in the occult, and I was hoping against hope he could explain the markings in the safe and on the cave walls. (Also, money was money.)

"A deal's a deal," Tripp said, hooking a carabiner to a knotted rope, attaching it to an anchor he'd set up, then throwing the free end into the darkness. He stood, with his shoulders thrown back, his fists on his hips, and smiled at Nicco, who was filming him from several different angles. "As long as you share any psychic insights you get down there so we can repeat them on our channel, then yeah, you can remain... *incognito*," he said, finishing with a little dramatic flourish. "And if those markings on the cave wall are as authentic as you say, you'll be helping us do what we do." He flashed me one of his signature smiles. "I think this is the beginning of a beautiful friendship."

I didn't respond, staring straight down into the black abyss.

"*Casablanca*? You ever seen it?"

I double-checked the rope's connection to my harness, hoping my silence would tell him this wasn't a movie trivia moment.

"Claude Rains? Humphrey Bogart? A misty night in northern Africa?"

"I can't believe I'm doing this again."

"Believe it, buddy," he said, clapping me on the shoulder. "We're about to go exploring!"

We slipped into the dark underside of the hotel, into the dank cave, then followed the path of shiny foil gum wrappers I'd left last time I was here. I gave the crevasse a wide berth. My light found a dark spot on the rock wall, the scooped-out shadow of the opening into the smaller cave.

I stepped over some scattered rock and entered.

When the light hit the symbols, they glimmered. Circles and lines and strange figures. I moved my beam up, over the twelve-foot ceiling, my light catching the white streaks and dots on a field of gray. Behind me came a chorus of *Whoa*s and *Wow*s and *Dude*s.

I swept right, then left...and stopped. *Blank spots.* On the walls, where there should have been symbols.

I walked up to a wall and touched the stone surface, cracked and half empty of marks. A crunch under my foot drawing my gaze down. Crumbled rock, there under my boot.

"This is amazing," Nicco said, sweeping his camera over the walls.

"Guys," I said. I knelt and picked up a handful of rock. Something white, like gypsum dust, came off on my fingers.

"How'd all those marks get up so high?" Tripp asked, turning in a circle, his head thrown back. "A ladder?"

"There's a problem here," I said.

Nicco took the GoPro off his head and turned it so he could talk into it. "Maybe they levitated. I mean, this place is nuts. And the question is, who did this? And was it even one person?"

"Hello?" I said, raising my voice.

"This must've taken decades to do," Tripp said, sweeping his beam over the walls.

"Would you two stop and look at me? This isn't all of it."

Tripp pointed his camera at me. "What do you mean, this isn't all of it? There's a crap-ton of marks in this cave."

"There are missing spots." I pointed my light to a damaged spot, and another. "There were symbols here!"

Tripp approached the wall, the hard angles of his face catching the light, making him look ghoulish. He reached out and touched it. "You're sure?"

"Yeah, I'm sure."

"So in the last few days, something came in here and destroyed pieces of this?"

"That's what I'm saying."

I glanced at the entrance. Thought of that thing I'd seen climbing in the darkness, when I was hanging on to the wall of the crevasse. Maybe it was out there right now. Maybe it was just a few feet away. Or Kit. Yesterday he'd come out of the mines, so satisfied with himself. Did he do this?

I took a few steps toward the hole and pointed my light out into the cave.

"Okay, buddy," Tripp said, gesturing to the symbol-covered wall. "Do your thing."

"What thing?"

"Feelings, premonitions, you know. Make the magic happen. Give us a little insight into what's going on here."

"Well, I can't offer the wall a cup of tea, so . . ."

"C'mon, you gotta loosen up! The tea leaves are just a crutch." When I didn't respond, he shrugged and reached into his bag for his camera. "All right, all right, I won't force it. But make yourself useful. Set up the lights, and I'll get some footage."

I turned in a slow circle, trying to figure out the puzzle. I imagined Kit, coming in here and wreaking havoc on this place, like he did the safe. It was the only explanation. But why?

I looked up at the ceiling, then closed my eyes and tried to make sense of it. The white dots moved on a field of black...I breathed in, and they trembled...like they did when I lay on the roof in winter, the fog of my breath clouding the air.

"They're constellations!" I said, opening my eyes.

"What?" Tripp said.

I went to the wall and pointed to what looked like a random dot. "See this?" I dragged my fingertip across the wall, over six more dots. "This is Leo. And this"—I moved higher and traced another set of dots—"Scorpio. And here's the Big Dipper."

He joined me at the wall.

"Whoa," Tripp said. "It's like one of those images you focus on long enough that the three-D image pops out from the chaos. And now I can't unsee it."

Constellations, all over the walls, mixed with other symbols. A much larger version of what I'd found inside the safe.

Nicco joined us at the wall and tilted his head. "That one doesn't belong there."

"Which one?" Tripp said.

Nicco made a small circle with his light. "Cyrus isn't anywhere near the Big Dipper." He looked into his GoPro. "I spent half my youth looking through a telescope on my roof. Geek power and all that."

Nicco babbled into the camera about stars while Tripp and I stood side by side, puzzling out the bits and pieces left. Andromeda. Sagittarius. Orion. Cancer. Draco.

"Why would Kit draw these?" I asked. Maybe he couldn't help it. Maybe he was like me, and someone directed him to do it in his sleep.

Nicco brought his camera down and regarded the wall thoughtfully. "Quinn, you ever been in prison?" he asked, in the same way someone would ask if I'd ever been to a museum or a movie theater.

"I'm seventeen."

"Juvie. Whatever." He stared at me, expressionless. "You seem like the type. Which is cool! I'm not judgey."

"What is your point?"

"All those markings. When you're stuck in one place for a long time, it's what you do to pass the time. You should have seen the wall next to my bunk at boarding school."

I did another sweep of the walls with my light. All those years alone. I could imagine it. Trapped in one spot forever, with nothing but chunks of gypsum and time on your hands.

Tripp tapped his fingers on his chin, his expression thoughtful. "I think you're off base here, Nicco. Why would Kit come back and destroy it? No, no, he didn't do this, which means…" He snapped his fingers. "It's a Devil's Trap."

It took me a moment to register the words. Devil's Trap.

Devil.

Tripp turned to Nicco. "You remember the place in Manchester?"

"How could I forget?" Nicco said, and they chuckled.

Tripp turned to face Nicco's GoPro. "So, folks, if you'd like to see what a traditional Devil's Trap looks like, check out episode forty-one." He winked and pretended to use his fingers as a gun, pointing at the camera. "Won a Webby, that one. You can't miss it."

"Can you guys turn that off a second?"

Tripp reached up and switched off both cameras, his expression sour. "You are such a killjoy."

"Are you saying Kit's some sort of…demon?" I asked.

"Not necessarily." He stared at the symbols, scratching his cheek. "And from these symbols—I mean, I've never seen a Devil's Trap with these markings before, so I'm thinking he's not, but he's something, all right."

Then he nodded to Nicco, who positioned himself in front of Tripp with his camera and flipped it on again. I made sure to stay far out of the shot.

"Traps for evil spirits have been used for, like, ever," Tripp said, walking slowly along the wall so Nicco could keep up. "Archaeologists are finding these kinds of things all the *time*. The Babylonians had their demon-catching bowls, and the Tibetans had their rams' skulls, which, if you ask me, is a super-awesome way to trap something, I mean, a ram's skull! And the Native Americans used hollow bones and moss...hell, in England a few years ago, they pulled up the boards of an old house to find a whole compartment carved with lines and symbols known to trap spirits."

Tripp stopped in front of the opening to the main cave. "But what's key to making a trap for an entity is that it has to be a never-ending loop that the spirit can't escape." He made a spiraling motion with his hand. Then he panned his camera over the walls, to the door etched with symbols that lay facedown, around the room. He stopped at the opening. "And here's the end of the loop."

For once, I wasn't sorry I'd brought him down here. I made a slashing motion across my throat.

He rolled his eyes, switching off the camera again. "What now?"

"The miners," I said, thinking of the entry in Hector's journal I'd read that morning. "Digging gypsum out of the hills, digging tunnels. Somebody busted down this wall, let Kit out without meaning to, and then—"

"—and then someone decided to trap him *again*," Tripp said, "but used the safe to do it. Which is why the inside of the safe is covered with the same symbols." Tripp crossed his arms, his expression turning perplexed. "Not sure how they got him in there, but there are all kinds of ways to lure spirits. Shiny objects like mirrors, trinkets, and in Europe they'd trap witches in vessels by placing hair and fingernail clippings and—"

"But why not just put him back in the cave?" I asked.

"This wall was completely destroyed. Hard to rebuild. But honestly, that's not the question we need to be asking." He flipped the camera on and turned it to face him. "Why did someone want to lock the spirit away in the first place? I mean, what did he do?"

Tripp and Nicco moved to the other end of the cavern, away from me. From the main cavern came the pattering of crumbling rock.

I froze. Just beyond the lip, the shallow hiss of breath, somewhere out in all that darkness. I stepped back a few feet. We had an audience of one, just on the other side of the wall.

"Honestly," Tripp said from the other side of the cave, standing next to Nicco and staring up at the walls in wonder. "I've never seen anything like this. And never this complex." He held the camera close to his face, so that all that would be in the frame was his eyes. "Whatever the spirit is," he said in a dramatic voice, his eye close to the lens, "if it needs a trap this complicated, the world is in for a wild ride."

CHAPTER
TWENTY-FOUR

From the Journal of Mattias Pilsner
March 7, 1933

I could've told Liam this would all come to nothing. Bad luck runs in this town as freely as the water.

One of the movie crew went missing last night. Mr. Fritz Von Jackassberg thinks they got on a bus and went home. Gypsum don't have a bus stop, or a bus. Fritz just won't face reality, because reality is, his movie ain't that good, and neither is his star, and now his people, people he's responsible for, are going off somewhere and getting themselves lost, or worse.

I'm writing this on the verandah of the Alvarado, during my smoke break. All those fools are singing and dancing inside, drinking themselves to death. Eva's draping herself all over the piano again, and Fritz is staring at her like she's a meal, and I'm thinking about what Mrs. Gonzales says about the water in the well, how it knows where her son is. And now I'm sure of it, *the way Liam and Hector haven't realized yet: whatever's happening will only get worse.*

———————•———————

Ollie and I pulled up in front of the Gypsum Lights Diner, where Macie's party was in full swing, red-and-green decorations and twinkle lights cutting a bright swath into the gathering dark.

Ollie put his newly repaired truck in park but kept the engine running. He tapped his fingers on the steering wheel, the green light from the dash reflecting a troubled expression.

"What?" I asked.

He turned to me. "Ever since you got back this morning from your little outing with the weirdos—"

"Here we go."

"—you've barely said a word. Don't wanna talk to nobody but June and Selena. But tonight you're willing to be Mr. Social Butterfly?"

I scratched my cheek and shrugged. I needed to talk to Mrs. Durbin, and Mrs. Durbin always came to Macie's Holiday Bash, and June said parties made her "more herself." There wouldn't be a better time. If I could try to read her, like I did last time, when I'd touched her arm . . . I didn't know if that was the Dark Place, but it was an omen, full of disappearing stars. I rubbed my arm, where the bite had scabbed over. It was better than trying to dip into the Dark Place again.

Of course, Ollie didn't need to know any of that.

"Guess I got stir-crazy."

Ollie looked through the windshield, into the diner, then grimaced. "Well, well. A.J.'s invited the mayor of Marfa to Macie's shindig."

A.J. stood at the counter, talking to a man in a suit. "What's wrong with that?"

"She's just so . . ." From the look on his face, I thought he would say *beautiful*. "So . . . ambitious." He finished that last word with an edge of bitterness.

"We goin' in or what?"

He reached toward the key. "Maybe we should go home. Put up the tree. Watch *Die Hard*."

"We're already here."

"Explosions," Ollie said, nodding sagely. "Explosions always make the holidays better."

I opened the door with a creak, shook my head, and stepped out into the cold.

Outside, the sky opened up with a bright scattering of stars. They seemed thinner than usual, as if far-off clouds were blocking bits and pieces of the night sky. Cassiopeia was still missing. But as soon as fear reared its ugly head, a soft cottony feeling came over me—and deep down, I knew it came from Kit, to distract me.

I opened the door to the diner and the world became suddenly brighter and louder, and about thirty degrees hotter. By the front door, the high school mariachi band played a hearty rendition of "Feliz Navidad." From the look of the crowd, all of Gypsum and a good part of Marfa had showed up to eat Macie and Enrique's tamales.

Macie and Enrique's annual Holiday Bash—aka Eva Durbin Appreciation Day, aka an excuse for A.J. to show off in front of the mayor of Marfa—was the event of the year. Macie presided over the tamale table, while Enrique kept the counter full of pecan pie, peanut brittle, flan, and sopapillas. Past the dozens of people stuffed inside the diner, in the back by the pool table, a black-and-white movie played on the flat-screen, a scene from *Passion's Gambit*. If I knew Eva, she was nearby, waiting for the moment her younger self makes out with Douglas Fairbanks Jr.

I pushed through the crowd to the counter. Enrique smiled and handed me a cup of eggnog. "Merry Christmas, Quinn baby!" He raised his voice. "Hey, the O'Briens are here!"

A resounding "Hey!" came from the crowd. I made my slow migration to the back to find Eva, stopping every two feet to get a hug or a clap on the back.

I passed a clump of people and June appeared, holding a plate topped with at least ten tamales. She wore a red Christmas sweater with a dancing Santa on it, which made me do a double take.

"I didn't know you owned anything that wasn't black," I shouted over the crowd swell.

June gave me an unreadable look, then a small close-lipped smile. "Go find Selena."

"Why?"

"She's got something for you." June stuffed half a tamale in her mouth and walked away.

I threaded my way farther into the crowd and Selena came into view, standing by the jukebox, in a serious conversation with Deputy Cruz, something about Gunter Moon and how they hadn't seen him in days (which didn't surprise me one bit, since he always went off on a bender around Christmas). She looked beautiful, her dark hair trailing down one shoulder over a red sweater with some sort of shimmer. And she'd put on makeup, I guessed to hide the dark circles from all the long research nights. And when she smiled...wow. She was a complete stunner. It almost made me forget the weirdness of the last two weeks.

Almost.

She saw me and did a double take. Her eyes brightened. "You came."

There was some expectation, there in her eyes. Like I was answering a question I didn't remember being asked. Over her head, I caught a glimpse of the next film clip, a scene from *Dark Destiny* with Lillian Gish. But before I could push past Selena and see if Eva Durbin was there, Selena had taken my hand and was leading me through the crowd.

"Wait, I need to see Eva first."

"No you don't."

She led me out of the diner, into the cold. She slipped her bag off her shoulder and unzipped it. "You want your present?" Her smile was contagious.

I peered into the diner. Nearby, June was filling up her plate again, tamales and bean dip and pecan pie in a pile. Mrs. Durbin wasn't going anywhere without her caretaker.

"Depends."

"On what?"

"Is it a book?"

"Of course it's a book." She pulled out a small package wrapped in red-and-gold paper. It had a fussy, complicated bow on the top, which I was guessing she'd watched a YouTube video several times to master.

We took down the tailgate of a nearby truck and sat while I unwrapped it. *Lonely Places: A Collection of Verse.* I flipped it open. Apparently, she'd given me poetry. I tried to hide my confusion, but she took in my expression and blushed, then looked away.

"I like it," I said. "Really. I like...lonely poetry."

Feeling awkward, I watched the crowd through the front windows. The mayor of Marfa had disappeared, and my brother and A.J. were standing by the dessert counter, actually talking—without throwing things.

"After what you said yesterday, I thought you'd like it."

I turned and met Selena's eye. She looked almost shy.

"Besides," she said, "I thought it would be nice if you didn't fail English this year, so...there you go."

I gave her a blank look. Yesterday?

She shrugged, crossed her arms. "The bookstore was out of Neanderthal poetry."

I put the book gently down on the tailgate, trying to find a way to make her feel less awkward.

"Me like. Book good."

She laughed, and the tension evaporated.

"I haven't wrapped your present yet, but I will." Which was a lie. I hadn't bought her a present yet, and I was pretty sure she knew it.

"It's okay." She waved my comment away. "Just don't fall off a cliff between now and New Year's and I'll consider us even."

We sat there, watching the darkness, the way the tourists did when they looked for spook lights. But the black that lay over the cactus was as still and empty as the bottom of a well. When I couldn't take it anymore, I turned toward the diner. In the back, the movie on the big screen was the tail end of *Swoon,* the movie Eva starred in with Clark Gable. The kiss faded to black, and a new clip started up, this time *Dead for Dollars.* Eva appeared on-screen, in all her sepia-toned splendor, rounding a boulder and surprising a group of masked bandits. Her expression morphed into dewy-eyed surprise, and the bandits dragged her off, through an arroyo, with the sun setting in the background.

As the bandits' horses became small and mountains rose up on the screen, an uneasy feeling swept over me. There in the corner of the screen, I could make out the outline of the phantom that made *Dead for Dollars* so famous. The naysayers always said it wasn't a ghost on the screen, just a weird bunch of prickly pear with some ocotillo behind it, stretching its knobby arms to the sky. I shivered and zipped my jacket higher.

"I almost forgot." Selena let out a half laugh. "All I could think about was...you know...presents..." She let out another awkward laugh. "It's a little weird, actually, how focused I've been on them. But I've been working the symbols on the cave wall, too. Talking to Tripp, who's actually not as bad as you've said."

"Just give him time."

"At first, I thought the symbols were all mixed up, but they're not. They're just the view from a different perspective."

She pulled out a notebook and turned to a page with a complicated sketch on it, which included planets and lines, and degrees and angles. She pointed. "See these constellations that form the Devil's Trap? I thought they were all mixed up, because none of the stars were in the right place. Capricorn was north of Gemini, Orion was south of Venus, that sort of thing. You know, random. But I was wrong. See? It's *not* random. It's like you're looking at the stars from another point in the universe."

"Whoa, that's weird." I paused, then said, "Selena? Pretend I didn't understand any of that. How would you explain it to...let's say...one of my chickens?"

"I don't know, but maybe whoever put Kit in the cave in the first place wasn't really from...*here.*"

"You mean, like Chicago?"

"Quinn."

"I know what you mean. But aliens? Really?"

"No, I'm not really thinking silver ships and little green men or anything like that."

"Then what?"

"I don't know. I'm still trying to figure it out."

"Wait a second." I turned the page and glanced over the symbols. The diagram of the Devil's Trap was complete. "You re-created the blank spots."

"Of course I did. I saw the whole thing before it got damaged, and then once I figured out the perspective thing, I filled in the gaps."

That meant if we ever needed to trap Kit, she could help us do it. Relief flooded through me. Selena was our safety net, our way out. She pointed to the page again, talking about stars, and all that relief disappeared. Kit had destroyed the safe. He'd destroyed patches of the wall. What would he do to Selena when he found out she had the whole thing stored in that beautiful memory of hers?

I took the book from her hands and closed it. "I want you to promise me something." I looked over my shoulder to make sure no one was watching. "Don't tell anyone else about this."

"Why?"

"The more people who know, the more chances for Kit to read their mind and figure out we still have a copy of the Devil's Trap."

I handed the book to her, and she slipped it into her bag. The earlier curious spark in her eye had been replaced with a dull sheen of fear.

"Not even June, okay?" I said. "And remember, the more emotional you feel, the easier it will be for him to read you. So just, I don't know, be icy."

"Icy?"

"Yeah, shut it all down."

She tucked a strand of hair behind her ear and looked away. "After yesterday, I can't help but be emotional. I'm kind of surprised you haven't mentioned it."

I was about to ask her what the heck she was talking about, but then I noticed something just above her head, in the sky. The space where Pegasus was supposed to be.

It was blank.

She started to open her mouth to say something, but I was already grabbing her upper arm, turning her around, pointing at the sky. Then we stood there, shoulder to shoulder, counting stars.

"Oh no," she whispered. "It's getting worse."

I turned her to face me. "Look, I gotta go talk to Eva, and…" I looked around the darkened parking lot. "I don't like you being alone out here."

She followed me back inside, and I managed to thread my way through the crowd without being waylaid. But when I got to the back, Eva Durbin was nowhere to be seen.

Suddenly, June came out of the crowd, her expression tense. "Mrs. Durbin is gone."

"What are you talking about?" I said.

"She's gone!" June threaded her hands in her hair, which was loose around her shoulders, stark against the black of her shirt. "She wasn't in her trailer. So I went over to her neighbors', and they all said they haven't seen her." She grabbed my arm. "Quinn, you gotta help me look. I…I was late, and maybe she got, I don't know, agitated…"

I looked down at her hand, and the arm. The black sweater. "Did you change clothes?"

June looked at me like I'd lost my mind. "Why do you care what I'm wearing? Didn't you hear me? Eva Durbin's missing!"

I grabbed her by both arms, looked into her eyes. "June, when did you get here?"

"What are you—"

"When did you get here!"

The people around us stopped talking and stared.

June shrugged my hands off. "Just now."

Selena pulled me aside, took in the expression on my face. "What's wrong?"

"That wasn't June," I said. "In the crowd. She talked to me, but it wasn't her."

Suddenly the walls closed in, like the sides of a refrigerator. The bright lights blinding, the faces of everyone I'd known all my life garish, the teeth too white.

Before she could ask me anything else, I pushed my way out of the crowd and into the night.

CHAPTER
TWENTY-FIVE

From the Journal of Hector Garcia
March 8, 1933
Half of the cows in Gypsum are missing. No sign
of predators or bits of hide or blood. Liam tells me
what's taken them is unnatural.

———————●————————●—

I didn't wait for morning. As soon as Ollie parked the truck in our
driveway, I headed around back toward the trail. Kit would be lurking
around the spring by now, I was sure of it. I walked past the tires full of
dying basil, past the chicken coop and—

A dark patch, there on the side of the boxy structure. I squinted to
make it out in the dim moonlight, and my step faltered.

A wide gash, torn in the wooden slats.

"Oh no."

I rushed over, pulled a pen light out of my pocket, and aimed it
through the splintered hole, heart fluttering in my throat. Maybe whatever it was had only gotten one of Gram's twenty, or maybe two, or...

The coop was empty.

Sick to my core, I scanned the yard for predators. No sign of anything. No piles of feathers. Just...gone.

I dropped the pen light. Laced my hands behind my head, like I could hold myself together that way, and turned in a slow circle. What the hell was happening?

A low warble drifted across the yard. I found Pumpkin huddled against the house, her black and white patterned feathers drooping.

Numb, I put the last of Gram's flock inside the garage, as if shutting a door could keep the things I loved safe when the world was unraveling. Then I took the trail away from the house, toward the spring. In the distance, Gypsum's downtown glowed faintly, the lights of the tree creating a halo at the center. And above it, the Milky Way moved slowly over the campgrounds and the desert and the world, a sweep of dappled light. And there, on the horizon, I saw it. The Big Dipper was gone. I couldn't deny it anymore. Bits and pieces of Gypsum were disappearing, big and small, and Kit was somehow at the center of it.

I walked past the cabin, where Nicco was a silhouette in the back, a bottle of wine in one hand, a phone in the other, arguing with someone. Some girl named Tracy. He was saying something about how she wasn't the person he remembered. That she'd changed. His voice floated on the chill night breeze. "I don't even know who you are anymore."

I guessed both of us had that problem, not recognizing the people in our lives for who they really were.

How long had Kit been doing this? If he could pretend to be June, he could pretend to be anyone. Ollie or June or Selena or...

My stomach twisted.

That comment she'd made outside the diner, about something I'd said the day before. Something that made her want to buy me a book of poetry.

He'd pretended to be me.

I passed the cabin and made my way down the hill and around a bend, wondering what else I would find missing along the way. Ahead, the Horse Crippler rising up, like the prow of an enormous ship. A dark figure stood near its base, arms raised to the stars.

I stopped, watching him. It looked exactly like that scene in *Dead for Dollars,* the ghost in the corner of the screen everyone claimed they could see.

I'd seen that figure somewhere else. In my dreams, in the visions that had come to me—to all of us—before June and Selena and I went to the Alvarado and started this whole thing. Back then, I thought it was just a memory of the movie, inserting itself in the vision.

After I'd stood long enough to lose the feeling in my fingers, I forced my feet to move again, toward the spring.

Kit must've seen me, because by the time I'd reached the base of the cliff, he had returned to his green armchair. A gas-fired camp lantern sat on a rock, just beside the dripping spring, nestled in the moss. The world smelled sharp and cold, like a copper penny.

We stared at each other for a while. "I hope you enjoyed the party."

His smile broadened. "Please forgive me, but I was lonely."

I watched his face, trying to figure out his expression. Kit could be anyone at any time. What Selena had said at the diner about Gunter Moon going missing slipped into my head. Maybe he'd been missing even longer than we thought, Kit putting Gunter's image on like a costume and walking around to keep us in the dark. And then there were all those people who'd gone missing from the movie set in 1933. Kit said he hadn't been out of the safe in ninety years, which would put him there right around the shooting of the film. Did he pretend to be them, too? So no one would notice they were gone?

Kit started to laugh. "Ahh, Quinn, you're thinking too much about all this."

"Seems like I haven't been thinking enough."

A feeling of calm swept over me, and for a second, a voice rose up. *You're overreacting.*

Eva Durbin had wandered off again, like she'd done when her caretakers had pulled into the rest stop and left her alone for five minutes. Gunter Moon was on a bender out in the desert. And Kit *was* lonely, wasn't he? Shouldn't I have some pity for him, the way I had pity for Selena after her dad died, for June? I was being rather selfish, after all.

Then I peered into Kit's eyes, saw the satisfaction there, and a jolt went through me. Another voice, screaming at me from far, far down the other end of a long tunnel, getting brighter and sharper, until it echoed against the walls of my skull, and my ears. And this one was all me.

Those aren't your thoughts!

"Kit," I said. "Just now, what I was thinking…"

He looked down at his hands as if he were examining his cuticles.

"Did you… did you put that in my head?"

He didn't answer. He didn't have to. How I'd acted since the safe had been opened, how I hadn't freaked out the way I should have, and neither had Ollie, or June, or Selena… and then there were the dreams I'd had for months before we'd even found the safe, the numbers, welling up, the desire to spin the dial. The picture Selena took, that dark shadow hanging over my shoulder, palms on either side of my head. And I stood there, under the cold overhang of the Horse Crippler, my hands hanging like deadwood at my sides, wondering how long he'd been doing this to us.

"Longer than you think," Kit said. He met my eye, his face clear and innocent.

"How long?"

Kit shrugged and sat back in the chair, lounging under the rock like it was the most comfortable place in the world. Like it was his living room. This whole desert, too, just a place to rest his feet.

He broke eye contact, then played with an unraveling thread on the arm of the old chair, like he was trying to make a decision. "I told you where to hide," he finally said.

The comment was so far out in left field, I didn't even know what to do with it. "What are you talking about?"

"That day you were playing hide-and-seek when you were six years old. In the desert. I told you where to hide."

The cold darkness of the refrigerator rose up in my bones. My fists, beating on the door. My breath caught in my throat.

"I can see you haven't forgotten. And I'm sorry. I'm sorry I had to do that to you."

"*You* told me to hide in the refrigerator."

"I nudged you in the right direction."

"Why? Why would you do that?"

His expression became defensive. "I nudged the sheriff, too."

"Nudged? What does that even mean?"

He gave me a look that said I was way too slow. "Just put a little idea, wriggling like a spider, right into someone's head." He reached out playfully, as if he would tap my temple, but I reared back in horror, my skin crawling. "So I nudged, and the sheriff found you before you…" He looked up at the ceiling of rock, at the place where the water gathered on the ceiling, dripped down on the ferns and stalagmite below. "I needed you to remember that feeling, when it was time."

The pieces were coming together, rising in me, like broken glass in my mind.

He leaned forward, his expression delighted. "Just like I nudged your gram so many years ago to teach you to read the cup, which was hard, I gotta say, back when the lock was still so tight on me…" He paused, as if he'd said too much, then leaned forward and continued. "Or like I nudged Enrique to check on the hotel last week, pushed him to call Ollie, then put a thought in Ollie's head that this was his next sure thing."

I listened to him, stunned. All this time, I thought it was my fault, Ollie finding that safe. But it wasn't. It was Kit's fault. Everything was Kit's fault.

Kit frowned, reading me. "I'm telling you now, because we have trust, you and me. We're friends now, aren't we? I don't want there to be anything hidden between us."

Rage built inside me, and I watched the water drip, because I couldn't look at him. A thought drifted in that said yes, we were friends. And I was so lonely, wasn't I? Since Gram died? Didn't I need friends? But the thoughts were soft, and quiet, and other words rose up in their place. And I said it before I could even think to hold the words back.

"I should never have let you out."

Kit leaned back on the chair, his eyes turning hard. He picked at the stray thread on the arm of the chair, a section of cloth that had been unraveling for twenty years. "You shouldn't have said that."

"Why not? You going to punish me?"

He didn't answer at first, though he looked like he might. And then Kit wasn't Kit anymore. A shimmer, a shift in his eyes, and his face re-formed into someone.

Ollie.

I forced myself to look at him, although my insides felt all worn out, just staring into my brother's eyes. Not because the mirage didn't look right. That wouldn't have been as horrible as what I saw now. Because it was perfect. I couldn't tell the difference at all.

"Stop it."

"You weren't in any real danger," he said.

"Stop it. You're not him."

"You know I'll always take care of you, Quinn. Haven't I always taken care of you?"

I keep my gaze on the ground. Reminded myself who he really was. Smoke and mirrors and distractions, lying to us and telling us what we wanted to hear, making us feel what we wanted to feel. I examined his face for a tell, the lie.

"I was out cold when they found me," I said. "My brain was completely oxygen deprived."

"I knew they'd find you in time." He tapped his temple. "I could see it." He sat back again, his eyes going distant. "I can see a lot of things. Not as well as you can, of course. But I see a lot."

"I still have trouble remembering things. Places. Details. I barely passed my junior year."

"After thousands of years of existence, I can tell you one thing for certain. School's overrated. You'll be fine."

I watched his expression for some remorse. For a second, I thought I found what I was looking for—but it seemed like he was just forcing the muscles of his face to *look* like guilt.

"I was a little kid," I said. "I never got over it. Neither did June. She thinks she was responsible for goading me into it."

He turned away, but before his expression closed, I caught a glimpse of something sly. And then I knew. That, too, was Kit.

"You made her feel angry that day. Put words in her head."

"I—"

"I thought we were *friends*. Friends don't lie to each other."

Kit pressed his lips together, watching me. "I suggested she bait you into it. You did the rest, of course. I never really *make* anyone do anything." He nodded, as if answering a question in his own head. "I knew if I planted that seed in you, and let it grow for a decade or so, it would yield the right fruit."

"But why?"

He leaned forward, his eyes intense. "I needed you to feel it. What it's like. To be trapped. To be in a box. So when it was time, you'd actually do it. *Let me out.*" His eyes reflected the lamplight. "I needed you to know how wrong it is to be alone like that."

Somewhere on the trail behind me, a voice called my name. Ollie. I turned to look over my shoulder. My brother rounded the bend in the trail.

When I turned to face Kit again, the mirage was gone. Kit looked like Kit. A few inches shorter, dark hair longer, his young fresh face looking up at me like...like...

Again, I got the feeling I'd known him longer than a week.

Deep down, in the place that read the leaves and knew the truth, that part of me remembered something about where I'd seen him. And I had the feeling I needed to hold on to that scrap of information, before it got swept away by the river of fear running through me, and whatever influence he had on my mind. I wanted to read him. Get him to take the cup, drink. And then I'd know for sure.

Kit stared at me curiously. "Quinn, I really am grateful. You don't need to be afraid."

With that he stood and walked past me.

Ollie stopped on the trail, just on the other side of the water. Moonlight glimmered over the surface, hanging heavy over us. The two met gazes for a moment. A challenge, crackling above the surface of the water like electricity. Then Kit turned and disappeared into the darkness.

I kept my thoughts blank until he was far away. Only once he was gone did I let the thought of me forcing Kit back into a Devil's Trap—this time one of my own making—out of its place in my head, turned it into a cold pinprick in my heart, quiet and sure.

CHAPTER
TWENTY-SIX

From the Journal of Liam O'Brien
March 9, 1933

Two people are missing. Guests are leaving. Fritz
is talking about pulling support for the Alvarado.

Everything I've worked for, gone in a matter
of days.

Even with all of Fritz's tantrums about leaving town, he's resumed shooting today. Said
tragedy helps sell films and brings in audi-
ences. Cursed sets and ghosts on camera. All of
it absinthe for the masses.

He wants tragedy? He's about to get it. I've
seen it, in my head, like God put the future in
there, telling me to do something about it. Change
it. I tried to warn Fritz to leave town now, before it
got worse, and he called me a charlatan, a snake
oil salesman. Then he went off with Eva and her
new toady to shoot the final scene of the movie on
MY land, in front of MY cliffs, like Gypsum and
everyone in it are nothing but a movie set to him.

Part of me, a petty little spot in the back of
my heart, is glad he won't last the week.

I didn't sleep again that night. When I told Ollie what had happened at the diner and the spring, he went quiet, then walked out to the porch with a six-pack of beer. My phone call to Selena resulted in what I expected, an awkward silence, along with a promise for more research, then texts every fifteen minutes with predictions and what-ifs. June's response was a dark joke about the world ending.

I felt like screaming into the phone. *Wake up! Can't you feel it?* But it wouldn't do any good. Kit had lulled them with his pitcher plant scent, with that sweet darkness that he commanded.

The texts finally died out around 4 a.m., with the last one coming from June, who couldn't stop worrying about Mrs. Durbin.

It's my fault she's gone!!

I crept downstairs, past the Christmas tree Ollie'd finally gotten around to putting up, and the stockings, past the few poorly wrapped presents Ollie and I had managed to scrape enough money together to buy for each other, past the kitchen island, where a letter lay open on the counter, another bill from the mortgage company, with IMMEDIATE ACTION REQUIRED stamped across the top. Next Christmas we'd be putting a tree up in our new rental in the Gun Barrel Trailer Park, next to Bill Winter and his loud family. If we lived that long.

Maybe Kit would move in next door. Take over Eva Durbin's trailer. As if we'd know it.

As if I'd ever be able to trust my eyes again.

I tried to go back to bed. The image of Kit, raising his arms to the sky, and the image of the phantom in the corner of the shot from *Dead for Dollars* superimposed themselves over each other. His face becoming June's, then Ollie's, then Gram's.

Just before dawn, when I drifted off into an uneasy sleep, Gram's face rose from memory. She'd know what to do. She'd pour me some tea, look into the cup, and tell me the possible futures, how to find the path to the best one, the one that didn't end up with Kit plugging himself into everyone's lives, the new family parasite.

A text from my brother woke me.

Get down to the Gas n sip – now

I threw on the clothes at the end of the bed and tore out of our driveway. A few minutes later, I rounded a bend in the road and the Gas 'n' Sip appeared. And I almost swerved off the pavement.

Half of the place, including the garage where Ollie and I brought his truck for tune-ups, was gone. One of the walls had been ripped off, leaving exposed rebar and chunks of concrete. I pulled up in front and shut off my engine, staring at the building in disbelief. The late-morning sun slanted its rays inside to the glass cases of drinks, the tumbled shelves.

Something huge had taken a bite out of Jim Betleman's store.

Inside, I found Ollie, sitting on an overturned milk crate, holding an open bottle of water in one hand, his phone in the other, his eyes full of shock.

"What the hell happened?"

He kept his eyes on the plastic bottle. "Jim Betleman's gone. His keys are on the counter. His car"—he pointed over his shoulder—"is in the parking lot out back."

"Did you call Deputy Cruz?"

"He didn't pick up."

"He always picks up. He's got an emergency line strapped to him when he's sleeping."

"So I called A.J.," Ollie said, leaning both forearms on his knees. "She was in a panic because both Deputy Cruz and the dispatcher are missing."

Next to Ollie was another milk crate, on its side. I turned it over and sat, stunned. Ollie scooped up a bottle of water that lay on its side a few feet away and uncapped it, then handed it to me.

Missing. Like Gunter Moon, and Eva Durbin. The college kids.

I took a deep drink and wiped my mouth, took in the gray outlines of the shelves. I'd been in the Gas 'n' Sip a thousand times. Now it was pathetic and tattered, a disorganized mess, like the aftermath of tornadoes I'd seen on TV. I lifted the water a second time to my mouth for a sip. I stopped halfway, a prickle of gooseflesh rising on my arms.

A tornado, like the one in 1933.

"A.J. sent June and her mom down to the station," Ollie said. "The place wasn't damaged, but it was empty. Cruz's patrol car was there. His keys, on his desk. His cell phone. A breakfast sandwich, untouched on his desk. So A.J. started calling people."

Ollie met my eye finally; the helplessness there sent a shot of panic through me. "Quinn, about a dozen people from Gypsum have disappeared."

———•———

I pounded my fist on the front door of Selena's house. No one answered.

I took out my key ring, hands shaking, and used the spare key. God, Kit could have gotten inside her head, figured out she'd seen the trap. That it was all stored in there. He'd destroyed the safe and the cave with the markings. If he knew, she was as good as dead.

Inside was nothing but a sink full of dishes and the lingering smell of Selena's lilac perfume.

I called Selena again. The message went directly to voicemail. She'd turned off her phone? She never turned off her phone. Maybe it was dead. No, she was one of those planner types, a girl who charged her phone at night. She was gone. Nowhere. All her things lying about. A half-full pot of coffee on the stove.

I texted June, who said she was heading over to the courthouse to check if anyone was still there—which I told her was a waste of time, since it was Christmas Eve and all the offices had closed up for the holiday—while A.J. was going to the library to check on Javier, because his wife had called to say he never made it to the Gypsum Lights for their lunch date and his phone was going straight to voicemail. She had no idea where Selena had gone off to.

The hope that had flamed in my chest died out. Kit knew. He knew she had the image of the cave in her head. I would never see her again, ever.

I sank down on her mother's couch and put my head in my hands. I was numb. Paralyzed. Selena was gone.

I didn't know how long I sat there, with a hole in my chest, staring at the pictures on the mantel. A group photo of the Garcias at a family reunion, Selena in the front row with her dark hair piled up in a bun, a laughing smile on her mouth. Then school photos and shots of her holding trophies. And at the end of the mantel, a framed shot of Selena in denim cutoffs, dripping wet, her black T-shirt sticking to her skin, wearing a triumphant smile. I stood next to her, shirtless and sunburned, giving the camera lens a smug look.

That had been taken about a year ago. When Gram was still with us, and the grass on Sheriff Garcia's grave had barely started to grow, it had rained more than usual, washing out the arroyos, dropping on the earth until all the cacti were fat with it. The blooms started up, miles and miles of cactus flowers, pink and vibrant red and pure white.

The campgrounds had filled up. Gram was happy. Ollie, if not happy, was at least distracted, what with the extra work of all those campers and avoiding A.J., who was in town to take care of her mom and her little sister, both still reeling from the funeral. Which meant Selena was at our house constantly, since the two sisters couldn't get along for more than two minutes put together.

I didn't remember how it happened, but in the middle of all that, the busy camping season and burying Gypsum's most beloved sheriff and third-quarter exams, June, Shep Betleman, Selena, and I ended up at the top of the Horse Crippler in cutoffs and T-shirts.

Selena peered over the edge, where fifty feet down, the spring had overflowed its banks, lapping at the fire circle of the nearest campsite. "You think the rain... is it really deep enough?"

"I think we won't know until we try," June said ominously. And then she stepped off the cliff, her chin up and her shoulders back, her face turned up to the sun, screaming all the way down.

We rushed to the edge. A splash echoed on the cliff wall. A few seconds later, June popped up, threw her arms out of the water, and whooped. "C'mon! It's fine!"

Shep went next, taking a running leap, his body rising up for a split second before he dropped like a stone out of sight.

Another splash echoed up to us. Selena backed away, putting one palm on her stomach, and looked at me.

I held up my hands in surrender. "This was your idea."

"I know."

I stood with her at the edge and imagined what it would be like to plunge into that chilly, breath-stealing water, so cold it laced a clamp around your chest. I was dying to do it. Selena was not.

"You don't have to, you know."

She kept her eyes on the water. "Yes, I do."

June yelled up from below. "C'mon, Selena! It's safe."

Shep's voice followed, barely audible. "No, it's not."

"It's mostly safe! Would you just unpucker and get down here?"

The minutes ticked by as Selena neared the edge, then backed away, over and over. The joyful whoops and splashes of Shep and June swimming below were almost too much for me. But if I jumped like I wanted to and left her, she'd be climbing down for sure. And somehow, I got the feeling she needed to do this.

After a mountain of indecision, Selena stopped moving and dithering, and we stood together, watching the horizon, where the crisp blue met the desert. On days like those, you could see to the ends of the earth, until the sky filled you up, turned your chest into a hot-air balloon, so full you could let go of the ground and float.

"You remember what Mr. James said in English class?" Selena asked. "When we were reading *The Outsiders*?"

I had to think for a second. I went to school. I sat in a classroom sometimes. Out here, it all seemed so unreal. "Yeah, sure. Don't go into burning buildings."

"Not that."

"Late papers are minus twenty percent."

"I'm serious."

I searched my head for tidbits from the book, the lectures, but they'd faded, become hieroglyphs and murmurs.

Selena kept her eyes on the horizon. "He said being young, like we are, is all about firsts, and that one day, you wouldn't have any more firsts. But if you were lucky, if you lived the right way, the only thing that would stop you from having new firsts would be your own death."

"Well, that's depressing."

"No," she said, keeping her eyes on the horizon. "It's not. It makes me feel better somehow. Knowing that all of your life can be that, full of firsts." A kind of peace lit up her eyes. "And who you share your firsts with, that's what matters."

She didn't look at me, but I knew what she was talking about. The kiss. That she didn't regret it. That she was glad it was me.

I held out my hand, palm up. She watched it for a few breaths, her eyes filling up with a joy I hadn't seen in months. She took it, and we stepped off the cliff together. We plummeted through the air, laughing at gravity. It looked like the water was moving toward us, rather than the other way around.

———————•———————

I put the picture down and turned to the front door, a stone in my chest. There were still people in Gypsum who were in danger, and I had to go. Undo the terrible thing I'd done.

By the door was an empty spot where Selena usually kept her bag of rock-climbing gear. Maybe I was wrong. Maybe she was...

I burned up the road with my motorcycle. Sprinted down the trail toward the Horse Crippler. My heart leapt when I saw her bag sat at the base. At the top was Selena, sitting in the theater seats, her rope trailing down the cliff, drinking out of her thermos.

I tipped my head back and cupped my hands around my mouth. "Come down, Selena. We've gotta talk."

"What?" she yelled down.

"Come. Down."

She shook her head like she couldn't hear me, although I knew she could. Then she mimed climbing and pointed at me, then put her hands together in a *Please* gesture.

When I gestured for her to rappel down to me, she got up, turned her back on me, and walked away, disappearing beyond the lip of the cliff.

I glanced over my shoulder, back at the trail leading to the house, and my motorcycle, then up at the Horse Crippler. I didn't have time for this. But I also couldn't let Selena stay in Gypsum one more minute.

I free-climbed the easiest route, pushing away Ollie's voice, which was telling me I was a fool for doing this without a rope. By the time I was moving from handhold to handhold, feeling the distance between me and the ground grow, I was so tense I couldn't concentrate. Where was Kit? Was he somewhere in town?

An image of Kit's face came, his self-satisfied smirk. Was that really Selena I was climbing to? Was she...

I banished the thought before it could take form and root. Focused on the next hold, digging my toe into the crack, shifting my weight, staying balanced. No, she wasn't dead. And I needed to talk to her, tell her to get out of Gypsum. Have her copy the Devil's Trap down for me and then go stay with her uncle in Terlingua where it was safe. Somehow, I would find a way to put Kit back in the Devil's Trap.

I worked my way up the cliff face, Selena calling down to tease me, telling me I was slow as molasses during an ice storm. And the image of her dead tortured me, her lying behind a patch of cactus somewhere, neck broken. Had I forgotten that somehow Kit had managed to kill someone when he was still in the safe? Now that he was out in the world, there was nothing he couldn't do.

The soothing thoughts that I usually heard were quiet. I guessed Kit wasn't bothering anymore to influence me. Which meant something.

I reached the summit. Pulled myself over the edge. Selena stood on the other side of the cliff, thumbs hooked into the loops of the harness at her hips, gaze out on the desert. Her rock-climbing shoes lay behind her. She stood barefoot on the rock, her dark hair loose over one shoulder.

"Selena, you are a hard person to reach."

"You know what I did today?" she said, not turning from the view. "I climbed this without timing myself. I just…climbed." She took a deep breath and let it out, like she'd been holding it for months.

"That's great, really. Selena, you have to get out of town."

She turned to look at me, her smile evaporating, confusion taking its place. "I can't leave right now."

"You have to."

I told her what I'd found at the Gas 'n' Sip that morning. How Jim Betleman and Deputy Cruz and at least a dozen other people were missing. Selena's face didn't change. She just listened, her expression as still as a pond.

"So you see, you got to climb down this cliff, go find your sister and your mother, and just leave. Head to your uncle's place."

"Are you leaving?"

"No."

"Then neither am I."

I tried to think of the right thing to say. To make her leave town. A cool breeze moved up the face, blowing her dark hair into her eyes. She reached up and brushed it away, tucking it behind one ear, her gaze set a million miles away.

"You could die."

"So could you."

"Selena—"

"You know, you're pissing me off. Who put you in charge of being the hero? Why do you expect me to run off to Terlingua while you stay here and figure this out? I can save myself. And maybe *I'm* the one who's going to make sure everyone's okay. I'm the one with the Devil's Trap in my head. Maybe I'm going to save *you*. You ever think about that?"

"I didn't…I just…"

"I don't need you to hold my hand anymore to get me to jump."

She leaned down to pick up her water bottle and uncapped it slowly, then took a swig, her gaze on the horizon.

Seeing the determination on her face, I knew I couldn't convince her to leave Gypsum. Then a current of doubt swept through me again. I was suddenly afraid she would change, her features would morph and slide, like a whacked-out carnival show, until she turned into Kit.

Selena pulled her gaze from the view, her eyes pinching when she took in my expression.

"What's wrong?"

"Can you name the two most serious mistakes that a lead climber makes during clipping?"

"Why are you giving me a test?"

I waited.

"Fine, weirdo. Back-clipping and Z-clipping."

I examined her face as a light of understanding lit her eyes.

"You think I'm not me," she said.

"He might be able to get other things out of your head, but he wouldn't get something like that. It has to be something you're emotional about."

"Well, you know how emotional us girls can be."

"You're not taking this very seriously."

"June said it's the end of the world. No point in crying over spilled milk."

Small in the distance, the Christmas tree in front of the Gypsum square was lit, its colored lights faint in the bright sunlight pouring down from a cloudless blue sky. We watched the landscape as a pickup truck made its way down the main road, kicking up a cloud of dust.

Then Selena tucked a strand of hair behind her ear and swallowed. "You know why I came up here?"

"I figured you were looking for Kit. Had some sort of plan or something."

"I came up here because of what you said to me the other day, when you recited that poem."

I swallowed, a stone forming in my stomach. "Selena, I—"

"I know it wasn't you. But what you said—what Kit said—was really beautiful."

"I'm afraid to ask..."

"He quoted Shakespeare."

"And you really thought that was me?"

She went on like she hadn't heard me. *"Love is an ever-fixed mark that looks on tempests and is not shaken."* She turned to me. "You were incredibly romantic. And yeah, I thought it was you. I almost kissed you."

Almost kissed you. Relief flooded through me. Then the relief faded, and anger took its place. *Almost* was too close.

"And then I got that call from you last night," she said, "and I felt so stupid..." A smile, sort of sad, touched the corner of her mouth. "I really thought that was you."

I watched her profile, and I had no idea what to say. I didn't know any Shakespeare. "Selena, there are a lot of things I love about home. The night sky. My front porch. Tater."

"Wow, so I'm competing with your cat."

"Just shut up and let me finish. I love Gram's house, and these theater seats, and hanging off a cliff with nothing but a rope between me and falling. But most of all, I love waking up every morning excited, because I know I'm going to see you."

She turned to meet my gaze, and the gold flecks in her eyes caught the light. A faint smudge of dust lay on her cheek, and on the side of her nose. I think that's what made me do it, believe it was really her. Then I closed the distance between us as the last shred of doubt fell away. It was really Selena. And for some reason, I'd been too afraid for the last year to leap off this cliff with her.

I reached up to brush away the dust, then pulled her into a kiss. A tumble of sensations hit me at once, electric and sweet and real, and for a second, I wondered if I was wrong. Maybe it wasn't her. Maybe it was Kit. But when she slipped her hands around my waist and pulled me closer, I told myself it was her, of course it was her.

The weight of all my worries pulled free and tumbled down off the edge of the Horse Crippler.

And I was flying.

I don't know how long we stood at the top of the world, getting lost in each other. Hours. Years. The scent of smoke came between us, drifting on the wind, and I'd smelled enough campfires to know this was something else.

I pulled away from her warmth and opened my eyes. Turned toward Gypsum. My stomach bottomed out. In the distance, a plume of gray cloud spilled into the air. Even from here, I could see the flames, leaping up from the center of town.

Main Street was on fire.

CHAPTER
TWENTY-SEVEN

We arrived at the edge of Gypsum to catch the final act. Two pickup trucks had parked sideways on Main Street to form a barricade, but just beyond it, four blocks away, rising in the late-afternoon sunshine, was a riot of flame. Pure destruction. And I felt it, as I stepped off the bike, as I went racing up the sidewalk, past a crowd of locals yelling at me to stop, past Sal and Macie and a dozen other people I'd known all my life, that we had all been so blind not to see this coming. That *I* had been so blind and helpless, and my second sight was good for nothing. And now people I loved were either dead, or about to be.

The Stoplight Café was gone. Like some huge hand had come from the sky and plucked it right off the earth. In its place was a tangle of wooden sidewalk. A jet of fire came from the ground, which had to be the gas line. The building next door was ablaze, and half of it had already been eaten up by flames.

The library. And my brother fighting with Enrique, who was trying to pull him back from the flames.

It took me a split second to put it together.

"Oh no."

Selena turned to me. "What?"

"June told me A.J. went to look for Javier at the library."

A stranger came out of the crowd at the margins and said something to me, but the roar of the flame was too much. Selena's face had moved from shock to terror. She started pushing her way through the crowd milling on the margins of the fire.

"Selena, stop!"

I tried to grab her arm, but she was too fast. Then, ten steps from the side door, she staggered back, choking on the smoke. When I reached her side, the heat was a lash to my face. My eyes teared, and as I drew a ragged, smoke-filled breath, Selena and I fell back, coughing.

Then someone's voice was suddenly in my ear, a stranger from Alpine, his meaty hand a clamp on our arms, dragging us away. "Are you crazy? You can't go in there."

A safe distance off, he stopped dragging us and let go, and the wind shifted, sending the acrid smell of smoke in a wave over both of us, along with a wall of heat. My eyes teared until I couldn't see a thing. Too hot. No air. Shouts reached me, a whirl of hellish activity I could barely see. A distant yell of sirens reached me, probably Alpine coming to the rescue.

Selena had her arms around her stomach, watching the building burn, crying. I blinked and wiped my eyes, and from the smoke emerged a trail of flame, hanging suspended over the street, slowly growing, crossing to the other sidewalk. A serpent of fire. Flaming its way through the air, magical and bright.

I stared into the smoke, trying to make sense of what I was seeing. Not a serpent. A Christmas garland, the one A.J. had hired Jim Betleman to hang above the street. On fire.

Enrique rushed back to the crowd, joining a few other members of the Gypsum volunteer fire department and Ollie, who were frantically pulling aside a pile of debris.

At first, I didn't know what they were doing, wasting time like that rather than putting out the fire. Then I realized they were still trying to find the fire hydrant.

God, we were all going to burn.

My body felt numb, my fingers like deadwood. Someone yelled that they'd found the hydrant. Enrique connected the hose and opened the valve, sending a torrent of water into the flames. But there was no way anyone had survived that fire. And A.J. was gone. Gone forever, like Gram, like my parents, like Ollie would be one day, and I couldn't stand the thought of any of it. Another mountain in my life, picked up from the horizon and snatched away before I was ready.

The small crowd milled behind us, and from it rose a chatter of voices, their words piled on top of each other and hard to make out, but I was able to put together what had happened. The Stoplight Café was there one minute, and the next it was gone, like it had never existed.

I stood, my arm around Selena, who was calling her sister, tears streaming down her face, saying, "Please, please, be there."

My heart was bottoming out, helpless to do anything, watching the Gypsum town library burn. Alpine's fire truck arrived and took over. With nothing left to do, Ollie joined us, met my eyes once, then braced himself on his knees, like he couldn't take it anymore.

The phone in my pocket vibrated. I glanced at the screen. It was Tripp, of all people.

where r u

A swell of irritation made me almost turn it off. This wasn't the time for him to call in his retainer. I tapped out a quick response:

911 in town – call me later

I slipped it back in my pocket, watching silently with Selena as the Alpine fire department put out the blaze.

Then Selena's phone buzzed with a text, and relief washed over her face. "Oh my God. It's A.J."

Ollie looked up, shock on his face. "She's okay?"

Selena nodded and laughed, wiping her eyes. "She's okay, she's okay." She hugged me, then looked at the text again, her smile falling. "She wants us to come to the Alvarado."

Another text buzzed in my pocket, and I pulled it out to look at the screen. Tripp again.

You have to come to the Alvarado

Second floor

Now

I'm not kidding

You're not going to believe who I just found

As I read the stream, I expected the last line to be something ridiculous. The skeletons of Bonnie and Clyde. Some other ghost hunter nonsense that had nothing to do real life.

And then I saw the name pop up on the screen.

• ———————— •

The sun sank behind the Alvarado, sending long shadows across the parking lot out front. The front doors yawned open.

I let off the gas, rolling to a stop next to June's bike, which lay on its side at the base of the stairs. Next to it sat A.J.'s SUV and Tripp's van, both dark and cold, the painting of the moon and clouds on the sliding door hard to make out in the failing light. At the unnatural stillness of the place, Selena's arms around my waist tightened, then unraveled when I slipped off the bike.

Ollie's truck pulled up behind me, and he stepped out, his gaze going up to the third floor. He looked determined about something, hopeful even. I hoped he got a chance to say whatever he'd come here to say to A.J.

I dialed Tripp's phone. It went to voicemail. "Not good."

"Maybe the battery died," Selena said, taking a few steps toward the front steps, then a few back.

"Maybe."

I texted him one word.

here

Selena squinted up at the windows, but they only reflected the setting sun.

I didn't answer, my gaze on the screen. No response.

The three of us stood at the base of the stairs, looking up into the darkened, hushed lobby, the familiar chandelier catching the yellow glow coming from the west windows, breaking it into prisms. The place smelled of dust and sunset. Above, the stars were beginning to show.

Ollie turned to meet my eye. "Do you believe him?"

"I don't know what to believe."

We entered the lobby, then climbed the stairs, like I had a thousand times as a child, looking for the wonder my gram always talked about. She loved this place, and now I'd opened up something in it, let something loose, and if I didn't do something, and fast, maybe all of this, the hotel, the town, the land she'd left us, all of it would be gone. And I felt it so deeply now, all of it about to slip away, that it was hard to breathe.

In the spa, we passed the rows of yawning tubs, then made our way down one hall, and then another, through that unnatural quiet. We turned into the hallway. And stopped.

A light was on, in the room down the hall. It was the same room we'd seen that first night, when June, Selena, and I had come here exploring.

"I'm having déjà vu," Selena said.

Tripp emerged from the room and stopped when he saw us, doing a double take. "You brought friends."

"Do you have any idea what's going on in Gypsum right now?"

"Of course I do. I tried to call someone to come get her, and no one picked up. I found a phone number in her pocket and called it, but that was just her caretaker. C'mon." He reentered the room and we all followed.

As I neared the open door, the first thing I noticed was how warm it was. The room I'd seen a few weeks ago had been transformed. The furniture had been righted. The broken window had been boarded up. A portable generator had been set up in the corner, by a bed that was spread with a thick flowered coverlet. A few books sat on the nightstand. Everything was swept and clean.

June and A.J. stood in the corner of the room, their attention on someone in an armchair, someone who had her back to me. I could already tell from the slope of her shoulders who she was.

Tripp had found Eva Durbin.

CHAPTER
TWENTY-EIGHT

March 4, 1933, Gypsum

Eva stood in a patch of darkness, far from the Alvarado, her silver heels in one hand, a bottle of champagne in the other.

She tipped her head back to look at the moon, which hung like a fat spotlight in the sky, shining down on her. Then she opened up her mouth and yelled, "Hope you rot in hell, Fritz Von Sturnberg!"

Eva took another swig, then threw the bottle over a patch of prickly pear. It made a satisfying crash.

She dropped the shoes, pressed her palms against her temples, and swayed to a tune only she heard. The moonlight shimmered over the rhinestones on her gown. A gift from the director. She laughed a hollow laugh.

"Sure, a gift. Thanks, Fritz."

"That's a terrible waste of good champagne."

She turned, startled. A man stood there by a ragged clump of ocotillo, which threw a spiny shadow over his face. He wore the simple clothes of a miner—tan shirt open at the throat, brown trousers, suspenders. Attractive, young. And he was staring at her with a look she'd seen a thousand times from men like him.

She shook her head, grabbed her shoes where she'd dropped them, and slipped them on, ready to head back to the party, the lights, all those gawkers.

"But I'm not like the other men," he said.

She froze, a current of unease passing through her. How close that was to an answer to her last thought. She turned to face him again. "I'm not in the mood for company."

He took a step back, as if to leave. "I can go."

In her next breath of cool desert air came the taste of something sweet. Just a touch, like a flower somewhere near, blooming. And it wasn't even April yet, when the desert came alive.

Suddenly she found she didn't want to leave at all.

The sweet scent passed, became dry desert air again, clean and cool.

"You know," the man said, standing casually with his hands in his pockets, "you're absolutely stunning."

"Yeah, that's what they tell me."

His mouth quirked. "And modest."

"What can I say. I abhor games."

"Abhor?"

"Yep, that's my word of the week. Abhor."

"How about this for *not a game*." He stepped toward her, out of the cactus shadow. His face lit up in a beam of moonlight. Handsome, mesmerizing. Her breath caught.

"In that dress," he said, his smile filled with a strange longing, "you look like starlight."

———•———

Mrs. Durbin didn't turn when I said her name. Her gray hair fell around her shoulders, brushed and neat, a white cardigan around her shoulders, along with a blanket. Her feet were tucked into carpet slippers. Not that she needed any of that. It was at least eighty-five degrees in the room.

Next to her, June knelt down beside the armchair. "Hey there," she said. "Quinn is here to say hello."

Eva turned her bright, childlike eyes up at me, and I got the impression, as I always did, of a young woman trapped in an old body. "There you are," she said.

"Hi, Mrs. Durbin."

Mrs. Durbin's watery gaze moved from face to face, unsure, and then settled back on me. "There you are." A spark of recognition flared. "Quinn."

"Yep, it's me."

"How's your gram?"

"She's fine. She's getting ready for Christmas." The words stuck in my throat.

"Good, good." She reached over and patted my hand with her own, which felt like dry sticks wrapped in warm parchment. Then she slipped it back onto her lap to touch the cover of a book.

Starlets of Pre-Code Hollywood.

I knew that book. It was from Gram's library. The two of them had paged through it together a thousand times, when Gram was well and Eva still had her mind. One afternoon rose above the others: Gram offering to read her cup, Eva begging off like she always did. And then Gram had taken out a good pen from the kitchen drawer and asked her to sign underneath her photo, in a section called "They Might Have Been," all Hollywood starlets who had a couple of good years and then faded. And there she was, splashed all over the page, in that gray silk dress covered in rhinestones, her hands folded under her chin, staring hypnotically into the camera. Eva had signed the page, looping her letters, but the pleasure in her eyes had just made me sad it was over for her.

And now Eva held the same book, and from the tear in the cover I *knew* it was ours. I had no idea what it was doing with Eva Durbin.

Ollie had crossed the room to talk to A.J., and now they stood off to the side, talking in low voices, Ollie's hand on her arm. For once, she wasn't pulling away.

Next to the recliner was a glass of water on a small table. June put a bendy straw in it and placed it carefully in Mrs. Durbin's hands. "I've checked her over, and she's fine. Not dehydrated, and she's clean. Fed. The place is full of supplies. Someone's been taking really good care of her."

I took in the box of tissues next to her, and the mini-fridge connected to the generator in the corner. "Yeah, but who?"

Tripp crossed his arms and watched Eva like he expected her to morph into something else. "I swear, I walked in and thought I'd found a ghost. It wasn't until I reached out and touched her that I realized she was corporeal."

"You mean alive?"

"Yeah," he said, tilting his head and looking at her oddly. "Alive."

"How did you find her?"

Tripp shrugged. "Came here to do our thing. Exploring the mines, taking footage. Nicco's still down there." Tripp zipped his jacket higher, as if the cold of the hotel was seeping through. His usual swagger and polish were gone, and in their place was an unsettled look. "I saw a light on, and I came up here, and boom, old lady sitting in room 336, where that director was murdered back in the day. Turns to us and says hello, easy as you please. Totally blew my mind."

Ollie gave me a baffled look, then went to the window to look out onto the cracked parking lot. Selena knelt beside the recliner. As Mrs. Durbin chatted with her about how nice it was that summer was finally here, Selena nodded in all the right places, then shot me a look.

"She's been gone two days," I murmured.

"I know," Tripp said, keeping his voice low. "But she said she's been with her 'boyfriend.'" He made air quotes around the word. "If we stay long enough, I think we'll find out more."

Selena moved toward the door and motioned me to follow. We stepped beyond the smothering heat of the room and moved down the hall.

I lowered my voice. "It has to be Kit. But why?"

"C'mere." She pulled me, stopping in front of one of the framed pictures. Three lines of people in a group portrait, their expressions caught in black-and-white. The *Dead for Dollars* director, Fritz Von Sturnberg, stood in the middle of the front row, chin tilted up. "Look who's in the back row."

I'd dreamt about that picture often enough, tumbling with all the other images of the hotel: the chandelier's teardrop crystals glimmering, the black-winged birds taking flight. Twenty people standing in rows of five, strangers from Hollywood and Gypsum locals, staring at the camera, frozen.

I searched the faces. And there he was, Kit, the only one smiling. A smirk, like he knew a really good joke and had no intention of telling anyone.

"*This* is where I'd seen him before! God, it was driving me crazy."

Next to him stood a familiar starlet, her blond hair in perfect ringlets, her arms behind her back. Eva Durbin.

The day Kit came out of the safe, he'd eaten half our pantry, then taken a book from our bookcase. *I hope you don't mind,* he'd said.

"This means he was a part of the movie crew when all those people went missing," I breathed.

Selena glanced over her shoulder down the hall, her expression calculating. "We need to ask her some questions."

"Good luck getting two words that make sense out of her."

Tripp's voice came from behind me. "I have an idea about that." He carried my backpack in one hand and looked from Selena's face to mine, his expression bright. "I know how we can find out what happened to Mrs. Durbin."

CHAPTER
TWENTY-NINE

March 8, 1933

Eva stripped off her gown, laughing at the stars, and dove into the spring. She didn't care about Fritz Von Sturnberg, or his promises, or her career, which was balanced on a knife's edge. Tip one way, fame. Tip the other, and it would all be over.

She and Kit swam in the black waters of the spring, under the cliff the locals called the Horse Crippler. This had become their secret spot, every night since they'd met four days ago. She could count the hours they'd had together on her fingers, but it felt like a lifetime. So much had happened, and her heart was so full she couldn't think.

Eva floated on her back, staring at the austere face of the cliff, black against the splash of the Milky Way. "They should call this place something grander, don't you think?"

Kit swam close and stole a kiss, his mouth warm. "I'll call it . . . Eva's Bluff."

"Oh, stop."

He circled her playfully, treading water. "I'm serious. And this whole desert, Eva Land."

"That's a terrible name for a desert."

He stopped next to her and floated on his back. "And all those constellations, I name them all . . . Eva."

She floated there, weightless, watching the stars tremble and shiver. Then Kit's warm arms were around her, his eyes glittering with starlight, and he kissed her again. His breath hot, and the water deliciously cold. For a second, she didn't want the stage, or the screen, or a million adoring fans. She just wanted Kit.

Later, they lay on the bank of the spring. Up on the hill, Liam O'Brien's house had only one light on. It shone in the dark like a lighthouse.

A bed of polished stones pressed into her back, and the water lapped at her feet. The hem of her dress was muddy and stuck to her skin, but she wasn't cold—even though the desert had lost the scorching heat that had earlier made her sweat off half her makeup, had Fritz yelling at wardrobe for the powder girl. No, this was perfect. She turned to Kit, who sat by the water's edge, one hand propping him up, the other's fingertips making lazy circles in the spring.

It was more than perfect.

Eva turned her head back to the sky, where the Big Dipper hung. Tomorrow she'd have to shoot the scene with the bandits again. Take direction from dear old Fritz. Her good mood evaporated.

Kit turned to her, his face unreadable in the shadows. "Fritz wants a little more than your best performance, doesn't he?"

She started. Somehow Kit always knew what she was feeling or thinking, even before she'd admitted it to herself. "He keeps talking about giving me the lead in the next picture, you know, real flirty and all, and when I brush him off, he gets a bit . . . distant. Talks about giving the role to someone else." She looked away and let out a mirthless chuckle. "Games. How I hate 'em. And Fritz, at the moment."

Kit kept his attention on the water, drawing a figure eight on the surface. "That's horrible," he said in a quiet voice.

She spread her arms wide. "That's show business," she said with a flourish and a smile.

Kit finally turned to her, his jaw set. "Are you going to . . ."

"No!" She leaned back on her hands. "Still haven't figured out what to do about it, though."

"I might have an idea." There was a darkness in his tone that she didn't like. Then he leaned close, his breath warm and sweet, and she forgot all about that.

"You know," he said, breaking from the kiss, "I've never loved anyone before."

"Me neither." Eva put a hand up and threaded it in his hair.

Above them, the Milky Way stretched out, like a bright wing.

———————•———————

It didn't take much convincing. A woman I'd known all my life, who never once let Gram or me inside her head, willingly took the flowered teacup and drank.

June knelt beside the armchair, helping her sip. Mrs. Durbin glanced up from time to time, her watery gaze traveling over the five of us, probably wondering why so many people had come to see her today.

Ollie had been difficult to convince, but after A.J pulled him out into the hall, he'd come back quiet and stone-faced, giving me a single nod before retreating to the other side of the room. I didn't know what she'd said to him, but even Ollie knew the world was unraveling faster than he could outrun it. None of us knew what to do next, and the answers might just be in Eva Durbin's head.

He leaned against the windowsill, his gaze on Mrs. Durbin, pity in his expression. "Does she even recognize any of us?"

"Not at sundown," June said. I didn't hear the sarcasm I usually got when she talked about Mrs. Durbin. There was a gentleness there now, like she was taking care of family. I guessed she was. And if Eva Durbin had lived in Gypsum for almost ninety years, she was family to me, too.

June helped her turn the cup again and sip. The cup shook.

Tripp stood across the room, apart from the rest of us, his camera off and pointing at the floor. His usual smile was gone, probably because I'd told him our deal was over if he filmed her. Eva Durbin might be a sideshow, but she was our sideshow, and I wasn't splashing her all over the internet without her permission.

A.J. sat on the edge of the mattress, next to Selena, watching Eva's hands on the cup. "I've never actually seen you do a reading," she said.

"There's not much to see. At least not from where you're sitting."

"This doesn't feel right," Selena said, wringing her hands. "Making her do this."

"You want to find out why the world is ending?" A.J. asked, her voice brittle. Selena didn't answer.

"Last sip, Mrs. Durbin," June said.

She smiled, looking from June to me. "It's good."

June helped her lift it the last time. "Yes, it's good."

I sat in the chair across from Eva Durbin, the only remaining member of the infamous *Dead for Dollars* cast, and took the cup from her hands.

Ollie caught my eye. A warning, there in his expression. *Don't go too far.*

Outside, the sun dragged itself down to the horizon. Half an hour before sunset. The shadows had grown long in the room.

The cup's white insides were lined with tea leaves. Patterns. A letter *G*. An ocean wave. An evergreen. Symbols I hadn't seen before. Somehow, I knew what they were, like a familiar face I could almost make out.

"Quinn," Ollie said, "what do you see?"

Suddenly everyone's eyes on me were too much. *Quinn, what do you see?*

And the world was gone. A burnt-out wick. An endless night. I stood in the Dark Place. Vast and empty. Free.

Two steps forward with my hands out, and I found the web. Sticky and familiar. I ran my hands over the symbols, caught in the web like curls of paper. Like shattered moth wings.

Find what I needed. Get out fast, before Kit came back. Before that thing on the other side of the web sensed my presence again and returned to finish what he'd started.

And then a voice came from behind me. "Quinn."

I turned, and the Dark Place was gone.

Four walls, wood paneling. An easy chair, a coffee table cluttered with perfume bottles and overflowing ashtrays and bottles of bourbon.

I was in the Gun Barrel Trailer Park, in Mrs. Durbin's trailer.

"Quinn, I'm right here."

And there she was: Mrs. Durbin, on her velvet fainting couch.

But she wasn't the Mrs. Durbin I knew. This was Eva Durbin the starlet, reclining on one arm, dressed in a white satin robe studded with rhinestones, her blond hair curled in perfect ringlets, face unlined and young. And she looked just like she did in the pictures, the ones she'd kept on her trailer walls all those years.

"I go on in twenty minutes," Eva said, "so let's get to it."

"On?"

"On set. You know. Hollywood stuff." She took a cigarette out of the silver case on the coffee table and inserted it into a long holder. Then she lit it and inhaled, looking at me from under thick black lashes. "Well, spit it out, boy. I don't got all day."

I went to the window and pulled the curtain aside. There was no concrete slab, no other trailers, no desert scrub, no Chinati Mountains. Just darkness. Vast. I strained to listen for movement, the dragging hiss and stumble of the monster, the one who'd tried to take a bite out of me.

"It's okay, Quinn. You're safe here."

"Where is here?"

She smiled and tapped her temple with a long lacquered nail. "There's a reason I've never let you read a cup for me before."

We eyed each other across the coffee table, through the smoke. Everything seemed so real, the sweet stench of tobacco, the feel of the shag carpet under my shoes.

I sank into the chair across from her. Behind me, through the thin walls of the trailer, the hum of voices from the set bled through. Voices. Workers carrying equipment. Hammering. Somehow, I was in Mrs. Durbin's head, *and* the Dark Place, at the same time.

"Mrs. Durbin—"

"Eva," she corrected me. "In here, I'm Eva."

"Eva, I need to know what's happening to Gypsum."

She inhaled and let out a long, smoky breath, shaking her head sadly. "Boy, why on earth did you let him out?"

I didn't answer, my stomach hitting bottom.

She took another delicate puff. "He's not actually *evil,* you know, but he can't help himself. He'll grow. Consume everything. Kit's like an invasive species that has a lot of food and no predators." At my confused look, she shrugged. "June watches a lot of Discovery Channel."

"And the constellations?"

"Yep. Gone. At least for now." She pointed the cigarette at me. "Your great-grandfather used to call him the Star Eater."

One look at my face and a small smile curled at the edge of her mouth.

"Yes, your family is tangled up in this too. Don't look so shocked. Liam O'Brien, Hector Garcia, and Mattias Pilsner." Her eyes brightened as she watched me soak that in. "You and Selena and June, I wasn't surprised you ended up friends. Your families have been in each other's business so long that you've got a bond. You'll fight, you'll complain about how June gets on your nerves, or that Selena is just too uptight, but you'll always come back to each other."

I tried to wrap my head around our ancestors dealing with this almost a century ago. Eva leaned on one arm, her cigarette smoke curling up from the tip.

"So he...eats starlight?"

"In a way, yes. Drinks it up somehow. Absorbs it. But once he's gone, the stars will come back. It's just the light he steals. The real problem is he'll absorb people, too, and buildings, whatever he can get. He's extremely hungry." She leaned forward. "You know, back in the day, Gypsum used to be a much bigger place."

The freak tornado. The earthquakes that swallowed up pieces of the land, made crevasses. The cleaned-up version in the local history books, telling stories of how so much of Gypsum was destroyed in the strange events in 1933. The old courthouse. The jail. Part of the Gun Barrel Trailer Park.

Suddenly, I felt sick to my core. I'd been talking to Kit, listening to him. My half-empty coop, the fact that I'd seen fewer animals around. The missing people. Gunter Moon wasn't sleeping it off in the desert. Deputy Cruz and his secretary didn't run away together. And Javier and the library...

As all of the realizations tumbled down on me, a cold certainty welled up, making its way down my arms until I went numb. "So we have to kill him."

She barked a laugh. "Good luck!" She tapped her cigarette on the ashtray. "We tried. But the best we could do was the safe."

"He destroyed the safe."

"You can use any container, big or small."

"But how do I get him to go inside?"

"*You* don't. The lock does that. That was me. The lock. We drew straws and I got the short one." She took another drag on her cigarette. "Though it don't work too good no more, what with my mind slipping like it has. Nothing lasts forever."

"I don't understand... what lock?"

She sat forward and poured herself a glass of water from a carafe. "Always did love your water. Until I knew." She set the carafe down. "The lock is a person. You do a thing, a kind of ritual if you want to call it that, and you make the marks on the container just so, and if you do, Kit can't get anyone to open the safe. He can't send dreams or send the combination or anything like that anymore. Can't make you so claustrophobic you can't help but open it. His influence becomes... softer." She looked uncomfortable as she said the last word, as if she knew firsthand what his influence was. "And don't you wait, boy. Don't you wait one more minute! The longer you leave him be, the bigger he gets, although people like us can't see it."

"So Kit has no idea you're the lock."

"Oh, he knows."

"But he's been caring for you, like he..."

"Loves me?"

"Yeah."

"Because he does. And I love him." At my confused look, she waved me away. "It'll take me too long to tell you the whole thing. Boy meets girl. Boy and girl fall in love on set. Girl finds out boy is really a monster who will destroy us all. Your typical love story." Then her eyes softened, and she pushed a blond curl behind her ear. "But my God, what a man he was."

Eva Durbin in love. I'd known her as crabby old Mrs. Durbin for so long I couldn't see her as anything else.

And loving someone that much and locking them away? That was even harder to comprehend.

"How do I get him back in the safe?"

"Just ask Bud."

"Why Bud?"

"Bud's the next in line. When I die."

"Bud Pilsner?"

"Is there any other Bud of note around here? Yes, Bud Pilsner."

"Bud Pilsner's dead."

She sat back on the couch, looking at me in shock. "Oh, that changes things." She sipped from her water glass. "Not too surprised, though, I have to say. It drove him into a state, it did. Bud started thinking he could escape his fate, if you believe in that sort of thing. Prepare for the day. Save himself. Save June. I'm guessing Bud blew himself up on one of his own mines."

I didn't have time to correct her, tell her who'd really killed Bud Pilsner. It all made sense now. Kit, he'd found a way. Probably planted some notion in Bud's head, that he could take the safe far away from here, drop it down a volcano or something. Then, when Bud got close…

"I always thought Bud Pilsner was just some unhinged prepper," I said.

"Oh, he was a prepper, all right. He just wasn't prepping for a government invasion. He was prepping for Kit." She sat up and slapped both her thighs with a familiar Mrs. Durbin gesture that meant she'd made up her mind. "But we still need to be moving forward. Get that boy in the box! And if I know Bud, he left June a message, or a journal, or a—"

"—a letter."

She stopped and met my eye, saw the realization there, and nodded. "That's where it'll be. It'll tell you how to put Kit back in and how to make a really good lock."

June had no idea, I was sure. If she had, she would have told us. Which meant that letter was still tucked away in her bag, unopened.

"I'd be real careful with June, boy, because she's meant to be the lock now, and if she dies, well—we made a promise back then, the four of us.

One of us dies, and there's no offspring, we go to the next family in line."
She leaned forward. "And it's age before beauty, so guess who's next?"

She must have seen the shock in my face, so she sat back. "I'd hate
to see Ollie pay the price I had to pay." She held up her hand to stop me
before I could ask. "And I can see your next question coming. Better not
to know what the price is ahead of time. And don't open that letter until
the last minute. You don't want him reading your mind."

A voice came from outside the trailer, calling her name. Her gaze
went to the door, expectant and excited. I couldn't see anyone past the
curtain, but a voice came again, something about a delay, that she'd have
to wait. The hope in her eyes dimmed, then melted into disappointment.

"What if there's another way?" I asked. "What if no one has to pay
the price?"

"Everything has a price, boy. You're old enough to know that."

"You said nothing in this world can kill Kit."

"Yep, that's the truth." She stubbed out her cigarette delicately.

"What about something from the Dark Place?" I asked.

Her expression changed to confusion. "The what?"

"The place we're in right now."

"Oh, is that what you call it." She glanced around the bright trailer.
"Not so dark to me."

"Maybe the thing that lives here can kill Kit. A real monster. It always
seems to know when I'm around." An itch started up on the back of my
neck, a certainty growing that it was on its way. I got up and pulled back
the curtain again. All there was on the other side was ink.

"That's why you're checking the window so much," she said, her eyes
set in the middle distance between us. Then she gave me a sad smile,
like she felt sorry for me. "I don't think this idea's going to work out for
you, boy."

"What if I draw it out, and pull Kit into the mines, away from
Gypsum and the people? Then nobody will have to be the lock. If we're
lucky, they'll destroy each other."

"Sit." I did. Eva patted my knee like the old Mrs. Durbin I knew.

"I could do it," I insisted, "let it out, and then if I'm lucky—"

"Ah, Quinn," she said. "You got it all wrong. My dear boy, you already let the monster out."

Then she stood, her robe flowing around her, and tapped me on the cheek. "Good luck. Or, as we say in the movies, break a leg." She moved to the door. "Or maybe don't do that, since he runs really fast."

Then she turned the knob and opened the door, gesturing for me to step out into the night.

I came out of the Dark Place slowly, the trailer shrinking until it was a pinprick of light, a distant star. The room in the Alvarado spun around me. Wallpaper. The faces of my friends, a blur of concern, mouths moving. A buzzing. And it wasn't the Dark Place putting cotton over my ears. It was panic.

My arm throbbed under the bandage, still healing. Pink skin, where his teeth had sunk in. I touched it.

The monster I'd sensed all these years, on the other side of the veil, the abomination with teeth that filled the corners of my nightmares. And Kit.

They were the same thing.

CHAPTER
THIRTY

I tried to speak. Tell them what Kit really was. *Walking around in a human suit all this time, but underneath it all it…* Selena tried to give me a glass of water, then looked into my eyes, like she was checking my pupils.

"Hey, Quinn! Snap out of it!" Ollie hovered behind Selena, staring at me. And beside him was June.

"Took you long enough," she said with false bravado and a small smile, worrying the blond braid over her shoulder.

She had no idea what was in store for her. Bud had left her more than a run-down house and a field full of land mines. She would become the lock, whatever that meant.

When she saw my expression, her smile fell.

Then Ollie's gaze slid up, over my head, and past me. Selena's gaze followed his, and she let go of my arms and sat back.

A familiar voice drifted to me. "What a delicious amount of emotion in this room. I can hardly hear myself think."

I turned to find Kit standing in the doorway.

He came in and set a brown paper grocery bag on a small table, then pulled out a six-pack of something with a blue label. Chocolate shake. A nutrition drink.

No one spoke or moved. Then Tripp's camera hand slowly rose, directing the lens at the doorway.

While Kit nonchalantly unpacked Eva's groceries, I blocked out what I could in my thoughts, channeling the coldest part of my emotions. A big fat zero of feeling. Without taking my eyes away from him, I wrapped Gram's cup in its dishcloth and shoved it in my backpack, then slung it over my shoulder. Like I was packing up to leave. Like there was absolutely nothing weird about all this, and it was just time to go. That's all. Time to head on home for dinner. The others started to follow my lead, awkwardly pretending it was just a party, breaking up for the night.

Kit set out the last items, a box of pasta, a jar of spaghetti sauce, and his gaze turned to me. "So you know what I am now."

My breath hitched in my throat, and I made myself answer. "Guess so."

"Good. I was tired of pretending anyway." He tilted his head, eyeing me, and the image I'd had at the cliffs returned: a predatory bird, sizing me up. Reading me. But then he froze, his hand on the back of Eva's chair, his eyes filling with disbelief. "You want to lock me away again."

My legs felt wooden, my hands numb.

His gaze swept over the group. "All of you do." He took a step back toward the door, the shock on his face slipping into something almost fragile, vulnerable.

Fear rose up in me like a bubble, ready to pop in my throat and send a scream out. Whatever sugary psychic drug he'd been sending out into the world was gone.

His shoulders slumped, and he turned toward the door. He was leaving. I willed him to keep going, slip through the door and disappear into the night, away from all of us. Selena leaned against the wall, shaking. The others stood staring, frozen. Even Tripp had lowered his camera.

Kit paused with his back to us, hand on the knob. "No, it's no good."

He dropped his hands by his sides; then he turned and pulled a handkerchief from his pocket. Leaning close to Eva's ear, he whispered, "You don't need to see this, sweetheart." Before he tied it around her face, a curtain of fear fell over her shining eyes, as she remembered where she was, and who was standing next to her.

Then he stood again, and the hurt I'd seen in his eyes only a moment ago had calcified, turned into something harder, with an edge. "I'll give you all a head start. New game of hide-and-seek." He gave me a pointed look. "Be careful where you hide this time."

I exchanged a glance with June. The others shifted uneasily, confused. Like cattle in their stalls, waiting for the chutes to open.

Kit twitched and rolled his shoulders like he was shrugging off a jacket. This time there was no shimmer. No mirage warping, no desert on a hot day, the horizon promising water holes and lies to draw you in. This was a stripping away, like he was peeling himself.

I stood, transfixed, Kit between me and the door.

Hide.

Run.

Climb out the window.

Instead I just watched, my lungs frozen.

Ollie pushed A.J. and June through the door. Then the others rushed into the hall. Kit's skin unspooled like threads, disappearing in wisps of smoke. Changing, growing. Bits of gray skin appeared. A flash of teeth.

A buzzing in my ears. A tug on my arm. Then the buzzing sharpened into a voice. Selena.

"Quinn!"

As if she'd broken a spell, I slipped past Kit—or what was left of Kit—and sprinted like I did that night, when June and Selena and I had come here for answers, when all this had started.

No, that wasn't when it started. I'd been running all my life. From this one thing.

We rounded the corner at full speed, the murky darkness of the hallways swallowing us, then the spa, the metal tubs glinting in the fading light that poured in from the windows. We sprinted down the grand staircase, a jackhammer of footsteps echoing against the vaulted ceiling. Ollie raced ahead of me, already halfway down. A.J., June, and Selena stopped at the bottom, near a bright circle that hovered like a spook light.

Not a spook light. A flashlight. And Tripp was at the base of the stairs, arguing with someone, pulling him toward the door, telling him to leave.

The light swung, hit me square in the eyes. I stumbled and fell, taking Selena with me. A GoPro camera light, on Nicco's forehead.

Suddenly Ollie was there, hauling us up, pulling us the rest of the way out.

"We gotta get out of here," he said. *"Now."*

Behind me, the *thump-thump* of running drifted down, a distant drumming. Growing louder. Echoing in the halls of the Alvarado.

Nicco pointed his light to the top of the stairs. "Is something up there?"

"Shut it off!" Tripp cried, dragging him toward the front door.

Nicco looked at him in complete shock.

A shadow shot out of the doorway to the spa. Moving fast. I didn't wait. Selena and I raced past Nicco and Tripp, out onto the porch.

I glanced over my shoulder just as a gray shape hit Nicco full force. A tumble of light swung across the ceiling. I stopped, turned back. I couldn't leave him. But Kit opened his mouth wider than I'd ever thought possible and sank his teeth into Nicco's throat. The blood. Kit's face dipping down to take a second bite. The screams echoing through the lobby.

Ollie grabbed my arm.

We bolted outside and down the verandah stairs toward the SUV. A.J. stood by the driver's door, stiff, stricken.

"What are you waiting for?" Ollie yelled, racing to her. "Give me the keys and get in!"

A.J. shook her head, her arms around her middle, like she was trying to hold herself together. I saw that the tires were flat, the engine torn to pieces. Ollie's truck was the same. My motorcycle, too.

The hotel grounds were dead quiet. All that reached us was the violent ripping of cloth, the crack of a bone.

Ollie signaled for us to follow him around the side of the hotel, past the gaping tiled hole in the ground that once was a swimming pool and behind the small pool house. Then he stopped, looking around him in the dusk, then at us, the wheels in his head spinning.

Selena leaned against the adobe wall and put her hands over her mouth. June walked in circles, hands behind her neck. A.J. braced herself on her knees like she was about to be sick. Tripp sat on the ground next to her, like his legs had just given out, his body shaking with silent sobs.

"We left him," Tripp managed to get out. And then he didn't speak again.

"Okay," Ollie finally said, the confusion in his eyes settling. "We run, fast as we can, head to the Gun Barrel Trailer Park. It's only a mile away."

I looked at the desert, which stretched out like a running track.

A.J. shook her head. "Wide-open space like that? What are you, nuts?"

"Okay then, we split up," Ollie said, "go in different directions."

"Then we won't all make it," A.J. said.

"Well, Ms. Mayor, if you've got a better idea, I'd like to hear it!"

A.J. threw up her hands. "We're doing this again?"

"Maybe if we hide," Selena ventured, her voice rising with panic, "he'll just pass by."

June stopped pacing and looked at her. "Hide? Really?"

"Well, I don't know!" Selena said, tears running down her cheeks. She turned away from her sister.

A.J. said nothing.

I peeked around the corner, at the back stairs leading to the second-floor verandah. "Someone can draw him back into the hotel, keep him busy."

"That's a sure way to get killed," Ollie said.

"No—a few of us can lead him into the old mines," June said. "That'd give everyone else a chance to get to the Gun Barrel."

Mines. The word sparked in me, grew to a flame.

I looked up into the sky. The moon was rising, almost full now. When the sun left us completely, the whole world would become a confusing pattern of gray and ink. Easy to take the wrong step.

Unless you had a really good guide.

I met June's eyes, and I caught a spark of recognition there, in the dying light of the sunset.

I turned my gaze west, toward Bud Pilsner's place, a steely determination growing inside me. "Actually, I've got a better idea."

———————◆———————

Ollie, June, and I raced across the dark desert into Bud Pilsner's field.

I had made Selena and the others promise to wait until Kit caught sight of us before they left their hiding spot. Right now, they were making for the Gun Barrel's distant lights. They'd be safe, I told myself. And we'd have June's eyes to guide us through the dark.

Ahead, June's silhouette was faint, and I struggled to keep up, Ollie bringing up the rear. I couldn't hear Kit, but I could feel him, gaining. Chasing me instead of Selena, A.J., and Tripp, which meant he didn't know yet what was in our minds—and he still didn't know what Selena held in her perfect memory.

Within a few minutes, I caught the rhythm of Kit's feet on the air. And I began seeing him in my head, the memory sharp as broken glass. His long, loping legs; the gray sheen of his skin; his mouth opening wide. The loud splash of blood on the floorboards of the Alvarado.

Out of the darkness ahead, battered signs materialized, spread out in an evenly spaced line. I couldn't read them in the dark, but I knew what they said.

NO TRESPASSING.

PRIVATE PROPERTY.

WARNING: EXPLOSIVES.

We blew past them, following June's path, the twisted line of safety between the hotel and Bud's house. A house with a garage and a truck.

The first explosion rocked the ground under me. I stumbled and fell. My ears rang, skin humming with the aftershock. I checked my arms and legs to make sure they were still there.

But it hadn't been me tripping the trigger. Only ten feet behind, dirt rained down in chunks. A dark figure struggled on the broken earth, his carapace skin gleaming in the starlight, horrible and beautiful. Confused, like a beetle thrown onto his back. One of his limbs jutted out at an unnatural angle. Then he stood, twisting his arm back into place like a grotesque doll.

I kept running. Zigzagging through Bud Pilsner's minefield, following the flash of June's blond hair into the night, stepping where she stepped, the sky pressing down on me like a heavy hand. The saliva in my mouth felt thick and hot. My head and hands went light, like I would pass out.

Another loud *snick* in the night. An explosion shook the earth, but this time I didn't turn to look. I flinched, bit my tongue. Tasted the tang of blood and adrenaline.

Ahead a boulder rose up, familiar. As a kid I would crouch there during hide-and-seek—before Bud lost himself in paranoia, made his land a deathtrap. I followed June and Ollie behind it and waited. Calming my mind, my emotions.

The night fell quiet.

Next to me, his back pressed against the rock, Ollie panted, his chest heaving. He turned to me, catching my eye for a split second, as if to make sure I was still alive. The porch light of Bud's house burned in the distance, across a football field of land.

June whispered, "I think we got him." She closed her eyes briefly, shaking her head, like she couldn't believe what she'd gotten herself into, then inched toward the edge of the boulder and peeked around the edge.

An explosion, this time so close my ears rang.

We took off, legs and arms pumping. The porch light grew larger, a beacon in a sea of sand and spines. We were nearing the edge of the minefield. Only thirty more feet of traps, and then a straight shot of flat-out running to the house.

But we were getting winded. June ducked behind a stand of creosote bushes thick enough to block Kit's view. We followed her.

We sat, panting. June's face was nothing but terror. I felt it too. Ollie looked worse. The last time he'd run this much, he was still in high school. Kit would catch him first on the straightaway, that was for sure. June and I would try to get inside, get the keys to the truck, but Kit would meet us in the garage.

And then there would be only one. I had a feeling Kit would leave me for last.

Kit's voice filtered through the creosote bush. Close, a few dozen yards to the left. "Why don't you all come out before I drag you out? More dignified that way."

I put a fist against my mouth and bit down. June and I exchanged a look, and the panic there told me she thought we were finished. It was a miracle we hadn't ended up in pieces already.

Before Ollie could stop me, I moved out of the shadow of the creosote bushes and showed myself.

Kit stood twenty feet away, his beetle-gray skin glimmering in the moonlight, speckled with what looked like mica chips. His mouth was a slash across his face, so wide it stretched almost to the sides of his head, where two dark holes lay on either side. He cocked his head.

Somehow, I found the courage to speak. "You really don't want to do this. I mean, we're friends, aren't we?"

"Friends don't lead friends through a field full of mines."

I edged backward, positioning myself to run. Hearing Kit's voice come out of that *thing*. It was too much. My skin prickled with loathing.

"Ah yes, people generally don't handle the real me that well. Eva only saw me like this once, but it was enough to cause a nasty breakup. I mean, she stuffed me in a safe." He shook his head. "She's easy to forgive, though. You? Not so much."

"You don't have to do this."

"It will be easier on you if I do this now, rather than later." His voice held a tinge of regret. "Then you don't have to see what happens tomorrow. Honestly, I should have just let you fall into the dark, like a shooting star. A kinder end, really. Oh well, what is it Selena says? No crying over spilled milk."

It took me a few seconds to put it together. Me, hanging on in all that blackness, about to plunge into the mouth of that crevasse. And the strange hand in the dark, helping me find my way. "That was *you?*"

"Of course it was me. I was heading to the cave to destroy the trap, and there you were, dangling off the wall like a wounded spider."

"Why?"

He shrugged, corded muscles rippling under his gray skin. He took a tentative step forward, looking at the ground as if it would explode any moment. "In a way, we're family."

Family? But before I could figure out what that meant, I noticed the small glimmers on his skin. There was a pattern. As if he were covered with…

Then Kit changed, his skin rippling. He looked like Kit again. Shirt and trousers and young, fresh face. "I'm not going back in a trap. You don't know what it's like to be shut away, folded up like a paper doll. And I think I can control it this time. Keep myself small. Eat less."

There was hope there, in his eyes. He believed what he was saying. I didn't. "What would Eva think if she saw you now, doing this to us?"

Even in the dim starlight, the change in his expression made me take a step back. "Don't talk about something you know nothing about."

"I know you love her. She wouldn't want you to do this."

"Eva isn't even Eva anymore. Time, the way it moves here… it's so cruel to all of you."

"You're wrong. She's still Eva. I talked to her. In the Dark Place. She was the Eva you remember. Young and beautiful and strong. And she told me she loves you."

Kit's eyes measured me in the dark. "You're lying."

"You can read my mind. You know I'm not lying. And she wouldn't want—"

"Quinn," he said, his voice quiet, without its usual dryness. "She abandoned me, just like you're abandoning me, because of something I can't help." The next sentence was spoken so softly, almost to himself, that I almost missed it. "It's why they left me here."

"They?"

Kit sighed, put his hands in his pockets. "You know what it's like, don't you? To be unwanted." His gaze moved past me to the rock where Ollie was hiding.

"Stay out of my head."

He shrugged and leaned against the boulder next to him, like it was the most comfortable place in the world. Like it was his living room. "But do you really want me to stop?" he asked.

Before I could answer, his features rippled. All of him rippled like a mirage on the highway in the full heat of summer.

Ollie. My brother—or what looked like my brother—leaned against the boulder.

"What are you doing?"

"Quinn, I'm sorry about the last six months."

"Stop it."

"When Gram died, I should have been a better brother. Understood what you were going through."

"Stop."

"But I was too wrapped up in myself to be what you needed me to be. And I'm sorry."

"Stop it!"

Kit's expressions, so like Ollie. He paused and pressed his lips together. "But isn't this what you wanted? To have me apologize?"

A voice rose up inside me, said *Yes.* Maybe that was him, his subtle influence. Maybe it was just me.

"Or this?" His eyes took on a wicked cast. "I know you better than you know yourself."

And with that last word, he changed into Selena.

We stared at each other across a stone's throw of desert. I wouldn't have been able to tell the difference. Not at all. And I knew that something like Kit shouldn't exist. That he was a walking lie. An illusion with teeth.

"I dream of you every night," she said. "I run my fingers through your—"

"Stop."

The smile slipped from Selena's face, and the illusion ended. In her place was the monster, the gray skin and slash of a mouth. "Enough talk."

I braced myself as Kit took a step.

The earth under his feet exploded.

The ground buckled. Then came a feeling of weightlessness, and I was falling, through the earth, into the darkness beneath.

CHAPTER
THIRTY-ONE

I woke in complete and utter blackness, disoriented. I'd been running. Starlight raining down. There'd been an explosion. Kit had tripped one. And now I was... what?

I opened my eyes as wide as I could. Nothing. I reached up to touch my face, afraid I'd find that my sight had been torn away by the blast.

A voice came out of the dark. "Quinn! Are you there?"

"Ollie? I can't see. I... I think I'm..." I ran my hand over my face, looking for damage. It was wet, and I tasted the copper of my own blood, but my face felt intact.

"No, it's not just you," Ollie said. "I can't see either. June? Are you there?"

There was no answer. The silky dark lay everywhere, and it covered my head. Kit had swallowed us. We were inside his stomach. I pressed my fists against my temples and squeezed my eyes shut. No, no, that wasn't it. But the air in my lungs felt like syrup. In and out, like drawing oxygen through a coffee stirrer.

"Ollie, where are we?" I managed.

"Wait a second."

Rustling. Ollie digging in his bag. A pinprick of light pierced the ink.

Immediate relief. My lungs opened up. Ollie stood a few feet away, phone in hand. The light burned like a fire against all that nothing, the best thing I'd seen in years.

Ollie's light moved, picking up the color gray. Rock. By the time I'd taken a deep lungful of that mushroom smell, the cold seeping into my bones, it finally clicked into place, where we were. The mines.

The light slid over the rough walls, until Ollie found a dark hole—the opening to a narrow tunnel, braced with wooden beams. Another search with Ollie's pinprick glow and we found a pile of debris, stone and clumps of earth and broken prickly pear. Half of a creosote bush stuck out of the mass.

The map from Selena's great-grandfather's journal came back to me, the faded, twisted lines, a honeycomb of mine shafts and caves below Gypsum. They reached all the way out to Gram's property, right underneath Bud Pilsner's land. And Bud Pilsner, the genius he was, had placed a mine right over a weak spot.

Ollie squinted at his phone screen and his jaw clenched. "I've got fifty-six percent left."

I slipped my backpack off my shoulders and unzipped it, searching for my phone. I found it and turned it on, squinting in the bright glow. Four percent. Great.

Ollie looked over my shoulder at the screen. "Haven't I told you a thousand times to plug it in before you go to bed? I have. I know I have. And look at this. Look where we are."

"Well, forgive me, Ollie, for not knowing we'd be trapped underground today." I turned off the phone and slipped it back in the bag. Something sharp scratched across my knuckles.

I tipped the bag toward Ollie's phone light. Something white lay at the bottom. A piece of porcelain. Small flowers.

Gram's cup, shattered.

Ollie barely noticed, pacing the walls and talking about how we were going to get out, if we could dig, if we'd kill ourselves in the process. He was doing what he always did, working out the problem by running his mouth. And I sat quietly, holding a shard so hard it cut into my palm.

There were a lot of horrible things about the last week, things that should have broken me. But this...finding the pieces of the cup at the bottom of my backpack, with the empty chip bags and school reports I still hadn't had the heart to tell Ollie about...this needle finally found the right spot.

Ollie lifted a piece of rock and threw it aside, then another. "Well, come on. Dig! Unless you want to sleep here?"

"Kit could be waiting for us. The minute we pop our heads above ground—"

"He's not gonna wait. He's off eating the town!"

Ollie was right. And digging was faster than wandering through the mines with my phone at four percent.

We chipped away at the wall of destruction, lifting it piece by piece, while Ollie talked on and on. I tried to shut out the possibility of the debris wall collapsing like a Jenga tower, covering us both and crushing our bones.

Nicco's face welled up in my mind, and I swallowed down the stab of regret that came with it. And where was June? I hoped she was up above, and then I hoped she wasn't, because then Kit would already have killed her. Had Selena and the others made it to the Gun Barrel? What would Gram say to us if she were here now? *You got yourself in a real hornets' nest now, Quinn. And how are you going to get yourself out?*

The scree shifted as I pulled a rock. My stomach twisted. I put it back. My stomach didn't uncoil until the grinding slide stopped.

"Watch what you're doing!"

"Good God, Ollie, can you stop correcting me for a moment?"

"We don't have a moment."

"I think we have a lot of moments. I think we're trapped underground with no idea of where that tunnel leads. I think June is dead..." My voice broke on the last word.

Ollie's expression shifted, the anger and hard-as-stone look melting.

Before he could answer, a murmur drifted toward me. It came from inside the pile of debris, near the trunk of the creosote bush, which lay under a thick blanket of desert dust and sand. The murmur became a moan. Ollie and I turned.

And then I heard my name.

I scrambled over to the pile and brushed away some of the bits. What'd I'd mistaken for the thick trunk of a creosote bush was part of an arm.

"June!"

Ollie and I dug her out, bit by bit, afraid we'd find her cut in half, or her legs crushed. But when we finally pulled her free, coughing and choking, the only thing wrong with her was a thousand scratches and a really bad attitude.

She stood on shaky legs and examined the ceiling and the walls. "No, uh-uh. Not happening. We are not in the mines."

"Yep," Ollie said. "We've gotta dig."

She coughed, then leaned on her knees, shook her head. "There's no opening that I saw."

I eyed the pile. "And we might make the whole thing come down on us."

Ollie pointed the light up at the impenetrable ceiling, swore under his breath. "Okay, I have to admit it. You're right."

June shook her head and swore, sweat and dirt staining the back of her T-shirt. Ollie's light reached into the well of dark for three or four feet before the void ate it.

I walked into the tunnel a few steps, tried to read that darkness, like I'd read the future. But I got nothing back but terrifying possibility.

CHAPTER
THIRTY-TWO

We walked toward what we thought was north, into *nothing*. So much black. The inside of a velvet bag. The bottom of the ocean.

Ollie's tiny phone light tethered me. That and the pain of the porcelain shard, pressed into my palm. *You are real,* the shard told me. But I laughed at the shard. Liar. Nothing was real anymore.

At a T junction, Ollie pointed the light both ways, his jaw clenched.

"I think the exit's less than a mile away," he said. "That wooden barricade is so rotten we'd bust through easily. No problem." Same old Ollie, winding himself up with an unhealthy amount of optimism.

"Left," June said, her gum popping increasing—which meant she'd chosen at random.

I glanced at Ollie's screen. It had fallen to thirty-two percent.

To keep the fear down, I imagined sunshine. Tall cliffs. Ropes and harnesses. The top of the Horse Crippler. But the darkness was too strong, elbowing its way in again, blowing its sweet breath in my face. I flipped the shard of Gram's cup over and over in my palm, pressed it against my fingers, numb from the cold. Neither Ollie nor June knew about what I'd found out at the hotel. And what was the price Eva was so cagey about?

"Hey, guys? I need to tell you something."

And I told them what Eva had said, word for word.

About Bud.

About how June would have to become the lock to keep Kit inside.

I finished, and June stopped in the middle of the tunnel, became so still for a second I thought she had vanished. When her voice finally came, disembodied in the dark, it was soft, almost awed. "So, all this time, Bud was trying to save me?"

"Guess so."

I couldn't see her, but I could hear her breath catch. Then she was moving again, faster this time.

"But just because people we never met made a pact, it doesn't mean we have to do it."

Ollie and I struggled to keep up with her.

"How do we even know how to do it?" she went on, her voice taut. "You know, the thing that locks Kit away again?"

"The letter your dad left you."

June's laugh echoed in the tunnel, hollow and bitter. "Which is now..."

"Somewhere in the Alvarado, yes."

A small side tunnel appeared on the right, and Ollie shined his light down it before leading us on straight. "If Kit's smart, he's already found the letter, destroyed it."

Selena's secret needed to stay secret a little longer, just in case Kit read June's mind. Still, I didn't have it in me to lie to her. Our footfalls echoed in the dark.

"I don't want to be Mrs. Durbin," June said, her voice small in the dark.

"You won't be."

"The price. What's it gonna be?"

"You'll never find out," I said. "We'll try to find another way."

"Everyone's always wondered why Mrs. D. stayed. Whatever happened when she...paid, I think it messed her up so bad she..."

It was the shake in her voice that made Ollie turn, his light a soft glow over her. Blond hair half out of her braid, eyes red. She barely looked like herself. She'd been crying in the dark, hiding from me.

"I mean, how'd she make herself do it? She was on her way up, and suddenly she throws it all away," she said, her words snagging. "I guess the lock gives and gives until she's all hollowed out." She sniffed, swept the back of her hand over her cheeks. Then she let out a laugh. "You know what Bud always said to me? He said, *Girl, you gotta learn. You gotta learn, girl, that sometimes you get to do what you* want *to do. The rest of the time? You do what you* have *to do.*" She shook her head. "I can't breathe. Quinn, I can't breathe."

I put my hand on her back, but she shook me off, started walking again.

"I want to have a family one day," she said into the dark.

"June—"

"I want to be *free.*"

"Stop, June." I caught up with her at a jog, grabbed her arm, and brought her to a stop. "June, June, look at me."

"Do you think it'll hurt?"

I stood close, looked into her eyes to steady her. She was terrified. "You're not going to be the lock. Okay? I . . . I would have seen it at least once if you were. In the leaves. But that's not in your future. I *know* the future, okay?" I smoothed the sides of her arms.

"And I know you're lying, Quinn," she said. "This isn't something you can fix."

We fell silent. I interlaced my fingers with hers. Cousin. Sister. Best friend.

With nothing left to say, we picked our way along the tunnel. Soft footsteps, the funk of my own sweat, the scent of peppermint gum, and the dry dust of the caves—I focused on that, and followed Ollie's shining star. Would we be lost here forever?

The minutes stretched, became hours. June had gone quiet, her face pale in the phone light, her eyes wide, like a rabbit caught in a bush.

I glanced at Ollie's screen, which was dimming. He reached out for my phone, and I gave it to him, so he could use my precious four percent.

His phone chose that moment to die. Ollie and I had a terrifying two seconds of pitch black before my phone's flashlight burned to life.

"I think we're almost there," June said.

This time, I didn't believe her.

We kept walking, moving through the ink of the tunnels, gypsum dust filling my nose, my lungs. Four percent shrank to three.

I cast a net for something to hold on to. Found myself back on the Horse Crippler. Selena and me, jumping off into the sunshine, yelling all the way down.

That last thought burned like a wick as we made our way through the tunnels. And then, suddenly, my three percent dwindled to nothing, and the light disappeared.

CHAPTER
THIRTY-THREE

The blackness closed in, like a cloth over my face. It wrapped tight over my eyes, my mouth, my everything.

I stopped walking. "June?"

"Right here."

I reached out blind. She took my hand.

"Can you get us out?"

She didn't answer, but her grip tightened.

Ollie, coming close, fumbled to take my hand. "Lie to us."

"No problem. I'll have us out in a jiffy."

"Thank you."

We walked. My feet touched the ground, my hand touched June's, and my lungs pulled in air, then pushed it out. That was all that was left of me. My flesh, my bones, even my eyes, all of it was gone, swallowed up by the eternal night. It was like the inside of Kit's stomach, I thought again. I pushed that idea away and tried to bring up the image of the cliffs, the sunshine. This time it didn't work.

"Quinn," June said, "you're breaking my fingers."

"Sorry."

Five minutes in, or an hour, or ten seconds maybe—I couldn't be sure, because time had become like an elastic band, stretching and popping—I started to see things. At first, a moving line of glowing green, snaking across the dark. Then flashes of something small and white, flying at my face. I closed my eyes to it, but the images kept coming, dying down and rising up.

The soft *plink* of dripping reached me. Another mirage, this time in my ears.

No, this was real.

It was cooler, and the air moved. A draft, a breeze, which meant we'd soon be outside in the starlight! June stopped with a sharp intake of breath.

"What's wrong?" Ollie whispered.

June backtracked us around a corner. She pulled me right, then left. Flattened us back against a wall.

A voice. It drifted on moth wings. At first, I couldn't make anything out. Vowels, consonants, floating like gypsum dust in the air. Also the drip of water...And an echo...Which meant a large space nearby. A cavern maybe.

The voice grew, became a song, piercing my ears like a sick lullaby I'd heard in my dreams for a year.

This is the Dark Place. I sing it.

There was a slur to the ends of the words. A syrupy little whisper that made my skin crawl.

Kit was here.

June's fingers tightened on mine until I couldn't feel my hand. Footsteps. She pulled us farther away, but the footsteps quickened, and suddenly they were right in front of us.

"Well, hello there."

And June's touch was suddenly gone.

A scrape of shoes on the rock came from my left, the thud of a fist connecting with flesh. Ollie grunting, yelling. June telling me to run.

Then a sickening crunch. Teeth on bone.

And June screaming.

I swung a fist, my eyes wide open and blind. I hit something that felt like stone. Had I hit rock? Or had I hit Kit? Either way, I flailed uselessly into the dark, trying to reach June, to drag her away. To save her. I had to save her.

An explosive tearing reached us in the dark, and June's voice cut off. Then a hand grabbed me from behind, pulling me off-balance. I fell back. I was being dragged. My brother was dragging me.

Instinct kicked in. I struggled, trying to piece it together. June silent, my bootheels scraping over stone—and Ollie, breathing harshly in my ear, dragging me away from that terrible, terrible sound.

A warm breath in my ear, then a low whisper. "We can't help her."

"Let me go!"

"She's already gone, Quinn."

"We can't leave her!"

"We have to go. Now."

Rough hands turned me, and then my legs were moving. Away from June. Away from the one person I never had to pretend with, ever. *Go back!* a voice in my head screamed. *Go back for her!* But I wasn't listening. And I hated myself.

We left her there and we ran. Hurtled into nothing, hands out.

Gone. June was gone.

My feet moved to my heartbeat, the pounding in my head. *I'm sorry, June. God, I'm sorry, I'm sorry. I'm sorry.*

One second the ground was there, and then it wasn't. For a bright moment, I saw a flash of the cliffs, the memory of Selena and me falling into sunshine. I thought I saw me dying.

Two seconds later we hit the ground below. A short drop, and a knife pain to my ankle. Then we were up, moving in the dark again. And selfishly, I wasn't thinking about June anymore—just myself.

My life was likely over. That thought spun slowly. Round and round. Life was over. Done. All my firsts complete. Maybe I would see June soon. And Bud. And Gram.

Then I heard another voice rising. This time it wasn't Ollie, or Gram, or Kit. This was all me.

You're not done yet.

Run. Fight!

Then I was dragging Ollie after *me,* my ankle white-hot with pain even as I ran. I turned right, then left, feeling along the walls.

Find a way out!

I imagined things. Veins of light, bleeding on the canvas of black. A floating journal, the one Selena had showed me, its pages flapping. A mouth, opening to swallow me, teeth closing around my face. Then came a fog of memories: Gram's clock, ticking in the empty living room. June and Selena and I, standing in front of the Alvarado, debating if we should go in. June's face, just before she left Eva Durbin's room. The Big Dipper, hanging low, its bright pinpoints bleeding and shuddering.

Minutes passed, stretched, became what felt like hours, as we pounded through the dark. The cold, damp smell of the cave faded. The familiar scent of dust took its place.

Somewhere up ahead, there was light. Faint, and distant, but real. The world around me grayed.

"We're almost out!" Ollie's breathing was harsh. But the tunnel ended, and we stumbled out into the open air.

Starlight. Immense and breathtaking. And the waxing moon, so bright it was like God had sliced a hole in the dark with the tip of a knife. I'd lived in Gypsum all my life, but it had *never* been this beautiful.

We limped west until we had at least a mile of rocks and hills between us and the mine's opening. I didn't realize Ollie's hand had left mine until the warmth was gone.

He sank to the ground, head in hands. I sat beside him, numb. Out of habit, I looked for June. For a split second, I truly expected to see her, her perfect vision picking up every detail of the desert. She would turn to us, her eyes lit up with mischief, and make a joke. Point the way over the hills. Tell us which way to go.

But June was dead.

And now it would fall to Ollie to be the lock. My brother.

I lay back on the hard ground, shame washing over me. She'd been dead less than an hour, and already all I could think about was myself. How this affected *me*.

A voice rose from the starlight, and for a second it sounded like her. *Marco.*

I spoke into the darkness. "Polo."

Our childhood game.

Ollie shifted next to me. "What?"

"Nothing, Ollie. I didn't say anything."

•————————•

To the right, the road to Gypsum snaked into the dark. A sign on the roadside gleamed in the moonlight.

Welcome to Gypsum
Population 1,021

We were just outside of town. Light flared up on the horizon. Sunrise? I blinked at it and rubbed my chest, confused. The sun rose in the west, but the orange glow lit the east.

"What the hell?"

Maybe Kit had changed reality, and everything was upside down now. Was he that powerful?

Ollie gave me a loaded look. Then without a word, we walked toward the glow in the east as it flickered. A stone settled in my chest. That wasn't the sun. Gypsum was burning.

I couldn't look at it, despair pressing down on me. Instead I blinked up at what was left of the Milky Way.

A highway to nowhere in particular. Gram's voice came from far away, from a corner of my mind. Not a memory. A message. *The night sky, she's like the inside of a cup. Makes you feel both big and small at the same time.*

My breath clouded the air, and the stars trembled like fireflies.

Rearranged themselves like tea leaves spinning in water. The white porcelain turned black. The dark leaves bright pinpricks…

And then Tripp's voice came next, telling me the tea leaves were just a crutch.

As Ollie walked beside me on the long road to town, I dug the shard of porcelain out of my pocket. The white gleamed in the pale light. I turned it, felt the edges. Selena's words came back to me too. *Maybe we can figure it out, what they did, back when this all happened.*

That was it.

The sky suddenly seemed the distant bottom of a pond, a well of beauty, a well of knowledge—all I had to do was reach out and dip a bucket into its depths, drink of that eternal water. I knew it. As sure as I knew Gram was gone and Selena wasn't, as sure as I knew I loved them both, I knew I could do this. And maybe, just maybe, the answers I needed lay on the other side. In the Dark Place.

You have to go farther. Cross over. You'll find it there, what you need to make this all stop. This voice sounded like June.

I stopped walking. Dropped the shard of porcelain into the dust. It barely made a sound. Ollie glanced back at me and turned, his expression puzzled.

Up above, the stars shimmered, and I searched for patterns. The serpent. A letter *N*. I imagined the sky god sitting up by the moon, sipping from the universe, tasting the sweet blackness there. And the darkness was sweet, but this time it wasn't a trap.

"Turn the cup," I murmured, my breath fogging the air. "Finish the last bit. Place it upside down on the saucer and put your hands over it."

Why? the sky god asked.

"I don't know," I murmured to the sky. "It's how my gram taught me."

Ollie walked back to me and grabbed me by the shoulders, searching my face with his worried gaze, his mouth forming words I couldn't hear. Then he followed my gaze up.

My fear was gone. Everything, my whole life, just a dream. *The letter* T. *A flying bird, then another, its wing folded, caught in a bush. A five-fingered hand. The insides of a dead sun. The outline of a seedpod...*

Ollie's breathing beside me ceased. My ears were stuffed with cotton. The stars faded, one by one, like Christmas lights popping out. Until they were gone.

I was in the Dark Place.

I stepped forward on the ground that wasn't there, breathed the air that wasn't air, until my fingertips brushed the sticky web. Took another step, sinking my arms to the elbows. Knowledge flowed over me, a cold, bright river current. Images came, futures of people I didn't know, mixed with the ones I did.

One more step. Excitement swelled in me, and fear. The web brushed my face.

More images. A skyscraper crumbling. A tide rising. The desire to know. I leaned forward and the web pulled against my skin, my eyelashes. I *would* finally know. Not just how to save Ollie and Selena, but all of Gypsum, everyone. And I wouldn't know just that.

I would know everything.

I moved through the web into the flow of the current, hanging on to the fibers of the web with one hand, a foot planted on the other side just in case I changed my mind. An ecstasy of knowledge swirled around me, filled my chest until it was about to burst open like a flower. One deep breath.

I pulled my hand free and stepped through, plunging into the icy water on the other side.

CHAPTER
THIRTY-FOUR

Vertigo squeezed my stomach like a fist. There was no ground. I had balled myself up like a child, my knees tucked into my chest. I was floating, spinning slowly.

How could there be this much nothing? Vast, like an ocean.

This was a mistake. I'd made a terrible, terrible mistake, but I would *not* die here, floating like a bit of seaweed in this sea of nothing and everything. I stretched my arms and legs into sticky blackness; yelled; tried to find solid footing. Punched at nothing.

My hand connected with soft flesh.

A weak grunt of surprise followed. I drew back, reached out again. Warm and solid. Cloth. I felt along the fibers to find a beefy shoulder under denim. The smell of cheap drugstore soap and stress sweat.

"Oh no."

"Quinn?" Ollie's voice.

"Ollie, I'm so sorry." I gripped him tighter.

"Where are we?"

I didn't want to tell him. That he was right. That I was dangerous. That I had always been dangerous, and now I'd killed us both. All I could manage was a simple statement of fact. "We're...in the Dark Place."

He pulled away. Next came a flurry of swearing. I found it oddly comforting. "I can't...where's the floor?!"

"I think we're lost."

He spun into me. I felt him stretching out his limbs, looking for ground.

"It's no use."

When I'd looked up into the stars, I'd had my hand on his arm. A connection. "I never thought it could happen this way, that I could bring someone with me." But an explanation didn't seem like enough right now, to make up for what I'd done. "I'm so sorry. This is all my fault."

He stopped struggling. Then a sigh. "No, it's not."

"Of course it is."

"You're not the only one who can *see* things, Quinn. Gram told me not to do it anymore, so I stopped."

"What in the world are you talking about?"

"You really think I was born into this family and I'm nothing but a walking meat sack?"

We floated next to each other, his vise grip on my shirt.

"Sometimes," he started, "when I'm asleep, I do this thing. Slip in and out of dreams. I used to slip into A.J.'s all the time, without meaning to. It's why we broke up. I mean, the *real* reason, not that nonsense about me being shiftless, which I am, but whatever."

"You're talking about astral projection, aren't you?"

"Yeah." He didn't seem happy about it. "So, like I said, this ain't your fault. It's just…" Another sigh. "An O'Brien thing. It's *our* fault. The two of us, staring at the stars side by side, half conscious. I'm thinking we just… slipped right over."

Time passed, maybe an hour, maybe a day, as I blinked into the dark and let myself feel the weight of what we'd done.

"Apparently, the universe can't handle two O'Briens." Ollie drew me into a rough side hug. It broke me in half.

When I opened my eyes again, in the distance, I saw light. Two pinpricks, like stars. They grew, crossing paths and switching places.

"Ollie, do you see that?"

The lights drew closer. And they weren't stars. More like spook lights, the ones I'd only heard about, seen drawings of in tourist guides and old books of fairy tales.

"You're not hallucinating. I see them too."

They grew, closing in, dancing there in the sea of black. They grew to the size of eyes, then stopped. One rose and moved back and forth, like someone stood far away with a lantern, lifting it high to signal to me.

I reached my legs down again, and this time I found ground. As soon as my soles touched, the familiar swell of gravity pulled at my bones. Next to me Ollie mumbled a curse in relief. We were standing.

"Maybe that's a safe haven," I said.

"Maybe it's the entrance to hell... but I'm not going to spend the rest of my life spinning nowhere in particular." His thick hand fumbled into mine again, and he squeezed.

"C'mon then," I said. "No use staying here, crying in the dark."

We walked toward the lights.

We walked for a long time, Ollie's warm callused palm my only anchor, and the lights my only goal. Sweat built on my back, soaking my T-shirt. But my ankle felt better. Tender, but not horrible. Like it had been healing for weeks. And the light, it waited patiently for us, hovering in the distance.

"Do you feel that?" Ollie asked.

I reached my free hand to the side. A feathery rasp on my fingertips—I was walking in a wheat field, palms touching the soft tops of the stalks. But they weren't really grain. They were little bits of the future, fragments and half-finished sentences. Each one held a whisper.

"I can hear them," Ollie said, his voice filled with wonder.

The whispers. Deaths and births and the voices of people on cliffs, yelling up at the sky as they plummeted toward the water. A swelling of joy, pain, then nothing—and a hundred other whispers rising up, clamoring to be heard. A flash came, followed by a series of images so bright they hurt. A city cutting into the sky, broken-backed, a steel mountain. A beach, stretched out like a pale arm. A blue sea. The inside of an airplane, the cockpit crusted with buttons.

The future grew around us, and I soaked it in. It lay in multitudes, each staff of wheat a possibility, a human life. I reached my fingers deeper into the stalks of wheat, a rush of pleasure flowing up my arm.

Then, in the kaleidoscope of images, I saw Kit.

A star, plummeting from the sky, hitting the ground, tearing a gash in the earth. Then Kit, lying on his side, gray and dotted with starlight, his claws curled up at his chest, eyes closed. Two monstrous shapes settled next to him, shadows enormous and fierce.

They struck fear in me so deep I couldn't shake it. I turned away before I could make them out, more terrified than I'd ever been. Just looking at them was a sin, and I would burn for it.

When I opened my eyes again, a door rose up, covered in writing—the one that led into the small cave under Gypsum. That monstrous shadow hand shut it. The pounding on the other side, the voice crying out...all that whimpering was Kit.

My skull, it suddenly felt ready to crack from the inside out, but I didn't want to stop. I reached my hands deeper into the stalks of wheat.

Kit, lying in the dark. All around him was the drip of the springs, the *plink* of the water from the ceiling landing on his gray skin, then snaking its way to pool beneath him. Years passed as the rock above him grew, slowly sharpening to a point. Stalactites. He lay unmoving, the pool growing, rivulets running over the limestone to join and drain away, become one, reaching fingers out into the caves, bubbling through to make springs.

Kit, his body and blood. His sweat. In the water.

In all of us.

It was why the water could heal. Why it led to long life. The water wasn't enriched by minerals, or sediment. It was *Kit*.

That was why I could see the future. Why June could see in the dark. And God, what else had that water done, over the years? I shivered in the dark. I could never, ever get away from him. Kit was a part of who I was.

Kit's voice rose in my head.

In a way, we're family.

Another voice came, echoing down a long tunnel. Saying my name. Telling me to stop. But the knowledge flowing through me, it was a river, rapids rushing through my head. It was enough for me to forget myself, to become something else. Something bigger—

Then, a slap across my cheek. *"Snap out of it!"*

I brought my arm to my chest, disoriented. "What happened?"

Ollie leaned close. "You wandered away from me, mumbling. Like you were possessed or something!"

I blinked in the darkness. The lights, the images, all gone. The spook lights lay in the distance, waiting. If Ollie hadn't pulled me back...

"It's bad enough you've got me stuck in a netherworld, but would you *please,* for the love of God..." Ollie grabbed the back of my shirt and started to drag me on, toward the lights.

I walked, keeping my fingers a few inches above the wheat stalks, trying to make sense of what I'd seen. Time stretched as we made our way through. Hours, years, millennia. Or maybe it was just a few breaths.

Family. Kit and me. Me and Ollie. All of Gypsum.

Tied together not by blood, but by water.

Gram's voice came back to me, in the Gun Barrel Trailer Park. *This well will never run dry. We're blessed, blessed with the land that God's given us.* Then her face turning to me, her hand still on the cup she'd read for Bill Winter, her warm smile lighting up the room. *You, my sweet boy, are a wonder.*

Everything I could do, my second sight, my ability to go into the Dark Place, all that came from Kit.

The wheat field ended before I could wrap my head around what it meant. And there they were. Two fist-sized spheres of light, hovering.

Ollie's voice drifted out of the dark. "Okay, now what?"

I reached toward them, then thought better of it. They glowed like tiny suns. The two lights moved toward each other, and switched places, like they were playing a game.

Gram called them will-o'-the-wisp. She told stories about the lights growing like flowers in bogs back in the old country, floating like fairies into the paths of travelers to lead them astray. Was that us? Being led astray?

The lights spread apart and grew. The smell of desert air wafted to us, and dust, drawn on a cool wind. More gravity, pulling us down. And the ground beneath us became rough and uneven.

The spook lights expanded, spread farther apart, intensified.

The growl of a car engine split the air.

Headlights.

With a rush of air, they grew until they blinded me. I pulled Ollie to the side just as the car came to a stop.

CHAPTER
THIRTY-FIVE

O llie and I scrambled back, just outside the headlights' glow. A car. Here. Was I dreaming? Around me grew the familiar landscape of the desert. The taste of grit—plus blood from biting my lip in the fall—said this was real enough.

The car was a dark shape, idling, a pool of light in front of the grille. Four car doors opened. I slid back a few inches into the brush.

The grind of shoes on the scree. The smell of cactus flower. The stars, quiet and shimmering through the scattered clouds in a swath of light. It all felt so real, like we were back in reality. Maybe we were.

The passengers rounded the car and stepped into the light.

All four of them were in thirties getups. One was a miner, in rough gray clothes. Two were men dressed like they were heading to a gala event—the taller one opened a silver case and slipped a cigarette between his lips, his tuxedo crisp and his hair slicked back, while the shorter one stood disheveled, his tuxedo tie dangling. The last, a woman, had her back to me, her hair twisted up like Eva's. I squinted. It wasn't her.

The disheveled man pulled his tie off and dropped it on the desert floor, like he wasn't sure why he'd come. The light caught his face, and I almost gasped.

I gripped Ollie's forearm. He turned to me and mouthed a word. *What?*

I leaned close to his ear. "That's Liam O'Brien."

Liam. Our great-grandfather, at Ollie's age, his face unlined and filled with determination.

The other man in the tuxedo glanced at Liam, then set his eyes in the distance and brought the cigarette to his mouth. The tip glowed orange, punching a hole in the dark. He exhaled loudly. "You're serious."

"Of course I'm serious," Liam replied.

The woman shifted, and the light illuminated her face. This time it was Ollie's turn to nudge me, but he didn't have to. I'd recognize her anywhere. I'd seen her picture on Selena's wall: her great-grandmother Camilla. And the other man, the one who was dressed as a miner, I'd seen that face a thousand times on Bud Pilsner's wall. Mattias Pilsner.

I leaned close to Ollie. "Is this a memory? Or is this really the past?"

The four of them stood watching something in the distance. I squinted. It was a cliff, one I hadn't seen anywhere near Gypsum, but the shape of it reminded me of a picture I'd seen once, on the wall of the Alvarado.

They watched it like it was about to get up and lumber away or open its rocky arms and reach for them.

Ollie leaned close. "Can they see us?"

"I don't know. Maybe it's just a memory."

The man with the slicked-back hair held up his hands, forming a square with his fingers. "This would be a great shot. Right here."

"Would you give it a rest?" Liam said.

"So we have to climb *that*," Camilla said.

"That's what Eva said," Liam said. "What we need grows at the very top."

The slick man in the tuxedo stuck his hands in his pockets and rocked back on his heels. "Good luck with that."

"We're not doing this without you."

The man took another drag of his cigarette, then exhaled. "I've never climbed anything except a set of stairs."

"It's either the cliff or the cave, Fritz. If you ask me, I'll take the cliff."

The familiar name was the last piece I needed. Fritz Von Sturnberg. The director! The one who went missing, then became a part of Alvarado history.

This had to be 1933. It was a clear night. And the stars. The stars... only a patchwork left, like moths had eaten away at the blanket of the sky.

"Look up," I whispered.

"Yeah, I see," Ollie hissed back.

I pieced it together as their conversation murmured in the dark. "Ollie, I think they're about to shut Kit away in the safe."

Fritz's voice rose above the others, angry. "How do we even know what to look for?"

Liam rubbed his palms together, slowly, like he was trying to remove a layer of soot. A familiar gesture, one I'd seen Gram make a thousand times. "Eva said we'd know it when we see it."

Mattias glanced at Camilla. "We should have brought Hector with us. He's a good climber."

"*I'm* a good climber," Camilla said. "And Hector's done enough."

Liam watched the cliff face. "Eva's in love with Kit."

"Yeah, so?" Camilla said.

"*So* maybe she's not being straight with us. Trying to protect him."

Camilla huffed a laugh. "I think she's made her choice. Come on. Let's get this done."

The men walked toward us, Mattias mumbling something about doubting Eva had the courage to "slip Kit a mickey," whatever that was, then Fritz laughing about how they'd be shocked at what a "girl like Eva" would do to save herself. Camilla made a disgusted sound in her throat as they moved past us, and we turned to watch them approach a cliff. It loomed like a battleship, taller than the Horse Crippler, taller than anything I'd ever climbed, the night sky above peppered with what was left of the stars.

And then a gasp, from Camilla. I turned to find her looking in my direction. She stepped closer, her shoes crunching on dry earth. Not looking through me. She could *see* me.

"Liam?" she said over her shoulder.

"What?" He turned, a silhouette.

"I see them."

"See what?"

"The spook lights."

And then she pointed right at us.

Before he could answer, the ground rumbled.

The cliff shook as the world tipped and the ground bucked. The woman stumbled, and Liam went to her, along with the miner, while Fritz stayed where he was, crouching, his hands over his head. A piece of the cliff sheared off and tumbled to the desert floor. I raised my arms against the rain of rock dust.

The world trembled and broke apart. Then what I saw, a hundred yards away, small in the cactus shadow, made me hold my breath.

A figure, arms stretched up to the starlight. Swaying and singing. His voice floated over the desert.

This is the Dark Place. This is the Dark Place. I sing it.

The ground rent with a terrible groan, as if the earth were the skin of some great beast. Kit's song rose up.

The Dark Place.

—————•—————

Kit's skin sparkled with patterns and pinpricks of light. Dots. Illuminations. Constellations.

That was what was *really* consuming Gypsum, taking out pieces of it, bit by bit. The Dark Place, leaking out of him like a dying star.

The earth opened wider. The cliff cracked, listing like a ship. I scrambled back, sprinted out into the desert, looking over my shoulder for one panicked second. The entire bluff of rock sank, tilted, then hit the desert floor with a thunderclap.

I stopped running, but not by choice.

I was stuck, like a fly in a web. Next to me Ollie struggled, suspended midstride, his eyes filled with panic. A pull on my insides began, like the dip in a roller coaster.

The rock that had crumbled to the desert floor rose, lifted by invisible hands. The rumble continued, but this time, the mountain grew from the earth. Shards of rock that had broken off flew up to rejoin their mother.

In the distance, Kit lowered his arms and vanished. I turned to the muddled voices behind me and found the four people moving backward, as if some enormous sky god had hit the reverse button on the world. They stepped back into the car, and it backed out, a billowing cloud disappearing as it went. The lights shrank, until they were gone.

The world went quiet and dark. Undisturbed. Light, on the western horizon, rising instead of sinking, time moving backward, until we stood, mouths gaping, blinking in the bright light of morning.

The force that had held us in place released us suddenly, and Ollie and I fell to the ground. We stood, both of us turning in a circle, trying to get our bearings. Blue sky. Sunlight lighting up the endless swell of tans and greens rolling away from us.

"Are we . . . are we home?" Ollie asked.

I turned in a circle. We were in the middle of a full cactus bloom. "No, look, it's spring."

My gaze went up, to the top of the cliff that towered above the desert. "This is what the lights wanted us to know. What we need is there, at the top of that cliff."

We both turned to the cliff that shouldn't exist anywhere in Gypsum, that I'd seen only in pictures. A tough route up the west side, zigzagging past scallops of smooth stone. Then overhangs, one after the other, to test all your upper-body strength. I'd never climbed anything like it, and it would take everything that I had to make the summit.

And neither of us had decent shoes. More importantly, neither of us had a rope.

CHAPTER
THIRTY-SIX

*A*n *act of faith. Faith in yourself. Faith that your equipment and your muscles and your will can work together to defy gravity, push you higher.*

I pressed my cheek against the cool rock, halfway up. Today, I would listen to Ollie's voice. I wouldn't let gravity do its work. Today I wouldn't let pain or my own pessimism distract me. I would climb. Put my fingers in any hold I could find and keep going.

Faith in your equipment. Today that was arms and legs. Sinew. Breath. *Faith in yourself.*

I hooked in a shallow hold with my fingertips, then shifted my weight, right arm trembling. Found a small ledge and rested. Above me stretched at least twenty feet of slim holds, few good places for my feet, which were already raw from the rough sandstone.

I took a breath, looking down the two stories my brother and I had already climbed. For hundreds of miles the desert stretched in bloom. Pale pink and trembling in the sunlight. Spring rains. The rare time when the desert blossomed, and it existed, here in the Dark Place, a section of time traced out by some sky god with a huge knife, then placed in this moment.

A sudden swell of vertigo hit me, and I pressed myself flat against the rock face until my cheek was numb with cold, then reminded myself what I was doing. Why I was doing it. Liam's words followed me up the cliff. *What we need grows at the very top.* I would find a way to make Kit eat it. After all, he ate everything he saw, so maybe he wouldn't even notice. If worst came to worst, he might just eat me while I was holding it.

Above me, Ollie's voice tumbled down, strained through labored breaths. "C'mon. We don't have all day."

Those four, the ones who'd driven out here in the middle of the night, had to a plan to stop Kit, and they'd come here to carry it out. And we could finally finish what they started.

I opened my eyes.

Don't look down. Don't think about your harness, back at your house, ninety years in the future. Or rope. Or good shoes.

Tipping my head back, I eyed the overhang jutting out twenty feet above me, its sandpaper undersides as rough as a cat's tongue. Ollie's legs dangled over the edge, disappearing as he pulled himself over.

A hold lay one foot above my right hand. I'd have to put all my weight on my right foot to do it, let the left side of my body untether from the rock, then balance for a split second and reach.

One breath and I released my left hand. One push, and a massive heave, and just as my right hand caught, my right foot slipped. I scrambled for a new hold, my heart leaping into my throat.

Ten more back-agonizing minutes, stretched as thin as piano wire, and I reached the first overhang. Gathering myself, I got a good hold and let my feet drift off the cliff face, then pulled myself up and over, arms shaking. The rock scraped skin, gouged through my T-shirt, and I kept going.

When it was over, I leaned against the rock, panting and shaking, then tilted my head to eye the next overhang.

From that point, the climb took over every part of me. I was flesh and sinew and effort. Breath. My body shifting an inch right, then left, pushing up an inch, muscles trembling. Ollie faded, becoming only a crumble of rock or a distant groan as he found his way. Even the destination fell away until I lived only in that handhold. Climb. Live. My heartbeat pounded in my chest like a pickaxe.

A cry above, and a small tumble of rock hit my head. I choked on the dust. Above, Ollie's foot disappeared as he slid over another overhang. A crack. My mouth went dry.

Then the rock above me gave way.

I pressed my cheek against the cliff face, eyes closed, the *whoosh* of stone, a breath of wind, plummeting past my ear, a delicate scrape on the edge on my bare foot. An inch closer, and it would have sent me flying off the wall.

I dangled by one hand. The ground below pulled on me. Bare feet scrabbling across the wall, I found my footing, and I could breathe again. Above me, where the rock had broken off, the path went smooth. Just above it, Ollie met my eye, his face stricken. My route had just crumbled. No one, not even an Olympic climber, could make that section of cliff.

I gave in to the urge to look down only once. Ten stories now. The desert flowed out, an ocean of spines and sand and blooming flower. Glorious and terrifying. My stomach swooped, tipped over the apex of a roller coaster. The distance from my spot on the cliff to the ground stretched like taffy. I shut my eyes and turned back to the wall.

If I fell, this world would not save me from myself.

I reached sideways, crab-crawling to a section of cliff with better holds. Ignored the thirst scratching at my throat. The pads of my feet, unused to climbing without leather, felt raw. Small cuts widened, until the sting of rock was the only thing I could think about. How I had to press myself into the pain, to keep from plummeting off the face.

I'm not sure how I made it up the last thirty feet to the summit. My hands slick with sweat, legs shaking. I moved from shallow hold to overhang, to another rough zigzagging path up toward safety. The image that helped me find the last ounce of strength was Selena's hand in mine, and the look of joy in her eyes just before we jumped off that cliff.

Suddenly, the top was only a foot away, the bright blue sky a beautiful stripe just above me. Ollie's face, and his voice. "I have faith in you. C'mon, you can do this."

Ollie helped me the last foot, his rough hand on my arm. I crested the edge and rolled over onto my back. The sunlight felt like rain.

Ollie knelt beside me, his T-shirt soaked with sweat, a cut on his forehead trailing blood. "Well, that was fun."

I laughed. "Thanks for dumping a ton of rock in my path."

"You're welcome." He squinted into the sunlight, scanning the summit's rocky landscape, which was dotted with cactus and blooms. "You ready to do this?"

I stood on shaky legs and wandered through the jagged stone and scrub. I'd never been this high above Gypsum before, thirty stories up. South, the Rio Grande snaked across the horizon, and to the northwest, the pale, bare Chinati Mountains. Gypsum lay below, or at least the Gypsum of ninety years ago, along with the smoking ruins of buildings in the outskirts.

Eva's voice came: *Gypsum used to be a much bigger place.* I eyed the destruction. If they hadn't shut him away when they did . . . whatever the spook lights wanted us to find, we'd better find it now.

I picked my way through cacti, their blooms pink and red, colors vibrant. We walked among them, searching.

The yellow petals sprouting from a prickly pear, the pink flowers of the lace cactus. The purple blooms of a horse crippler. The desert lit up with its splendor, just like it always was after the spring rains, when Gram and I picked the fat blossoms, the cool morning air crisp on my tongue. And when I opened my hands to show her what I found, she'd put her warm palm on my shoulder and tell me I done good.

Everything was the ordinary kind of beautiful, though, plants I'd seen every year of my life. Ollie called me over to look at the violet flower on a clump of hedgehog cactus. It was enormous and perfect, but again, it didn't feel right.

Then a patch of shadow caught my eye. Not a cactus. A plant, small with pale silver leaves. Small white flowers grew from its center. Easy to miss.

And all my years gathering with Gram, I had never seen this. "Ollie, I think I found it."

Ollie came to stand beside me, eyeing the small plant. "You sure? It doesn't look like much."

He started to reach for it, and out of instinct, I held up a hand. Moved in front of him. A feeling. Maybe even a premonition.

"Give me a second," I said.

I crouched, hesitant to touch its leaves. As my shadow passed over the plant, the small flowers opened at my touch. A sharp scent reached me. Tangy and sweet. Familiar, like the smell of the Alvarado at night.

A puff of pollen released. I coughed and my eyes stung. As I knelt there, the blue sky picked up speed, like the world had been spun like a top.

I coughed again, Ollie's hand on my back, his panicked voice in my ears. Dust maybe. And a tickling sensation, there in my chest.

I coughed again, wondering if I should pluck it up by the roots, fold it in some cloth, tuck it away. And how would we even climb down? Weakness spread through me, helplessness.

"Quinn! What's wrong?"

I rubbed the spot above my breastbone. A spike of pain swelled, then faded, then swelled again. "I don't know."

At my next cough, I realized it wasn't the dust. It was the pollen. In my lungs.

Overhead, the clouds blurred, became streaks of light. Ollie gripped my arm as I coughed. My lungs itching, something clawing. His voice came at me down a long tunnel. The ground melted.

This is the Dark Place, a voice said to me. *The Dark Place. Sing it with me.*

The sky darkened until stars appeared, spinning and whirling. I squeezed my eyes shut, the sickening feeling of the roller coaster swinging through me, and when I opened them again, everything had gone still.

Beside me lay Ollie. Above, the night sky, around me silhouettes. I recognized voices. Selena's. A.J.'s and Tripp's. All of them leaning over us like spirits, come to take us home.

We were all dead. Had to be. Then I caught sight of a familiar sign, a quarter mile away, pointing to town.

Welcome to Gypsum
Population 1,021

The smell of smoke filled the desert, and the sharp pain of my ankle said we were out of the Dark Place. Empty-handed.

A swell of bitter rage filled me. I'd had it. Growing in the rocks only a foot away. But I'd hesitated, and we'd been ripped away, thrown back into the real world with nothing to show for it.

I turned my head to see if Ollie was okay, only to find A.J. with her arms around him, her face buried in his neck. Ollie wrapped his arms around her, murmuring something into her neck.

A bright light flashed in my eyes. Selena, peeling back my eyelids and shining her penlight.

I coughed, batting her hand away. "What on earth are you doing?"

"You're okay!"

"Yep," I said, coughing again, smoke from Gypsum burning my lungs. The way Selena and Tripp were acting, I'd just come back from the dead.

Selena helped me sit up. Tripp examined my leg.

"How did you find us?" I managed.

"June. She wandered out of the mines, and we were driving the roads, looking for any trace of you and…" She went on, but I couldn't focus, because breathing had become difficult.

"That wasn't June," I tried to say, words barely making it past my throat.

Selena leaned closer to my face. "Ollie, something's wrong. He's turning blue."

The tickle turned into a sharp pain. I clawed at my shirt.

Ollie untangled himself from A.J., and his shadow loomed over me. But all I could think about was the pain in the center of my chest. I pushed his hands aside, scrabbling at my clothes, tearing apart my shirt until I reached bare skin.

My vision blurred, until the moon hanging above my chest became a spinning disk of light, the edge sharp enough to cut.

Ollie knelt next to me. I watched my skin swell, below my breastbone, something pushing its way through my skin.

A burst of agony. A tearing, and I bucked as a single sprout pushed through my chest. I gasped, trying to scream. A trickle of a moan came, a wheeze, as the tendril became a shoot, thickened into a stem.

Somewhere, as if coming down a dark tunnel, came the voice of Eva Durbin.

The price.

Blood streamed, hot and warm, down my sides, and the others knelt around me, panicked and helpless.

I lay there on the desert floor, trembling under the watchful gaze of the stars, the stem unfurled into a perfect silver leaf, and another, sprouting from my chest.

CHAPTER
THIRTY-SEVEN
Kit

*T*his is the Dark Place, I sing it.

I walked down Main Street, the night sky pouring into me, making me bigger, stronger. All around me, a riot of flame. Acrid smoke. A wave of heat. The night air bursting with shouts, fire trucks arriving, sirens blaring.

I never wanted this.

Shadows darted against the orange glow, and I moved past them, blending in, looking like one of them. The shadows became people, trying to put out a blaze that had taken half of the courthouse.

I could feel it, the need to raise my arms to the sky and sway and dig in that gaping hole in the universe for more. Always more. My skin glistened with points of light, mica chips in a riverbed. My disguise flickered, and a tumble of voices and screams and darkness erupted around me, like some crowded corner of hell.

Yes, fear me. I don't blame you.

Tonight, I am a monster. And look at what I've done to you.

The ground bucked. A crack widened. In front of the courthouse, the Christmas tree tipped, its string of lights popping, and tumbled into the darkness.

Merry Christmas, Gypsum. And Happy New Year.

Chunks of concrete flew up and toward me, sinking into my center. Somehow, I'd broken the water main. One deep breath, and somehow it had broken. Now small figures moved about, trying to douse the flames with buckets.

A drop of rain on a fire. The crowd parted, and a man came toward me, against the flow of traffic, brandishing a shotgun. It was torn from his grasp and flew into the maelstrom; then he flew off his feet, toward the hideous black hole I had become. Another drop of rain, but still the fire inside me raged.

Another body flew into me, and I wanted to shut my eyes and forget. Maybe it wasn't really me, doing this. I could pretend. Light up the movie screen in my mind and sink into a fantasy. But all I could feel was that endless well of nothing.

The world lit up with panicked voices as parts of the earth tore away. A man at the edge of the destruction pointed a camera at me. Let him. Let him record it all and put it out in the world, the cry of the earth tearing and the fire's tongues eating what was left of it.

The smell of the caves wafted up from below, mixing with the dust. And then, just when I was about to finish them all...

Sunrise.

My weak time. It spilled over the horizon like molten rock, stretching its fingers into corners and lighting up all the destruction I'd caused.

I sat on the steps of a building that was no longer there—the hat shop? The police station?—as the smoke drifted around me. The night died out like an ember.

I'd done this. A surge of regret moved through me. Eva. Would I tell her what I'd done? Would she forgive me? It wasn't like I could stop. And hadn't I helped Quinn, and Ollie? I'd relented. I'd forgiven.

For now.

I got up and walked toward the edge of town, toward the Alvarado. Please, just one more day here before it all ended, before the space inside me begged for the rest. Maybe I just had to try harder. Wasn't that what they used to tell me, before they left me here? When they were still trying to train me up?

Willpower. Just try. Can you just try, little one?

One more day with Eva. Hold her hand. Maybe she'd let me into that place in her mind, like she used to when she first locked me away. Let me sit on her couch and smoke her cigarettes and pretend. If I couldn't help myself, if I failed, I would save her for last, spend as much time with her as I could before the whole world went out.

No one stirred on the streets, but miles away, cars hummed on the freeway. A large truck. Probably another fire truck from Alpine, or maybe El Paso, and police, and the press, all coming here to see the destruction and stop it. As if they could.

I'd made it to the edge of town when the whisper began. *Kit, can you hear me?*

I stopped in the middle of the street. Checked behind me. I was alone. *Kit.*

It was coming from inside my own head. And I was almost certain it was Quinn O'Brien.

"Well, this is new."

I followed the voice, which spoke to me in whispers, passing a few frightened people clinging to the shadows of the few remaining buildings, the man with the camera watching and recording.

The Gypsum Lights Diner.

Through the windows, the empty tables were visible, the long bar with the stools and the grill. The doors to the bathrooms at the back.

There in the middle sat Quinn O'Brien, as calm as could be, with two cups and a white porcelain teapot.

He motioned me in, his expression unreadable. As I pushed through the door, I realized that his face wasn't the only thing that I couldn't read. His mind was now walled off. I probed his thoughts and found nothing but a thousand locks, keeping me out.

I hesitated, my hand on the knob. Something felt off. But there he was, with that strange expression, egging me on.

I could leave. Or finish him. And then...

And then what? There would be tomorrow, then the void. The loneliness so deep, it tore me apart with wanting. What could it hurt, to talk to him one last time? I was wrong about Quinn being hard to forgive. I could forgive a lot, considering.

When I entered, the Christmas bells on the door jingled. The place smelled clean, like a knife's edge. In the back booth sat Quinn's brother, Ollie, and Quinn's strange friend, Tripp. They stared at me with wide frightened eyes. It had been much better when they didn't know what I was.

I pushed inside their thoughts, but it was a confused mass of fear. They were grieving June. But in all that, I caught the edge of another thought, one they were trying to hide. Worry, for Selena, but I couldn't suss out why. Quinn hadn't told them what he was doing here.

Quinn nodded to them. They stood and left through the back door, moving out into the alley beyond. Ollie was last, looking over his shoulder at Quinn like he'd never see him again.

Quinn sat calmly, both hands resting on the table, jacket open, a blood-soaked bandage on his chest. His face was pale, like he'd been through hell and more. He gestured to the chair across from him. "Have a seat," he said, his voice hoarse.

"Why would I have a seat?"

"Because you miss me."

I glanced over my shoulder at the empty street. A rumble of a truck rolled past, the fire truck from El Paso, plus two police cars. They kept going, and the rumble died.

I sat. "What kind of pie did Macie make today?"

"She left town. With Enrique, I hope. If you didn't eat him, that is. But there's some apple left over from two days ago." Quinn nodded toward the counter. "Over there, under the glass."

"Two-day-old pie here is better than fresh pie anywhere else."

The edge of a smile crept onto Quinn's face. "Ain't that the truth."

We sat quietly, watching each other. He didn't seem nervous. Again, something was off.

"When you go to the Alvarado," Quinn said, "you won't find her."

I sat back in my seat, startled.

"She's somewhere safe."

I probed the minds closest to me, on the other side of the diner's walls. But they knew nothing. I searched for Eva in all the confusion, but her mind was so weak now, so numb. She wasn't anywhere.

"Tell me where she is."

"I don't think so."

"I'll kill your family."

"Kill Ollie and you'll never see her again."

His eyes stayed steady. Truth.

Quinn placed his hand on the teapot handle, his gaze on me. "I need to read your cup." He reached over to pour for me.

"Why do you want to do that?"

Quinn shrugged. "Because I want to know."

"Know what?"

"Everything. If I read your cup, I will."

The clock above the stove ticked steadily, the eyes of the cat moving back and forth. A pressure built inside me. I tried again to pierce the membrane between me and Quinn and failed.

"You've been to the other side," I said. "I can see it. On your face. You're different now."

That seemed to bother Quinn, and he stopped pouring for a moment, then continued.

"You know, once you've been to the other side," I said, "you can never go back."

Not long ago, that would have rattled Quinn. But not now. He kept pouring the tea like it was nothing at all.

"I'm not mad anymore," I said.

"Good to know."

"Not at all. You want to lock me away. Leave me. But I get it." I looked at my hands, flexing them, palms up, read the lines there. "They left me here too, so I guess I should get used to it."

"They?"

"If you didn't like me, you're *really* not gonna like them." I waited for Quinn to ask for more. He didn't. Instead he watched patiently, unreadable.

"You ever had a goldfish, Quinn?"

He shook his head.

"You win it at a carnival, bring it home, love it. Then your mom starts complaining that the tank smells, and you're sick of feeding it. So you find a lake and just dump it in."

"I'm guessing in this scenario, you're the goldfish."

"But the goldfish, it's not supposed to be there. So it grows, and grows, and then there's another goldfish, and they breed a million of them. Soon, all that lake is just goldfish. Of course, I'm just one, but I'm a pretty big goldfish."

Quinn set the teapot down, watching me with something like pity. "Are you saying you were some kind of pet?"

I shrugged. I wasn't sure what I was. "It feels good to talk about it. You know, with a friend. Now that it's all almost over."

He pushed the cup toward me, and I stared at it, lifted it. The tea leaves swirled inside, drawing me in.

"You drink," he said. "I read, and then I'll tell you where she is."

I knew what he was trying to do, and it wouldn't work. He thought there'd be an answer, inside me. An Achilles' heel. But Bud's letter was gone, burned. And the other way to lock me up? That had disappeared long ago, buried in an earthquake in 1933. It was sad, really, his efforts.

"I love this place," I said, "and all of you."

"I know."

"I'll try harder. I will. Maybe it will work this time."

"Just drink."

"You're wasting your time."

"You want to find Eva?"

"Of course I do."

"Good. Then drink."

"If I do, you promise you'll tell me where she is?"

He nodded, a familiar honesty shining in his eyes. He meant it. He would take me to Eva.

I lifted the cup to my mouth and drank. If I failed, if I couldn't help myself, maybe I would save Quinn for second to last, hold out as long as I could. Family, after all, was family. Would I tell him, though? Before the end came, why he'd always been able to see the future so clearly? Why the world of second sight opened up for him like a flower at midnight? Maybe I would tell him. He liked secrets. It was in his nature.

At the first sip, I could sense, rather than see, the swell of relief coming from Quinn. He rubbed his chest like it ached. A trickle of blood made its way under the bandage.

"You have a terrible poker face," I said.

"So I've been told."

"You're going through a lot of trouble for a reading."

"Turn the cup as you drink," he said, lips tight, face blank.

I finished it and put it back on the saucer. "Ah, refreshing."

"Now turn it upside down and put your hands over it."

I rolled my eyes and pulled at my collar, then put my hands over the cup. "Is this okay? Do I need a doily? My, my, you are a prissy one."

"How do you feel?" Quinn asked.

"Fine."

But I wasn't fine. Heat crept up my neck, and I swallowed down the swell of vertigo. The ground beneath me shook, like a train was passing nearby. I clutched my chest; my eyes felt full, my stomach worse.

I knew what this meant. But he couldn't have. I opened my eyes, my vision blurry, and turned over the cup. Inside, the leaves formed a familiar pattern.

Stars. Constellations.

The trap.

I dropped the cup. It shattered. Turning, I found the chair across from me empty.

The metallic grind of an unoiled hinge came from behind. Quinn was there, opening the door to the diner and slipping through. The door shut. Now on the other side of the glass, he met my gaze.

The ground trembled, tearing my heart in two, and the posters and autographed pictures tumbled off the wall, chairs toppled, glass shattered. Grease spilled out of the deep fryer onto the floor, filling the diner with its thick scent.

And now I could see it, written faintly over the walls, just a sheen in daylight. Symbols—the symbols from the cave walls—trapping me like a bug in a jar.

The destruction multiplied, and panic rose in my throat. No air. None at all.

Quinn held my gaze as he reached up and turned the lock.

The diner fell away around me, folding like paper. Darkening like iron. Just a dream. It had to be.

I stood in disbelief as the world shrank, squeezing me into the shape of a cube, filling me with sand like a doll. Endless miles of desert sand, in my lungs and my veins—

Then the diner re-formed. Chairs, booths, pictures of movie stars. Eva's young face, caught in sepia tones, her fingers curled under her chin.

My prison.

I sat and whimpered, shedding the last of who I pretended to be, scratching at the inside of the door to the diner, then yelling and pounding.

I could change. I could! If they just understood that, they'd let me out! And this time, they'd never let me go.

CHAPTER
THIRTY-EIGHT

The night after I locked Kit away in the diner, A.J. and Ollie put caution tape around the perimeter.

The next morning, Gypsum residents started arriving, trekking in from the countryside, coming in from whatever place they'd been hiding. Selena's uncle came in from Terlingua and erected barricades in front of the parking lot. Sal Lumpkin made a sign on some old particleboard.

DO NOT CROSS LINE. DANGEROUS CHEMICALS.

Hundreds of Gypsum's residents showed up, then pitched in to seal the place off to the world.

Most of the town didn't know what had gone on in the diner, what was now trapped inside. No one spoke of it, but everyone seemed to understand what they had to do. Ollie called it communal instinct. But me, I knew what it was. We were all connected, from living on the land, from drinking the water that had soaked up so much of Kit's energy over thousands of years.

As I nailed the last board up, I looked through the dark glass. The electricity was still down. In the corner booth, by the jukebox, was a dim shape, vaguely human. It hunched in the shadows. Just before I lifted the board to cover the last window, I caught movement, a spot of inky darkness in the gray light. A hand reached out and touched the jukebox. The lights flared on.

I hammered in the first nail. Johnny Cash's "Ring of Fire" bled through the window.

Ollie and I exchanged a glance.

"You sure he can't bust out of here?" Ollie asked.

"I'm sure." I didn't know how I knew, but I knew. "What I did, and the symbols Selena drew on the walls—he can't open the door. Not as long as I'm alive."

Ollie rubbed a hand over his stubbled chin. "I thought the power to the diner was off."

"It is."

Ollie and I decided to take what was left of the safe out of town. It was a shell now, and Kit had torn it to pieces, but I didn't want it rusting in the junkyard.

And when we tried to leave, that's when I found out the price Eva Durbin had been so sly about.

I leaned against Ollie's truck. My chest still ached, although the place where the plant had sprouted right out of me had healed over miraculously, leaving a pale pink scar in a starburst. While Ollie and Enrique loaded the pieces of the safe, I touched the spot, my mind spinning through what had happened to me.

What *had* happened? I expected to be dead, or feel different, or something. But all I felt was tired, and like I wanted to stay in bed for a few days.

Tater came out from under the porch and sniffed at my boots, then gave me a strange look. She'd been glued to me since she was a kitten, so it was odd, her slinking away.

Enrique and Ollie had almost finished loading the safe, which was now as light as any other eighty-pound piece of furniture, and just as docile.

My phone buzzed, and for a second, I thought I'd see June's name. But it was A.J. I answered it, bitter disappointment coiling in my chest. I'd fixed a lot, but there were limits.

"You still okay?" was the first thing out of her mouth.

"Just sore."

"Good, because tomorrow I want you to go on a road trip with us, to LA. Tripp's driving."

"What's in LA?"

"According to Eva Durbin, everything."

"Wait...she wants to leave Gypsum?"

"I can't get her to stop talking about it. She's trying to leave the trailer right now...hold on, Mrs. Durbin, let's pack first...yes, we're leaving soon...I promise!" A.J. lowered her voice again. "Anyway, she almost got on my bike earlier, telling me she was heading west. Unless I tie her down, I don't think I can get her to stay in Gypsum more than a day."

I touched the starburst scar on my chest. In the background, Mrs. Durbin asked who was on the line. Then her voice rose, saying I couldn't go with them.

"Quinn?"

"It's just strange, after a lifetime of refusing to leave, that Eva would leave now."

"Well, it's about time, don't you think?"

"You don't think she'll throw another fit?"

"Not unless we miss the exit for the Cracker Barrel."

I hung up, a strange unease rising in me. Ollie slipped into the driver's seat and gave me a *Let's get to it* nod.

By the time we'd reached the YOU ARE NOW LEAVING GYPSUM sign, I rubbed the sore spot on my chest, nervous. But I didn't explode. Or grow tentacles. Relief flooded through me. Maybe the price had skipped me. Maybe I'd caught a break in the world's worst lottery.

A few miles later, I drifted off in the passenger seat, dreaming of glass boxes and blue skies.

Until the pain woke me.

My cheek was pressed up against the window, the tans and greens of the desert a blur. And my stomach churned, like I was about to turn inside out.

A tree, there in the distance, a half mile ahead. Lone and scraggly, but something that didn't grow in Gypsum.

I rubbed my face, uncapped my water and took a sip. "Ollie, can you put on some music?"

"Like what?"

"I don't care. Anything."

Something about my voice made Ollie turn and give me a worried look. He flipped on the radio, and an old country song warbled through the tinny speaker by my leg. Dolly Parton. Something Gram would have loved.

I closed my eyes, listening to the rumble of the truck, trying to sing along, but my stomach was squeezing like a fist had taken hold. Bile rose in my throat. My palms tingled.

By the time Dolly was telling me why Jolene shouldn't take her man, we got to the tree. A patch of green. As we passed, I could feel its skeletal branches tearing at my arm.

Ollie glanced over at me, his forearm resting on the steering wheel. "You okay? You look pale."

I wasn't okay, but we needed to keep going. I nodded, because for once in my life, I was going to leave Gypsum. Take this monstrous box and all its bad memories beyond the city limits.

I rubbed the sore spot on my chest, where the plant had broken through, and a voice rose that sounded a lot like Eva's. *How are you even here?* I glanced in the rearview mirror at the road behind me. It was empty, and the urge to turn the car around and head back rose in me, so powerful I almost grabbed the wheel.

The world became a discordant tangle of Ollie yelling at me, Dolly Parton hitting high notes, the engine growling. The road in front of me blurred, moved in a swish of browns and the gray asphalt of the highway, all of it melting as the truck swung in an arc.

Faint, and from somewhere inside my mind came Eva Durbin's voice. *I told you so.*

Before I blacked out, I think I told Ollie to keep driving. But my words were nothing more than a burble of sounds, like I was surfacing from water. Then the voices of the song and my brother became as light as bubbles, until they were gone altogether.

———————•———————

I woke up in the Dark Place, breathing air that wasn't there, standing on the ground that didn't exist. Vast. Filled with ink.

But no longer empty.

Instead of an abyss around me, lines of webbing spread out from me. Everywhere, into the dark, for miles. Then I looked down, and panic rose in me like a tide.

That enormous web that spread into the darkness, all of it came from the starburst on my chest.

I reached down to touch it, my hands shaking, the place where my skin and the web met. Threads as tough as leather, gnarly and twisted. No, it wasn't a web. It had *never* been a web. All these years—that was my mind, making up something to make it make sense.

They were roots. And I was at the center.

I pulled at them, but they held fast. Grabbed a bunch in my fist and tore, swearing and crying, telling myself it wasn't what I thought it was.

And from nowhere and everywhere came a whisper. "Come in, boy. Come in."

I stopped and turned to the sound of Eva Durbin's voice. The trailer floated there, in the ink.

I walked up the stairs to the stoop and opened the door, the smell of mothballs and chicken soup blowing past, then fading quickly. In its place came the smell of perfume and cigarettes. Eva Durbin lay on her couch, drinking from a crystal glass so ornate it looked like a jewel. And so did she, young and vibrant, her blond hair curling at her temples.

She watched me with unreadable eyes. "Seems like you found your way here all right this time."

I stood watching her through the cloud of curling smoke, rubbing my chest, which felt normal now, just skin and bone and muscle. "What just happened to me?"

She nodded sagely, the familiar old Mrs. Durbin's expression on this young face. "Yes, I would think you'd be like this now."

And from under the overflowing ashtray, she pulled a letter. On the front the word *June* was written in a slanted hand. As soon as I took it from her hand, the name disappeared, and in its place came another.

Quinn.

Gram's handwriting. The loopy Qs. The stutter in the letters I started to notice a few months before she died.

Eva touched the back of my hand gently. "This was supposed to arrive in your mailbox a few days ago. Kit made sure it didn't."

"How did you get it?"

She gave me a mysterious shrug. "Being the lock has all kinds of advantages. You'll find out." She looked down into my hands, which were gripping the letter tightly.

Dear Quinn,

If you are getting this letter, it means the Pilsner line is gone. And I'm sorry, because I know how much June meant to you. But you're going to have to be there for Ollie, now that he's the lock. Lucky for him, he doesn't have the same wanderlust that you do.

I'm sure you figured out a long time ago that Gypsum is not a normal place. People here are special, like you and me. June and her family. Selena and her family. Anyone who's lived here for generations has gifts born of the water, even if they don't know it yet, and Ollie's will only grow. I don't want either of you to be afraid of this. Change is wondrous, if you live long enough to see it happen. Your brother is a wonder, just like you.

Now, about the safe. If you don't know what I'm talking about, good. Don't go looking for it. No one knows the combination to the safe anymore, and that's by design, baby. And I have to warn you about something.

Now don't get me wrong, your gift is a good thing. Your sight is as pure as starlight, no matter what Bud Pilsner says. But when Eva starts to fade, you need to keep out of the Dark Place for a while, just until things are settled and Ollie takes her place. What lives in the safe has his fingers in the Dark Place, and he will try to manipulate you.

Eva has given you all the details by now, and I hope you'll have time to process all this before she dies. Just remember not to open the safe, under any circumstances, no matter how much it tells you to. With the Pilsner line gone, the guardianship of the safe will pass to the oldest child in the O'Brien family: Ollie. If we die out, it goes to the Garcias. What our ancestors did to make this pact between the families, that's lost to us now, but those bonds are strong, and they won't break.

I'm writing this at the kitchen table, and I can see both of you, out in the driveway, working on the motorcycle you two fished out of the junk-yard. Honestly, it does my heart good to know Ollie has you, which will take the sting out of what he has to do. When you graduate and go off to have your adventures, you make sure to come back to see Ollie often, since he can't go with you. But this trust we give Ollie, all of Gypsum has given him, it's sacred. Ollie's sacrifice saves us all.

I miss you, my sweet boy. Always remember that you are a wonder.

Love,
Gram

I looked up from the letter. "What does she mean? What sacrifice did Ollie make?"

"Well, it's all mixed up now, isn't it? Because you took his place. I don't know how you did it."

Sunlight. The premonition on the cliff. Telling Ollie to wait while I took a closer look at the plant. "I don't understand."

She leaned forward. "It means, boy, that you can never leave Gypsum. Never. You're here for the long haul."

I let go of the letter. The pages fluttered to my feet. Eva's words floated around the trailer, but I couldn't hear her over the rush of blood in my ears.

I threw open the door of the trailer and ran into the dark. Blind and hurtling, like that first night long ago, when June had left me and Selena in the hallway of the Alvarado. I didn't know where I was going, and I didn't care.

At that moment I wanted to see the cliffs of our campground more than anything in the world, and suddenly, there they were. Real and solid, like I was home. Rising up like a battleship in the night. Eva's voice followed me down the trail, and I ignored her, ignored the panic rising in me, and disbelief, until I reached the base of the cliff and started climbing with no ropes, clawing at the rock to get away from that truth, Eva, and the words written in a letter June never got to read.

You'll be tethered here, like Eva has been, for the rest of your life.

I clung to the cliff face, climbing recklessly. I didn't care if I fell, plummeted down, and hit the earth at ninety miles an hour. I was no different than Kit now, stuck in a space too small for me.

When I reached the top, I looked over the desert. Sweat and pulse and breath in my lungs, the summer sun warming my face. It looked so real, so close to the real thing, I almost couldn't tell the difference. As good as one of Kit's illusions. This time, coming from inside me.

Eva's voice came from behind me. "Running won't help you, son."

I turned, and the desert was gone, and the cliffs. The paneled walls of Eva's trailer rose up, and Eva lay on her couch, smoking through her long-handled filter, her young face watching me with a placid, pitying expression.

I sank down into the chair across from her, suddenly exhausted, heartsick. "This is why you never went home."

She nodded.

"Why didn't you tell me? What the price would be."

She sighed and put down her glass. "If I told you too much, Kit would know. He'd get inside your mind. I had to send you in there blind."

"Maybe I would have made a different choice." I thought of that motorcycle trip to Canada. The one thing in my life I was sure I needed to do. "Maybe I would have just left town. Maybe I would have let Ollie become the lock."

Her smile was sad. "No, you wouldn't have."

The choice Eva made...she knew there would be a price, and she went into it blindly, like I did. "All those years, we just thought you liked it here."

She shrugged. "Gypsum. Hollywood. Oh yes, I can see why you thought I'd be torn."

"Is there a chance I can change this?"

"Never." She put out her cigarette. "Never. You actually don't *exist* once you get too far out of town. The boundary is the edge of the underground springs. Without them, you'll start to fade, like I did every time they tried to take me away."

I looked over my shoulder at the trailer door. On the other side lay the Dark Place. I guessed when I came out of it, I'd be back in the truck, and Ollie would be shaking me awake. I looked out into the darkness, too numb to understand what this meant. At that moment, all I wanted to do was go home and sleep.

Eva stood with a swish of white silk and came to sit on the armrest of my chair, then put a hand on my shoulder. "It's all right, boy. Sometimes doing the right thing doesn't mean you get to go out in a blaze of glory. Sometimes, you just have to stay, and live. It's harder, you know, to just live."

A voice bled through the walls. "Eva, it's time now. We're ready for you."

She sighed. "Finally."

She took in my expression and her eyes softened. She reached out to touch my hand. "Gypsum's not such a bad place, you know."

She squeezed my shoulder again, and although she looked young to my eyes, her hand felt as thin and dry as deadwood. She walked past me and stepped out into the night, letting the Dark Place swallow her whole.

CHAPTER
THIRTY-NINE

*T*hree months later

I clung to the cliff, ten feet from the top of the Horse Crippler, one hand hanging on to a small limestone lip, the other going for a biner at my waist. I clipped in and secured myself with a nylon strap from my harness, then leaned back, hanging at the top of the world.

North, over the rolling desert toward Gypsum, construction rose up in patches. A new courthouse and library, and new shops—all funded by grants A.J. had gotten from Uncle Sam—dozens of workers hammering and lifting and putting Gypsum back together, nail by nail.

Life in Gypsum, despite the destruction and unexplained events of Christmas Day, *kind of* went back to normal. Most people had been too focused on running like hell to notice where the destruction was coming from, so when the news vans arrived, most locals looked into the camera and shrugged.

It was a twister.

It was an earthquake.

It was a broken gas line.

And the strange video circulating around the web? That had to be doctored, the locals said. It was amazing what you could do with special effects software these days. Make a man look like he was a black hole, drinking in chunks of concrete through his mouth and chest like magic.

The fifteen people who'd gone missing were never found, and the posters nailed up on telephone poles and on the sides of buildings had become tattered. A lot of folks still held out hope, though, that the missing would wander in one day from the desert with amnesia and a good story to tell over coffee at the Gypsum Lights Diner.

I knew different.

My phone buzzed in my pack. I slipped it out and found a text from Tripp.

got another client for you

I slipped it back in my pack without answering it. I would. As I had for the last three months. Meeting up with Tripp's friends for all kinds of psychic shenanigans, stuffing money in my pockets like a bandit. After the two videos Tripp had made went viral and word got out that I was the town's psychic, everyone had a theory about how I was involved. Then the requests for readings came pouring in. It took a month to make enough to get Ollie and me up to date on the mortgage. By the time summer came, we'd have the house renovated, two more cabins, and a new website to go with the new business: Starlight Campgrounds and O'Brien Brothers Rock-Climbing Tours.

The phone buzzed again. This time it was Ollie.

You ever coming home for dinner?

Nah, you guys have fun

We made lasagna. You should come by. Got a present for you.

Next time

Ollie and A.J. still needed space. When I'd offered to move out and into the cabin, they'd made a big show of asking me to stay, but in the end, I knew what they wanted. When two people finally admit they can't be without each other, they don't need an audience.

I looked west toward the house rising on the hill, which had just gotten a fresh coat of white paint, plus a STARLIGHT B&B sign at the end of the drive. On the porch swing, not too far from the coop, where Pumpkin and her new brood were pecking the dirt, Ollie and A.J. sat taking in the evening air, his arm slung around her, her head on his shoulder. He lifted his hand and waved.

At least life had worked out for one of us.

By sunset, I'd made a fire in the stone circle outside my cabin and watched the night fall over the campgrounds, turning the western horizon a deep purple.

Down the trail came the rhythm of boots, one set, and I'd know the pattern anywhere. I slipped the phone back into my pocket.

Selena rounded the bend in the trail, wearing jeans and a white T-shirt, blue backpack slung over one shoulder, her dark hair glowing in the firelight. She nodded her hello and went around the side of the cabin to grab the camp chairs. Then she set a plain paper bag by my feet, the word *Present* written in Sharpie on the side.

"Is it someone's birthday?" I asked.

"C'mon, you're eighteen. Stop being such a hermit. You need to celebrate." She held up the plain brown bag. "If you haven't guessed, this one is from June."

I sat up. "Wait...what?"

Selena took in my expression, my confusion. "I just thought...I don't know, if I picked one that was supposed to be from her, you'd..." She put the bag down. "I guess I don't know how to say goodbye."

I picked up the bag. Inside were two packs of chewing gum and a new carabiner. It was *exactly* what June would buy me.

A lump formed in my throat. Selena needed this ritual. I guess I did too.

"Thank you. This is perfect."

Once the sun had set and the universe spread herself above me like a million fireflies, quiet fell over the world. The two of us sat, watching the desert until the stars wheeled across the sky, the sparks of the fire rising to join them. This place, it was home. I loved it like I loved Gram, or Ollie, or Selena and June. But it was a place to come home to. That meant that sometimes, you left it. At least you were supposed to leave it.

Wasn't that what young people did? Leave the nest to explore, then come home for Christmas?

I bit my tongue, because Selena had heard enough of my moods, and I listened to her talk about school, the new sheriff who'd come from Alpine, how Ollie and A.J.'s new romance had pleased Aunt Macie enough that she added their prom picture over the stove, right next to hers and Enrique's.

Then Selena got to the point. "We think you're spending too much time alone."

I stirred the fire, the red embers glowing. "Who's *we*?"

"Me and Ollie. And A.J. And Macie."

"So, everybody."

"You sound cranky. Do you really want to end up like Mrs. Durbin?"

"I already ended up like Mrs. Durbin."

Selena leaned forward. "It doesn't have to be that way."

I stirred the fire some more. "Yeah, Ollie said the same thing."

Selena's eyes shone in the firelight, and her expression was unreadable. She'd given me space after what happened at the diner, and I was glad. At least I told myself I was glad. June's words came back to me, about O'Briens never knowing what they wanted. But June was wrong. One thing I knew for sure: I didn't want anyone to be anchored to one place because of me.

Selena gave me a soft look and fished in her backpack, pulling out another present. From the look of the perfect wrapping, it was definitely from Selena.

I took it suspiciously. "Is it a book?"

"Sort of."

I unwrapped it. A small leather journal. Blank inside. A little pen tucked into an inside pocket.

Selena interlaced her fingers and wrung her hands, watching me like I was a skittish horse. "I thought maybe you could…"

"Write poetry?"

"Write it out, you know, what's going on in your head. I hear it helps."

I nodded, staring at the cover, wondering if it could be that easy. Just write it out. It was what my ancestors did.

She gave me a knowing look. "And I saved this one for last." She reached back into her bottomless backpack and pulled out a box wrapped in newspaper, a copy of the *Gypsum Times*. "Ollie told me to give this to you. Said you'd know what to do with it."

I unwrapped it and lifted the lid off the box. Inside was a thick stack of papers held together with a binder clip. I scanned them, confused.

"These are the old mortgage documents."

Selena leaned forward in her camp chair, squinting in the firelight, tilting her head to read the front page.

I held them up. "This is a strange thing to give your brother on his birthday."

She picked up the box and a smile lit the corner of her mouth. She pulled out a book of matches. On top of the stack was one single sheet of paper, folded and tied with twine. I unfolded it. Small print and lots of numbers. At the bottom, a red stamp said PAID IN FULL. At the top was a message handwritten from Ollie.

Thought you'd like to do the honors.

"What did it say?" Selena asked.

I smiled and lit a match. "It said *Happy birthday*."

Selena fell asleep on my porch in a hammock, but I was wound up. No, I was floating. No more bills hanging over our heads. Gram would be proud. Of both of us.

While Selena slept a few feet away, I got up and put on my boots. Stared at the journal, on the camp chair, then took it on impulse. Wandered out into the starlight and stood in a clearing, letting the sky light me up with pale fire. A billion suns, so bright they'd vaporize you in an instant. But everything changed with distance, and time.

My chest ached, and I rubbed the scar, although if I was honest with myself, that wasn't why it hurt. So I walked. At first, I thought I'd just walk to the Horse Crippler, but then I saw the cliff's massive back rising up, under the rind of the moon, and I kept going.

A mile of desert passed, my breath fogging the night air, my boots marking a path across the desert so familiar to me it had become a mother. Cactus shadow and rock, quiet and multitudes of suns, all of it my home, the home I'd saved, protected.

Sometimes you just have to stay, and live. An ordinary life. That's what Eva meant.

I wandered a trail toward the mines, then stood at the mouth, staring into the darkness. There was nothing ordinary about Gypsum.

The rock near the entrance had a flat spot, what Gram would call a good seat for the show. I sat, thinking about her, and how she'd held my hand when I was small and pointed to the sky and taught me about right and wrong. If she saw me now, she'd tell me to just get on home. She would have put her thick arm around me, given me a squeeze, and said everything would be all right.

And June, she would climb with me. Stand in the dark and call my name, lead me out of the tunnels. This time, I was the one who left her behind.

I opened the journal and wrote. Then I put my face in my hands and wept, thankful I didn't have an audience. Time passed. The world stayed silent.

I dropped my hands, looked up at the sky.

This time it was so easy to enter the Dark Place. I watched the nebula, bright and clear, focused on it. It opened for me.

The Dark Place wasn't dark anymore. A landscape, like home, but not quite like home. All the edges had blurred, like a faded photograph, the world turned sepia.

I stayed there, watching the mountains, the clouds move across the blue-black sky. The cliff above the mouth of the mines stretched up toward the starlit sky, and I gave in to a sudden urge to climb.

I walked back to the cabin, arriving just before sunrise. Selena was still asleep in her hammock, her lashes a dark curve on her cheek, her hair lying over one shoulder as she lay there, breathing.

"Hey," I whispered, kneeling beside the hammock. "Wake up."

Those eyes fluttered open, and Selena's mouth curved into a sleepy smile. "Good morning."

I leaned down and kissed her, without thinking about it, for once without regretting it or wishing I were somewhere else.

She was the first to pull away, her hands still wrapped around my neck. "You look better."

"I am."

She searched my face, looking for clues.

"Let's just climb. Before the sun is up. So we can catch everything when it's just beginning."

Within five minutes we had our gear and headed to the base of the Horse Crippler. The darkened rock slid under my hands as I pushed myself up, rising higher, until my lungs were filled with the joy of it. This place, it was home and I loved it.

I reached the summit. Took off my shoes and stood on the edge of the cliff in my bare feet. Then I fished in my pocket for the note I'd written June, the one I'd torn out of the first page of the journal, and read it again, with Selena looking over my shoulder.

"Quinn, that's beautiful." Selena's voice broke on the last word.

"Thanks."

Selena sniffed. "June would totally roll her eyes at that."

I smiled, my throat constricting.

I stood on the edge, with a hundred words I could never say to June burning on the page, and thought about what makes someone the kind of person who stays. If you inherit that, or if you choose it.

What it meant to love something more than you loved yourself.

I let the wind take it. It drifted and spun, down the cliff face, until it lit upon the surface of the spring and floated there.

We watched the speck of white drifting on the dark water. Then Selena sat beside me in the theater seats, her head on my shoulder. Together we watched the sun rising over the Chinati Mountains, my heart so light I was sure it was made of air.

ACKNOWLEDGMENTS

Writers don't create a book alone, despite what the romantic stereotypes suggest. Writers are part of a wider team of creatives who bring a project to life, and I honestly couldn't do this without my people. I love my people.

First of all, I have to thank DFW Writers' Workshop, a group of writers who has inspired me, critiqued me, torn my pages apart, and helped me put them back together. They tell me when an idea is good, when it's not, and they tell me not to give up. In particular, I want to thank Brooke Fossey, Brian Tracey, John Bartell, Dana Swift, Alex Martinez, Helen Dent, and Lauren Danhof. Without their help during revision, I wouldn't have been able to see this story clearly. Even more people at DFW Writers' Workshop have given me moral support on this project: Larry Enmon, Russell Connor, Sally Hamilton, Blair Lovern, Rosemary Clement, Allen Crowley, Colin Holmes, BJ Sloan, JB Sanders, Carolyn Rae Willamson, David Jones, Karoline Chapman, Becca Seifert, Sara Mensinga, Karen Farrell, and Harry Hall. And thank you to the talented Lauren Lanza Osias: your marketing help and moral support has kept me from losing it several times. I could go on for days about how much these wonderful people have done for me, and there's nothing I wouldn't do for them.

I want to thank Amy Bishop-Wycisk, my agent at Trellis Literary Management, for shepherding this project back when it was just a weird pitch idea and a chapter about three teens breaking into a haunted hotel. You saw the potential in it, and in me. Your eye for developmental editing is truly amazing.

To my friends, thank you. So many of the exploits of June, Selena, and Quinn come from my time with my dear friend Adrienne Knutson, back when we were car-less teens getting in trouble in Garden Ridge (minus the ghosts). Adrienne, you're the best partner-in-crime ever. My friend Hannah Head: your enthusiasm for my work always makes me feel like a rock star. Thank you to my Thrillertique group at ITW: you helped me troubleshoot that first chapter with fresh eyes when I really, really needed it. My beloved Zetta Brown: your talent and wit have been constant companions through all this. And Night Song: thank you for helping me think about this idea on the ground floor, and your guidance has always been gentle and supportive.

All the folks at Holiday House deserve a huge round of applause. My editor, Mora Couch: you have been a champion of this project from the beginning, and your thoughtful, careful edits have helped me through when I doubted myself and my own writing ability. The Holiday House marketing department—Sara DiSalvo, Michelle Montague, Terry Borzumanto-Greenberg, Alison Tarnofksy, Anna Abbell, Tiffany Coelho, and Saskia den Boon—thank you for helping get the word out, and thanks to Kerry Martin and Chelsea Hunter for bringing together a design that is really stunning. A huge thank you to the production team—Lisa Lee, Judy Varon, Rebecca Godan, and Emma Swan. It takes a lot of talented people to put a book together, and I'm so grateful to everyone.

Thank you to my family, both the Lutzes and the Browns. Like the O'Briens, there aren't many of us, and any time we're together is a gift. Thank you to my daughter, Robin: you are one of the most creative people I've ever met, and you remind me to take myself less seriously. Your cheerful "what ifs" and unending enthusiasm for weaving stories reminds me why I do this in the first place. Most of all, I need to thank my husband, Russell. You have been the one to hear me obsess about a scene that didn't work (over and over) and let me bounce ideas off of you until something stuck. You're brilliant and kind, and your support during this whole process has kept the project from falling off a precipice more than once.

There's one final person to thank, who's not here with us anymore—my aunt, Barbara Houghton. Eva Durbin's quirkier characteristics, as well as her frustrated dreams, are based on you, Aunt B. Thank you for always hanging in there, and for your forgiving heart. You are deeply missed, and I hope you're experiencing the best do-over ever right now.